Lesley THOMSON

the death chamber

HEAD of ZEUS

First published in the UK in 2018 by Head of Zeus Ltd
This paperback edition published in the UK in 2018 by Head of Zeus Ltd

9 7 5 3 1 2 4 6 8

A catalogue record for this book is available from
the British Library.

ISBN (PB): 9781786697226
ISBN (E): 9781786697196

Typeset by Adrian McLaughlin

Printed and bound in Great Britain by
CPI Group (UK) Ltd, Croydon CR0 4YY

MIX
Paper from
responsible sources
FSC® C020471

Head of Zeus Ltd
First Floor East
5–8 Hardwick Street
London EC1R 4RG

WWW.HEADOFZEUS.COM

To Lisa Holloway and Juliet Eve with my love

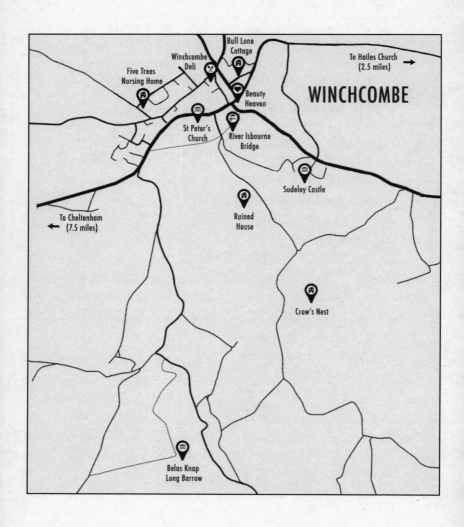

WINCHCOMBE

Bull Lone
Cottage

Winchcombe
Deli

Five Trees
Nursing Home

Beauty
Heaven

St Peter's
Church

River Isbourne
Bridge

To Hailes Church
(2.5 miles) →

Sudeley Castle

To Cheltenham
(7.5 miles)
←

Ruined
House

Crow's Nest

Belas Knap
Long Barrow

In his opinion one of the chief defects in detective stories – for he was given to busmen's holidays – was that authors made their 'sleuths' like unto the angels, watching for days without, so to speak, taking their eyes off the ball. It was not so in real life.

—JOHN GALSWORTHY *Over the River*
(The Forsyte Saga, volume nine)

I am the family face;
Flesh perishes, I live on,
Projecting trait and trace
Through time to times anon,
And leaping from place to place
Over oblivion.

The years-heired feature that can
In curve and voice and eye
Despise the human span
Of durance – that is I;
The eternal thing in man.
That heeds no call to die.

—THOMAS HARDY 'Heredity'

Prologue

Saturday 11 June 1977

Cassie Baker ducks into the back of Mick Spicer's souped-up Ford Escort Mark 1. Her mum shouts from the gate, 'Find your little sister and be in a taxi by ten!' Lauren Spicer cranes around from the front seat and the friends exchange a look. By ten the party won't be started.

Trudy Baker yells, 'Don't spend that taxi money on drink. *Don't* drink!' As Mick accelerates down the lane, she adds something about not making a racket when Cassie gets back. The girls laugh. Lauren Spicer's tempted to shout, *Cassie won't be coming back.* She says to Cassie, 'Would we drink?' Mick tells them, 'Behave!'

In Cassie's bead-encrusted clutch-bag is a bottle labelled Chucklin' Cherry. It's filled with Smirnoff vodka. She calls back to her mum, her words snatched into the night, 'I'll be *good.*' Famous last words.

Cassie's thinking just how good she'll be. Juggling the vodka bottle she applies lipstick. Mick floors the accelerator on a bend, sending Cassie's eye shadow compact under the seat.

Mick drops his sister and Cassie outside Winchcombe's community centre. Later he'll lie and say it took him twenty-five minutes to get to his party in Cheltenham from Winchcombe, although speeding fifty miles an hour most of the way, it was nearer fifteen.

Like the town's main streets, the community centre is decked out with Silver Jubilee bunting for the Queen's twenty-five-year-old reign. Fabric flags sodden by the rain that afternoon sag drunkenly from the shingles. From inside comes the muffled throb of 'Tiger Feet'… Through steamed-up windows, red and yellow lights – strobing out of step with the beat – resemble flames of an inferno.

A banner is slung across the gable: 'Winchcombe Youth Disco'. Tottering up to the entrance on their crepe-soled platform shoes, Cassie and Lauren take turns with the Smirnoff. They cling to each other, ostensibly for support, but neither girl wants the other to get there first. Cassie's eighteen and Lauren's sixteen, so in a sense Cassie's always going to get there first. Lauren's in a skimpy cotton skirt and sparkly tank-top. The shiny black dress Cassie's borrowed from Lauren reveals jutting contours of a strip-thin figure. *Tonight's the night*, Cassie hums to herself.

In the hallway Winchcombe's youth bellow out Mud's 'Tiger Feet', pushing and nudging in an unruly queue. A whiff of fresh paint in honour of the Queen deadens the summer air.

With vodka-fuelled impatience, Cassie laboriously tells the flinty-faced woman selling tickets (the bossy cow made her shifts at the Co-op a torture) that her ticket's paid for. Mrs Glover, in Jubilee bowler hat and Union Jack cape, sternly rips a ticket off her reel and informs Cassie that no one has paid for her and waits in stolid silence until Cassie hands over twenty pence. The disco is kids' stuff, she's only come to keep an eye on Karen who was there as soon as the doors opened like the goody-two-shoes she is.

Lauren is pouting at her reflection in a glass-covered notice-board. Amidst the usual business of Keep Fit Classes, Monthly Bring and Buy sale and Scout meetings, are announcements scattered with a riot of exclamation marks: 'Exciting Events for the Jubilee!' 'Royal Coffee Morning! Share your memories of our Queen!!' Cassie shoulders through double doors into the hall. Adjusting her cape, Mrs Glover doesn't see Lauren slip in behind her.

Momentarily dazed by lights and the thundering bass of 'Disco Inferno', Cassie scours the crowd. She can't make out faces. She pushes through the press of bodies and as the track melds into Stevie Wonder, she starts to dance. A group of boys huddled by the DJ's desk, too sober or shy to hit the floor, are mesmerized by Cassie's writhing moves. It's as if she's held by invisible arms. Lauren joins her and they move in unison.

The DJ, with Noddy Holder bushy sideboards and chequered jacket, is old enough to be the grandfather of everyone in the hall. It doesn't stop him watching the girls watching the boys watching Lauren and Cassie.

Lauren whispers something in Cassie's ear and Cassie gives a curt nod. She is dancing nonchalantly now, a bored expression on her cool even features. Half the girls in the hall want to be Cassie. Most of the boys, and some of the girls, know she's out of their league.

An hour later Cassie retreats to the table of twiglets and plain crisps. She takes a pull on the cherry drink bottle. Heatwave's 'Boogie Nights' is 'their song'. She turns her nose up. The hall smells like the school gym, it's not the place, this is only a rehearsal for the real thing. She smiles to herself as the vodka burns her throat.

Time moves slowly when you're counting the minutes. An hour later, when the Sex Pistols rock the speakers and, in a frenzy of pogoing to 'God Save the Queen', Cassie is splashed by sparkling Corona and subterfuge Party Four, she leaves.

She is stumbling past St Peter's church when the bells strike ten. Twice she veers off the kerb into the road. The second time a car hoots and the driver swears. Her vision blurred by vodka and with only one thing on her mind, Cassie is oblivious.

Cassie Baker has known Winchcombe all her life. Her ancestors are buried, headstones illegible, in the St Peter's church graveyard. Numbered amongst these dead is Cassie's great-grandmother who a century ago died of apoplexy in the doctor's surgery, now the Lloyds Bank, on Abbey Terrace. Cassie's not going to let that happen to her. Being Donna Summer, she sings in perfect tune as she lurches down Vineyard Street heading for her future.

She pauses by the bridge over the River Isbourne and briefly dizzied, leans on the parapet and gazes at the blackness below.

'Night, gorgeous!' a man with a Sid Vicious hairdo and complexion, his arm around a woman with punky blue hair, whoops at Cassie. His girlfriend elbows him and he gives an exaggerated groan.

Years later, divorced and with a paunch, Kelvin Finch will claim the distinction of being the last person, apart from the murderer, to speak to Cassie Baker.

Cassie wrenches off her shoes and carries them dangling by the straps. Making faster progress, she doesn't care that tiny stones cut her bare feet as she passes the gates to the castle.

On the Old Brockhampton Road drifts of moonlight appear and disappear between clouds. Hawthorn hedges casts shadows so intense they might be chasms in the tarmac. Cassie's used to the dark, but tonight a sudden fear prickles. Her dad drives home this way. What an idiot! If he sees her, *where's your baby sister and look at you… done up like a tart…*

She passes the field where, as a kid, she saw Bambi nibbling moss, or so her dad said. Then the five-bar gate with the outline of the stand of trees that march like soldiers. She'll take the short cut at the next gate. Although Winchcombe is in her bones, the morbid light presents dips and inclines that are foreign to her. She stops and looks back down the lane. Framed by branches is St Peter's church, the view adorns crinkle-cut postcards of Winchcombe but now has the quality of a nightmare.

Something's coming. Her dad's van. Cassie flattens herself into the hedge. Headlights trace the twists and turns of the lane and rising from the 'hidden dip' they catch her in their glare.

Bright spots blind her. The van judders to a stop. One brake light glows red. 'Boogie Nights' is playing in Cassie's head; it's as if the figure coming towards her moves in time to the music.

Chapter One

June 2016

Four fifteen. Afternoon. Stella Darnell crossed the hospice car park and led Stanley into reception.

'Thank goodness you're here, Stella!' Wendy the receptionist greeted her. 'Mrs Hogan's driving the nurses bonkers asking when you're coming. She *loves* you!'

'That's good. I mean…'

'I know what you mean! Patty's still with us. Vicky reckons that's down to you. She says you're doing wonders for Patty. I can believe it!'

'You OK?' Wendy had been on Stella's cleaning team before retiring and becoming part-time receptionist at the local hospice.

'Mustn't grumble.' Wendy smiled. 'Although I do! Can I give Stanley a little something?'

Stella watched her small apricot poodle sit, paw raised, eyes fixed on the approaching liver treat. Wendy's home-made treats, sealed into bags with hearts on them, were a bestseller in the little display of sweets, crisps and greeting cards beside the desk.

Stella Darnell, MD of Clean Slate, a successful cleaning company in West London, had been volunteering as a hospice befriender for three months. She sat with patients, talking or just keeping them company while giving respite to friends and family. Stella's friend had died there the previous year. Since then, Clean Slate had cleaned the hospice at a hefty discount, but Stella wanted to offer something personal. Jackie, her PA, keen to get Stella away from long days in the office, came up with the idea.

Emboldened by her chat with Wendy which had diffused Stella's ever-present trepidation around the fact of death, Stella headed for the ward.

'Given up on you!' An elderly woman lying propped against a stack of pillows waved a hand. 'Look at these two, snivelling like the babies they once were. Kids! Go and get a coffee!'

A man and a woman in their forties, tight white faces and combed dark hair fixing them as siblings, mumbled thanks to Stella and hastened from the room.

'When you're dying, you're supposed to take stock of your achievements. Those two are mine. Lord help us. Wobbly lips, glum faces. I'll be cremated. I don't want them lamenting over my grave,' she nodded emphatically. 'They were the same with school journeys. At least this time when I go some teacher can't ring for me to come back!' She glowered at Stella, daring her to protest. 'Stanley *here*!' She gave the bed sheet a slap.

Without hesitation or need of a home-cooked treat, Stanley flew up onto the bed and flopped beside Patty, head on paws. He too was a volunteer. As a PAT dog (Pets As Therapy), he submitted to fuss on the laps of patients and their families. Patty Hogan might be insensitive with humans, but she was a dog-whisperer when it came to Stanley.

'Off we go, Stella Darnell.' Patty was dying of bowel cancer. In the two weeks since her admission, Patty had become Stella's favourite patient.

'Ignore her when she's nasty about people, especially her children. Go with it,' Vicky, one of the nurses – and Stella's new friend – had advised before Stella's first visit to Patty. 'Best know her bark is as bad as her bite and you'll both get on fine.'

Stella was used to cantankerous and exacting cleaning clients. When one such client had demanded Stella scrub behind the bath panel and wipe inside the light fittings (electricity off) Stella considered her day made. Befrienders didn't clean and Patty Hogan's eyes were tired; Stella must read to her.

That afternoon, Stella, whose own reading centred on hygiene equipment catalogues, was to finish the first volume of The Forsyte Saga. Stella had come round to thinking, despite the story not being true (Stella liked facts), it was quite realistic. She had clients like Soames Forsyte who wanted value for money. Patty Hogan called him a monster, as if she knew him personally.

'I'm off.' Vicky looked in on her patients – whether they were conscious or not – at the end of her shift. She'd told Stella, 'I never know who'll be there next time I'm in.' Vicky left Patty until last because if Stella was there, Vicky said she too liked being read to. As she'd said to Stella, 'Mum read stories to me when I was little, I read my kids my old faves: Worzel Gummidge, Narnia and Five Go Mad at the Hospice!'

'Sit down, Vicky.' Patty waggled a finger at the chair where her son had been sitting, then motioned for Stella to continue.

'"... The thistledown no longer moved. The dog placed his chin over the sunlit foot. It did not stir. The dog withdrew his chin quickly, rose, and leaped on old Jolyon's lap, looked in his face, whined; then, leaping down, sat on his haunches, gazing up. And suddenly he uttered a long, long howl.

'But the thistledown was still as death, and the face of his old master.'"

Unlike the thistledown, the words on the page did move. Stella blinked and her voice cracked. A hand appeared. Vicky handed her a tissue.

'Blow and carry on,' Patty Hogan instructed with her eyes closed.

The last sentence was something about summer coming, but as she read it, Stella made no sense of it. She closed the tatty paperback and, wiping her nose, glanced at Vicky. Vicky didn't look bothered. Stella guessed that as a nurse she was probably used to people dying in real life, never mind in books.

'We'll start *In Chancery* next week.' Patty Hogan dismissed them and moments later she was asleep.

'I didn't know Old Jolyon was going to die,' Stella said when they were standing by Vicky's car in the hospice car park. 'Maybe I should have missed out that bit.'

'I'd guess Patty knows those novels by heart, it won't have been a shock. Besides, she's not scared of dying. Her children would pretend she's going to get better if Patty didn't keep giving them tasks for her funeral.' Vicky jiggled her car key. 'Saying that, whatever she says, I don't see Patty being here for book two.'

'She seemed fine.' Stella was taken aback. When she'd realized there were eight more volumes in The Forsyte Saga, she'd taken this as insurance Patty would stay alive to hear them.

'Her colour wasn't great.' Vicky flipped up her fob watch. 'Speaking of offspring in denial, I must pick mine up from Roddy's mum, they'll be thinking they can watch TV all night. I meant to say, I love Clean Slate! Our house is a show-home after Anne's been. You're a life-saver, Stell!'

Stella had been reluctant to take out a cleaning contract with Vicky. On one of their dog walks (Vicky had a black cockapoo called Bing, named not after Crosby, but a rabbit on the BBC's CBeebies channel), Vicky had asked Stella to break her 'don't clean for friends' rule. When Stella scoped Vicky's house to determine the requirements, she'd noted the large number of books. Books gathered dust, but she wouldn't charge extra.

'I saw that on telly.' Stella had pointed at *Worzel Gummidge* next to paperbacks by C.S. Lewis. Vicky's children were three and four years old. Stella hadn't started reading until she was six and had stopped after passing A-level English.

'Those are my old copies, I forgot they were there.' Vicky had frowned. Stella knew it was because Stella had commented on personal items. A sternly underlined rule in Stella's staff manual was that cleaning operatives refrained from remark or judgement of clients' possessions or décor. Stella could have kicked herself.

As Vicky's bright yellow Jeep Renegade left the car park, Stella's eyebrows knitted at the memory. She sat in her van looking out at the River Thames. On the far bank was Mortlake Crematorium where they'd gone for her dad's funeral. Like old Jolyon, there'd been no one with Terry when he died, not even a dog. She wondered if Stanley would howl when she died. She turned in her seat. Strapped onto his jump seat, Stanley was dozing. By the time she was old, Stanley would be dead. Unless she died young. Lucie May – her dad's ex – would say it was too late for that.

Stella knew Vicky drew the line at murder, real or fictional. Soon after Stella started at the hospice, a doctor who'd read she'd solved cold cases asked her about them while they were making tea in the staffroom. Saying she 'couldn't talk about murder', Vicky left the room. Stella understood; she too avoided talking about murder.

Six p.m. Stella was going to supper at Jackie's. Jack would be there. Galvanized by this prospect, Stella reversed the van out of the bay.

Six thirty. Evening. The shadows of trees on Shepherd's Bush Green lengthened. Sunlight reflected on the windows of a slow-moving bus sent a searchlight across Clean Slate's two-roomed office. The windows, shut against the carbon monoxide fumes of idling rush-hour traffic, rendered the room stuffy with the accumulated heat of the day. It was a Hobson's choice between poisoning and suffocation.

Jackie Makepeace was determined to have her report on potential office space ready for Stella the next morning. Resistant to change, Stella avoided the subject of 'relocation'. However, their poky premises above the mini-mart were unsuitable to receive the growing number of corporate clients and they needed more staff to service them. As it was, there wasn't space for Jackie, her assistant Beverly, Stella, and Stella's mum Suzie Darnell, who worked part-time maintaining their database. Jackie would be firm. Clean Slate must move.

With the help of her brother-in-law Barry, Jackie had identified several buildings in West London and at that moment was pasting in a link to premises in Hammersmith – a converted 1930s furniture warehouse near Wormwood Scrubs prison. While Stella would like the gleaming décor and high-level security, she'd quibble at the need for the café with Wi-Fi on the ground floor 'for exclusive use of tenants'.

Jackie pulled the report from the printer and took it into Stella's office. It was usual for Stella to be at her desk at this hour, but she'd embraced befriending at the hospice and indeed had gone every day for the last fortnight. She'd also made a friend. Jackie liked the sound of Vicky, a specialist palliative-care nurse who had encouraged Stella out of the office for walks and lunches. Stella was circumspect about making friends, so Vicky was a good thing.

Stella was to be at Jackie's for supper. Roast lamb and trimmings prepared by Nick, Jackie's younger son. Despite it being spring, Stella wouldn't be lured from her office-lair on the promise of a rocket salad. She was a meat and two veg woman. Actually, Jackie smiled to herself, Stella was a microwaved shepherd's pie without veg woman. Jackie was working on that.

She caught the time on Stella's wall clock. It was a plastic monstrosity in the shape of a vacuum cleaner Beverly had, as a joke, shown Stella in a catalogue, and which, taking an instant liking to it, Stella had ordered online. Jackie laid the paper on Stella's keyboard. She did a sweep of the outer office. Kettle unplugged, milk in fridge, photocopier off. Beverly's computer was glowing, the Clean Slate logo – underscored with the dash of a small-handled brush – floated about the screen. Jackie tutted and switched it off.

Jackie was startled by tapping. A face, half obscured by Clean Slate's sign, was peering through the wired glass in the door. She felt a flicker of annoyance. No matter how often they were asked, the insurance brokers upstairs left the street door on the latch. Anyone could walk in. Clean Slate was on the first landing and couriers expecting signature invariably interrupted with parcels for the brokers. This explained Stella's considering office security a priority. Jackie was thinking that at least she'd locked this door when it opened and the stranger walked in. Jackie sighed inwardly, she'd forgotten to take it off the latch after Bev had gone.

'Stella Darnell?' A woman in her early forties, bobbed hair tucked behind her ears, in a white denim jacket, tight black trousers and the sort of high heels that felled your arches scowled at Jackie as if they had already fallen out badly.

'No, can I help you?' Jackie adopted a bright smile. 'Jackie Makepeace, I'm Stella's PA.'

'I have to see Stella Darnell.' The woman flicked a look at Stella's door on which was Beverly's laminated notice, 'Stella Darnell, Managing Director'.

'She's not here, I'm afraid. I wonder if I could help?'

'It's not cleaning.' The woman gave a flick of her hair with red nail-polished fingers; sprayed into shape, it didn't budge.

'Is it a case?' Jackie enquired softly. Another reason Clean Slate needed to move to a larger office was that, besides offering cleaning, Stella had decided to take the business of being a private detective seriously and offer it as a service.

'Yes.' Smoothing her hand over and over her flat stomach, the woman appeared suddenly indecisive. She darted glances about her as if concerned they could be overheard.

'May I ask your name?' Jackie posed a simple question to get the woman to open up.

'Lisa Mercer. It's not for me. It's nothing to do with me.'

She fiddled with a silver pendant resting on her tanned chest. Her lips, matching the nails, were a pencil dash. Lisa Mercer took care of her good looks.

'I see,' Jackie said, although she didn't.

'Paul Mercer asked me to come. He's my father.'

'Do sit down, Ms Mercer.' Jackie wheeled out Beverly's chair from her desk.

Lisa Mercer remained standing. 'It's about… do you remember Charles Brice? He was arrested for the Bryony Motson and Cassandra Baker murders in—'

'I remember.' As if the windows had been blasted, air seemed to be sucked from the room. Jackie knew who the woman was. She gripped the sides of her keyboard. Lisa Mercer was the daughter of the detective.

Chapter Two

New Year's Eve 1999

The public toilets in Cheltenham had the look of a morgue. The Victorian urinals, pocked by cigarette burns, that lined the tiled walls were elegant masterpieces of waste design. Opposite two oak stalls were sinks big enough to bath a baby.

A man in a Harrington jacket, black T-shirt and baggy black and grey check trousers, his blonded hair styled to tip over ice-blue eyes, was using the corner urinal. Finishing, he stepped off the plate and moved to a sink. He massaged a cracked tablet of carbolic under a torrent of scalding water without generating suds. Fluorescent light revealed lines around the mouth and eyes that, despite the boyish hairstyle, put him in his forties.

He was still sluicing his hands when a middle-aged man strolled into the chamber. Tall and suited in black, he nevertheless lacked the sartorial care of the man at the sink. His jacket bulged with change, his hair needed a wash and a cut and his shirt was escaping from his waistband. He went to the cubicles and tipped each door wide with a forefinger. Ascertaining they were empty, he returned to the exit.

'Nice to see you wash your hands after taking a piss, Charlie Brice!' His voice was a low rumble.

'This is a surprise.' Clenching his bottom lip between his teeth, Brice smiled as if the surprise was a good one. He pulled at a grubby roller towel until he found a lighter grey section and, finger by finger, dried his hands. Without turning around he said, 'Inspector Mercer. Happy millennium to you too!'

'Detective *Chief* Inspector.'

'Hanging out in toilets win you a stripe?' Charlie Brice turned to Mercer. 'Last time we met I think you were rescuing a cat from a tree? Or no, was it when you tried to do me for not having a cab licence? Bad luck there!'

'Where is she?' Mercer snarled.

'Have we done with pleasantries?' Brice made to leave, but Mercer was blocking the door. 'If you don't mind me saying, you're looking jaded for the last night of the century—'

'Where's Bryony Motson? Tell me now, you little shit, or so help me...' Mercer twisted a fistful of Brice's T-shirt and pulled him close. 'We got a witness saw you with Bryony in the Sun in Winchcombe. She left the pub in your taxi. Where've you got her?' Knuckles white, Mercer jerked Brice until their faces were an inch apart.

'I don't keep track of my fares.' Brice was laconic. 'Eeeuch! Extra-strong mints, what habitual misdemeanour is that hiding, Chief Inspector?'

'Where is she?' Mercer's shout bounced off the ceramic walls. He let go of Brice and kneaded his fist as if preparing for a punch.

'I wish I could help.' Brice was pleasant. 'I haven't seen Bryony Motson since I dropped her at her flat the night I had a drink with her. She didn't want a second date. Mystery to me, I've a way with the ladies! *Say lah vee*!' He exaggerated a London accent.

Thirteen days ago, on 18 December Bryony Motson, an eighteen-year-old Abbey National teller, had left a nightclub in Cheltenham. She bid her friends 'Happy Christmas' and went to catch the late 'Bingo' bus to her home in Winchcombe nine miles away. She hadn't been seen since. The case passed the golden twenty-four hours, when evidence is intact and memories are fresh, with no solid lead. Then Mercer's slot on *Crimewatch* yielded two nuggets. An elderly woman, walking her Pekinese in Pittville Park, had found the girl's fake Fendi handbag in a bin. A matching Fendi purse contained fifty pounds cash. Mercer reckoned that the money lessened the possibility, slim as it was, that Bryony had gone off on her own accord. She had a good job and had just moved into a flat share. The cash suggested kidnap. But not for monetary gain. Mercer would not assume murder while there was a chance of life.

This investigation – Operation Banyan – was personal. Bryony Motson's father Brian, manager at the Lloyds Bank in Winchcombe, had helped Mercer wisely invest his Gold Cup winnings a few years back. His money doubled, Mercer built a games room onto his house in Bishops Cleeve. Every detective needs an injection of emotion when long days and nights with no leads is crushing body and soul. Mercer was fuelled by the idea: suppose it happened to a daughter of his?

On *Crimewatch*, he'd told Nick Ross how, when Bryony Motson left the nightclub she'd been wearing stone-washed jeans, a black velvet top and, despite bitter cold, no coat. Mercer – who liked his wife in high heels – opined that the girl's high heels would have prevented her running from an assailant.

The driver of the last bus to Winchcombe that night told police he'd passed the Pittville Park stop – a request – without being hailed. Nor had anyone fitting Bryony's description got off outside the police station – Bryony's stop – where the bus terminated at 23.06. Mercer's team traced every passenger on the bus. The two men and a woman corroborated the driver's story. When Bryony Motson said goodbye to her friends on 19 December, she might as well have walked off the planet.

Paul Mercer knew from experience and stats that a victim was likely to be dead within hours of going missing. Yet he kept faith. His gut told him that Bryony was alive. This was a 'crime in action'.

Nugget number two: five thirty on 31 December, His head

aching and reluctant to go home to change into his suit for the ball, Paul Mercer was at his desk in Cheltenham police station. He was brooding on how life was complicated when his phone rang. A woman in the foyer was asking for him.

Many times in his career Mercer had wished for the 'Robinson Crusoe Witness', who, cut off from news, doesn't know they're sitting on treasure. Lindsay Bennett, a pretty primary school teacher in her thirties, had been in bed with flu for over a week, too sick to watch TV or listen to the radio. *'I thought I was dying!'* Mercer had his castaway.

On the evening of 13 December – a Monday – Bennett had done her marking in the Sun Inn on North Street. *'You don't meet people stuck at home.'* She'd noticed the man because she fancied him and had hoped, because of the obvious age difference, that the young woman with him – who she now knew was Bryony – was his daughter. Irked by this, Mercer was nevertheless grateful for her detailed description. *'He had blue eyes like Malcolm McDowell, my Mum's fantasy man!! I hoped he was her dad so I'd be in with a chance!'* She'd even noted a half-moon scar on the man's cheek and – bless her – the telephone number on the taxi in which he and the girl had driven away. It was solid circumstantial. Mercer's team identified the man as Charles Brice, a local taxi driver. Operation Banyan lit up.

Fifteen minutes later a patrol radioed in. Brice had stopped to pick up a chocolate bar from a shop opposite Cheltenham Library. Ten minutes after that, Mercer spotted Brice's taxi outside the public toilets near the library. He'd told his police driver to wait and jumping out of the car, strolled into the toilets.

'You're coming to the station.' Mercer's voice rang in the tiled room.

'You're kidding. This is the best night in my life for fares!' Now Brice was concerned. 'Then I've got a party to go to. Unlike you. Or is the Gents your idea of a good time?' Adjusting the crutch of his trousers, his gaze travelled over the officer's face as a lover's might.

Detective Chief Inspector Paul Mercer did have a party to go to. He'd promised his wife that this year he'd get to the police black-tie ball at the golf club. A new century and a new start to a marriage faltering because he was always missing, assumed working. Tomorrow they'd treat their twenty-three-year-old daughter Lisa to the *Saturday Night Fever* musical at London's Palladium. Apparently, when she was little, Lisa loved the film. Mercer was confused: he couldn't keep up with what the girls liked.

He led Brice out of the toilets to the squad car where a young WPC sat in the driver's seat. A rough hand on the back of Brice's head, Mercer pushed him into the back seat and slammed the door shut. He paused by the kerb and breathed in a lungful of night air. He had a Nominated Suspect. He'd locate Bryony Motson and return her to her dad. He'd do a press conference in a blaze of glory. He'd hit the golf club in time to dance to 'The Lady in Red' with his wife of thirty years as the bells rang out for 2000. He'd caught the perfect case to end 1999. *Thank you, God!*

Humming the Bee Gees' 'Staying Alive', Mercer rested his palm on the car. He loved this bit, when pieces of the proverbial jigsaw fitted. Brice knew Bryony: opportunity. She'd jilted him: motive. A taxi gave Brice a legitimate reason to give Bryony a lift. Means. As a taxi driver Brice was trusted. Years in the force told the detective that, sharp, clever and plausible, Brice fitted the profile of a killer. Brice had kidnapped a young innocent girl. Mercer would make him pay.

'What have you done with Bryony?' Mercer got in the passenger seat beside the WPC. He put up a hand to pause her from starting the engine and addressed Brice's silhouette in the rear mirror.

'Why do you think I know anything?' Charles Brice sounded curious.

'Cut the crap. Tell me where she is!' His fingers curling and uncurling on his lap, Mercer wanted to rip the man's head off.

'I met Bryony Motson in the Sun, like your witness said. We clocked each other. She let me buy her a drink. She took a few off me, but who's counting. I kept to orange juice as I was driving. After that, I drove her to her flat where I left her. I gave her my number. She never rang. She was a nice girl, I'm as upset as you she's gone missing.'

'So upset you didn't tell us you'd been for a drink with her? Christ, it's been all over the news.' Mercer told himself no daughter of his would chat up strangers in pubs.

'What was the point? Bryony was at work the next day. How was me spending an hour in the pub with her going to help you?' Brice sounded weary.

'Where were you on the eighteenth of December?'

'I had a Birmingham airport drop, then a pick-up from there to Tewkesbury.' Brice gave a jaw-cracking yawn. 'Can I go please, Mr Policeman? This is wasting time for us both.'

'You answered promptly. Can you name every fare you've taken over the last fortnight?'

'The eighteenth's my Aunty Phyll's birthday. I popped in on her. You're a family man, you understand. She's moved into that old people's home your mum runs. I guess you'll end up there one day!'

'Can your aunt confirm that?' Mercer snapped his head around, sure from his voice that Brice was smiling, but the man was looking out the side window, apparently unaware he'd touched a nerve.

'I also remember that date because it's when Bryony disappeared. It's not like you think, I wasn't busy hiding her in a drainage shaft!'

'What the fuck does that mean?' Mercer reached up and flicked on the interior light.

'An expression, officer.' Brice rested blue eyes on Mercer. It seemed to Mercer he was gazing right into his mind.

'Why specify a drainage shaft?' Mercer's mind went to Cheltenham's sewerage system. *Christ!*

Brice spoke so quietly Mercer didn't catch it.

'What?' Every second was the difference between finding a terrified girl trapped in a dank cellar – or a drainage shaft – and a corpse. Brice must know Mercer had nothing concrete, that time was on his side.

Brice laughed again and in a Tommy Steele accent said, 'Innocent till proved guilty, guv!'

'If you don't say where you've got Bryony the papers will make your life not worth living. They'll camp outside your door and tail you wherever you go. They'll harass your "Aunty Phyll". They'll make your family suffer. Tell me where she is, it'll work for you in the long run.'

'Sir, I think we should be at the station for this,' the WPC muttered to him.

'I know what I'm doing, *Constable*!' Mercer snarled at her. Yet she was right. He wasn't sailing close to the wind, he'd hit a hurricane. Yet what he'd told the girl was true, he knew exactly what he was doing.

'You didn't answer my question,' Brice remarked as if he hadn't heard the exchange.

'What question?'

'I asked if you wanted a New Year's prezzie?'

Mercer's skin prickled. He'd always been able to get suspects to confess. 'Go on.'

'I heard about a girl.'

'Don't play games, Brice!'

'I can show you.'

Mercer could think on his feet. A kidnap demanded fancy footwork. He dismissed the WPC and eased his bulk behind the wheel. 'Let's go.'

Charles Brice directed Mercer along the dark road to Winchcombe. They drove in silence, passing Cleeve Hill and the golf club where Mercer should be right now. As they reached the lights of the town, Brice instructed Mercer to turn into Corndean Lane. After some minutes he directed him down a dirt track off to the left marked 'Private'.

Thick woodland closed off the sky. Through gaps between trees of ash and oak Mercer glimpsed the distant lights of Corndean

Hall. If Brice tried anything, no one would hear. Mercer dismissed this. The dank wooded tract was the perfect setting in which to hide Bryony Motson.

The car headlamps illuminated a sharp bend and to his right Mercer saw a sheer drop. He gripped the wheel. One jerk and the car would plunge down, the few bushes and saplings struggling to reach the sunlight wouldn't halt the trajectory.

'Stop here. We'll have to walk the rest,' Brice told him.

'You stay in the car. I'm not stupid.' Mercer pulled into a clearing by a stile and cut the engine.

'You'll never find it by yourself. I'm hardly going to run away!' Brice might have been giving the advice of a friend.

Mercer saw the sense in that. He made Charles Brice climb the stile ahead of him and then stand still. He shone his torch in Brice's face to blind him. Once he was over the stile, he shoved Brice onward and stumbled behind him along a muddied path. The cold weather had frozen the ground or walking would have been impossible. They came to another stile.

'I know this place. This is Belas Knap!' Mercer directed the torch past Brice to a grassy mound within a low stone wall. 'It's a bloody Neolithic long barrow. An ancient burial place. If this is a wind-up—'

'A copper with historical know-how! No wonder they promoted you! *Early* Neolithic as it goes.' Brice nimbly jumped over stones jutting from a wall to the other side. 'No wind-up, but it may be a wild goose chase.' He was halfway along a path that skirted a grassy mound rising above the wall.

Forgetting Brice could get away, Mercer knelt before one of the chambers in the long barrow and shone the beam around the interior. The sides were lined with flat, narrow stones interlocked along the same principle as the drystone walls dividing fields and gardens across Gloucestershire. At the back of the chamber was a huge stone. Mercer crawled into the mouth of the hole and touched the boulder. 'This bloody thing's granite, how could anyone be buried there?'

'Sandstone, actually. If my source is to be believed, a body's wedged behind that blocking stone. Frankly I reckon this is a waste of both our time.'

'Blocking stone? What are you, an effing archaeologist? If this is where you've got Bryony, so help me I'll—' Mercer's voice reverberated in the cadaverous dark.

'I wanted to be an archaeologist when I was a kid, but you have to go to university and—'

'Shut up and help move this bloody thing!' Mercer rested the torch on the chamber floor and gripped an edge of the stone.

Brice crawled in beside Mercer. Using the weight of their bodies as leverage, they heaved on the boulder. It shifted centimetres.

'Ouch!' Mercer's knee exploded in pain. He fell backwards, rubbing furiously at the cartilage.

'You were kneeling on a shepherd's crown.' Brice was holding a small rounded stone to the torchlight. 'See that hole in the centre?'

'A crown?' As the pain in his knee subsided, Mercer tried to attune to the slightest cry from deep within the mound. Yet even as he listened, he knew that the stone was wedged too close to the wall for more than a trickle of air to seep in. Bryony had been missing for thirteen days. He yelled, 'Bryony!'

'She's not here!' Brice was calm. Too calm. 'A shepherd's crown was left inside long barrows to send the dead on their next journey and—'

'Shut it! Get here and pull when I say!' Mercer got a hold on the stone slab again. When Brice was back in position he counted, 'One, two, *three*!'

Brice was a younger, stronger man and his pull was more powerful than Mercer's. Instead of to one side, this imbalance caused the stone to topple forward. The men scuffled backwards as the lump of sandstone crashed down, just missing them.

'Oh!' Charles Brice groaned as a rank smell of earth and decay wafted out. The stone had revealed a cavity the size of a travelling trunk. Mercer's first thought was of a foetus curled in the womb. He didn't need to be an archaeologist to conclude that the body interred in the cramped space wasn't Neolithic, early or late. Neither was it Bryony Motson.

So it was that only hours into the twenty-first century, Detective Chief Inspector Paul Mercer, aged fifty-three, with an exemplary career in the force and a year until full pension, faced two kinds of abyss. One was literal: behind the 'blocking stone' was a deep hole within the ancient monument. As white-suited forensics worked in the glare of spotlights, Mercer stared at what the pathologist would call an 'articulated skeleton'. The other was the vertiginous reality of his decision not to arrest Brice in the toilets and interview him under caution. A decision that some would say cost Paul Mercer his life.

Chapter Three

The setting sun turned the spans on Hammersmith Bridge to spun gold and made jewels out of jagged glass and shards of plastic on the Thames foreshore. The tide was ebbing; as Jack teetered on a brick by the river's edge, a strip of mud between his brick and the water broadened.

Jack meandered up to the retaining wall. The bricks were livid green up to the tidemark. He disliked this shade of green and looked away. Above were the gardens of Hammersmith Terrace. Iron mooring hoops and giant reinforcing bolts in the wall were mute witnesses of the crimes and misdemeanours of over a century.

Tall, wearing black trousers, black lace-ups, mussed dark hair falling onto his forehead, Jack Harmon might be a 1940s academic. He was actually a driver for London Underground's District line. The dead late shift. Preferring the darkness of his cab, he seldom sought the sun. An exception to this was the odd cleaning shift he did for Stella.

His phone was ringing. It wouldn't be Jackie wondering where he was. She'd never call. She let him be.

'Hey, Bella!' Jack affected nonchalance. Bella had dumped him months before. She'd told him he needed to get over his mother's death. After that, if he wanted to, he could call. But when he had called, Bella hadn't believed he was over it. Nor had he. Had she changed her mind? What did he feel about that? He found he was staring at the green slime. He blinked and transferred his gaze to the receding water.

'Where are you?' Bella always asked where he was. One of the problems in their relationship had been that he never wanted to tell her. Jack gazed out over the molten-flecked Thames. If he said he was by the Bell Steps, Bella would know he was there because of his mother and hang up. Jackie had suggested he tell Bella there are some things you never get over. There was no point trying to change him.

'Out and about.' He missed their nocturnal walks. He missed nestling in Bella's studio watching her create intricate botanical drawings. But had he missed *Bella*? 'How are you?'

'I'm pregnant.'

A motorboat scuttered past in the direction of Barnes Bridge. The wash rippled over the mud. Jack covered the mouthpiece in case Bella guessed he was by the river.

'Are you by the river?'

'Yes!' As if he'd got there inadvertently. 'Pregnant? That's great. Congratulations.' He supposed he was pleased. Bella had never had steadfast love, children loved you whatever. Jack quelled irritation that she'd so quickly replaced him with another man. 'Do I know him?'

'Know who?'

'Your partner. The father. It's wonderful.' Jack warmed to his theme. Bella was letting him know she'd moved on. A final twist of her scalpel. He'd seen early on in their relationship that it would be inadvisable to make an enemy of Bella. Then he'd gone and done exactly that.

'Yes, you do know him,' Bella breathed in his ear. 'It's you.'

The mud along the base of the retaining wall had dried to grey clay. Jack had read newspapers from that July day in 1981. It was likely his mother had cried for help, but by the Thames, in the middle of a Wednesday, no one heard. She was found by a man walking his dog. Minutes more and she'd have been washed away.

'Jack, you there?'

'Pregnant? How?' Jack swept a hand down his face. 'I mean I haven't seen you for five months.'

'Do I need to explain the facts of life?' Bella sounded upset.

'Of course not. But we took precautions.' No they hadn't. Bella was forty-nine, she'd be fifty next year. She'd stopped having periods. She'd said it was a liberation. He hadn't needed condoms, another liberation. He'd noticed she'd put on weight, but assumed that their split had made Bella comfort eat.

'It seems I can still conceive.'

'That's lovely. That is, if you think so?' *Idiot.*

Without noticing Jack had returned to the shoreline. He picked up a flat stone and sent it skimming over the water. It bounced two, three, four, five times. He'd done that with his mummy, never with Hugh, his father. He imagined skimming stones with his own child.

'Bit late if I don't think it's lovely. I'm due in a fortnight.'

'In a *fortnight*?' Jack whipped around. The beach was empty. As empty as it had been that July day. He'd never supposed he'd be someone's dad. He wasn't sure he had it in him. After his mother's death, his father acted like Jack was in the way. Jack stopped being someone's son. 'Why didn't you tell me sooner?'

'I wouldn't be telling you now, 'cept Emily said to. Now I've told you, I'll go.'

'Emily was right, I'm terribly glad to know. I'll be there with you Bella, all the way.' His heart swelled with the grandiosity of the moment.

'You will *not*! I didn't ring so you could be Wonderful Daddy. I don't need you swooping in with lavish presents and swooping out like a Superhero. My own father did that before he got bored with me.'

'I won't be like that. I'll be "hands on".' The sun sent last piercing rays across the ragged beach.

'I don't want you involved. It was a mistake to tell you, I knew you'd try to muscle in.'

'You can't do this on your own. I want to be there.' If he said he loved Bella, she might relent. She'd once told him no one had ever said that to her. 'I want to be there for the two of you.'

'It's not the "two of us".'

'What do you mean?' Bella had a new partner. Jack felt a flash of pure jealousy. He didn't want another man – or another woman – bringing up his child.

'There'll be a boy and a girl. I'm having twins.'

Jack sat on the Bell Steps and watched the tide turn. From the Ram pub came shouts of laughter. If he called for help no one would hear. If they did, they'd assume a hoax because he looked fine. He wasn't fine. He was going to be a father, but his children would never know him. An hour earlier he'd got a text from Jackie. Three kisses. A sign she hoped he was all right and was welcome if he felt like it. Jackie always got it right. He couldn't go. She wouldn't give him advice, she wouldn't say it would be all right. Jackie never said anything she didn't mean or couldn't know was true. He couldn't face Stella. Jack felt a shot of anguish. Bella's news cast him into a new darkness. He couldn't tell Bella he loved her because he was in love with Stella. He couldn't tell Stella he loved her because if it didn't make her run screaming, that he was to be a father certainly would. At best, Stella was indifferent to children.

Jack stayed on the beach where, in 1981, his mother was murdered and where, in 2011, he'd first met Stella Darnell. An ending and a beginning.

It grew dark. A waning moon rose in the sky. From the road, a street lamp sent shadows down the river stairs. When the rising water reached Jack's step he got up. The pub was closed.

Rubber-soled, his shoes were soundless as he walked into the subway beneath the Great West Road.

In the bleakly lit tunnel, Jack Harmon stared at the blue tiled walls as if in a trance.

Chapter Four

The Shogun took up two spaces outside the house. With a mix of exasperation and affection, Jackie patted the spotless paintwork. Barry Makepeace, her brother-in-law, rich, generous and, Graham said, 'full of himself', took up more than one space in all senses. She'd forgotten he was coming. Stella and Barry were not her first choice of guest combination. Barry, the world's most charming flirt and Stella, a reticent creature baffled by a compliment.

Her key in the lock, Jackie paused. There was another reason she'd rather Barry wasn't there. All the way home she'd struggled with how to tell Stella about Lisa Mercer's visit to the office. Barry's presence increased her dilemma.

'... there's comprehensive breakdown cover built in...' Barry's voice boomed down the passage.

She was greeted by wafts of roasting lamb tinged with lemon: her son Nick was a better cook than either of his parents. Jackie stepped into the kitchen and into a scene of domestic bliss. Stella was washing pots and pans that wouldn't go in the dishwasher. Anyone else and Jackie would have made them sit still with a glass of wine, but Stella was most content cleaning. Stella's dog Stanley shot out of his bed and bounded over to Jackie. On hind legs, he stretched up to her, reaching her knees, to have his ears scratched. Nick was trickling red wine from a bottle into a frying pan bubbling with what he called jus and she called gravy. Graham, her husband of some thirty years, lounged at the table drinking Beck's from a bottle. He preferred a glass, the 'cool-man' act was for his older brother's benefit. Jackie felt a burst of keen love for the man for whom sibling rivalry was alive and well after nearly sixty years. Barry had pushed aside cutlery for a sheaf of documents. Beer bottle clasped, he was reading out the benefits of the insurance he'd got for Nick's Chrysler PT Cruiser. Her son was twenty-five and an actor which should have meant a premium in four figures, but Barry, an adroit and successful broker, was quoting Nick a far smaller sum.

'Is that legal?' Graham muttered.

Barry winked over his beer bottle. Jackie believed he kept within the law. He might be Flash Gordon fused with George Clooney, but Barry's bargains had saved her family and Clean Slate thousands in motor and property insurance. Tonight, Barry was kitted out as if for a tropical beach in a short-sleeved shirt pattered with palm leaves and open to reveal tufts of still-brown chest hair. His matching hair was cut long on top and short at the sides, a flattering style that would suit Graham, who stuck to a number two.

'Where's Jack?' Jack Harmon, being a train driver, was punctual to the half-minute. Illusive and a loner, he never turned down supper at hers. Definitely not if Stella was coming.

No one heard the question.

'… shame about you being an actor, Nicky lad. If you were a pen pusher like your dad, I'd have lopped off even more cash!' Barry boomed at his nephew.

'I'm not a pen pusher…' Graham muttered.

'Good work, Uncle Baz.' Nick went on stirring the gravy. Jackie fretted; Barry liked fuss for his largesse. Nick didn't detain himself with the detail of tax, insurance or bills. Jackie dreaded it was the fault of indulgent mothering. Yet their oldest, Mark, was, if anything, too responsible. One son saved for a rainy day that never came, the other lived as if there was no tomorrow.

'Saved *us* money.' Graham contemplated his lager.

'What we *all* mean is, Barry, you're a star!' Jackie had been saving the Makepeace brothers from the dynamic of Barry bossing Graham and of Graham kicking against it since they were teenagers.

Barry raised an eyebrow at his brother. 'If you left the council, you'd earn ten times over!'

'It's not all about money.' Graham took the bait.

'Enough!' Jackie flung her arms around her husband's neck. 'When Nick goes to Hollywood, he'll treat us all!' Her faith in her son was endless. Maybe that was the trouble.

'You're late,' Graham muttered. Meaning he'd had to deal with Barry.

'I got caught by a last-minute client.' Jackie blurted out what she'd planned not to say. She went to Nick and, leaning against him, ruffled his immaculate hair, noticing again that he was thinning on top. That was from her side of the family: Graham and Barry had thick heads of hair. Nick offered her a slurp of his gravy on a spoon. 'Mmm, delicious!' Her sense of well-being returned. *Her boy.*

'All right, Stell?' Jackie wandered to the sink and grabbed a cloth to dry a saucepan. Stella didn't 'do' kissing. Jackie puffed out her cheeks to her as a signal she'd forgotten that Barry was coming. Stella seemed unbothered, although were she a poker player she'd never reveal her hand. 'Have you heard from Jack? I expected he'd be here by now.'

'No.' Stella tipped out the washing-up bowl. 'Who was the client?'

'What client?'

'You said that's why you were late.' She snapped off the rubber gloves.

In relation to cleaning, Stella missed very little. Jackie poured herself wine. Playing for time, she took a sip.

'Have you seen Barry's new motor?' Accidentally, Graham's timing was perfect. 'See what he spends his commission on?'

'It handles rough terrain,' Barry told the room.

'Give over, Gray.' Jackie sat down next to Graham. 'I saw the Shogun! You can take us for a spin. Not now!' She stayed Barry's hand as he swiped his keys off the table.

'He needs to get home to Yvonne.' Graham drained his bottle and, getting up, pulled another from inside the fridge door. The kitchen clock said half seven. Jackie checked her phone, Jack hadn't texted.

Proffering a gold Montblanc pen, Barry called, 'Come and sign your life away, Nicky old son!'

Stanley jumped onto Jackie's lap. Stella sat down at the table. *Where was Jack?*

Nick wiped his hands on a tea towel and whipped it onto his shoulder, before flourishing a signature along several dotted lines. 'Stay to dinner, Baz, there's plenty.'

Barry signed beneath, with surprisingly cramped handwriting for such a larger-than-life man, and slipped the contract into his snazzy Italian briefcase.

'Who was the client?' Stella asked Jackie again.

'Someone called Lisa Mercer. You haven't seen my dahlias, have you!' A panicked diversionary tactic.

'No,' Stella agreed. She never noticed flowers.

'Mum, they're gone, remember? The slugs didn't even leave stalks.' Nick was being sensitive, but right then Jackie could have tossed her wine over him.

'Mercer?' Barry was soaping his hands at the sink. 'Wasn't that the name of that copper?'

'Paul Mercer,' Graham, who was bad with names, offered promptly.

There was a beat of silence.

'Was it a cleaning job?' Like Stanley with a bone, Stella wouldn't give up.

'No, er, she...' Jackie was too aware that she could not handle rough terrain.

'Is this one of your cases?' Barry loved that Stella was a detective. It opened a whole new avenue of insurance potential.

'I'll tell you later,' Jackie said to Stella under her breath. Barry was the last person she wanted involved. No, not the *last* person...

Barry got another beer. He was staying for supper.

Nick put a bowl of mashed potato and another of roasted parsnips on the table.

'Start serving yourselves.' Jackie sounded desperate even to herself.

'What did Lisa Mercer want?' Stella asked.

'I'm texting Jack.' Jackie jumped up and headed into the hallway.

'Underground Man's got a better offer.' Barry didn't care for Jack who, although they'd never met, he reckoned was 'one sandwich short of a picnic'. Despite this, Jackie wished Jack would arrive. Being annoyed by Jack might encourage Barry to leave.

Where are you? The question never worked with her sons. Jack was her 'third son'. She deleted it and sent three kisses. Jack would know he was wanted.

'What did Lisa Mercer want?' Stella persisted when she returned.

'She wants you and Jack to prove that her father – he's a detective – was right about his suspect in the Bryony Motson and Cassie Baker murders.' Jackie had the sensation of looking over the edge of a very high building.

'You're kidding me!' Barry scoffed. 'That's done and dusted.'

'That detective, Paul Mercer, doesn't think so.' Jackie stared into her wine glass.

'Ex-detective,' Barry corrected her. 'He got it wrong about Charlie Brice being guilty.'

'You don't know that.' Graham picked at the label on his beer bottle. Nick was clattering at the oven.

'Who were Bryony Motson and Cassie Baker?' Stella asked.

'Who wants what? Rare, medium, well cooked, there's something of everything.' Nick laid down a plate on which sat a leg of lamb spiked with garlic and garnished with lemon and sprigs of rosemary. He brandished a chef's carving knife, the blade glittered in a bar of evening sunlight.

'Sweetie, it looks fabulous. Doesn't it look fabulous, everyone!' Jackie cried. 'Don't let it go cold!' Warm air drifted in through the French windows. The hot oven made the room warmer still. Nothing would go cold.

Chapter Five

'How in hell did you get in?' Bella barred the way to her artists' board as if shielding her drawing from Jack.

'Up the stairs.' Jack wished he could bite back the apparent sarcasm. An empty cereal bowl was on the window sill. Bella ate her breakfast at Kew's Herbarium. That would change when she became a mother. 'Josie waved me in.'

'She shouldn't have.' Bella's eyes glittered with rage. Her cheeks were rosy, her mass of curly hair fanning out, Kate Bush style. Jack felt a stirring of attraction. Bella was a beautiful woman, especially when angry, which she was often.

'Everything all right here?' A man, hands in a baggy cardy and the sort of maroon cords Lucie May allied with insanity, hovered by the cabinets which divided Bella's drawing area from the rest of the artists' room. He peered over a pair of pince-nez, an affectation, Jack thought.

'Hello, Brian.' He flashed the elderly illustrator his best smile.

'Yes thanks, Brian.' Bella began straightening her tools, a sharpened pencil, a rubber, a fine-nib pen. The scalpel.

Jack saw he'd messed up. He should have called Bella and asked to meet. She hated surprises. In many ways she was like Stella. But then that was the point. She'd been second best – third best counting his dead mother – and Bella knew it.

Stella's company cleaned Kew Gardens. In his Clean Slate polo shirt and a flash of his lanyard Jack had easily blagged his way in.

'Did you tell Josie we'd split up?' Jack baulked at the term. He saw now that he'd never really considered him and Bella as together.

'It's none of her business.' Bella snatched up the scalpel. 'It's nothing to do with you either.'

Best not say that Josie had called 'Congratulations' as he crossed to the stairs.

'Bella, we need to talk.' He glanced at Bella's pregnant tummy. She'd put on weight generally. It suited her. She must be at that 'blooming' stage, he hazily supposed.

'I have nothing to say.' Bella began sharpening a pencil and shavings flew up like confetti.

Bella's drawing was a large seed, she'd shaded the rounded surface with dots. Every dot would be faithful to the original. Bella Markham was Kew Gardens' best illustrator, she lectured internationally and was never out of work. Where was there in her life the time to care for children? *It's nothing to do with you.* He felt an ache in his solar plexus. 'Please, Bella, I'll be there. You can't do this on your own.'

'I've done my life on my own so far, a couple of kids isn't going to stop me. For the last time, I want you nowhere near me. Near *us*. These babies don't need someone who sneaks around streets at night and never answers his phone. I had an absent father, it won't happen to my kids!'

Stung, Jack didn't point out that an absent father was exactly what his children – *his children*, crazy notion – would have. Bella had said 'these' as if the babies were nothing to do with to her.

'Please go, Jack.' Bella perched on her chair, she looked out at the Thames. The sadness in her voice cut him.

Sunlight sparkled on the water. It was a classic summer's day, yet Jack was huddled in his overcoat.

'Bella—'

'Go!' Bella raised her voice.

Before Brian the Protector could reappear, he left the artists' room.

Jack was passing the red telephone box outside the Herbarium when his own phone beeped.

Is there a time you could come to the office? Sx

Since their last case Stella had been putting a kiss after her initial. He texted, *Now. Jx*

Chapter Six

'Have biscuits, Jack, as many as you can eat.' Beverly whipped the wrapping from around a packet of digestives and placed it on Jackie's desk beside Jack's tea. Stork-like on one knee-high booted leg, she enquired solicitously, 'Would you like anything else?'

'You're all right, Bev.' Jack prised out two digestives. Munching, he settled into what was Suzie Darnell's chair when she was in. He looked at Jackie at her desk sipping from her 'World's Best Mum' mug of Nescafé. 'Sorry I didn't make it last night.'

'Not to worry, Jack. We missed you, didn't we, Stell?' Jackie's two boys knew to ring if they were cancelling. Jackie forgave Jack anything in his sleeveless jumper, crumpled shirt, reading glasses on the end of his nose and hair rumpled. He wasn't like Nick or Mark. Nor, this morning, did Jack seem like himself. What was wrong?

Stella's office door opened. She came out and, murmuring thanks, took a Clean Slate branded mug of tea from Beverly. She perched herself on a low wheelie stool by the tea trolley. Clasping a Coke, Beverly checked the answer machine was on – they wouldn't take calls – and returned to her desk opposite Jackie's, popping the can and taking a swig.

'Where were you last night?' Stella rarely asked anyone about their private life. Jackie knew she'd minded Jack's no-show.

'At the river.' Jack bit into his third digestive.

Stella would get the significance. The Thames was where Jack's mother used to take Jack when he was a small boy and where, thirty-five years ago, she had been strangled.

'We've got a new case!' Beverly crowed. Although she dreaded the meeting, Jackie could have kissed Bev for unwittingly changing the subject. Jack suffered enough.

'Murder?' Jack took three more biscuits and offered the packet around. When no one took one, he levered out another. Jackie wondered when he'd last eaten.

'Jackie met a potential client. Her father's a detective,' Stella said.

'A sign!' Jack hooted in a spray of crumbs.

'How is it a sign?' Stella resisted Jack's reliance on fateful markers. Although as Stella and Jack got closer, Jackie had seen her resistance diminish.

'He means she's like you,' Beverly said. 'You're the detective's daughter. Awesome!' She rocked back in her chair.

'That's coincidence.' Stella furrowed her brow.

'Jack says there's no such thing as coincidence.' Since they'd co-opted Beverly to help with cold cases, she'd soaked up every bit of information and advice Jack and Stella uttered. 'It *is* a sign.'

Jack asked Stella, 'Have you accepted the case?'

'I didn't meet Lisa Mercer. I was waiting for you before we decide,' Stella told him.

Jack regarded his tea. He'd be irritated to be the last to know. Jackie wouldn't remind him he'd have known if he'd come to supper.

'Please take us through your meeting with Lisa Mercer,' Stella asked Jackie.

Jackie slid her notepad forward. 'Mercer's father was a detective chief inspector in the Gloucestershire Police until 2000 when he was dismissed for gross misconduct.'

'What did he do?' Beverly was scrubbing clean a whiteboard

that took up the partition wall of Stella's room. She drew a line across the middle in red marker.

'It's more what he didn't do.' Jackie scanned her notes although she recalled every detail. 'I'll start at the beginning.'

Stella and Jack settled in their chairs as if they were in for a bedtime story. Beverly stood, pen ready. The team was all here, I should be enjoying this, Jackie told herself.

'Two eighteen-year-old girls disappeared from the town of Winchcombe in Gloucestershire. The first was Cassie Baker in 1977. Then, in 1999, Bryony Motson went missing.' She paused for Beverly to write up the names on her timeline. Bev – a purveyor of metaphorical fairy dust – framed each in a heart. 'Cassie left a Queen's Silver Jubilee disco on the eleventh of June 1977 and was last seen on a bridge leading to a lane on the outskirts of the town where she lived. Her family didn't worry because she'd run away several times. She was eighteen, they had no right – perhaps no desire – to fetch her home. Her younger sister admitted that Cassie had mentioned meeting a "heart-throb". Cassie's best friend Lauren was pissed off, they'd always planned to go to London together. Cassie Baker had escaped Winchcombe for the pull of the big city on her own.'

'My mum would go ape if I went off like that.' Beverly noted the party and the last sighting on her timeline.

'Nothing was heard of Cassie Baker for twenty-two years until Bryony Motson vanished in 1999.'

'What happened then?' Jack smacked his hands of crumbs and embarked on another biscuit.

Jackie expanded on the notes she'd taken when Lisa Mercer was there. 'At half eleven on December the eighteenth 1999, Bryony Motson, a teller with the Cheltenham branch of the Abbey National building society, left the Pandemonium nightclub with two girlfriends. She headed to a nearby stop to catch the last bus home. Bryony was an only child. She lived with her widowed father in a village called Broadway. She had recently left his house and moved into a flat share in Winchcombe.

The flatmate didn't worry as Bryony often stayed out late with friends. Nor was she concerned when Bryony didn't come home at all that night. But when the Abbey National left a message on the answer machine on the Monday – the twentieth – asking if Bryony was ill, she rang the police.'

'The first twenty-four hours of a disappearance are critical. In both cases for these women, the period was squandered.' Stella was writing in her Filofax.

'What was the flatmate's name?' The pen top clamped between her teeth like a cigar stub, Beverly's speech was blurred.

'Jenni Wiles. Sadly, she died of cancer two years ago so you can't talk to her,' Jackie told them. 'It's going to be hard to talk to anyone. Lisa Mercer reckons that her dad's continued investigation of the murders isn't popular, the town wants to move on. She told me "Winchcombe welcomes walkers, not private detectives".'

'Were there no leads?' Stella asked.

'Yes. I'll concentrate on Bryony Motson, you'll see why.' Reluctant to recount the story at all, Jackie considered how to arrange the narrative. 'On the twelfth of December, six days before she disappeared, Bryony was seen in a pub in Winchcombe with a taxi driver. They left together. The witness, a woman, said the man was very good-looking. Jenni Wiles, the flatmate, told police Bryony had mentioned a man who looked like a film star.'

'Could have been fantasy.' Jack unwrapped the last biscuit. 'No one's as good-looking as a film star.'

'Except a film star.' Beverly put 'film star' in green marker under Bryony's name.

'Bryony hadn't told the friends she went clubbing with. Nor was she with a man that night,' Jackie continued.

'So then this taxi driver wasn't important enough to talk about? Like I said, perhaps it was a fantasy,' Jack pondered.

'She told Jenni Wiles,' Beverly reminded him.

'Bryony hardly knew her flatmate,' Jackie said. 'She could have been testing out the information, making it feel real. Jenni Wiles didn't probe, I imagine Bryony's friends would have demanded every detail. The witness said the taxi driver reminded her of that actor, Malcolm McLaren. No, McDowell.'

'A film star,' Jack murmured.

'That's our man!' Beverly stabbed the air with her pen.

'Hold your horses.' Jackie turned a page in her notebook. 'Paul Mercer was positive that it was. He identified the driver as Charlie Brice, aged forty-one, with a police record. He believed he was keeping Bryony Motson alive somewhere.'

'A record for doing what?' Jack was looking at her, Jackie glanced away. Jack was a mind-reader, she didn't want him reading hers.

'When he was nineteen, Brice nicked a pair of Dr Martens from a shop in the King's Road. In London.'

'Hang on!' Jack balled up the biscuit wrapping and hurled it into the bin by the photocopier. 'The police suspected Brice of murder because he'd shoplifted?' Jack liked to play devil's advocate.

'Not just that. He'd been seen with Bryony Motson and looked like this Malcolm McDowell.' Beverly woodpeckered the whiteboard with her marker, making a scattering of dots around Brice's name. 'Since Bryony was seen after this Brice took her home, it's only a circumstantial connection.'

'Read this.' Stella handed everyone a sheet of paper.

It was an article from the Gloucestershire *Echo* dated January 2000. Jackie should have expected that; ever thorough, Stella had done research. In the ensuing quiet as they read, Jackie heard traffic on Shepherd's Bush roundabout. The familiar grinding of engines and bursts of horns didn't reassure her. Since last evening, Jackie had been propelled into a nightmare.

BRYONY KIDNAP.
MAN LEADS POLICE TO BODY

When detectives picked up taxi driver Charles Brice on suspicion of kidnapping Abbey National teller Bryony Motson, he denied kidnapping the missing girl. Instead, he took Paul Mercer – the officer leading Bryony's disappearance – to Belas Knap, a Neolithic burial chamber above Winchcombe. Mercer expected to find the girl – an attractive eighteen-year-old – alive. But when they moved a rock from an entrance into the ancient long barrow they discovered the skeleton of an adult female. Through recent dental work, police have identified Cassandra Baker, an eighteen-year-old girl last seen in 1977. Trudy and Ralph Baker believed that their daughter had run away to London. Although in over two decades they had heard nothing from Cassie, they supposed her married with children. On two occasions the family were told of vague sightings of Cassie. An old school friend had spotted Cassie in London's Carnaby Street, someone else told Trudy she'd seen a 'spit of her' on a beach in Lanzarote. It turns out that Cassie Baker never left Winchcombe. Charles Brice has been arrested for the murders of Cassie and of Bryony Motson. Bryony's body has not been found.

'A few steps up from stealing footwear!' Jack breathed. 'It's a total change of MO.'

Jackie wanted to agree. 'Brice insisted he'd been told about Cassie's body by a drunk taxi passenger weeks earlier. Matthew Craven, an estate agent, lived in Winchcombe. He was flash with money and full of himself. Charlie Brice hadn't believed him, he'd been more concerned Craven would throw up on the seat. When Paul Mercer accused Charlie of kidnap, he remembered what Craven had said and, as he put it, "tried to get Mercer off my back".' Jackie flourished the article. 'Brice led Mercer to Belas Knap.'

'Knowing where a body's buried is an indication of guilt. Odd ploy to choose to convince Mercer he was innocent,' Jack said.

'Mercer was convinced he'd landed a serial killer. Charlie had murdered Bryony Motson *and* Cassie Baker. "Like all his Christmases had come at once," Lisa Mercer told me. However, after twenty years, forensics could only confirm that Baker's

DNA matched her family. With no other clues, like Bev said, it was circumstantial. Mercer had to let Brice go,' Jackie said.

Jack rested his chin in a cupped hand. 'Did Craven admit he'd confessed to Brice in his cab? It was one man's word against the other.'

Stella chimed in. 'Matthew Craven had been Cassie's boyfriend until they split up weeks before she vanished. He admitted to hiding her body in the mound. He also confessed he'd put a small stone with a hole in it beside her body. Craven said it was a Neolithic custom to keep Cassie safe on her next journey.' Stella paused at the obvious irony. 'Craven never actually confessed to murder. Craven's new girlfriend – Lauren Spicer – had claimed he was with her at the Jubilee disco when Cassie disappeared. When Craven told police about the stone, Spicer withdrew her alibi. She'd covered for him because she'd believed him innocent.' Stella was up on the facts, Jackie observed.

'Basically nothing linked Brice to Cassie Baker's murder except his taking Mercer to the disposal site.' Jack sat back in his chair. 'Circumstantial or not, I'm tempted to go with Mercer's view. He is the obvious suspect for both murders.'

'Craven was found guilty and sentenced to life-imprisonment.' Stella drew a line in her notes. 'Charles Brice was never tried and is free to this day.'

'That means Brice could have murdered more victims in between Bryony Motson in 1999 and Cassie Baker in 1977!' Beverley whirled around from her heavily populated timeline.

There was silence as the team digested this possibility.

'Not if he's innocent,' Jackie maintained. 'Paul Mercer is certain that they put away the wrong man. In his mind, if Craven was involved at all, he was the accomplice. Charlie killed Baker and framed Craven.' Jackie swilled back her coffee. It was cold, she didn't care.

'When making up a story, for plausibility splice it with shreds of truth. A drunk man in a taxi is a trusty chestnut.' It sounded like a recipe. Jack was speaking from experience, Jackie suspected him frequently of being economical with the truth. A man impelled to go on nocturnal walks through the city, Jack harboured secrets.

Now Jack asked, 'Wasn't Brice at least charged with kidnapping Bryony Motson?'

'No one's ever been charged.' Stella looked up from her notes, 'You think Charles Brice was innocent, don't you Jackie? That's what you said last night.'

Had she said that? 'I, er, it doesn't matter what I think, I'm not the detective.'

'While Craven was on remand, a fellow prisoner claimed he'd confessed to him. That, and the fact he admitted telling Brice where Cassie Baker was buried, meant he got life.'

'Craven is in prison on the say-so of a convicted felon and a man who the SIO considered the prime suspect.' Jack fiddled with a cufflink. Although his clothes were crumpled and frayed, he took sartorial care.

'It's harder to prove innocence than hide guilt.' Stella would be offering one of her dad's pearls of wisdom. 'Mercer made an error going with Brice to Belas Knap. He's quoted saying he *knew* Bryony Motson was alive and had to put her safety first. If he'd arrested Brice, the taxi driver would exercise his right to silence. Mercer was sure Bryony was alive and the situation was time-critical. He didn't follow the Police and Criminal Evidence Act and read Brice his rights. PACE says if you suspect someone you must arrest them, take them to a police station and offer them a solicitor. Anything Brice told Mercer *before* his eventual arrest on Belas Knap was inadmissible.' Stella glanced at the answer machine. She disliked missing calls. 'Bryony Motson's father – Brian – gives interviews saying that Mercer waiving the rules stopped her killer being brought to justice. Officially, it's an open "No Body" murder investigation. In reality, the case is cold.'

'Lisa Mercer wants to you to prove that it's Charlie Brice. She said something like, if her mum were here she'd want Mercer to die happy,' Jackie finished up and folded her arms.

'Weird what makes people happy.' Beverly surveyed the white-board.

'Mercer would be righting a wrong.' Jack raised an eyebrow. 'It would be atonement.'

'Craven denied the cell confession. He'd asked to be kept in solitary confinement to avoid someone trying to cash in with a "confession story".'

'People get punished for crimes they didn't do,' Beverly said. 'In primary school, I told a teacher I'd stolen the money which was found in my big brother's pocket. I had to do the times-tables in a corner and my mum was called up to the school. Maybe this Matthew Craven is innocent.'

Jack twirled his specs by an arm. 'As I see it, we have two options. Go all out to prove Brice guilty of two murders and make our client's dad happy. Or follow the evidence and discover who murdered Cassie Baker and Bryony Motson. The outcome might be the same. Or it might not.'

'If Lisa Mercer only wants us to prove her father's hunch, I vote we refuse. We work with an open mind.' Stella got up. 'There's one way to decide.'

'Which is?' Jack asked.

'Let's go and see this so-called detective's daughter.' Stella was already out of the door.

Chapter Seven

Long and winding, Bollo Lane connected the London boroughs of Chiswick and Acton. Houses gave way to industrial units of concrete and galvanized metal which housed, variously, an auctioneer's, a wood yard, an international shipping business, the local Royal Mail sorting office. A long stretch of fence topped with barbed wire bulged against the pressure of burgeoning scrub. Two cranes towered over a building site enclosed by a hoarding that promised 'Stylish Apartments and Houses with Incredible Views'.

The satnav said they were three minutes from the address Lisa Mercer had given Jackie.

At Bollo Lane's level crossing, Jack watched a westbound District line train clatter past. 'What "incredible views"? There's little to see from my cab. Ooh, except the London Transport Museum, we must go there.' He pointed down a road on their left.

'Isn't that more for kids?'

'Everyone. It would be great to go with children when they're no longer babies,' Jack said.

'A child wouldn't be a baby.' Stella bumped the van over the crossing. Jack put things in the oddest of ways. The satnav said they'd arrived. Stella pulled in by a row of Edwardian semis. Lisa Mercer was staying with a friend who lived on the end of the short terrace. Plastic sheeting shrouding scaffolding ballooned in the breeze. Inside the gate a bulk bag of sand slouched beside a delivery load of paving bricks. There was no sign of a builder. They picked their way to the front door around a plastic bucket brimming with blackened water and four wheelie bins. Stella rang the bell.

They'd agreed she'd lead. Jack said that with Mercer and Stella both having detectives for fathers they'd find synergy. Stella doubted this, but agreed because she wanted to lead.

'You're Stella Darnell.' The woman on the threshold made it sound like an accusation. 'Who's this?'

'Jack Harmon.' Jack put his hand out. Perhaps the woman didn't see because she was looking at Stella. She didn't take his hand.

'Jack's my colleague.' Stella sensed a first hurdle.

Lisa Mercer was dressed as if going to work. Her bright red cotton skirt-suit suggested work was for an airline or car rental company. Matching red high heels brought her within a few inches of Stella and Jack's six foot. Longish blonded hair was fixed with spray that Stella's keen hyper-olfactory nose identified as Paul Mitchell's Freeze and Shine.

'I expected just you.'

'We are a team,' Stella said stoutly.

'You'd better come in. Tea, coffee?' The offer was peremptory. Stella refused.

'Tea please,' Jack chirped from behind her.

Mercer left Stella and Jack in a front room filled with a component sofa in white leather angled to face a gigantic television. Diffused light filtering through the sheeting outside made the leather seem whiter still, an ethereal quality accentuated by frosted panes in the window. Stella, who prized privacy, had been considering putting something of the same in her windows. Jack had said it would be like being trapped in an iceberg. She heard buzzing and stared, with incredulity, as Jack's outstretched legs slowly rose.

43

'This is *fab*.' He'd activated the reclining mechanism at his end of the sofa.

'No!' she hissed.

'You said look relaxed. You've got one your end too.' Jack was fair.

'Not that relaxed.' Although not great on nuance, Stella had seen something of herself in Lisa Mercer. A woman of action with the minimum of fuss, Mercer would deplore lounging about, even if the furniture invited it. Stella hadn't brought Stanley because the poodle could be unpredictable, snouting out food behind furniture and embarrassing clients. She'd forgotten Jack was unpredictable.

A scan of the room told Stella whoever did the cleaning was top notch. A finger test on the coffee table confirmed this. The television was glossy black. A gold tinted mirror above the fire-place shone with a recent polish. Stella reminded herself she wasn't there to do a cleaning estimate.

She caught movement. On a shelf was one of those cats with the flapping paw that looked like it was forever begging.

'A Maneki-neko,' Jack observed happily. 'A Japanese talisman that brings luck. We should have one in the office.' He pressed a button and his feet descended to the floor.

Never mind luck, the constant up and down gesture – begging or waving – made Stella feel she could never give the cat enough attention.

Mercer entered carrying a mug of tea and a plate of biscuits on a tray. Stella noted the air of brisk competence with vague approval; it added to her building portrait of Mercer as a woman who got things done. Maybe Jack was right about synergy.

She fished her Filofax from her rucksack. 'Jackie Makepeace outlined your case, but it would help if you talked us through it.'

Jack was baring his teeth at Stella. Momentarily perplexed, Stella remembered it was a sign. He wanted her to *Smile!* She shot a smile at Lisa then, job done, wrote the date at the top of a clean page.

Unsmiling, Lisa Mercer gave Jack his tea. She sat on the edge of the last segment of the seating, her high heels clacking together. She dashed an imaginary speck off her lap. 'My father was a detective, like yours.' She eyed Stella severely as if this shared experience was Stella's fault. 'Unlike your father, sixteen years ago, one year shy of thirty years' exemplary service and with a medal for bravery, Paul Mercer was dismissed for gross misconduct.'

'Bravery. That's impressive. What did he do?' Jack leaned over and took a Bourbon biscuit.

'He wasn't even on duty. He stopped a man from attacking a tourist outside Gloucester Cathedral and got knifed.' Lisa Mercer made the intervention sound careless. 'He got stabbed. '"Hero Cop Dad!" Great dad if he'd bled to death!' She pecked on a biscuit, a hand underneath to catch crumbs. 'Ego was his downfall. He got a wash and blow dry for *Crimewatch*!' Munching, she shielded her mouth.

'Ego?' Stella asked. Psychological terms were Jack's territory. 'I understood his down— that it was his failure to caution Charles Brice.'

'Two counts were upheld.' Lisa held up a finger. 'One: Paul Mercer thought he knew better than the judge, he played PACE roulette and lost. The judge decided that anything Brice told him before they found the girl's body was unusable in court. Two: he was a media tart who thrived on the oxygen of publicity. The case would be high profile, he was all set to be Nipper of the Yard. Brice had to be his man.' Perhaps seeing Stella's perplexity – was Nipper a dog? – she said, 'Joe Mounsey. He led the Moors Murders. Mercer wanted to be in the true crime books like Mounsey, have his memoir ghosted, *Thirty Years of Violent Crime*, the perfect Christmas present. The Baker and Motson murders would ensure him a place in the detectives' Hall of Fame.' She took another biscuit. 'Fame? I should coco! Everyone's heard of the detective who let a murderer walk!'

'You seem a tad annoyed with your father.' Jack was congenial as he took another Bourbon. A 'tad' was putting it mildly, Stella was thinking.

'Paul Mercer is responsible for Brian Motson failing to get closure for his loved one. They managed to pin the Baker murder on her boyfriend Matthew Craven, but no one's been charged with Bryony's death. Paul Mercer was a crap husband, a crap father and a crap policeman. They couldn't fault his paperwork,' Mercer added inconsequentially. She patted at her hair with the flat of a manicured hand. 'He was married to the force. It divorced him. The only person he cares about is Charles bloody Brice. Mum left Paul Mercer the day after they found that Cassie Baker in the long barrow. Three years ago, she died of cancer. He killed her, he broke her heart!' Lisa Mercer's head twitched as if a fly had landed on her. Two red patches appeared on her carefully made-up face.

'If Brice had been arrested his lawyer would have advised him to remain silent,' Jack said. 'Your father going with Brice to Belas Knap meant he found Cassie Baker's body. It allowed her parents to have a funeral.'

'He'll tell you that. It's his justification for what he didn't do. Trudy Baker's grateful. Cassie's dad Ralph lives in my nursing home. Half the time he can't remember he has kids and most of his life he had trouble remembering he had a wife! I don't blame that Brian Motson for complaining to the Police Complaints Authority. Paul Mercer ruined his life. The poor man would kill Mercer if he could. Mercer always flew solo. Until he crashed and burned.' Lisa Mercer finished her biscuit and hugged herself as if preventing the possibility that she too might kill her father. 'He claims he's on the side of the victims. He has both eyes on himself.'

'The pressure during an investigation is intense, long hours without a break. Family is often a casualty.' Stella found Lisa Mercer's referring to her father by his name disquieting. Not least because she herself had thought of her father by his name too.

Lisa Mercer glared. 'So you were fine when darling Daddy ducked out of family outings, cinema trips or was a no-show for birthday parties? I'm betting he did all that!'

'My dad worked hard.' As a child Stella had wished she could miss her own birthday parties. Terry had indeed cancelled treats and broken promises, which infuriated her mum. She didn't remember minding. Since his death in 2011, Stella had gradually come to understand her dad – she too put work first.

They needed to change tack. Stella needed to signal Jack. Their strategy had been to be neutral about Mercer's contravention of PACE. Easy for Jack, he said he'd have done the same thing. Stella, a stickler for rules, would have issued a caution regardless of whether it silenced Brice. Jackie had described Lisa Mercer as annoyed with her father, but she appeared to loathe him. If they were nice about Mercer, they would alienate Lisa. Treading carefully, Stella asked, 'You want us to help him?'

'I don't give a toss what you do!' Lisa Mercer scrutinized her nails, pressed against a palm.

Stella was wondering what to say when Lisa Mercer dispensed with the dilemma.

'He's dying.' Mercer pursed her lips. 'He's got heart failure. He's a walking time-bomb, could have a massive coronary any time. He's housebound. Won't let me help. He could move into my nursing home, it was his mother's before I took it over, everything laid on, he'd have the best room. Instead, the local beautician does his shopping. Thank God Mum isn't here because ten to one she'd have come back to service him.'

It wasn't lost on Stella that Suzie Darnell had left Stella's dad or that Terry Darnell had died of a heart attack. 'Jackie said you'd like us to help your father.'

'Help him? Like I say, I don't give a stuff, I'm the messenger. Mercer wants you to catch this man.'

Stella took a breath. 'We don't undertake cases on that basis.'

'What basis would that be?' Lisa Mercer was steely.

Unnerved by little, Stella was unnerved. 'It could be your father is wrong about Charles Brice. He mightn't have murdered Cassie Baker or Bryony Motson. It might not be Matthew Craven either, maybe he's serving time for a crime he didn't commit. It could be someone else altogether. We never limit focus at the expense of every possibility.'

'Lovely for you!' With finger and thumb Lisa Mercer checked the corners of her lips for crumbs.

'If we find evidence linking Brice to what happened to either of these women, it'll emphasize that your fath— Paul Mercer's failure to arrest him stopped him being in prison years ago. It might attract more criticism. Is that what he wants?' Stella knew it was OK for a person to insult their own family members, but not for others to join in.

'He wants to be proved right! That's all he cares about.'

'You said he's ill?' Jack said.

'One month at the outside.' Lisa Mercer gave a jerk as if this was news to her.

'That's not long.' Stella meant the extent of Mercer's life, but his daughter took her to mean the case.

'Long enough to see there's no point,' she snapped. 'This is money for old rope. All you have to do is check for anything he's missed and keep an eye on Brice. Mercer's convinced that now he's housebound, Brice'll make a slip. Pie in the sky, if you ask me. The man hasn't in all these years, why he should now...'

'We'd need everything from the investigation up to when Paul Mercer left the police.' Putting down a caveat, Stella again avoided the word 'downfall'. She had a bad feeling. Jackie hadn't seemed keen they take the case. Stella was beginning to see why.

'He has all the files.'

'He has the files?' Stella echoed.

'Don't sound shocked! I read your father made copies of his unsolved cases. It's what they do. They can't let go.'

'He was a perfectionist.' Stella had never articulated this. Jackie suggested Stella try being less perfect, that would, she said, be good enough.

'That'll give us plenty to go on!' Jack was hearty.

Stella and Jack had solved two of Terry Darnell's investigations from papers Stella found in his house when he died. Periodically, she ventured into the attic and dusted a last set of boxes. She hadn't opened them. Although illogical, it was too much like walking in a dead man's shoes. From now on she'd find her own cases.

'What will happen when… if he—' Stella began.

'Drops dead!' Mercer raised an eyebrow. 'You quit. Why go on?'

'To discover the truth?' Jack suggested amiably.

Lisa Mercer stared at him. 'Paul Mercer is your client. Not me. I'm only talking to you now for Mum's sake. She left him, but if she were here, she'd hire you to give him peace.' She glared at the waving cat.

'Would she want to see it through after his death?' Jack persisted.

'She's dead so no she wouldn't,' Lisa Mercer uttered fiercely with bewildering logic. 'If that puts you off, fine!' She got up. Jack got up too.

Stella gathered up her bag. It struck her that Lisa was no more keen than Jackie they take the job. Stella wasn't either. She was appalled to hear herself say, 'We'll collect the papers from your father. Where in London does he live?'

'Nowhere! He lives near me in Winchcombe and while you work on this, so will you.'

Stella saw the get-out. 'We can't leave—'

'We prefer to get a feel of the crime scene. To live and breathe the scene of the life, the murder and the deposition. To tread in the steps of the dead and the living.'

Stella gaped at Jack.

Lisa Mercer handed her an envelope. 'Address of Paul Mercer and of where you're staying. Not in great nick but fine for a month. It belongs to one of my old people. He won't sell, even though the land's worth a mint and he'd stop fretting he's poor as a church mouse if he did. Mercer paid rent for it upfront. My one satisfaction is I've screwed some cash out of him for a harmless old gentleman whose sons never visit him.'

'Is Winchcombe a city?' Stella heard her voice from a long way away. Absurd question, she knew it wasn't.

'No. It's a village in the Cotswolds. I grew up there. Hated it then, nothing to do at night or weekends. But I admit now that it's got its charms. Not that you'll be sightseeing!'

'I can't leave Lon—'

'Sounds perfect!' Jack said.

Stella was a Londoner born and bred. The countryside was messy, muddy and defied cleaning; an alien landscape she'd rarely had call to visit. Outside the house she made a last-ditch objection, 'Won't Mr Mercer mind us taking over his case? I mean we're not actual detec—' She caught Jack's warning look.

Lisa Mercer looked at Stella. 'Didn't I say? He asked for you specifically.'

'Why me?' Stella's van gleamed in the sunshine. In a minute they'd be driving away. 'I'm afraid we can't—'

'Yes!' Jack grabbed Lisa Mercer's hand and shook it. 'We'll do it!'

'You're the wonderful Terry Darnell's daughter! He says your dad called you a chip off the old block. "Any daughter of Darnell can't go wrong." Running a care home doesn't cut it.' Lisa Mercer looked baffled then, snapping into action, she closed the front door on them.

'Why did you agree?' Driving back along Bollo Lane, Stella kept her voice level.

'How could you refuse?' Jack was rolling one of the cigarettes that as far as Stella knew he never smoked. His silver cigarette case balanced on his knee, he licked along the paper.

'I can't take time off work. No way can I move to the country.' She might have been invited on a Polar expedition.

'Yes, you can!' Jack rounded on her. 'You can do emails, talk on the phone, Skype. You don't need to be there. The only thing you can't do is clean and Jackie keeps saying to concentrate more on the business. She says you should take more time off. You have a team of cleaners.'

'We can't get more clients then have insufficient operatives to fulfil the service.' Flurried by Jack's outburst, Stella resorted to business-speak.

'Face it, Stella, Clean Slate doesn't need you!' Jack bellowed.

Stella dipped along back streets into Duke's Avenue. Clean Slate had clients in there, she'd cleaned a house on the right last week. They passed Chiswick Library where she used to go with her dad. He'd borrowed a book on the Braybrook Street shooting of three policeman in the sixties. Stella had read it twice over. Her mum said it was no story for a little girl. Her parents, who had stopped speaking even when Terry handed Stella over after his access weekend, had spoken that day. She'd crouched under a table in her mum's living room being a birdwatcher in her hide of chairs and blankets.

'It'll give her nightmares.'

'She had nightmares when Babar the elephant's mummy died. She asked about the police. It's her history, I was searching for Harry Roberts' gang the day she was born!'

'Don't I know! Took you weeks to bother to see her.'

'That's not true!*' her dad had bellowed.*

'That's not true!' Stella shouted. 'Clean Slate *does* need me!'

'Crap! Jackie's trained up Bev. Beverly is practically running recruitment. She's a bright young woman.' Jack was a tennis player whacking an ace Stella couldn't return. 'You're a detective. *It's time you acted like one!*'

'I'm a cleaner!' The words reverberated in her head.

'Ring Lisa Mercer and tell her that her father is wrong. Terry was wrong. You're not a chip off any block. Stick to your mop and bucket!' Jack snapped shut his cigarette case as Stella stopped at the junction for Turnham Green station.

'Let me out here, please,' he said.

After Jack had gone, Stella sat through a traffic light change as she gazed at the newly rolled cigarette on the empty seat.

Stick to your mop and bucket!

Chapter Eight

'Emma's going to finish with Nick.' Jackie took a sip of Sauvignon Blanc, feeling the cool liquid travel through her. She tipped back the lounger and put her face in the sun. There, she'd spoken her fear out loud.

'You always say that.' Graham sat in their Jack and Jill seat. He was swiping and dabbing at his tablet. A surveyor by day, he relaxed in the evenings by creating houses on 3D CAD software and furnishing them with tables, chairs and pictures. Pretend dream houses, although he said he had his dream house.

They'd had supper in the garden. At eight o'clock it was still warm. 'She didn't come to dinner last night.'

'Nor did Jack.' Graham was concentrating on his screen.

'Emma always comes with Nick.'

'He said she had a cold.'

'Emma's never ill. She's as strong as a horse.'

'You complain you never see Nick on his own, that he's dependent on Emma,' Graham said.

'She's good for him.' Jackie gazed out across the lawn. When he got in from work that evening, Graham had mown it. She had enjoyed watching him taking the machine up and down, making stripes like in the adverts. She wanted Emma to love her son the way she loved Graham. Still in his office trousers, shirtsleeves rolled, Graham looked as sexy as he had when she first fell in love with him. He and Barry were good-looking and good company, she wished they got on better. Her own Makepeace boys – Nick and Mark – were as handsome and, unlike Barry and Graham, they were close. Jacky thought back to last night. At least the brothers had agreed about something. Both advised that Stella and Jack leave the Winchcombe case alone. Jackie took a breath. 'Stella's going to Gloucestershire.'

Graham lowered his tablet.

'They're leaving the day after tomorrow. They'll stay in Winchcombe – actually, it's a bit out of the village. Mercer's giving them his files.' The words tumbled out. The sun was going down, but Jackie felt her face burning. She reached for her wine. 'Mercer's dying, his last wish is that Charlie is put away.'

'You said Stella would refuse.' Graham spoke as if it was a promise broken.

'She did. She hates to be away from the office or to leave London. Jack persuaded her. More than persuasion, the poor lad rang me earlier in a right state. He shouted at Stella! Can you imagine? Those two never fall out.' Jackie finished her wine. 'A good thing, I told him. A spot of friction's no harm. Those two tiptoe around each other!' She heard herself chattering as Graham's face darkened.

'That ex-cop's obsessed. It's too late now. Why rake it all up? Why did you tell Stella? In front of Barry?'

'So I shouldn't have said Lisa Mercer came to the office? I never lie to Stella.' She glared at Graham. 'Barry would have found out anyway.' Had she lied to Stella?

They were silent. Jackie heard the rumbling approach of an aeroplane. A car door slammed in the street. A bee buzzed in the lavender bush, above the chitter-chat of birds, a pigeon cooed. *You fool you, you fool you*, her grandad used to claim they were saying. Summer sounds. More gently, Jackie said, 'Gray, it's time this was put to bed. Charlie has a cloud hanging over him. We all do.'

Graham banged his beer glass down on the slatted table, spilling lager. 'You think Jack and Stella can solve a case that the police couldn't?'

'You said yourself Stella and Jack's solve rate rivals Martin Cashman's!' Jackie watched beer drip through the slats onto the patio.

'When they prove Brice is the killer, what then?'

'Not "when", "if",' Jackie said before she could stop herself.

'*When.* If Stella refused the case, how come they're going to Winchcombe? Since when does Jack decide? Stella's the one with her head screwed on.' Graham drained the rest of his lager. 'How dare he shout at Stella? When you think what she's done for him!'

'She's not his boss. They're a team,' Jackie said. 'Jack's done as much for Stella. You know that!'

'Why are you arguing?'

Nick stood in the open doorway. Her normally immaculately turned-out son had forgotten to shave.

'Haven't you got a show tonight?' she asked.

'I'm off sick.' Nick's voice cracked.

'You don't look sick.' Graham was never off sick. *Nor was Nick*.

'You don't look great.' Jackie eased out of the lounger. 'What's the matter, love?'

'Emma's left me!' Nick burst into tears.

Chapter Nine

Jack had told himself he must do what Bella asked and leave her alone. But tramping along the towpath towards Kew Bridge, his feet had other ideas. They guided him under the bridge, up from the towpath and along Ferry Lane.

At night, Kew Gardens was closed and, apart from staff going to Kew's estate office, few drove to the car park at the end of the lane. It was ten minutes after midnight, Jack was alone. Two hundred metres along, he climbed onto the river bank and peeped over the wall. A solitary light burned on an upper floor of the Herbarium. Bella was in the window of the artists' room, seated at her drawing table.

He should be happy he was going away with Stella. Less than thirty-six hours ago it would have been a dream come true. A sign! The two of them sharing a house, shopping together, sleeping under the same roof, working on a murder case. But Stella hadn't wanted to leave Clean Slate and now he'd shouted at her she would decide not to go. Fancy saying that Clean Slate didn't need her. *Cruel.* Clean Slate was Stella's life. What right had he to undermine that? After all she'd done for him.

Jack moved behind a tree, his gaze on Bella's window. Even if she looked out, Bella wouldn't see him. Jack Harmon knew how to be invisible.

Bella had told him he'd have no part in his children's lives. They would never sit on his lap or hear his stories. He would never sing the lullabies that played – like a stuck record – in his head. He would never pass on his mother's love, or the ghost memories of childhood that he couldn't trust.

He should never have used her father against her. Jackie had played it down when he told her. '*Stella appreciates honesty. Don't beat yourself up…*' He hadn't told her the bit about Clean Slate not needing Stella. Jack had been going to tell Jackie about the twins. But he couldn't admit that Bella wanted him nowhere near 'these babies'. He couldn't bear to see Jackie being careful not to agree with Bella. No good mother would want Jack Harmon near her children. He was damaged goods.

Jack froze. Bella was looking out of the window. Breathing evenly, he tried to think of nothing. The trick was to be nothing.

Bella didn't need to see him to know he was there. In the dead of night, she'd walked along this lane with him. She kissed his neck, unzipped his flies, unbuckled his belt… Jack wondered if his children had been conceived on this river bank. *Water babies.* A joke he could never make to them, hardly a joke.

Bella knew he was there.

His phone buzzed. *Bella.* He fumbled in his pocket. He looked up at the Herbarium. Bella was back at her drawing board.

'Fancy a nippet, Jackanory?' Lucie May, the *Fulham and Hammersmith Chronicle*'s war correspondent, claimed never to sleep.

A nippet – gin and tonic – was exactly what he wanted and Lucie May was the woman he'd most like to have it with.

Jack was in Lucie's 'Murder Room'. The last time he was here the walls, plastered with photos of a murder victim, had given the room an oppressive air as if the murder had been committed there. He'd been glad that Stella was with him.

Months later, the walls were white and bare and smelled of

a synthetic lemon fragrance. Adept at papering over cracks to hide inconvenient truths, Lucie had done no actual decorating to the house since buying it five years before. Until now. What was she up to?

He wished Stella was there now. Relations were strained between the two women, but Stella cut through Lucie's smoke-screen (since she'd given up cigarettes, no longer literal), and laid bare Lucie's scheming.

'Chin-chin, Jacko!' Lucie handed Jack a gin and tonic and clinked her own glass against it.

Lucie's unforgiving lifestyle – working through the night sipping nippets with days spent chasing stories regardless of risk – had taken their mental toll. Despite her faults (ruthless, vengeful, competitive…), Lucie was dear to him. Jack couldn't bear for her to get ill.

'Endora! Say "I love Lucie!"' Lucie was talking to her bookshelf.

Perched on a pile of books and magazines on true crime a bright yellow, puff-chested budgerigar was preening itself on a copy of *The Job*, the police in-house publication.

'Where did you get that?'

'Not *that*, darlinka! *Her!*' Lucie crooned at the budgie. '*Endora!* Say "I love Lucie!"'

'*Endora!*' the bird said.

'Garry gave me a present! He's forgiven me for being a naughty neglectful aunty!' Lucie poked her face up to the bird and made kissing noises. '*Nort-ee Arnt-ee!* Meet my new feathered friend.'

'Endora?' Jack reflected that, like Stella, Lucie could surprise him.

'Garry named her. Sweet, isn't it?' Lucie tried again, 'I love *Looo-ceee!*'

Lucie and her nephew had a precarious relationship. Garry was no doubt aware that Endora was the cantankerous elderly witch in the sixties show *Bewitched*. Lucie would make a magnificent witch.

'What a nice present.' Now that Jack was ensconced in the

Murder Room, he didn't feel in the mood for company. Except Stella's. Would Stella speak to him again?

'*What a nice present.*' The bird was eerily faithful to his voice.

'Gave it, sold it, 's'all the same,' Lucie said airily. She sat on the office chair at her desk and swivelled it to face Jack.

Lucie May, a bundle of contradictions, liked fuss from her sister's family while portraying herself as the roving reporter without a tie in the world. She could swoop on them with lavish gifts, or grumble that she had to go to her sister's birthday meal. The budgerigar was a development. Jack hadn't known Lucie in charge of a creature and was concerned Endora wouldn't thrive under her lack of care.

'I've got a scoop, Jacko!' Lucie spun around on her chair, her finger to her lips. 'If you say a word Endora will peck you to pieces.'

'Of course not.' Lucie and her scoops. Jack took a sip of his nippet. A double gin, if not a treble.

'Matthew Craven's being released. And I'm the only one who knows!'

'Who is Matthew Craven?' Jack realized he knew exactly who he was. Keeping his face expressionless, he gulped his drink, wincing as the alcohol burnt his gullet.

'Nice try, Mr Poker-Face Drawers!' Lucie crunched on a carrot. 'Baz Makepeace says you and PC Mop are going to catch that Brice fellow.' She trilled at the bird, 'Say "I love you!"'

There followed an expectant silence as Jack and Lucie watched the budgerigar nibble its feathers.

Without having met Barry but on the basis that Jackie and Stella liked him, Jack was wary of Graham's brother. Naturally he and Lucie knew each other, the press reporter and the businessman was the symbiotic pairing of PR and pounds. Lucie knew everyone and, it seemed, found out everything. 'How do you know Craven's due for release?'

'Sshh!' Lucie tapped the side of her nose. 'When Matty Craven steps out of Long Lartin a free man the day after tomorrow expecting to slip into obscurity, guess who'll be there to hold his hand!' She gave a corncrake cackle.

Lucie wasn't the only person who knew about Craven's release. Whatever he'd told his daughter, Paul Mercer hadn't asked for Stella only because he was dying. He too must have heard about Craven and, Jack guessed, it had galvanized him to put Brice inside instead. Whatever, Stella wouldn't be pleased that Lucie was on the case. If Stella was still on the case…

'Mercer was at Terry's funeral. Thin as a pikestaff, sheet-white, looked deader than Terry! You didn't see him?' Lucie swivelled 360 degrees in her chair, snatching another carrot from a bag of M&S crudités on her desk as she spun past.

'I was looking after Stella.' *No one looked after Stella.*

'*Sure* you were, baby!' Lucie fixed him a basilisk glare.

You underestimated Lucie at your peril. 'I wouldn't have known Mercer if I had seen him at the funeral. I only heard about him today.'

'Keep up, Jacko! It's a detective's business to leave no stone unturned,' Lucie cried. 'I was on that story in 1999.'

'How come? The women lived in Gloucestershire.'

'Charles Brice grew up round here. He went to school in Hammersmith. I spotted that.' Lucie gave a modest shrug and contemplated Endora who in turn contemplated her. 'Paul Mercer liked to swagger and shove. Judges Rules was his playground, the man was gutted when PACE came along in the eighties, it cramped his MO. Smart officers like Terry saw that Code C gave freedoms.' Lucie tossed the end of her carrot at a waste-bin a metre away and missed.

'How did it do that?' Jack asked although, his spirits leaden, he didn't much care.

'PACE spelt out in black and white the dos and don'ts. Terry read it on the Tube to work. We'd be in bed, all passion spent, when he'd rattle off the Codes of Practice, section numbers on detention, interview procedures, what a turn-on! We were like an old married couple!' With another revolution on the chair,

Lucie looked briefly wistful. 'Terry'd say make the rules work for you.'

'Terry stuck to the rules. Like Stella,' Jack demurred.

'Stella likes to think he did.' Lucie stirred her drink with a devil's head swizzle stick. 'Paul Mercer cut corners like origami. Terry said he was an ace interrogator, he built rapport with hardened villains so they chattered like canaries – or budgies – spilling inconsistencies until they hung themselves. Brice's hint about where that body was buried was gin to a spider to Mercer.' Lucie hooked the lemon from her glass and ripped it to shreds between her teeth.

Lucie's ability to judge character was little better than Stella's, but her description of Mercer tallied with his daughter's so Jack was inclined to trust it. Feeling his mouth shrivel at the sight of the lemon, he looked away and saw that not every wall was blank.

Hero Cop Slips Up in Bryony Motson interview, *Murderer of Cassie Baker and Bryony Motson Walks Free*, *Killer Goes on Shopping Spree*.

A picture below the last headline showed a man with lithe build in jeans and jumper outside a branch of Aldi. He was flanked by two men who must be prison guards and carried a bulging plastic bag. A photograph on the nearest cutting was of Charles Brice. Arrest photos made everyone look guilty, but still Jack recognized the sardonic stare of a man who rode suspicion like a surfer. The man in the picture had something to hide. His eye roved to a couple of privately taken snaps. In both photographs, Brice was some twenty years younger than in the police mugshot. In one, Brice, hair blonded by sun, smiled off camera with the even teeth of an actor. Jack recalled the conversation at Clean Slate's office that morning. The primary school teacher had said Brice resembled Malcolm McDowell. *A film star.*

Lucie was researching for her scoop about Matthew Craven's imminent release, a matter of hours Lucie said. An obsessed ex-cop overseeing Jack and Stella's investigation was nothing to Lucie May's attentions. If they did work on the case together, they would have two people looking over their shoulders. Jack's heart sank.

'Brice was a bit of all right, wasn't he!' Lucie whipped out of her chair and opened a cupboard next to Jack's chair. She tilted the bottle of Hendrick's at him.

Jack shook his head, he felt drunk.

'When are you off?' Lucie enquired in a by-the-way tone.

'Off where?' He stalled her. Pointlessly.

'Winchers, Jackaroo! For your month in the country!'

How could Lucie know that? 'Tomorrow.' He glanced at his watch. It was after midnight. 'Today. But we might not be going. Stella has Clean Slate.'

Eyes narrowed over her glass. 'And you have the London Underground. Listen, Jonathan-Justin, if you can't make it with Sexy Sherlock amongst the sheep and cows, you're not the man I know you are.' She even knew his middle name.

'We'd be working on the case.' In his discomfort, Jack sounded haughty.

'Sure you would, bubsie!' Snorting, Lucie swivelled to her desk. A sign for him to leave.

'Good luck with Craven.' He stopped in the doorway.

'No such thing as luck, you know that. It's putting in the graft. I'll be outside Long Lartin first thing the day after tomorrow. Early bird catches the worm that's turned.' She did another spin on her chair.

Jack went down the stairs. From the Murder Room he heard Lucie's wheedling falsetto, 'I love Lucie. I love you be-est!'

Silence. The bird had opted for 'No Comment'.

Chapter Ten

The sun burning through the early-morning mist made phantoms of houses on Chiswick Mall and tinted the Thames mercury silver. The swirling mass played tricks with dimension and the eyot causeway appeared to lead into the slate-white sky.

Stella was walking with Stanley. Bruised after Jack's anger the day before, she had shunned her usual company of dog walkers in Ravenscourt Park. Jack had had a point. Her mum – and, once upon a time, her dad – said if you did a thing, do it well. If Stella accepted murder cases, she was a detective. Yet a month away from the office – from cleaning – was a lifetime. Jack said Clean Slate could do without her, but, Stella brooded, could she do without Clean Slate?

Before Jack got cross with her, they'd agreed she'd collect him from his home on the Kew towpath at ten a.m. That was in three hours' time. Google Maps said the journey to Winchcombe was two hours, five minutes, allowing for delays call it two and a half. They'd be there by lunchtime. Stella, for whom the countryside was the Amazon jungle, was keen to arrive in daylight.

Before Jack's outburst, Stella would have been pleased by the prospect of two and a half hours in the van with him. Now she felt dread. What if he'd changed his mind and wouldn't come? She'd been shocked by his telling her off, as she saw it. Jackie had once told Stella she suspected Jack carried 'dark emotions he daren't express'. Stella did think if *her* mum had been murdered when she was little she'd be scarred for life. There was lots about Jack she didn't get and wasn't sure she wanted to get. He walked in streets after dark. He'd stayed in people's houses without permission. On the plus side he held down a job, two jobs if she counted cleaning. She'd begun to think that Jackie was wrong about the 'dark forces'. Then Jack had got furious with her. Stella recalled his pupils, black and fathomless. He was a stranger. A stranger she was about to share a house with in the middle of nowhere. Maybe it was for the best if Jack decided not to come.

Stella didn't see the cyclist emerging from the fog or notice he rode on the pavement. She had paused for Stanley to sniff along cobbles outside a house. It prompted a memory. When she was little her dad had let her try to walk on these cobbles, her small sandalled feet wouldn't balance on the rounded stones.

Go on, Stell, that's my girl!

Stella was jolted on the shoulder.

'*Fuck* off!' The cyclist's shout was amplified in the suspended quiet.

Stanley barked and yanked his lead, trying to chase after the man.

Filled with an uprush of anger, Stella whipped around and shoved at the cyclist. She was too slow. He had got clean away.

The sun was a yellow disc. The eyot had solidified across the water, reeds on its shoreline rustling in the breeze. As the mist evaporated, colours resolved into yellow lines and signposts, the water tower appeared behind the brewery.

Stella's shoulder throbbed where the man had shoved her.

Standing on the cobbles, Stella reflected that, at eighteen, when she'd refused to join the police and be a detective she'd denied Terry his greatest wish. Jack said the dead watched over the living. Stella found this alarming, but if the dead were watching, then maybe her dad would see she was being a detective. Thinking this, Stella formed a plan.

'That's assault! We should report him.' Jack was indignant.

Shaken by the experience with the cyclist, Stella had unpacked and repacked and got to Jack's house ten minutes late.

'He expected me to move out of the way.' Dimly, Stella heard that Jack had said 'we'. She hadn't meant to tell him, but it was something to say. She glanced around the living room. There was a pile of clothes and books on Jack's dining table. He hadn't packed. He wasn't coming. This, combined with finding him in bare feet clasping an electric toothbrush had, as if she'd caught him naked, plunged her into perplexity. Stella recognized head-on she needed Jack to come with her. She couldn't be a detective on her own.

'It's likely he had mental health issues or was on drugs. Or both. It's good you're going away.' Jack detached the brush from the holder.

You're going away. Out of the back window Stella saw row upon row of small bushes. Keen to forget the cyclist and, she realized, delay Jack telling her he wasn't coming, she asked, 'What's that?'

'My new box maze!' Jack clapped his hands. 'Brilliant, don't you think?'

Stella had got lost in Hampton Court maze when she was a child. She did not think it was brilliant. 'Are you opening it to the public?'

'No. It's for me and my friends.'

Stella hadn't thought of Jack having friends. 'How long will it take to grow?'

'Next year the branches will meld.'

'You can see over the top, it'll be easy to get out.' Stella tried to be tactful. Obviously Jack hadn't thought of this.

'It's not about finding your way out, it's the mystery of walking within.' Jack joined her at the window. 'It's a place to wander in, to wonder. To *be*!'

'Oh,' Stella said.

A book of music lay open on the piano. The instrument had belonged to Jack's mother. Beethoven's *Pathétique* meant nothing to Stella, but Jackie had told her his mother would play it to Jack after she'd put him to bed. The room was cluttered. A squashy old velvet sofa, a leather armchair, two occasional tables. Shelves in the chimney alcoves were stuffed with books. On the walls were oil portraits of stern relatives, Jack's 'Dead Ones'. Lucie May said Jack's family, on his father's side, 'went back generations'. Jack's great-grandfather, Barnaby Rokesmith, might have glanced up from consultation of a technical drawing. The Rokesmith men had been civil engineers. Jackie said Jack drove over bridges and through tunnels he dreamed he'd built. Barnaby, with sleek dark locks and eyes so alive someone might be peeping through the canvas, was Jack in a frock coat.

Jack had lived in the dilapidated house on Kew towpath for six months, but unlike her own place, it was like he'd always been there. He had done scant renovation, but as Stella had felt on rare visits to Jack's previous house, it was forensically clean. He wiped away dust, polished surfaces and removed cobwebs, so that a place was not just spotless, it was a home. He had arranged the squashy cushions so that Stella, who rarely relaxed, wanted to flop onto the sofa. A light fragrance pervaded the room. Stella traced the scent to a vase of white roses on the front window sill. How odd that Jack had bought himself flowers.

'Sit on the sofa.' Jack was a mind-reader. 'There's rumoured to be an Anglo Saxon saint buried in Winchcombe called St Kenhelm. The village was the capital of Winchcombeshire, population five years ago about five thousand. Catherine Parr is buried in Sudeley Castle on the edge of the town. We know about Belas Knap, the Early Neolithic burial chamber where Cassie Baker was found.' Jack was fitting his toothbrush into a leather washbag that nestled in a canvas grip by the living-room door.

Jack was coming! Stella felt a flood of happiness.

'Wikipedia says: "St Peter's Church, in the centre of the town, is noted for its grotesques." How wonderful!' Jack zipped up the grip and swung it onto his shoulder. He turned to her, 'Stella, about what I said, I'm so sorr—'

They were startled by a bang on the front door. Stanley barked and, claws skittering on the floorboards, scampered into the hall. Stella chased after him and fastened on his lead before pulling open the door.

A figure in voluminous black, eyes shielded by large sunglasses, loomed in the porch. Stanley leapt at her, mewing piteously. Stella registered his, 'I've found a friend' cry. Yet the figure – a woman – reeled away from him in pantomime horror.

'Down!' Stella instructed Stanley. Unusually, he obeyed. Stella recognized the woman. Bella Markham was not a friend.

'It's you,' Bella observed with less enthusiasm than Stella felt.

'All right, Bella,' Stella acknowledged gruffly.

'I want to see Jack.'

'I'm here.' Jack put down his bag. Stella grabbed it.

'Stell, it's heavy,' Jack protested.

'It's fine.' Stella barged past Bella. 'See you in the van. Bye, Bella.' She didn't wait for a reply. Now she knew where the roses had come from.

Stella loaded the grip into the van, strapped Stanley into his seat and got in. She spread the road atlas over the steering wheel. The van had satnav but Stella liked a tangible overview. Without taking it in, she traced the route with her finger. Jack was back with Bella. Stella hadn't gathered who'd left who – some months earlier – or why. Jackie had told her they'd split up, for once Jackie was wrong.

Stella glanced up in time to see Bella Markham striding out of the alley, skirts swishing. She crossed Kew Green to a black convertible Mini parked by the pond. Stella prepared to wave, but Bella zoomed past without apparently seeing her. By the time Jack mooched around the corner, hands in trouser pockets, the Mini was on the South Circular.

'All right?' Stella laid the atlas in the well by Jack's feet.

'Fine and dandy! I'll navigate.' Jack picked up the atlas.

Stella decided not to mention that the page Jack was scrutinizing covered the outskirts of Edinburgh.

Chapter Eleven

'Hey, girls, how's it fadging?' Barry Makepeace breezed into the Clean Slate office.

Jackie was on the phone. She flattened a palm against the mouthpiece and did a 'keep it down' motion.

'Would you like a drink, Mr Makepeace?' Beverly scooted out of her chair.

'Only if it's a beer!' He flung himself into Suzie's chair and stretched out his legs. A tall burly man with a big personality, Makepeace filled whatever room he entered.

'You can have my Coke,' Beverly offered.

'You're a sweetheart, but I couldn't steal it from you.' Grinning, he tugged loose his bright yellow tie. The room also filled with the tang of his aftershave.

'All right, Baz.' Jackie was off the phone. 'Bev, that woman with five cats in Chiswick High Road wants an estimate. Would you go?'

Beverly gaped at Jackie as if she'd gone mad. 'Stella does estimates.'

'She can't do them all,' Jackie told her. 'Remember to over-estimate the cleaning time. Customers suspect we stint on quality if you quote low. No compliments on furnishings, décor etc., you'll make her nervous. You *see* only what needs cleaning.'

Barry pulled a face. 'With five cats there'll be plenty needs doing. Isn't keeping that many a sign of insanity?'

'We're not about judging how our clients live either.' Jackie was stern. 'It's a sign of a large pet food bill and that's all.'

'"Think cleaning, not compliments."' Beverly intoned a phrase from the Clean Slate handbook that she was proud to have invented.

'When you're done, Bev, maybe you'll do one for me.' Barry eased the back of his neck, turning this way and that.

Beverly reddened.

'Enough, Barry,' Jackie said.

'I'm serious. My new apartments are ready for cleaning. Bev could go with Stella and see how the boss works. She'll make sure Stella gives me a discount, won't you?' Besides insurance deals and bargain vehicles, Barry had ventured into property development. Graham prophesied that one day his brother's burgeoning empire would come crashing down.

'Stella always gives you a discount,' Jackie retorted.

'Go kick arse, Bev!' Barry watched Beverly slip on her 'customer-facing heels' and stalk out of the office.

'I'll look at the flats,' Jackie told him. 'Stella's away.'

Abruptly serious, Barry leaned towards Jackie. 'You said she wouldn't go.'

'I was wrong.' Jackie hit a button on her keyboard and the printer began spewing out paper.

'There's nothing to find so they won't find it.' Jackie tapped the pages together and stapled a corner.

'What's baby bro say?'

'He's annoyed I told Stella.' Jackie didn't say that since supper the night before last, Graham had hardly spoken to her. If Nick wasn't staying – unable to eat and inconsolable – Jackie could have sorted it. She and Graham rarely argued and when they did, made up in minutes. Her sister said having no rows wasn't natural, but she'd had two divorces.

'Why *did* you tell her?'

'Mercer's daughter would have reached Stella eventually.'

'I hope you don't regret it.' Barry headed out of the office.

'Don't wind Graham up,' Jackie said to the closing door. Graham was already wound up.

The telephone rang. Her mind elsewhere, Jackie prattled a sing-song greeting into the receiver, 'Clean Slate for a fresh start, Jackie speaking. Hello, how can I help you?'

Chapter Twelve

'NO T8X. A political statement. That's rare.' Jack noted in his book the number plate of a Toyota Grand Vitara in the outside lane. The fifth personalized registration he'd spotted since they'd joined the M40.

'Why do people do that?' Stella said.

Never would Stella intentionally proclaim her personality on a vehicle or even in her house where most walls, painted a safe white, were bare. She didn't suspect that her studied anonymity revealed her as risk-averse, tidy and methodical. Ironically, Stella did have a personalized plate. Barry Makepeace had acquired a job lot – CS1 to CS6 – for Clean Slate. By choice, Stella's van had no company logo. She'd been taken aback when customers – those aware of her murder cases – assumed CS1 stood for Crime Scene Investigation.

'Look, 8ARTR3! That has to be today's best.' Jack pointed at a blue car in the outside lane with an 'F' decal above the bumper.

'Why?' Bless her, Stella was trying to appear interested.

'Jean-Paul Sartre, the French philosopher. How bonkers is that! And that's a Citroën. No British driver would name a plate in honour of a philosopher. Bertrand Russell, Mary Wollstonecraft, I don't think so...' Jack glanced up in time to see a sign flash by. 'Can we stop at the next services? I could do with a pee.'

'No problem. Please would you get me a large skinny latte?' Stella flicked down the indicator. 'Extra hot.'

Minutes later Jack was weaving his way through the cavernous mall, bewildered by the cathedral clamour underpinned by George Michael urging him to have faith. A giant Sky News screen showed Donald Trump campaigning for the US presidency. Jack eased past queues for Starbucks, a salad bar, motorway-dazed travellers window-shopping at a mobile phone concession and clustering around the McDonald's tables.

There was one urinal free, Jack fumbled at his flies as he made for it. As his pee hit the steel panel, he returned to Bella's visit. Seeing Stella she'd said, 'You didn't take long to get it together with *her*!' Bella had been voicing her fear that he'd always loved Stella. She'd seen by his hesitation that she was right and stormed off without saying why she'd come. Jack might have reassured Bella by saying that after his outburst to Stella the previous morning, he and Stella were speaking with the politeness of strangers. Was Bella going to tell him she'd changed her mind and he could be a proper father to his babies after all?

Stella. Jack shut his eyes. He had no idea how to tell Stella about the twins.

He soaped his hands under hot water. He was now convinced that Bella had been about to propose they get back together. He'd blown it. The drier – 'Air Fury' – blasted him with a high-pitched whine. He'd read that these machines damaged children's hearing. His hands still damp, Jack left the toilets.

He shuffled forward in the long queue at Starbucks. Idly he watched people coming into the mall. A thirty-something woman in a waist-length cardigan and stretch jeans shepherded children – a boy and a girl aged about five – towards the loos, an arm on their shoulders. The boy was clutching the crutch of his blue combats. Jack wondered if he himself had ever been to a service station with his mother. All his memories of her involved the back garden and the river. He'd take his twins to the Gent's. No way would he let his daughter go off by herself, he'd keep her safe.

When he reached the counter, he took two packets of biscotti, paused and pulled out a third packet.

'Large skinny latte, please.' Jack's smile was lost on the cashier. Pen hovering, she didn't look at him. 'Extra hot please.'

'Name?' the woman barked.

Name? Jack kept his 'footprint' light. He never gave his name in public.

'Stanley.' He bounced on his heels.

The woman scribbled 'Stanley' on the cup in black pen, added 'X H' and passed the cup to a barista.

He moved to the other end of the counter to wait for the latte. The little family were back. The mother was stopping the boy pawing at the glass protecting the pastries. Jack nearly dropped the biscotti. The children were twins. He felt a plunge of despair, Bella had said he belonged in the dark. He'd never be in a service station with his children.

Two women were staring at him. Had he spoken his thoughts out loud?

'Stanley?' The barista, a young Asian man, his hair short at the sides and combed forward on top, who'd succeeded in transforming his Starbucks jacket into a fashion item, was holding up a cup. 'Skinny latte mate?'

'You didn't get one?' Stella slotted her drink into one of the holders. He saw her see 'Stanley' scrawled on the side. She didn't comment.

'I changed my mind.' Jack wasn't going to explain that seeing two children with their mum had made him forget that he'd wanted a flat white.

As Stella followed exit signs around the sprawling car park, an old-fashioned telephone ring came through the van's speakers. She turned up the volume on the steering wheel: 'Stella Darnell.'

'Lisa Mercer. Please go and see my father the minute you arrive, he's keen to get going.'

Chapter Thirteen

The ancient Saxon town of Winchcombe had changed little from the sepia-toned photographs hung on the staircase wall in the old town hall. A vintage Bentley parked in a pool of lamplight outside one of the cottages of mellow Cotswold stone on North Street might easily have been there in 1916 as a century later.

Even in broad daylight, sun blazing onto pavements with myriad hollyhocks growing between the cracks and sending gleams of light off four-by-fours rumbling along the main street, Winchcombe achieved a timelessness.

Instinctively, as if dictated by the gentler pace, Stella touched the brake to slowly drift past shops which recalled Hammersmith in the seventies. A sit-up-and-beg bike laden with loaves and rolls was propped outside a bakery. There was a dog bowl outside the pet shop. The summer air smelled of batter from the fish and chip shop that was opposite a post office. People lingered in groups chatting, or sipped drinks at tables outside the Winchcombe deli. Stella looked away from the Co-op. Since her dad died outside the Seaford branch down on the Sussex coast, she'd avoided the supermarket.

Paul Mercer lived on Bull Lane. Barely more than an alley, it was between a boutique festooned with hanging baskets, and a gift shop. Stella wouldn't risk scraping the van against the stone walls. Ignoring the satnav, she went next right into Chandos Street which, lined with more cottages, wasn't much wider than Bull Lane.

They found the car park described in Lisa Mercer's instructions. Oddly, for a no-nonsense woman, Lisa had added in brackets that when he was a boy her grandfather kept his horse here in what, a hundred years ago, had been a meadow. Jack was delighted by this detail. Stella, who had never so much as ridden a donkey on the beach, was glad there were no horses there now.

Jack waited while Stella fed two hours' worth of change into a machine by a bin overflowing with cans, food cartons and used poo-bags. Stanley lifted his leg against one of the hollyhocks growing by the car park.

Unlike most others, Mercer's house was built of reddish brick and squeezed between two cottages like an afterthought. A sign in the window warned 'DO NOT PARK!' in capitals. Mercer's instruction was heeded: Stella noted that his tiny dwelling was the only one without a car parked hard up against the cottage walls. Winchcombe streets weren't constructed for modern-day traffic.

Jack knocked on the door, the wood red, faded to pink.

'Maybe he's out,' he said, after a full minute.

Stanley tilted his head as if he'd heard something.

'Mercer can't go out,' Stella reminded him.

'He's in there.' Jack pressed his ear to the door. Stanley growled. 'He's shouting something.' He went to the window and cupped his hand to the glass. Then, 'Ah yes, got you!'

'What's happening?'

'There's a key safe. He called out the code.' Jack unlatched a side door.

A dank passage led to the back. A path ran between the cottages and the back gardens. The garden next door to Mercer's was a riot of colour, a trellis arch trailed some flower or other, Stella only knew roses and hollyhocks. A green-stained plaster dolphin spouted water into a pool. The sound might have been pleasant, but in the country silence (no voices, no music, no planes, no ringtones; no familiar London sounds), Stella found it unsettling.

Even when mobile, Mercer hadn't been a gardener. Moss-covered concrete ended with a brick shed, the door on one hinge. A flowerpot full of cigarette stubs was beside another brimming with dead ivy.

Jack returned the key to the safe and followed Stella as, gingerly, she ventured into Mercer's kitchen. They were enveloped by the odour of reheated food. Able to identify a brand at fifty paces, Stella sniffed another smell that buoyed her. Paragon kitchen sanitizer. The disinfectant was heavy duty for a domestic space. She warmed to Paul Mercer.

The ceiling barely gave headroom. Instinctively, Stella ducked. Sunlight flared over a spotless gas cooker. On a counter was a kettle, a jar of Co-op instant coffee, and a replicate of the Sharp microwave with wood-effect control panel that Stella's mum had in the eighties. No dust, no dirt. Someone had deep-cleaned the kitchen. Stella sniffed again. Lithofin Power-Clean, she used it for a shopping mall client. It was a mallet to hit a pin but, she guessed, that Mercer, like Terry used to filthy crime scenes, maintained stringent hygiene standards at home. She brightened further.

In the living room, disinfectant was spliced with Gillette's Cool Wave. The aftershave Terry had worn. Stella's heart flipped.

'Mr Mercer?'

But for the observant flicking brown eyes and the brown hair touching his collar, Stella would not have believed the mountainous man in a riser recliner, carpet-slippered feet swollen, was the man with the policeman-good-looks in photos sixteen years ago. Mercer's liver-spotted skin had a sallow tinge like old newspaper. Pudgy fingers with gnarled nails worried at a blanket spread over his capacious lap.

Mercer was hemmed in by a table on wheels straddling his chair. It was laden with files, a dirty dinner plate and fork, a bottle of lemonade, drinks glasses and a pill box. Mercer's bulging stomach was a shelf for papers he'd been reading. Stella knew heart failure caused build-up of body fluid, the lungs filled with water so, if the heart didn't pack up, death was by drowning. Mercer was sixty-three, two years younger than Terry when he died. Yet Mercer looked older than Terry had then. If there was luck, Terry had been lucky to go suddenly and not end up like Mercer, helpless and immobile.

'If you want tea, you'll have to get it. I could, but if I do I'll be too knackered to talk.' Mercer nodded at a shabby divan against a wall of Cotswold stone. 'Have a seat.'

'Shall I make you tea?' Stella fleetingly wondered why not plaster the wall. It must be like living in a cave.

'Your dad comes through that door with a bottle of JD.' He wheezed. 'Terry whistles as he walks up the lane. I always know it's him.'

Disconcerted by Mercer talking about Terry in the present tense, Stella sat down on the divan. Jack joined her. Stanley jumped on her lap. She tried to picture her dad in the poky cottage. He used to whistle when he came in from work, she'd forgotten.

After he died, Stella would get the impression Terry had left a room seconds before she entered. This occurred less since she'd chosen to live in his house, bequeathed to her, instead of visiting to clean. She had never before actively wished he'd stayed in the room but now that wish was strong. If Terry would burst in with a bottle of Jack Daniel's, he'd handle Mercer. That this couldn't happen made her unintentionally combative. She launched straight in, 'What makes you so sure Charles Brice killed Cassie Baker and Bryony Motson?'

'Brice knew Cassie in 1977. He was staying with his aunt here. He was living in Winchcombe by December 1999 when Bryony was last seen alive. He fancied both girls. He let slip how Bryony rejected him. You can bet Cassie did a swerve – by all accounts that girl knew her own mind. The life and soul, she lit up a room. Her and Lauren. Brice doesn't take "no" for an answer. He's perceptive, he manipulates. Too clever and brim-full of confidence. It's in his eyes, devil's eyes.' Mercer rattled his papers and muttered as if they'd argued with him. 'Terry agrees.'

How could Terry agree? Perhaps his illness had affected his mind. Stella remembered her manners: 'This is Jack. Jack Harmon, my colleague.'

'Good to meet you, sir. We're looking forward to working for you.' Jack jumped up, grasped Mercer's meaty hand and shook it.

'Glad to have you on board. As your dad knows, Stella, investigating a death is a delicate matter. You've got the family to consider, they're your first duty. You assign a liaison officer, but it doesn't let you off. The family have to know *your* face, to trust *you*. Get involved. Don't listen to guff about being objective, if you don't care in here.' He thumped a fist against his heart. Not wise, Stella worried. 'Then who's working for the dead? Dig deep. Feel their pain, suffer their loss. It's the hardest part. Reassure the family you'll do everything in your power to find who murdered their loved one. I promised Cassie's mum Trudy I'd bring Cassie's killer in. Terry'll tell you, I keep my word.' The papers in one hand, Mercer gripped his chair as if he might tip out of it and succumbed to a bout of coughing.

Stella reached for the lemonade, but although he'd gone puce, Mercer waved it away. Clearing his throat, he gasped, 'Brice still visits Cassie's disposal site. Five times in January and three in February.'

'How do you know?' Jack asked.

'I follow him, keep him under covert surveillance. Did. I haven't been able to since this thing got me. He'll slip up now he thinks I'm out of action.' With rasping breaths, Mercer waved at the files on the table. 'It's all in there, my decision log, path reports for both girls, witness statements, press releases, interviews... Two cases twenty years apart, one killer.' He subsided into another cough.

If Brice was the murderer, Stella thought, he was clever enough not to have made a mistake in sixteen years. She doubted new agents staking him out would cause him to put a foot wrong.

Terry's voice was clear to her, as if there after all, as good as echoing Mercer:

'*A murder victim isn't responsible for their death. The killer is to blame. But the way a victim lived, their cares, their choices, can yield clues to why they died. Get to know the victim, meet their families and their friends. Get under their skin.*'

'We'd like to meet the families of Cassie Baker and Bryony Motson.' Stella nodded.

'I'm the devil incarnate to Brian Motson, he dobbed me in to the PCA. Said I let Bryony's killer walk. He won't talk if he knows you're working for me. That's a shame, because like I told him, I'll get Brice. That man planned that murder, hid the weapon and disposed of it afterwards. But even the clever ones trip up in the end.'

'What about Ralph Baker?'

'What about Ralph Baker. Thick as a bucket of plaster, him. He does the heartbroken father bit, but consider this, never between the seventies and the millennium did he go looking for his precious daughter. Nor was he there for Cassie when she was alive. Him and Cassie were at each other's throats hammer and tongs. To give Brian Motson credit, he was a doting dad, still is. I was gobsmacked when he complained. He sorted my mortgage when he was at the bank.'

'Given Cassie was rumoured to be in London, if Brice hadn't taken you to Belas Knap, you'd never have found Cassie Baker's body.' Stella saw the intrinsic unfairness in the affair. Mercer wasn't corrupt. In 1999, he'd worked tirelessly to find Bryony. He'd enabled the Bakers to give Cassie a funeral. But when a murder case is unsolved, Terry said someone had to take the rap. First in line was the detective who failed to find the killer. Especially one who'd broken the rules from day one.

'I made the right decision. It was a live kidnap situation. Brice isn't your common or garden villain. He's from London.' Mercer implied this was a factor in Brice's guilt. 'He came to Winchcombe in the seventies to milk his aunt. He soon learnt Phyllis Brice couldn't be played. He knew he'd be a suspect, so he turned the light on Craven. Brice fooled the police and he fooled the courts. He didn't fool me. It's your job to get him.'

'We will keep an open mind—' Stella began.

'Start with Trudy Baker, Cassie's mother. She was on top of the world to have her girl home, she'll meet you. Lisa'll set you up with both her and Ralph. He likes Lisa.'

'What do you think happened to Bryony Motson?' Jack asked.

'Same as Cassie, he's buried her somewhere he thinks we're too dumb to look.'

Stella considered that, as Motson's body hadn't been found, Brice had hidden her well.

'The wisest place to bury a body is in an existing grave. We searched the two long barrows out at Hazelton near here. Like Belas Knap, archaeologists excavated them in the seventies. Nothing there.' Mercer rested his hands on his stomach. 'Bryony's here. It's a matter of time.'

'Here?' Stella echoed.

'In Winchcombe. Here's what happened. Bryony missed the last bus. She hailed a taxi. The taxi was driven by Brice. Her bad luck was compounded. She'd been in his taxi before so she trusted him. She even went out with him, to the Sun Inn on North Street. He takes her up to Cleeve Hill, tries it on, there's a struggle and—'

'You believed Bryony Motson was abducted so you didn't arrest Brice.' Stella felt cruel as she reminded Mercer of his mistake.

He steepled chubby fingers. 'Hindsight's a detective's enemy. I did think that. Now I know Bryony never made it out of that cab alive. Mark my words, like Keith Bennett's still buried on Saddleworth Moor, Bryony is out there on Cleeve Common in an unmarked grave.'

'You think Brice could have been in on it with Craven?' Jack asked.

The disgraced detective looked at Stella as if it were she who had spoken. 'Craven isn't a killer. He's not even a killer's accomplice. Go to the prison. Talk to him.'

'We don't have visitors' rights,' Stella reminded him. As unlicensed private detectives, their scope was limited.

Mercer pushed back his hair. 'You can do it.'

'We're too late,' Jack said. 'He's being released in the morning.'

Stella wouldn't have believed it was possible for Mercer to look worse. Pricks of perspiration appeared on his pale skin and dampened his hair, as if he'd stepped from a shower.

'You got that wrong, lad. If he was being let out, I'd have been told. I still have friends out there.' He waved towards the window at the empty street.

'So you didn't know?' Jack looked surprised.

'I'm sure you're right. When a high-profile murderer is let out of prison it's headline news.' Quick to mollify, Stella wondered what Jack was playing at. Getting Mercer riled would not help.

'Exactly.' Mercer was short of breath. 'You talk to him. He won't budge for me. Brice has him in a vice. Craven says he put a stupid stone with a hole in with Cassie to "make it better for her". I've told him I know he didn't do it. He just has to tell us it was Brice. Matty won't budge.' Looking at Stella, Mercer panted, 'You'll do it.'

'What does – did – my dad think?' Mercer had tantalized Stella with the notion of Terry alive. She didn't know what made her ask the question; would knowing help?

'Terry says it's—' Mercer spluttered and his bulk shook with terrible convulsions. 'Read *everything*. Back. Here. Nine a.m. *Sharp.*'

Stella got out her phone. 'I'm calling your daughter.'

'*Put that away!*' Mercer shouted with surprising volume. 'I don't want them interfering.'

'Them?' Jack said.

Gasping, Mercer pulled a wad of banknotes from a pocket in the side of the recliner. 'Here.'

'What is that for?' Stella asked.

'Expenses. I'll top up when needs be.' Eyes shut, Mercer rested his head against the cushion. 'Two-fifty. Don't go mad.' Winded, he stretched towards Stella, ignoring Jack who was closer.

Stella took the folded bundle of twenty-pound notes from Mercer and slipped it in her rucksack. Jack was filling a carrier bag with bulging files.

Mercer's chest rattled as he pushed out each word. 'Get. That. *Bastard!*'

Stella looked to where the pudgy finger pointed, almost expecting Charles Brice to be there at the window. For a second she saw the younger man whose action – or lack of action – had divided the nation into those who supported the detective for finding Cassie Baker's body and those who'd lambasted him for waiving the rules.

As they returned along Bull Lane to the car park, they were deafened by an ear-splitting roar. It ricocheted off the walls of the cottages and seemed to contract the air. Shielding his eyes from the sun with a hand, Jack squinted upwards. 'It's an RAF transport plane coming out of Brize Norton. I guess we'll hear a few of those while we're here. Who says the countryside's quiet!'

The plane thundered across the clear blue sky and away behind trees that peeped above chimney pots. The rumble, resembling a prolonged explosion, died to silence.

In the distance in every direction were hills. Some dotted with blobs that Stella realized were sheep. Winchcombe didn't join up with somewhere else like Hammersmith. It came to a stop, beyond which were fields. Stella found herself longing for the hectic traffic outside her office window.

In the car park – thankfully no longer a field – Stella recalled her question to Mercer. Who had Terry suspected murdered the women? Mercer had mentioned that Terry agreed with him about Brice's appearance, not his guilt. Had Terry believed Charles Brice killed Cassie Baker and Bryony Motson?

The answer must wait until tomorrow.

Chapter Fourteen

Jackie hesitated on the landing. She could hear murmurings from Nick's bedroom. He was on the phone to Emma trying to save his relationship. Going by the marathon calls he'd made since he'd arrived, he'd be a while. Although if it went badly he'd want to talk to Jackie. In his late twenties, Nick still believed his mum held all the answers. He told her his secrets. Sometimes more than she wanted to know. Her family treated her as the depository for their secrets. No one wondered if she had a secret.

Graham had gone to a meeting in Hertfordshire – he'd told her why but she hadn't taken it in. They were getting on no better than Nick and Emma. She had heard him say he'd be late home.

She released the hatch to the attic. She tried to grab the ladder but it was centimetres out of reach. It was a family rule that no one went up into the attic if alone in the house. Nick would help, but he'd ask why she wanted to go up there.

Jackie went into Mark's bedroom which, since he'd moved out, was their shared study. She wheeled the office chair onto the landing and positioned it beneath the hatch. She clutched the banister and hauled herself onto the chair. It spun around until she was looking down on the drop to the stairs below. She lightly pushed against Nick's closed bedroom door. The chair rotated to where she wanted it. She was being monumentally stupid.

She might easily lose her balance and pitch over the banister rail. Slowly, she raised her head to the hatch and grabbed the ladder. As she lowered it, the chair scooted from under her and crashed against the study door jamb. Jackie leapt clear. Leaning against the banister, she was grateful that, when a friend lost a front tooth extracting a loft ladder, Graham had fitted theirs with a stalling mechanism. She waited. Nothing. Nick would be oblivious if she lay unconscious outside his bedroom. So much for not being alone in the house. She climbed the ladder into the attic.

When they'd bought the house thirty years ago, they'd planned to convert the attic. But while the children were growing up they'd struggled to meet the mortgage. Now it was paid off they could afford the extension, but with Mark and Nick gone (almost), they had ample room so there was no point.

The attic was littered with disused toys, a one-armed Action Man rested on a bag of footballs, amidst sections of plastic goal-posts. Tangled in the netting was an acoustic guitar and Nick's bear Micawber. Jackie hesitated. He might like that. Absurd, she stopped herself retrieving it. His electric bass guitar from various teenaged bands lay beside it. There were at least four old computers they'd didn't dare chuck away in case one held some vital file. Boxes were stacked under the eaves, full of photo albums from their boys' childhoods and their own, tools inherited from both their dads (and Jackie's mum had been a dab hand with a drill). There were ornaments stuck in the limbo between display and disposal. Stella knew a declutterer. Jackie's mood darkened. No amount of decluttering could change the past.

On the far side of the attic, Jackie found what she was look-ing for.

The army surplus shoulder bag she'd lugged about in her sixth form. Biro scrawls covered the canvas, CND logos, 'Peace', 'Love' 'Che Guevara', 'The Who' and a heart with initials in it that had been so effectively blocked out it was impossible to read them. Jackie didn't have to try. She knew what they were. Sitting on a box of old bedding, she unbuckled the bag and tipped its contents onto the floor. Out slid a wallet of Boots-developed photographs, four diaries (Letts Schoolgirl) and a strip of photo-booth pictures. She picked this up and dropped it as if burnt. She glanced towards the hatchway. She was hidden by boxes. The house was silent. Nick was still on the phone.

She opened the Boots wallet and, heart thumping, flipped through the photographs. Most were of fields with sheep. In one a track wended its way into hills. Another showed a cluster of houses and a church. The last photo was of a group of young people outside a house with a black front door. Two young men wore flared jeans, James Taylor hair and tie-dye T-shirts. Arms folded, they lounged against the wall of the house. One was particularly nonchalant, his legs crossed at the ankles. The other, with a stubbly chin, rested the sole of his boot flat against the wall. A third, hands thrust in drainpipe jeans pockets, frowned at the two men. Jackie herself frowned at the girl in a Biba smock, loon pants and monkey boots. She shoved the pictures back into the wallet and shovelling everything back into the bag, struggled up, stifling a groan at her stiffened legs. She swung the bag across her chest, got her phone from her jeans and stabbed the keys.

'Jax, all right?' Barry's voice seemed to carry around the attic.

'I need to talk to you,' she whispered.

'Fire away.'

A chinking. Barry would be having a whisky or ten. He drank steadily, but like Lucie May with her nippets, alcohol barely affected him. She believed that, law-abiding, Barry never drove when he was over the limit.

'Not *now*.'

'Mum, you up there?' It was Nick.

'I'll pop into the office,' Barry said.

'No. I'll text.' She cut the line.

'Mum!' Nick sounded concerned.

Jackie crossed to the hatch. Barefoot, Nick balanced on the bottom rung of the ladder. He did a mock-cross face. 'What happened to "Don't go up into the attic on your own"?'

'You were on the phone.' The sort of weak excuse her boys used to give when they'd been naughty. His emotions worn on his sleeve, Nick was every inch the jilted partner. Aside from tearful outbursts, he still hadn't shaved (though he had styled his hair). Yesterday's shirt hung crumpled over designer jeans. He was a younger, untidier Graham. Jackie was suffused with love swiftly followed by guilt. *Bad Mother.*

'Who were you talking to?'

'No one.' Too prompt. Nick hadn't inherited his acting skills from her. But with no reason to suspect his mum would lie, he accepted her answer.

'You should have called me to help. Why are you up there?'

She should have anticipated the question. Intent on her mission, Jackie had no answer.

'Nothing.'

'Nothing?'

Jackie looked about the attic. She lit upon the electric fan they'd bought for her mum in her final illness when she was either too hot or too cold. 'I'm getting Grandma's fan.'

'Let me.' Nick was up the ladder before she could stop him.

Teetering at the edge of the hatch, Jackie bundled the canvas bag behind her. Sick at her deception, she manoeuvred round to prevent Nick seeing it.

'What's this?' Nick picked up the photo-booth strip. He held it up to the light bulb dangling from a rafter.

Black and white with a curtained background. In the first shot a girl, late teens, with long hair and heavy eye make-up, features bleached by the flash, stared above the lens. In the next one she was open-mouthed in horror, caught unawares when the shutter snapped. Number three, she was half out of the frame and a boy with long hair, about the same age and hugged by the fur collar of a parka, grimaced at the lens. Lastly they were locked in a kiss, the boy doing a two-fingers sign behind them.

'This is you!' Nick exclaimed.

'I was young.' Jackie snatched back the strip.

'Who's the guy? I thought Dad was your first love.' Nick sounded accusatory.

'He was.' Jackie folded the strip over again. About to tear it up, she changed her mind and stepped away from Nick, stuffing it in her jeans pocket.

'Careful, Mum!' Nick pulled her back from the hatchway. He saw the fan. 'You mean that thing? It's huge, you'd never have managed it by yourself.'

'It's not heavy.' Jackie was indignant. She went to the gym twice a week, she could have managed the fan with one hand.

'Why do you want it? There's one in the sitting room and in the kitchen.' Nick might be poleaxed by grief but his observational skills were not dimmed.

'Oh, you know, in case. The main thing was this.' Jackie grabbed the bear from the box of toys and held him to her chest. 'I found Micawber!'

'Ah!' Nick took the bear from her. 'Yes!'

As Nick was being Christopher Robin gazing lovingly at his bear, Jackie pulled off the canvas bag, ducking under the strap, and tossed it out of the hatch. It sailed over the banister and landed, with a thump, on the stairs.

Nick shot around. 'Did you hear that?'

'No. Yes. It was the heating.' She flung herself down the ladder. The heating was off, but Nick wasn't practical, his brother Mark wouldn't have swallowed the explanation.

'Where do you want it?' Halfway down the ladder, Nick hugged the fan like a dancing partner, the bear stuffed in his waistband. His every move was as if choreographed.

'In the study please, love.' The bag was on the half-landing, all Nick had to do was glance down and he'd see it. She leaned on the rail, blocking his view. 'Plug it in for me, see it if works.'

Jackie rushed down the stairs, whipping up the bag, continuing to the hall. She crammed it in her workbag. It barely fitted, but Nick – or Graham – wouldn't notice. The front door opened.

'Hi! All right, darling!' Jackie heard herself shout at Graham.

'There's already one in the study, Mum.' Nick was coming down the stairs.

'One what?' Graham laid his briefcase beside Jackie's bag. It seemed to her his gaze lingered on it.

'Mum wanted the fan from the attic. I caught her up there!' Nick folded his arms. Normally Jackie would have been pleased to see her heartbroken son smiling. Now she wanted to shut him up.

'You went up there by yourself?' Graham was looking at her strangely.

'Mum wasn't alone, I was there.' It never annoyed Graham how their sons took her side. 'Anyway, listen, I've got brilliant news!' Nick might be about to take a bow. 'Me and Emma are back together. I'm going *home*!'

In both his parents' minds was the dull observation that their son no longer called their house his home.

'Brilliant!' Jackie said at last.

Filling the kettle for tea, she reflected that with Nick gone, there would just be her and Graham. For the first time in over thirty years Jackie wasn't sure what she felt about that.

Chapter Fifteen

'They buried a time capsule under the town hall in 1999,' Jack
remarked as Stella negotiated a tight junction onto Winchcombe's
high street. 'Loads of businesses and shops in the town con-
tributed things that presumably represented everyday life, like
beer mats, a wooden clothes peg and a Nipper mousetrap. My
favourite is doll body parts and a plaster cast of a gargoyle.' Jack
gave an exaggerated shudder. 'Apparently a dentist donated a
scalpel – when would they use a scalpel?'

Two wreaths leant against the war memorial although it was
months since Armistice day. Jack knew that small communities
missed their dead. It was the dead who had brought Stella and
him to Winchcombe. He gestured at the bag of papers next to
Stanley's jump seat behind him. 'It'll take more than an evening
to read all that.'

'We'll have to, Mercer will expect 101 per cent.' Obeying the
satnav, Stella swung the van down a road called Vineyard Street,
lined on both sides by picturesque cottages. They'd stopped at
the Co-op and bought a bottle of Jack Daniels. Stella was being
a chip off the old block, Jack thought.

'That's rich from a man sacked for gross misconduct.' Jack
doubted that Stella was any happier than he was about being

at the ex-detective's beck and call. At least she seemed to have forgotten his mentioning Craven's release. Stella would also not be happy that Lucie May was on the case.

'How come you said Matthew Craven was being released?' Stella asked.

'He annoyed me. He's so certain he's right.' Jack peered out of the window as he tried to gather himself. 'Ooh, that must be the bridge Lisa Mercer mentioned. Cassie Baker was last seen here alive on the night she was probably murdered.'

'So it's not true?' Stella was not to be distracted.

'Lucie May told me.' Jack felt himself heating up. He stared over the stone parapet at an allotment, rectangles of soil planted with staked sweet peas and runner beans, lines of rhubarb and lettuces. 'She said she had a scoop. But you know Lucie and her scoops.' He barked a laugh. 'It won't come to anything.'

'We'll ask her what Craven told her. This only works if we're a team.' Stella was seldom so sanguine about Lucie May.

'Did Cassie live around here?' Jack felt disquiet. Never had Stella referred to Lucie as in their team.

'Her parents' house was at the top of the Old Brockhampton Road. There are no records of her booking a taxi as her mum said she told her to. It's assumed she walked or thumbed a lift and was picked up by her killer.'

'Unless the killer was the taxi driver, Charles Brice.' No wonder the huge bag of papers didn't faze Stella, she was familiar with the case.

'He was only nineteen then. He didn't have a cab licence.'

'It's strange, don't you think, that her parents believed Cassie had left home,' Jack pondered.

'Her best friend – Lauren something – said Cassie talked about going to London to work. Her sister Karen said she'd boasted she'd met a man she called her heart-throb. Plus she didn't get on with her dad, he was strict with her. Karen said some clothes were missing from her room. Don't forget she'd run away several times already.'

'What's the evidence that the heart-throb was Charles Brice? Just that he looked like a film star?' Jack asked.

'That was Bryony Motson's flatmate Jenni Wiles.' Stella was patient but Jack felt bad for muddling up the two murder victims. He must know Cassie and Bryony as individuals in their own right.

His thoughts were interrupted by the satnav. They had 'reached their destination'. Stella braked outside the gatehouse to Sudeley Castle. Jack felt his spirits lift. He'd always wanted to live in a building with battlements.

'It can't mean up there,' Stella said.

'It's where Catherine Parr lived,' Jack said again. 'Builders discovered her tomb while they were renovating the chapel.' He'd read up on Winchcombe at least.

'It won't be there. I'll keep going,' Stella said.

As they continued along a leafy winding lane, the voice repeated that they had arrived and then resorted to 'Turn around when possible'.

Every so often a five-bar gate offered a snatch of a field, some with crops; in others sheep grazed. The lane petered out into a track leading up an incline to a dead end. A signpost said 'Winchcombe 2½'. Disorientated by endless hedgerows, Jack had the impression they'd come at least ten.

'I suppose a postcode covers a wider area here than in London.' Stella's tone sounded foreboding.

'Perhaps that's it.' He craned to look through metal gates on their right. On a drive was a racing-green Jaguar and a matching green Range Rover. A detached house backed onto a field of corn or wheat; it looked like a picture in Jack's boyhood Ladybird book *The Farm*, which in the confusion of leaving he'd forgotten to pack.

'There's people living there,' Stella said with evident relief. 'And there.' She pointed to a sprawling farmhouse amid outbuildings set back to their left. Three rusting cars were parked at angles as if their drivers had abandoned them in a hurry. 'We must have missed the turning.'

She manoeuvred the van around, avoiding ditches each side, and went back along the lane at crawling pace. The hawthorn hedge gave way to coils of barbed wire. Beyond these was a fence. The house was obscured by woods, no wonder he hadn't seen it the first time. Jack recognized the judicious planting choice of holly, hawthorn and nettles. Whoever had lived here knew how to deter intruders.

Stella pulled onto a verge by tall iron gates topped with yet more barbed wire, hauled her rucksack through the seats and dug out a piece of paper. '"Double gates lead onto a driveway. Use key to unlock." Yup, this is it.'

'It looks abandoned.' Jack felt his own foreboding mounting.

Stella spoke on a sigh. 'Lisa Mercer said it was empty. That explains the security. The owner doesn't want squatters.'

'There's someone there!' Jack exclaimed.

Stella reversed a metre.

'There!'

Just visible between trunks of oak and ash and a thicket of bramble a man stood stock-still. He was watching them.

'He's probably the caretaker.' Jack tried to sound perky.

Involuntarily, Stella stepped on the accelerator and the van bunny-hopped forward. She pulled on the handbrake. 'Lisa Mercer never mentioned a caretaker. It doesn't look cared for.' She turned off the engine and climbed out of the van. Taking the key from her Barbour jacket she unlocked a sturdy padlock that held the gates together. Jack got out and began pushing them open.

Groundsel and forget-me-nots had grown through a gravelled drive. Stella took the van through and stopping metres up the drive, waited while Jack locked the padlock. He didn't know if he felt more secure within the gates or out on the lane. Who was locked in with them?

Although it was mid-afternoon, a canopy of trees made it darker. Bushes encroached onto the drive, branches clattered against the van, Jack shut his window to avoid being lashed by a bramble. Her lips pursed, Stella held tight to the wheel as she drove over potholes.

Around a bend in the drive they came upon the caretaker, arms outstretched in welcome.

The man wore a flouncy blouse and bright green trousers, all topped with a straw hat. His face was indistinct so Jack couldn't read his expression, whatever, he was fed up that the man was there. He'd counted on time alone with Stella when, marooned in the country, they could get back to where they'd been before he upset her.

Stella exclaimed, 'It's a scarecrow!'

'He's looks real,' Jack said as they drew alongside the straw effigy on the drive. Close up, Jack's heart rate increased. The figure was chillingly lifelike. 'Odd place for him to be. There's nothing to scare here.'

Stella didn't reply. She wouldn't be interested in a scarecrow.

Around another bend they came upon the house. A rickety sign – 'Crow's Nest' – confirmed they'd come to the right place. The building was half-timbered with a hip-gabled roof and an extension that, while in keeping with the house, gave it an off-balance look. There was a dip in the slate roof as if a giant hand had pressed upon the tiles. Latticed windows and white-icing stucco gave it a fairy-tale appearance. Not in a good way, as Beverly would have said. Jack's neck prickled. The scarecrow wasn't there to shoo crows – or any bird – away from plants: there were none. Nature had reclaimed the garden. Sooner or later, it would reclaim the house too. He looked back down the drive, half expecting the scarecrow to appear.

Stella unlocked the door, which creaked ominously when she pushed it open. They were greeted with a heavy musty smell.

'Something's died in here.' Stella was matter-of-fact.

Jack felt his dread take shape.

Off a spacious hallway panelled with oak was a dining room with a long oak table and mismatching chairs. Jack went through a doorway on the left. A sitting room stretched the width of the house in which the only furniture was a sofa before a vast stone fireplace in a wall of Cotswold stone and a leather armchair. Although it was sunny, the latticed windows let in little light. The air was damp and chill. Thinking it foolish to separate, he went to find Stella.

She was unlatching a ledge and brace door at the end of the hall. Inside was a steep staircase. In what amounted to a cupboard, the cloying smell was stronger. Jack reached for a Bakelite switch and flicked it.

'The electricity's off. Where did Mercer say the fuse boxes were?' he said.

'There's none,' Stella said.

'There's a light switch, there must be lights,' Jack insisted.

'There's no electricity. Lisa's instructions say it was cut off. We've got calor gas canisters for cooking and candles for light.' She sounded cool about what Jack considered a disaster.

Stella trotted Stanley up a protesting staircase into the darkness above. Her voice sounded hollow. 'Mercer says there are five bedrooms, this one has an en suite.' She stood aside for Jack to enter a room with a vast four-poster bed with a pink counterpane.

Three windows gave a panoramic view of hills, although here, too, scant light seeped through the leaded glass. Jack glimpsed the battlements of Sudeley Castle. There was an oak wardrobe of similar grand proportions to the bed. Although a wood he liked, the preponderance of oak was lowering his already low spirits.

Stella unfolded Lisa's instructions. 'Sheets are in an airing cupboard on the landing.' She sniffed the air and pulled a face. 'We should have brought our own.'

En suite was a posh term for a lavatory with no seat and a corroded overhead cistern. The deep roll-topped bath with lime-encrusted taps sent Jack back to boarding school. With no hot water it would take many kettles and pans to fill and the water would cool on impact. A wooden foot-grid by the bath promised verrucas and other horrible foot conditions.

'You sleep here.'

'Mercer wanted you on this case. You should have it...' Jack trailed off. It didn't sound like selfless generosity. Stella never took the best for herself, she'd concluded that the other rooms were worse.

He wondered if Mercer's expenses could stretch to a B and B.

'I probably get up to pee more often than you,' Stella said.

'*Oh!* Right.' Stella never mentioned bodily functions, hers or others. Jackie blithely grumbled about hot flushes and bladder infections, but Jack had come to imagine vaguely, that like the Queen, Stella never went to the loo. Absurdly he felt stirring in his pants and, in case Stella noticed, left the room.

Two of the bedrooms were bare, in another was a double bed dwarfed by another large oak wardrobe.

'Or you could sleep here. It's smaller so it might be warmer,' Stella suggested.

Jack did *not* want to share with the nasty wardrobe which was like the one in which he'd hidden from his grandmother when he was little. Actually, not so little. 'Let's see the others.'

At the end of the passage were stairs to an attic. Tacitly, in agreement, they didn't go up. Returning along the corridor they found another lavatory and in a separate room a bath as chipped and dirty as Stella's en suite. She opened a door next to her bedroom and sprang back. The stink was overpowering. Stanley grew excited.

Claws up, a crow lay amongst grey ashes in a grate, its eyes cold and unblinking.

A hand clamped over her nose and mouth – Stella would know the smell was particulate – she muttered, 'It's come down the chimney and got trapped.'

A fir tree hard by the window allowed only a faint greenish light through the diamond-shaped panes. The illumination was enough light to see that the black feathers were crawling with maggots.

'That's strange,' Stella said.

'What is?'

'Lisa Mercer said no one's been here for months. This door was closed, yet there's no bird droppings on the bedding or the floor.' She went to the window. 'The bird would have tried to fly towards the light to escape, but there are no impact marks, of its beak or body, on the glass.' She shook her head. 'Or...'

'Or what?' Jack didn't need to ask.

'Or someone placed it dead in the fireplace, which is obviously ridiculous.'

'Obviously,' Jack agreed weakly. 'Maybe it died and fell down the chimney. I guess it explains why this place is called Crow's Nest.'

'Yes.' Stella returned to the passage.

'I'll have this room,' Jack announced.

Stella stopped at the top of the stairs. 'You sure? What about the...'

'With the window open and after I've buried the crow, it'll be nice,' he assured her. The room was cosy with a view of an orchard behind the house. It would, he told himself, be nice.

'The one with the double bed is bigger. Or have the en-suite one, seriously.'

'This is perfect.' Jack couldn't say he wanted the room so that the distance between them was only the thickness of the wall. The dead crow was a sign. And, he knew, not a good sign.

Chapter Sixteen

Stella and Jack spent the next two hours settling in. She unloaded her Clean Slate equipment bag from the van and set to, cleaning the house. With no electricity, they couldn't use the Henry vacuum kept in the van. Unfazed, Stella whisked about the rooms with a broom and soon the floors were dotted with heaps of dust and debris like molehills.

The large kitchen was equipped with a stove connected to a calor gas canister, a battered deal table and a walk-in larder. Jack wiped out a leaning cupboard with mesh apertures in the doors and lined each shelf with rose-scented paper from a roll in Stella's bag. He told her that she'd covered every eventuality. Stella, who never went anywhere without the means to render any space germ-free, was ever ready for dirt, mouse droppings, feathers or far worse. While Jack was more than discouraged by the filth and stagnant odours, Stella could only feel something approaching comfortable in this remote house in the countryside after giving it a good clean.

She sluiced floors and vigorously polished furniture. She aired sheets and blankets over kitchen chairs arranged on a patio outside the kitchen. Jack pegged rugs to gnarled apple trees in the orchard and beat them. He tried to clean the windows, but dirt had encrusted the glass and he could make little difference.

Sunlight streamed through the open doors and windows, twittering birdsong from the woods filled the house in which scents of polish, air freshener and many other cleaning products was carried by the through draught. Stella, Jack noticed, had a spring in her step. She had arrived.

They decided to go for a walk; Jack said it was important to get the lie of the land. Stella had brought a map, but she was aware that Stanley needed a walk so agreed.

Stella noticed that they both gave the scarecrow a wide berth as they passed it on the drive. It was stupid, but she couldn't shake her first impression that the straw man was real, that, wide-brimmed hat shading his features, the tall and imposing figure was the caretaker.

Stella let Jack and Stanley through the gates and snapped shut the padlock. She turned at a rustling sound. A breeze sent a flurry of dried leaves along the lane. Stella quelled the ghost of a fear.

'Left or right?' Jack hovered on the lane – he looked unwilling to go in either direction. The image of the dead crow and the scarecrow in her mind, Stella considered driving home to Hammersmith.

'Right.' Stella remembered passing a stile as they drove in.

They ambled along the hot lane. No one passed them, on foot or in a car. They lingered while Stanley rooted in a ditch or nibbled at juicy blades of grass along the verges. They heard the tweet and chirrup of birds and bees buzzing in hedgerows. The whistle and chuff-chuff of a steam engine was a ghost noise. Stella hazily supposed that Winchcombe's line wasn't electrified. Despite these sounds, her impression was of silence.

Stella was finding the lack of people and field after field stretching on and on under a huge sky disturbing. Worse, she couldn't place the country smells. The delicate scent of wild rose and the muskier odour of cow parsley were foreign to her.

Unmoved by the idyllic summer scenery, Stella hadn't forgotten why she and Jack had come to Winchcombe. In the last forty years two young women had disappeared in this town, pretty enough to decorate the lid of a biscuit tin. If Paul Mercer was right, the murderer lived within a mile of where they were walking.

'You could let Stanley off, there aren't any animals.' Jack stopped by a telegraph pole on which a crudely painted sign said, 'Footpath'. The board had tilted so the arrow pointed skyward.

'Cows can kill you. Six people a year are trampled to death by them.' Stella told him she often listened to *Farming Today* on the radio as she travelled to work. In rush hour on Hammersmith Broadway, the information had been merely interesting, now it had critical relevance.

'Blimey!' Jack stopped. 'You have been doing your homework. Isn't that on at about half five in the morning?'

Stella hadn't thought of the programme as homework. Now she tried to dredge up any other facts that might help them. There had been something about not leaving dog poo where sheep could eat it but she couldn't remember why. She returned to the point in question, 'Stanley might run away.'

'Where could he run?' Jack waved at the expanse of grass.

'Anywhere.' The possibilities were endless. 'He could go home. There was that dog who ran hundreds of miles back to its owners.'

'You're his owner and you're here.'

Stella unclipped Stanley's lead and watched, heart in mouth, as he broke into a gallop, ears flapping, tail like a flag.

Able to deftly guide a cleaning trolley between office desks and around water fountains, Stella and Jack trudged gingerly in the alien landscape. Stella mismanaged a stile and reached the other side facing the wrong way. Jack scuffed his Jones and Crockett brogues slipping in mud. Stella's footwear – her 'cleaning' CAT boots – was at least sensible, but she kept tripping on the uneven ground and with each step felt a blister developing.

Only Stanley was at home. He belted along the track of flattened grass, diverting hither and thither after the myriad scents.

His agility classes paying off, he sailed over brambles and trotted along a plank across a stream that led to yet another field.

'We could get lost. Everything looks the same,' Stella whispered, although surely they were alone.

'Not if we keep to the path and keep looking behind.'

Stella whirled around. 'Do you think we're being followed?'

'No! I was thinking it's what to do in unfamiliar terrain. The way back looks different to the way forward. We should check what it looks like the other way and notice landmarks so we can find our way back.' Jack was whispering too.

Stella thought it looked the same either way. But she made a mental note of a tree in the corner of the field. Her dad had given her a book on trees, so she could at least name them. The tree was an oak and, judging by its girth and the roughened bark, was over two hundred years old. She felt briefly fortified by this fact.

'That's our lode star.' Jack pointed at Sudeley Castle, honey-coloured in the late-afternoon sun. 'Ooh, what's that?' He blundered towards the oak tree.

Stella was appalled he'd left the path. He was trespassing. In London, walls and railings, signs, pavements and streets defined where you could and couldn't go. Scared of losing Jack, she stumbled after him over the clods of earth.

Within low railings were the remains of a house, built, like most of Winchcombe, of honey-coloured stone. Hollyhocks, aquilegia and marigolds choked by nettles and bindweed, were remnants of a garden. Ivy draped remaining walls and brambles twisted in and out of gaping windows, moss-covered roof slates obtruded from the soil.

A sign read, 'Danger, Keep Out!' Jack vaulted the railings and strode off to the tumbledown building, calling happily, 'A ruined house! Someone's begun to renovate, the mortar's recent, hmm, not that recent, maybe they went bust. Shame, it's a terrific setting.'

He stepped through a doorway in a wall and glided through the 'rooms', respecting absent walls as if the house was intact.

This was his element: any minute and Stella expected he'd start chatting to a ghost.

It struck her that pretty much the only difference between this house and Crow's Nest was that Crow's Nest had a roof. They were staying in an old house in the middle of fields and woods. Why had she agreed to take a case in the country? She breathed in through her nose. Smoke. Someone had lit a fire here. She looked around her. There was no one but Jack there. She became aware that she could no longer hear birdsong. Or insects. It was truly silent.

'Jack, it's dangerous,' Stella shouted. She imagined a landowner with a shotgun or some other untold rural peril involving adders or angry cows.

'We need a map,' Jack called back gaily.

Like Stella, Jack was a Londoner. Unlike her, he was drawn to empty buildings, haunted, he believed, by lives lived. In Hammersmith Stella could close her mind to his exploits. Not here. Against her judgement she climbed the railings and went after him.

'We've got Google,' she said when she reached him. Jack was a devotee of Streetview, although in Winchcombe there were fewer streets to view.

'Not when the juice runs out.' He was crouched before a fireplace that had probably been the living room. The smell of smoke was stronger. 'We'll orientate ourselves while it's light and learn the topography. Our murderer will know every contour, every path and holloway, every hedgerow and stream, every meadow, the woods, crevices—'

'Brice comes from London.' Stella's chest tightened. They'd have no email or phone. No internet access. She'd taken no electricity in her stride, they could heat water for cleaning and washing. No amount of boiled kettles gave them Wi-Fi.

'He lived in Winchcombe when he was a teenager. What you learn when you're young becomes part of your DNA.'

'I can't imagine knowing this place well, it's all grass and trees and hedges,' Stella said. 'Jackie said the Cotswolds is wealthy and I've seen more four-by-fours here than in Kew. Yet in a few hours we've found two abandoned houses.'

'There are empty houses in London. Ghosts live everywhere,' Jack added inconsequentially.

'In 1977 I'm sure that someone lived here. It's close to the lane where Cassie Baker was likely abducted. So it's in the vicinity of a crime scene. Whoever was here might have seen or heard something. They might have been here in 1999, too, when her body was found.'

'There were no windows facing the lane so they couldn't have seen anything from the house. But if Cassie cried for help, it's possible they'd have heard.' Jack stared off towards the lane. 'Or they killed her themselves, of course...'

'We need to establish who lived here. Mercer will probably know.' Uneasy, Stella tried to orientate herself. 'Isn't Belas Knap over there?'

'Yes, it is.' Shading his eyes, Jack looked towards a hill covered in woodland. 'I suppose one good thing about the countryside is not much changes. It would have looked like this in 1999, even in 1977.'

'Nothing stays the same. Farming practices change, different crops are sown, trees are coppiced or felled, hedgerows destroyed for increased mechanization.' Stella remembered *Farming Today* once more.

'Good point. That stand of five trees marching down the middle of the field suggests there was once a boundary. And the Old Brockhampton Lane can't always have been "old". Presumably it once went to Brockhampton. I suppose the people who lived in this house are long dead.' Jack sighed.

'What was that?' Stella jumped. She looked for Stanley, a barometer of danger. He was on the other side of the fence, basking in a tractor rut.

'What was what?'

'I heard something.' The five trees did look as if they were marching.

'It was some animal. We'll have to learn the soundscape of the countryside too.'

'Let's go.' Stella looked out across the fields. Winchcombe looked like a toy town amongst the hills, the church tower high above the higgledy-piggledy houses. As she looked, she heard the bells ring for five o'clock. The chimes and the view were quintessential ingredients of an English village, but to Stella they might be the signs of a nightmare. The quiet was too quiet. Beneath the beauty lurked something distinctly bad.

She strode back across the field, got over the stile – back to front – and stopped, grabbing Jack's shirtsleeve. 'There's someone there!'

'Where?' He moved closer to her.

'By that oak tree.'

'It's a shadow of a branch.'

Stanley began to growl.

'It's not a shadow!' Stella gasped.

Stanley barked and before Stella could grab him, bounded towards the tree. Before he got there, he came to a halt and gave a howl. A dreadful cry that belonged in Stella's nightmare.

'He's seen something.' She belted after her dog.

'Stella, no, wait, it might be—'

Stella saw who it was. Or rather what it was. 'It's a scarecrow!'

'What's it doing here?' Jack joined her.

'Scaring crows.' An afternoon in the country had taught her this much. She should feel better but she didn't.

'This field's laid to grass, there's been sheep grazing here.' Jack kicked at a lump of dried dung with a muddied brogue. 'There's no need to scare birds. We came this way, I don't remember seeing it.'

'"We don't see what doesn't interest us."' Stella quoted one of Jack's sayings back to him. Except she had noticed the oak tree. There had been nothing underneath it. She took a few steps towards the figure, its arms outstretched.

'Jack, it's the same scarecrow.'

'So it is,' Jack breathed. 'Worzel Gummidge!'

'What?'

'You remember those books about a scarecrow who walked crab-wise and lived in the ten-acre field? He was always moving about the village.'

Stella had seen the TV series. 'That was a story, it wasn't true. Someone's moved him. *It.*'

'Possibly. Possibly not.' Jack shrugged.

'Definitely!' Stella hurried on along the path. Jackie had said Jack gave names to things to make them friends that wouldn't hurt him. When aged ten, Stella had seen *Worzel Gummidge* on television, she'd been scared. A rational reaction, Terry told her.

'It could be a sign.' Jack caught up with her.

'It's not for scaring birds.' Stella's heart was going ten to the dozen. She paused beneath the footpath notice on the telegraph pole to get her breath. 'It's there to scare *us*. Someone doesn't want us working on this case.'

Chapter Seventeen

'I'll start with Cassie Baker, you read up on Bryony Motson then we'll swap.' Stella was arranging Mercer's files into piles on the table.

Jack had found seasoned logs in an outhouse and suggested he light a fire. Stella objected; after the hot journey and Mercer's stuffy cottage she welcomed the chill in the old house. But when the sun dipped behind the hills, the temperature dipped too and she changed her mind. She was impressed when Jack got the wood burning, her vague understanding of setting a fire involved liberal use of firelighters and they had none. She helped Jack drag the oak table in from the dining room to consolidate the heat.

Their supper was one of Jackie's curries mopped up with hunks of peshwari naan. Stella wanted a clear head so refused one of the bottles of Merlot they'd bought in the Co-op.

It was half past eight by the time they'd eaten and cleared up.

Stella's cleaning earlier had helped her befriend Crow's Nest. She was lost in the fields and woods, but she knew every nook and cranny of the house. The polished gleam on the oak table calmed her. The fire had taken the chill off the room and the scent of lavender air freshener laced the air.

Jack fitted six candles from a bundle he'd found in a kitchen cupboard into Wee Willy Winkie holders made of tin and lined them along the table. They sat each end and spread the papers between them. Stella felt more ready than she had all day to take on the case, or, since they were keeping an open mind, both cases.

After supper, Stella had gone round the house closing windows and doors yet a draught from somewhere made the candle flames flicker and there was a roaring sound from the chimney. The text on the closely typed documents danced as shadows trembled. She wished she'd brought her head-torch. She was nervous of knocking over a candle – even with no dust, the wood-panelled walls would send the house up like a tinderbox. After an hour the candles had burned halfway. There were two candles left from the bundle. In London Stella relied on her phone's torch, but they must conserve battery life for calls. As it was, 4G fluctuated as often as the flames.

They hadn't pulled shut the heavy brocade curtains which, too heavy to take out and beat, were greyed with dirt and cobwebs. Whoever moved the scarecrow – over supper they convinced themselves it was village kids – wouldn't be sneaking about in the dark. Now Stella wasn't so sure. She glanced up at the diamond-shaped panes. The glass was black as coal.

Stella had read Mercer's decision log, the running account a senior investigating officer keeps of every development in an investigation. After the major errors that later lost him his job, Paul Mercer had followed procedure to the letter. When Forensics had unearthed Cassie Baker's skeleton from Belas Knapp and he'd finally cautioned Brice, Mercer had secured and preserved the crime scene, albeit it was twenty-two years old by then. Even after two decades, in 1999 there might still have been some physical evidence, not contaminated or destroyed. Careful killers made mistakes, leaving traces – fabric threads, a strand of hair – that placed them on the end of a murder chain. Not, it seemed, Cassie's killer.

He'd appointed a murder team, including a bone expert and

a soil expert. He held regular briefing meetings with his team and kept the press informed. (Unfortunately too informed, it transpired.) As Lisa had said, Mercer was hot on administration, every minor decision was recorded and cross-referenced.

X-rays of Cassie Baker's skull had matched X-rays obtained from a dentist still working in Winchcombe in 1999, but according to Mercer's scribble in the margin he had retired. He'd extracted her wisdom teeth a month before she vanished. Stella found herself mulling that had Cassie known she was going to die she might have avoided the operation. Stupid; if Cassie'd known she would be murdered... she was thinking like Jack.

Stella knew once a crime scene was established it was vital to find witnesses. This included tracking vehicle index numbers and capturing details of anyone nearby. Knocking on doors was tedious, but Stella remembered Terry's advice about 'good old-fashioned legwork'. With a team of two this wasn't possible. They'd start with interviewing key people...

The Bakers had assumed Cassie – described by her head teacher as lively and popular with classmates – had run off to London.

Stella pulled a rolled-up pad of flip-chart paper out of her rucksack and cleared a space on the table. She laid out the photo of Beverly's timeline that Jackie had taken and printed up. Stella would have preferred to set up a spreadsheet with the timeline, details of witnesses, suspects and the crimes, but her laptop didn't run on steam. She must do with pen and paper. She transcribed the timeline onto several sheets of paper and began to blu-tack them on the wall by the door. Jack jumped up and helped her. Soon the length of the room was papered with the timeline.

Stella started a list headed 'Suspects'. At the other end of the table, Jack began one on a fresh flip-chart sheet.

At the top Stella put Ralph Baker. According to his statement, Cassie's father was in Bristol the night his daughter failed to come home. Baker admitted he'd stayed in a flat in the St Paul's area rented by a woman with whom he was having an affair. The woman corroborated Baker's alibi. His wife Trudy said that 'all she knew was he wasn't with his family'. Terry maintained that an alibi from a parent or partner was no alibi. Stella listed both parents as suspects and added their whereabouts to the timeline.

Jack was contributing to the timeline from 1999. Brian Motson, Bryony's father (another obvious suspect), had been at a Rotary Club dinner in Burford on 19 December. He lived in Broadway, a village between Burford and Winchcombe and further still from Cheltenham. On the face of it he was clear. Nevertheless, Jack added Motson to Bryony's suspect list underneath Charles Brice.

'Why did Brice lead Mercer to Cassie Baker's grave?' Stella squinted at Jack over sputtering candle flames. 'Nothing else links him to her. Why put himself in the frame? It looks like a sign of guilt.'

'Some serial killers deliberately leave clues because they want to be stopped.' Jack didn't sound convinced.

'If so, surely he'd have made sure he was caught. There was insufficient evidence to charge him with Cassie's murder, and none he killed Bryony Motson.' Stella leaned over the papers and blew out the candles in the centre of the table. They needed to maximize the time they had light. The remaining flames died down, plunging them into semi-darkness.

Stanley gave one of his gurgling growls, a particularly unsettling sound.

'What's the matter?' She tried to keep her voice level: dogs picked up fear. The little poodle was in the gloom outside the ragged circle of light. Her sense of connection to the house achieved by cleaning into every corner had ebbed. Shadows had crept closer, the air no longer smelled fresh. Worse, she couldn't decide what it smelled of.

'We'll have to get used to Stanley hearing unfamiliar noises. There'll be all manner of wildlife out there on the prowl,' Jack said.

Stella didn't want to think of any creature out there in the infinite dark. She pictured the scarecrow stalking the drive. Or worse, someone carrying the scarecrow. Blowing out the candles was false economy, she could barely see to read. She peered at her watch, one gadget unaffected by no electricity. Two o'clock. It was Saturday. They'd been working for over four hours. Fending off tiredness, she made herself focus on the task. 'Cassie sounds like a handful, running away, bunking off school, and Trudy's statement says she was caught shoplifting from the Co-op when she was thirteen.'

'She was an adventurer, sounds like she had gumption.' Jack looked at Stella over his glasses. 'How very sad that she didn't make it to London and the life she appears to have wanted.' He returned to the paper he was reading. 'Mercer's marginalia says that the Sun Inn where Brice had a drink with Bryony has closed, it's an antique shop now. I can't find anything here to contradict Brice's claim that he never saw Bryony after dropping her off at her flat. Imagine if I was found murdered, you've been seen by several witnesses with me, that doesn't make you my killer.'

'I'd never kill you.' Stella thought her heart had stopped.

'Quite, but there'd be loads of evidence pointing to you. Just saying, Brice could be innocent.' Candlelight played on Jack's cheekbones, flickering flames made his brown eyes glitter. Jackie said he could be a model. At the time Stella had considered this was overstating things, but in the candlelight, Jack might have stepped out from *Vogue*. He was right: she'd told Jackie about Jack being angry with her. They would have been on CCTV outside the services and on the M40. Mercer saw them together. If Jack were found dead, she was the obvious suspect. However cross he got with her, she would never want to murder Jack. He was talking.

'... Bryony left the club in Cheltenham. Listen, this is unbearably poignant. Bryony's dad told Mercer's team that he'd won her this teddy bear at the Winchcombe Mop Fair when she was ten. She kept it with her, even as an adult. When the police found her handbag in a bin it was empty apart from fifty pounds. This is the *Daily Mail*: "... fighting tears, a distraught Brian Motson described how the bear was 'Bry's best friend – apart from me.

She carried it everywhere, it was in her handbag. Whoever has got her, at least let her keep it.'" The missing bear fuelled Mercer's conviction that Bryony had been kidnapped and was alive.' Jack whipped off his specs and sat back. 'I know we discussed this, but surely Bryony would have told her friends about the film star, Brice or whoever?'

'Not everyone tells their friends who they like.' Stella was Jack's friend yet he told her little. Were they friends? Jack confided in Jackie. Beverly had known he was going out with Bella and that they'd broken up. Jackie and Beverly probably knew they were back together. For Stella, usually so circumspect, Bella's appearance on Jack's doorstep was proof enough of this. She'd made it fact. Stella briefly admitted to herself that she'd told no one who she liked.

Jack and Stella read on in silence, both perfectly still in their chairs. Jack with one leg tucked under, Stella upright as if at her desk. The candles burned lower. The windows rattled. Stanley, curled in his bed by the fire, huffed and sighed in his sleep. The fire died in the grate.

'Cassie dumped Craven a couple of weeks before the Jubilee disco. Or so he claimed.' Stella broke the silence. 'A woman selling tickets at the disco saw him kissing Lauren Spicer at the disco. Lauren was Cassie's best friend so that must have been awkward.' Stella put Matthew Craven and Lauren Spicer on her list of suspects.

'Maybe Karen killed her and invented Heart-throb Guy. She would guess their parents would think Cassie had gone to London.' Jack sucked on a spectacle arm as if it were a pipe.

'Mercer's put question marks against Karen's statement. But obviously he cleared her of suspicion.'

'Cassie Baker's sister said she told her about a heart-throb and Bryony Motson's flatmate says Bryony met a man who, quote, "could be a film star". The Sun Inn witness saw Brice with Bryony and noticed Brice resembled Malcolm McDowell, a film star. In both cases there's mention of an unknown man. Strange parallel, don't you think?' Jack crammed on his specs and added 'Film Star Man' to his own suspects.

Stella rubbed her eyes, aching from lack of light. Solving a crime held similarities to a deep clean. The removal of a stain depended on the type of stain, the surface stained and the length of time since the spillage. Wounded by Jack's anger and determined to be a detective, Stella was studying Terry's dog-eared copy of the police's 'Murder Investigation Manual'. It was out of date but murder didn't change.

To know about the culprit a detective had to discover how the murder was committed, who had motive and means. Terry had told her female killers tended to use knives and men their fists. Men often appealed self-defence for murder. An option not open to women whose killings were often premeditated: a violent husband had to be overcome unawares. Cassie Baker's skull had been hit with a blunt instrument, which Stella knew suggested opportunism. Her murderer had grabbed whatever was nearest, a lump of wood or a brick, and wielded it with great force. Stella agreed with Jack, Cassie might have broken rules, she'd been dishonest, but although Cassie was long-dead, Stella had a strong sense of a young woman unafraid to take on the world. Stella would quite like to be like that, she let herself think.

The choice of what the manual called the 'disposal site' suggested knowledge of the area, understanding of, and familiarity with, the long barrow thingy. Had Stella not seen a diagram of Belas Knap in Mercer's notes, she'd envisage the burial chamber as a cart on wheels. Someone had known Belas Knap was the perfect place to hide a body. Craven had placed a stone with a hole in it next to Cassie, an ancient rite, he'd said in his statement, calling it a 'shepherd's crown'. How many killers were up on Early Neolithic history or whatever that was? Stella turned her attention to Cassie's best friend.

'Lauren Spicer runs a beauty parlour in Winchcombe. Let's meet her. Friends can become enemies.' She began another list of interviewees.

'Why doesn't Mercer suspect the people Bryony Motson worked with, never mind her flatmate Jenni who failed to tell the police for two days? It's often your nearest and dearest who murder you.' Jack held a document dangerously close to the candle flame to read it. 'Brice had an alibi for the night Bryony disappeared! Mercer didn't tell us. He visited his elderly Aunt Phyllis then claimed he took a passenger to Birmingham airport. The cab company and the aunt confirmed it. He was at the airport when Bryony left the nightclub. He'd have had to drive like the wind to get to Cheltenham in time to abduct her.'

'Not impossible. If Bryony had missed the bus maybe she started walking and Brice saw her on his way into Winchcombe. Like we said, Bryony would have trusted him.' Stella saw that the fire had gone out. The room was chill and the smell – another dead crow? – was stronger.

'We'll need to stand up to Mercer.' She gave a sigh. 'He'll have us tailing Brice at the expense of others; for Cassie's murder we've got Karen and their parents Ralph and Trudy, then there's her best friend Lauren Spicer and ex, Matthew Craven.'

'For Bryony there's her two clubbing mates, CCTV has them going off in the opposite direction to Bryony, but that could have been a ruse.' Jack flapped the flip-chart paper. 'Her father Brian – what if she went back to Winchcombe that night and he killed her? Then, we only have flatmate Jenni's word that Bryony didn't return to the flat. People have killed because they're sick of doing all the washing-up. Finally, there's the film star who may or may not be Charles Brice.' Jack puffed out his cheeks.

'Yes, if Bryony didn't take part in the cleaning rota, maybe Jenni got angry.' This was as close as Stella could get to understanding a motive for murder. 'But Jenni Wiles has died.'

'She was alive then.'

'We have to keep this doable. Let's stick to the father and Jenni Wiles as suspects for now.' 'The Murder Manual', and Terry, advised establishing parameters for a murder investigation. 'And obviously Charles Brice.'

'You said Lauren Spicer's brother gave Cassie and Lauren a lift to the disco,' Jack said.

'Mick Spicer.' Stella nodded.

'He could have been Heart-Throb and dumped Cassie or she dumped him or maybe he was married and she threatened to "out" him. They rowed, he killed her.' Jack's candle died, blotting him out.

'Spicer's alibi is iron-clad, he stayed in Cheltenham that night. There's no mention he and Cassie dated.' Stella stifled a yawn.

'Is there any reason why Matthew Craven is discounted as Bryony's killer?' Jack pondered. 'He worked in Cheltenham as well as Winchcombe. He could easily have been at the same nightclub as Bryony.'

'We shouldn't discount him for both murders. The morning after Cassie didn't come home, Craven was seen on Corndean Lane by a farmer harvesting a field. Corndean Lane's a route out of Winchcombe and, specifically, it passes Belas Knap.' She flapped a paper. 'Lauren says in her statement that Craven told her he wished Cassie Baker would go away. That points to revenge. It's why Lauren retracted her statement that they'd been together all night. She was actually with her mum, but being sure Craven hadn't killed Cassie, wanted to help him. Craven had no alibi. The jury sent him to prison.' Stella watched as Jack put more wood on the fire. 'Not least he knew she was dead.'

In the distance, Stella heard the church bells. They weren't so far from civilization. She squinted at her watch, 2.45 a.m.

'Craven never claimed to be guilty or innocent. After admitting that he left the shepherd's crown stone with Cassie, he resorted to "No comment".' Stella stuck her list of suspects on the wall below the timeline. 'We could be looking for two killers. Brice was a cabby born in London, nothing says he was up on ancient history and no one saw him with Cassie.'

The sliver of a new moon was dimmed by bright stars. The church clock chimed four quarters, they reverberated through

Winchcombe's deserted streets and backways. A pause. The bell tolled the hour three times.

The sound carried to the Bull Lane car park where an LED lamp-post, working on a movement sensor, cast bleak light across the tarmac.

In Crow's Nest, the house a hulk in the thickening dark, the wick on the last candle fizzled into the moat of hot wax and, as if pinched between invisible fingers, the flame went out.

Chapter Eighteen

The cold water thundered onto his back like hailstones. Vigorously Jack soaped himself, counted to three then, reaching blindly through the water, turned off the tap. Fully awake, his skin tingling, he debated getting away with a shower every other day. No. Cleanliness wasn't so much next to godliness as vital while living with Stella. At least it was summer – in winter the water would be icy.

As he was dressing Jack heard skittering and froze while he was doing up his shirt. Rats? Jack could take on a cold-blooded killer in the dark, but was nervous of long-tailed rodents. The door swung open. He met the accusatory stare of brown eyes within a furry face. Stanley was expecting a walk.

Two hours earlier, as dawn was breaking, he and Stella had stood on the landing outside their bedrooms. Jack had surreptitiously tried to entice Stanley in to sleep with him. Stanley would keep him warm and be good company. But the little dog had trotted after Stella without a backward glance.

Now, claws clipping on worn treads, Stanley was Jack's shadow as he tiptoed downstairs. He checked his pockets for poo-bags and biscuits, fastened on Stanley's lead and left the house. His watch said half past six.

Outside, the heat was building. The air was fresher than

London. Yet Jack pined for the claggy odour of river mud. The hills far away sharpened a longing for vistas interrupted by tall buildings. If he told Stella she'd think him absurd.

'Come on, Stanley.' Jack girded himself.

The way through the woods was dark and chilly. Jack imagined the densely growing trees inhabited by dryads and nymphs who meant him only good. It didn't work. The closely grown trunks and interweaving branches either side of the drive were unsettling.

He set off along Old Brockhampton Lane away from Winchcombe. After a few minutes he came upon a rusting iron kissing gate. He lifted the loop of blue twine holding it shut and let Stanley snake in ahead of him. The hinges gave an eerie shriek. Jack tensed.

In the field beyond, the rising sun picked out each blade of grass. Dried cow pats, encrusted and crumbling, suggested there hadn't been livestock in the field for several days. Jack had been alarmed by Stella saying cows could kill. As if they didn't have enough to contend with. He'd used precious battery and Googled it. Stella was right. The advice was to free your dog – cows didn't like dogs – as a decoy. Bad idea. Stanley would be trampled by a stampeding herd. As he watched the apricot poodle lift his hind leg against a thistle, Jack knew he'd die before Stanley came to harm.

The path wound up a slope. Looking down, he spied the ruined house he and Stella had come across the evening before. In London his sense of direction was acute, but now, despite going in the opposite direction to the house, it was in front of him. He'd walked in a circle. Stanley, perhaps sniffing familiar scents, belted away towards the ruins. By the time Jack caught up, Stanley was pattering about the rubble-strewn rooms.

There was a buzzing. The blue-white sky was empty. Berating himself – he must get used to the wildlife – Jack climbed the railings – after little sleep and with no Stella to impress, he didn't vault them – and stepped over the one-time threshold. The buzzing was louder. It was someone in a light aircraft, probably on their way to work. The sound was insidious, irritable and probing. His solar plexus tightened. A shadow flitted across the concreted floor. Instinctively he flinched. Stanley flew into a fury, hurling himself upward as if he too could fly, and barking at the top of his voice.

A shape passed across the fireplace set in the wall of Cotswold stone. A helicopter. It was the wrong scale. Keeping out of sight of the empty windows, Jack peeped around the crumbling stone. *A drone.*

Jack knew enough about surveillance equipment to recognize a multi-rotor drone. It could be there for only one reason. He was being watched. He snatched up Stanley and scrabbled for cover at the back of the house. He crouched behind a water tank. For a moment he thought the drone had gone, the air was still, he felt surrounded by silence. Then the buzzing grew louder. How was it possible to experience silence and noise at the same time? Jack tried to breathe and, crawling to the edge of the water tank, risked a look. The drone was descending. Stanley barked. Jack clamped a hand over the dog's woolly muzzle and shielded his eyes under his arm. Having none of it, Stanley struggled violently.

'Ssssh, Stanley! It's a frie-*end*. Just a little drow-*wone*,' Jack soothed. Whatever else, the drone wasn't a friend. Jack felt a flash of horror as he imagined bashing Stanley on the head to stop him giving away their position. As if he divined this, Stanley went limp and Jack felt a sting of remorse. The buzzing was angry. The pilot was homing in on him. *Where was the pilot?*

Clutching Stanley to his chest, keeping low, Jack skirted the tank. He flung himself over a drystone wall into a field that, planted with oil seed rape, was a dazzling yellow. Keeping to the fringe of the crop, eyes smarting from the bitter smell, Jack ran until he reached a hedge. The buzzing was insistent. He kept from his mind the futility of his efforts. Wherever he tried to hide, the drone would catch him in its crosshairs. He pushed through the hawthorn and fell into a ditch on the other side. Struggling to his feet, Jack couldn't see the insect-like machine.

Any minute now it would regain height. He and Stanley were sitting ducks. He couldn't hear the engine. The only sound was blood pounding in his ears.

Something crossed the sky above him. Jack shifted Stanley to his shoulder and smashed through brambles and cow parsley to run along the edge of the field. Again, he allowed himself a breather. The shape in the sky was still there. It was a crow. A crow!

The chimney of the ruined house wavered in the heat. The sky was clear. The crow flew off towards the lane. Jack's legs hardly took his weight. He was trembling. Skilful at sloughing off those who had followed him through dark London streets, he had never had to combat something above him before.

The fields beyond the hedgerow of blackthorn and hazel merged with the whitening sky. Stanley nosed amongst a scattering of wood anemone and buttercups growing close to the hedge. Tilting his head, he was following every move of a fat furry bumblebee as it dipped into the flowers. There was no sign of the drone.

As morning sun warmed the air, Jack shivered. He didn't scare easily, but he was fearful now.

Jack was securing the gate at the bottom of the drive when Stanley tugged his lead taut and wrenched Jack's hand away. He dropped the key. Stooping to retrieve it, he saw what had aroused Stanley's curiosity. Hidden in the grass was a cigarette end. More than one. Jack counted three. The butts were on the inside of the gate. It was possible that one might blow over, but not three. They were crushed as if they'd been ground out by a boot. It had rained in the night, but the filters were dry.

In London a pile of cigarette butts in a gutter tossed from a car ashtray was a common sight, but why here and why only three? It didn't take detective skills to infer that someone had been here smoking. Jack scoured the woods. There was a ragged gap in the trees. With binoculars he'd have an uninterrupted view of the house. He bent down. Twigs were snapped and the grass was flattened. Someone had stood for at least the time it had taken to smoke three cigarettes. It was the caretaker. *There was no caretaker.*

Jack let Stanley off his lead and traipsed after him through the tunnel of oaks and ashes. At the bend of the drive, where they'd first seen it yesterday, was the scarecrow. Arms wide, he grinned toothlessly at Jack.

The trees were still. It was hot now. Scouring the shimmering hills, Jack couldn't make out the lane. If you wanted to watch Crow's Nest, why stay all the way down there? With little sleep, his mind was playing tricks on him.

Jack smelled bacon cooking. The day righted itself. With sprightly steps he followed Stanley to the back of the house. He stopped in the doorway of the kitchen. Stella was teasing sizzling rashers about a frying pan with a non-stick slice. Her hair, combed and glossy, was newly washed, she'd braved the cold shower. Buttered bread lay on plates beside a cafetière of coffee and a bottle of tomato ketchup. Stella had made breakfast. Jack felt unalloyed joy.

'Just in time.' Stella slid two slices of bacon onto a slab of bread. 'I rang Cassie Baker's mother. She can see us at eleven. We'll go after we've talked to Mercer.'

Jack's phone vibrated. It was an image text. *Bella?* She used to send pictures of her latest botanical drawing. It wasn't Bella.

Jack gaped, uncomprehending, at the photograph. Framed within the image, Stella was buttering bread beside the stove. Behind her, the cafetière was empty. In the picture she had yet to make the coffee.

The photo had been taken nine minutes ago. *At precisely the time the buzzing had stopped by the ruined house.*

'Two rashers or three?' Stella touted a crispy strip of bacon balanced on the slice.

'One please,' Jack said, his appetite gone.

Chapter Nineteen

'We need to talk,' Jackie announced as soon as Graham came into the kitchen.

'What's there to say?' Graham sounded resigned, sad even. 'You could stop this.'

'You were there, you know I couldn't lie. It would have been wrong to say nothing. We – you and me – have to tell them.'

'You know what, Jackie? I don't have to do anything. You're office manager for a cleaning company. Get real, it's not *Murder She Wrote*!' Graham slammed the mug onto the table, spilling coffee onto the William Morris patterned cloth. He turned to the door and barrelled into Nick.

'I'm off!' Misery, then joy that Emma wanted him back, had rendered Nick oblivious to the weighted silence that had descended on his parents since the night Stella and Barry were there for supper. Sporting a light brown suede jacket, matching narrow-leg trousers and pointy buckled shoes, Nick was a restored man. 'Any chance one of you guys could drop me at Gunnersbury? Got to be in Clerkenwell for eleven.'

'We're not going—'

'I'll take you.' Graham slipped past Nick to the hall.

Jackie watched him swipe his car keys off the shelf. 'When will you be back?'

'Life-saver, Dad!' Nick came and clasped Jackie by the shoulders. He kissed the top of her head. 'Mum, thanks for everything. For being *you*!'

Before she could reply, Nick had grabbed his suitcase and was chasing down the path after Graham.

The night before, Jackie had set three places. Bowls, mugs, spoons. She'd got in Shredded Wheat for Nick, his childhood favourite, Graham had cornflakes and there was muesli for her. Now she mopped up the coffee and, piece by piece, cleared away the untouched breakfast things.

She poured herself a coffee. Somehow, a Clean Slate mug had found its way home. Jackie sat at the table and sipped the coffee, absently tracing twisting stems in Morris's design with a finger. After so long living there, the sounds in the house were part of her. The boiler fired up, crockery rattled every time a car passed. The radio still on in Nick's room was playing Neil Diamond's 'Sweet Caroline'. Barbara next door must have the same station, because, hanging out her washing, she was belting out the bit she knew '*Sweeeeet Carol-line...*' lah-lahing the rest. Jack said synchronicity was a sign. Her neighbour's exuberance pitched Jackie deeper into gloom.

Had Graham forgotten their weekend ritual? After breakfast they would walk to the end of the road and into Chiswick House grounds. Strolling arm in arm, they'd discuss their boys and make plans for the weekend. In the café she had a skinny latte, Graham liked a flat white. They shared the newspaper. Later, they cleaned the house, Jackie prepared the evening meal and Graham mended broken plates, rewired lights; she could rely on him to fix the household snags. Not this time.

Pushing sixty, Jackie was too aware that anything could go wrong any time. She'd supposed it would be illness or accident. Nick broke his leg last year, Graham had a prostate scare. But she and Graham, childhood sweethearts, were solid and for ever. When she dared contemplate a scenario without Graham, he'd loved her until he died.

This alone-ness, with Graham there, but not there, was worse than death. She'd been blinkered. No one could rewrite the past.

Chapter Twenty

Jack and Stella arrived at the little house in Bull Lane as the church clock struck nine. Clutching the bottle of Jack Daniels, Stella knocked on the door to give Mercer warning, then went down the side passage. Jack opened the key safe and removed the keys.

An empty foil dish and the cardboard sleeve for a low-calorie shepherd's pie lay on the kitchen counter. Mercer hadn't cleared away his supper things. The microwave door hung open. Stella shut it. Jack saw her resist cleaning up smears of food on the counter.

With a brisk rap, Stella opened the sitting-room door. 'Hello? Mr Mercer?'

They were hit by a stench. Mercer was in his armchair. A plate at his feet, the knife and fork and congealed lumps of potato were scattered on the carpet.

He was asleep, lips parted, pyjama jacket straining at the buttons over his swollen stomach. The smell was a rich mix of piss, shit and shepherd's pie. Mercer's trousers were damp at the crotch.

Backing away, Jack was astonished when, placing the Jack Daniels bottle on the table, Stella knelt down by the elderly man and whispered softly, 'Mr Mercer, it's Stella. Shall I get you some fresh things?' Stella was used to unsavoury scenes abandoned by those who'd created the mess.

Jack, on the other hand, was eager to leave. 'Shall I call Lisa?'

'And say what? He's refused to let her help. See if you can find clean clothes upstairs.' Cool in a crisis, Stella wouldn't even consider this a crisis.

Jack was at the top of the stairs when Stella called, 'Jack. Come back.'

She had pushed up Mercer's sleeve and was holding his wrist. 'He's died.' She placed Mercer's inert arm on his stomach and, getting to her feet, took her phone out of her combat trousers. 'He's in rigor. He's been dead some hours. You call the emergency services. I'll ring Lisa.'

Mercer himself told them yesterday never to shirk telling the family their loved one was dead. Stella knew what it was like to receive the information of her own father's death. Lisa Mercer had claimed to hold scant affection for Paul Mercer, but his death must surely affect her.

'We'll wait until Lisa gets here. Then go back to Crow's Nest and pack. We can be in London for lunchtime.' Stella had snapped into brisk efficiency.

If he dies you're off the job. Lisa Mercer's words. They were going home. He could see Bella. He could persuade her he'd be a perfect dad. Not all fathers were like hers had been. He'd be there for his children. Jack dialled 999.

Once they returned to London, Lucie would take over the investigation. Once they were back in their lives – not on a case – he'd have no chance to show Stella he believed in her as a detective. He believed in *her*. Jack was clear. He wanted to stay in Gloucestershire, he wanted to work with Stella to find the killer – or killers – of Cassie Baker and Bryony Motson. Together they would bring Cassie and Bryony justice.

He wanted to live with Stella in Crow's Nest, just her and him with Stanley in the middle of nowhere.

'Hello? *Hello?* Which service do you require?'

Jack gave the address and details of the situation to the operator.

'I was thinking...' he said when he was off the phone. 'We've done so much work on this. Maybe we should stay on and try to solve it?'

'Lisa said it would be over when Paul Mercer died. His finances will be frozen and Lisa doesn't want us to investigate, she won't pay.' Stella was patient.

'Mercer knew he was dying. He asked for you, he trusted you because you're Terry Darnell's daughter. He never said anything about stopping when he died. OK, we don't owe him, but would Terry want you to abandon it?' Low ploy. It was his last hope.

Perhaps Stella had become aware they were in the presence of a dead man. In shadow, Paul Mercer might have closed his eyes the better to listen. Or it was Jack's evocation of her dead father, because she appeared to relent.

'We'd have to work for nothing.'

'I've got my salary from London Underground. It's not like we've been paid much as detectives before, is it.' Careful. Stella couldn't be pushed.

'Jackie won't like it.' Stella cradled the phone in her hands. 'She didn't seem happy we were leaving London.' As this occurred, she added, 'Odd, she often says I need country air.'

'Call it a holiday.' Jackie was a stumbling block; Stella took her advice to the letter. So did he. Jackie had seemed reluctant to see them go – Jack had presumed it was because she'd miss them.

'Whatever, I need to call Lisa. My phone's about to die, may I use yours while I have enough battery to look up her number?'

He handed her his phone.

'What's this?' Stella was holding up the photograph of herself making breakfast.

'I, er...' If he told her about the drone – or the cigarettes – Stella would decide the case was a matter for the police. She'd leave Winchcombe without a backward glance.

'Did you take this?'

'Ye-es.' He bit on his lower lip and tasted blood.

'Without me knowing?'

'Not exactly, I thought you did. No, in fact, that is...' Jack advised Stella that, if in a fix, open your mouth and see what comes out. *Crap advice.*

'Lisa? Stella Darnell.' She stood up straight. 'I'm very sorry to tell you that your father has died.'

Stella didn't dress up a drama. Jack heard chatter through the earpiece. It sounded as if Lisa Mercer wasn't drawing breath.

'... they're on their way. We'll be here...'

More chatter.

'Heart attack? I'm not a doctor, but given his condition...' Stella moved to Mercer's body and lowered the phone. Jack had the crazy notion she was going to pass it to the dead detective so he could talk to his daughter. She bent down at Mercer's feet and gathered up the cutlery and laid it on the plate. She peered beneath the chair.

'I can't see a note. He may have tried to phone you, we can do last number redial...' Stella sounded dubious.

Lisa Mercer was asking Stella to check for any sign that, in his last hours, Mercer had tried to communicate with her. Jack knew that one, he'd spent a lifetime looking for proof that, as she lay dying, his mother was thinking of him.

A black police-style notebook was tucked between Mercer's body and the chair arm. Jack reached for it. Stella stayed him. She delved into her combats and pulled out silicone gloves and flapped them at him.

Stella was being a detective. Jack nearly whisked her about the room in a foxtrot. Instead he snapped on the gloves and slipped his hand down the side of the cushion, extracting the notebook. He flipped to the last pages. For a sick man, Mercer's handwriting was bold. No message for his only daughter, right up to his death as in life, Paul Mercer had been concerned with the two women who had haunted him for sixteen years. Most of the contents was reiteration of the facts of Cassie and Bryony's last days. Bus numbers, their routes and times, their known actions, what they were wearing. The contents of Bryony Motson's bag: lipstick, tissues, Tampax, painkillers, fifty pounds in cash. On another page was a shopping list: shepherd's pie, baked beans, lemonade. It was, Jack guessed, Mercer's own. The rest of the notebook was blank. Jack was about to close it when he saw writing on the inside cover.

Unlike the rest of the pages, the handwriting was faint and spidery as if the letters and symbols were the last thing that Mercer managed to write.

$$\text{L=MC ??} \quad \text{SBHH = L/GS? TC} \checkmark$$

Was this a dying man's message to Stella? More likely, like most people, Paul Mercer had believed himself immortal and had scribbled the figures as a reminder for when Stella arrived.

'… I understand. We'll bring the key to your care home… No, we're not expecting remuneration, we hardly got going…'

Stella was dropping the case. Jack stared unseeing at the black book. The pale silicone made his hand look as lifeless as Mercer's. He wandered into the kitchen. The door to the stairs was open. On an impulse, he ran up the stairs. Stella wouldn't sanction him poking about in the house of a corpse. He had only minutes.

A tiny bathroom overlooked the unkempt garden. On the sill was a cut-throat razor, a tube of shaving soap and a toothbrush with crushed bristles that looked as if Mercer used them to clean the grouting. It was dry, as was a towel hanging behind the door. It was likely that Mercer had died after eating his shepherd's pie.

A candlewick counterpane covered a single bed. Jack opened the wardrobe and released a whiff of camphor and rancid sweat. The hanging area was crammed with white shirts, crisply ironed. Below were three pairs of polished black lace-ups. Still wearing the gloves, Jack pushed the clothes along the rail. He slid out a drawer at the bottom and sifted through underwear, socks, pants and vests. By the bed a travelling clock was three minutes fast. Jack remembered Stella saying her dad kept his watch three minutes ahead. So did Stella. A train driver, Jack had to know the exact time.

There was a creak. Jack was ready to tell Stella he'd needed the loo, but he had no excuse for being in Mercer's bedroom. Stanley. Jack glared at him. In reply, Stanley pattered across the threadbare rug and, flattening himself, hind legs as if hinged back, tried to snake beneath the bed.

Jack bent down. The floor was thick with dust. Stanley recognized assistance and retreated expectantly. Pinching his nose to stop himself sneezing, Jack scrabbled under the bed as far as he could reach. He felt a hard object. It was wedged between the floorboards. He worked it until it came free and, sitting on his haunches, examined his find. A tube of Clarins eye cream. Stanley lost interest. Jack was interested to know that Mercer had cared about his skin.

In the bathroom he yanked the chain as backup that he'd used the lavatory. He felt bad; even if she believed him, Stella wouldn't like it. Clean Slate's manual stipulated, *Staff must not use clients' facilities.*

Stella was talking slowly and clearly. She'd picked up the ruse of dictating texts from her friend Tina. Jack was used to getting messages with the words 'Question Mark' and 'Full stop' when the software didn't convert the instruction to punctuation.

'Mercer dead full stop case cancelled full stop coming back full stop stella ex'

She must be texting Jackie. It was definite. They were leaving. He returned downstairs.

'Lisa Mercer's on her way. I'll meet you at the deli in Winchcombe, the one with the tables outside.' Stella knew what he'd been up to. She was getting him out of the way.

On the way out, Jack gathered up the shepherd's pie sleeve and carton from the counter. Outside, he tripped on something.

The flowerpot of fag ends. Except there were none, someone had cleared them away, leaving pockmarked soil. Jack felt he had cigarette ends on the brain. Opening a blue wheelie bin, he tossed in the packaging. Amidst newspapers and a number of beer bottles – Mercer had drunk Donnington's – there were other shepherd's pie cartons. Like Stella's father's, it seemed the ex-cop's diet was limited. Jack was about to shut the bin when he saw a Starbucks coffee cup. When – or how – had Mercer gone to a Starbucks? There wasn't one in the high street. There was scribble on the side. He reached in and flipping the cup read it. *Grant*. The boxes for 'Large', 'Skinny' and 'Cappuccino' were ticked. It had to be a sign.

Since they'd left Mercer yesterday he'd had another visitor. Grant. Yesterday Mercer had wanted to tell them something. Now he was dead. The Starbucks cup was more than a sign. It was a *clue*. It told Jack that Paul Mercer had been murdered.

Chapter Twenty-One

Nick and Graham had been gone two hours. Even in bad traffic it didn't take that long to get to Gunnersbury and back. Unable to sit, Jackie had tidied and vacuumed, even though a potential Clean Slate cleaner had been tried out the day before and left every room spotless. Now she was keeping an eye on the door as if staring at it would make Graham walk in. She'd stopped herself texting and asking when he was coming home, she was nervous of his reply. Or of getting no reply. She was a love-sick teenager again.

Jackie was rarely home alone. Graham dropped her at the office in the mornings. Even when Nick's relationship was going well, if he'd failed an audition he'd come home and soothed himself by cooking up delicious recipes. If Emma was away – a TV floor manager, she was frequently away – he hung out with them. Jackie liked that Nick found his middle-aged parents good company, until Lucie May had accused her of keeping Nick tied to 'his mummy's apron strings'. Lucie's default mode was waspish, her sting wide of the mark, but her comment still niggled at Jackie.

Listening out for Graham's car, she fretted that she had, as Lucie said, clipped Nick's wings. He and Mark were so different. When they'd started school, Mark trotted off eagerly without a backward glance. Nick had cried – the same desolate wail of recent days – when she handed him over to the infant teacher. Only when he was cast as Jesus in the Nativity play had he skipped in willingly. They'd had it again at secondary school. No crying this time, instead Nick had bunked off. He was caught stealing foundation powder from Boots in Chiswick High Road – to add to his actor's make-up – but before the manager could call the police, an off-duty police officer had intervened and got the manager to contact her. On the bus home, Nick confided to her that he wanted to go back to his primary school and be in a play. She spoke to his new school and he joined a drama group. He'd never looked back. Nick needed to act. He also needed to be loved and adored. Mark was married and expecting a child. He was living in Liverpool and they hardly ever saw him. Would she know her grandchild? She hadn't liked seeing Nick distressed, but had enjoyed being able to fuss over him. Had she mummified him in apron strings? Were Lucie May a mother, Jackie doubted her children would get any attention. Her thoughts were buzzing like angry insects.

She was startled out of these thoughts by her phone. A text. *Graham*. Ridiculously nervous, she opened her phone. Stella. As usual, her text read like a telegram.

Mercer dead. Case cancelled full stop coming back. Stella x

Relief coursed through her. Stella and Jack would find another case. Life would go back to normal. Jackie flicked on the kettle, took cups down from the cupboard. Galvanized, she set about washing the kitchen floor. They could go out tonight, try out the Chinese on Chiswick High Road. Call it a date. Jackie hummed as she worked.

Chapter Twenty-Two

'We could be on the road by one and, as it's the weekend, in London by three.' Stella bumped the van over the potholes through the wood up to Crow's Nest. 'I'll ring Cassie Baker's mother and say we're not going.'

'Are you sure?' Jack said.

'Lisa Mercer wants us gone. We'll never find a B and B, it's already the holiday season.' Stella was reluctant to leave the job incomplete but would welcome constant hot water, lights and Wi-Fi. And the last straw, 'My phone's about to pack up. There's nowhere to charge it.'

'There's something I haven't told you,' Jack said.

'What?' He was going to tell her he was back with Bella. Stella didn't consciously experience jealousy. Jackie had once suggested that she might find it hard to share Jack with Bella. She'd dismissed the notion. Yet that morning, hearing Jack leave the house with Stanley, she'd guessed he was going to phone Bella where she wouldn't overhear. Stella had distracted herself making breakfast. When she'd seen the picture Jack had taken of her cooking she'd been pleased.

'I didn't take that photo of you.'

'Oh. Right.' Jack would be embarrassed that she'd seen it. But spying was the sort of thing he did and at least snapping her was harmless. Terry had taken lots of photographs of her and of his cases. Quelling vague disappointment, Stella resolved to take more pictures – of suspicious places – when she charged up her phone. A detective must be observant at all times.

'Someone else took it and sent it to me.'

'What do you mean? I would have seen the person taking it.' Stella heard the illogicality, she hadn't seen the photographer.

'It wasn't a person, it was a drone.'

Stella listened unbelieving as Jack told her he'd been tracked by a drone at the ruined house.

'I'd have heard it,' she countered. 'I've seen a drone, it sounds like a vacuum cleaner in the sky.'

'They can be silent,' Jack explained. 'I think I was meant to hear it. Like the scarecrow, the drone and the picture are warnings. But it came up on you by stealth. Someone is going to huge lengths to get rid of us.'

Stella parked the van by the side of the house. 'A drone and a scarecrow aren't huge lengths. It could be a teenager who got a drone for their birthday.'

'I wonder if it's Brice.'

'Paul Mercer was after Brice for years without finding anything to incriminate him. I doubt Brice is bothered by us. Besides, he doesn't know we're here.'

'I found this in Mercer's recycling bin.' Jack handed Stella a plastic bag. Inside was a cup from Starbucks. 'Someone was bothered enough by Mercer to kill him.'

'Who's Grant?' Stella held up the cup. She should do more checking in bins. Being a detective meant getting dirty. She examined the bag. 'And whoever he is, why should he want to kill Mercer?'

'To stop Mercer talking to us.'

'We have talked to him,' she pointed out.

'Only because Lisa asked us to go earlier. Maybe Grant didn't know. He killed Mercer last night, or this morning, to stop him seeing us today as originally arranged.'

'Mercer had chronic obstructive pulmonary disease, he could have died any time. It's a stretch to find an old coffee cup and call it murder.'

'There's these.' Jack pulled two more plastic evidence bags from his pocket.

'Cigarette ends. Were these in Mercer's bin?'

'That one was. I found the other ones down by our gate. Whoever smoked those ones was watching the house last night. I doubt it was kids, they'd have been bored out of their skulls. Whoever was prepared to stand there for a minimum of twenty minutes had patience. I got the other ones out of Mercer's bin. They were in a flowerpot by his door, someone had cleared them away. They're the same brand, do you see?' Jack laid all the bags on the dashboard. 'Stella, someone wants us off this case. If we judge an action by the outcome, they've succeeded.'

'They have not.' Stella got out her phone and began texting.

'Are you cancelling Cassie Baker's mother?' Jack asked.

'No, I'm telling Jackie.'

'Telling her what?'

'We're staying. We won't be fazed by a drone or a mangy old scarecrow, and certainly not a murder. Solving murders is what we do.' Stella pressed 'send'.

Jack had a funny look almost – *not possible* – like he was trying not to cry.

Her phone gave a tooting signal. It was her alarm. 'We're due at Trudy Baker's in fifteen minutes.'

Chapter Twenty-Three

'Paul Mercer is a flippin' saint! I'm only seeing you because he asked me. I'm sick of reporters barging their way in asking questions like, "Do you miss your daughter, Trudy?" Idiots, I miss Cassie every day of my life.'

On a blue and pink sofa, in boot-cut jeans and a pink and blue stripy blouse that matched the furniture, Trudy Baker sat with her legs crossed and arms folded. She ejected saccharine pellets into her coffee and pushed a plate of doughnuts across the mosaic-topped table to Stella and Jack, seated in pink and blue armchairs opposite. Jack had deliberately gone for the pink, Stella disliked that colour.

Trudy Baker lived in the house they'd seen when they arrived the day before. The Range Rover had gone, but the racing green Jaguar was parked outside. Lines in the ground suggested that it had been newly raked.

Jet-black hair, nails polished the pink in her sofa, skilfully applied make-up, if heavy on the eye-liner; but for a smoker's tell-tale grooves around the mouth Jack would put Cassie Baker's mother late fifties, not seventy-four.

On the primrose-yellow walls were prints of a jetty in a calm sea, another of a ship against a cloudless horizon. Above Trudy Baker was a print of ornamental starfish and shells. None of it was Jack's taste but he warmed to the effort taken. A TV, volume muted, was tuned to a jewellery shopping channel. From a music system came the silky tones of Perry Como crooning 'It's Impossible'.

'Have a doughnut.' Trudy Baker thrust the plate at Stella.

'No, you're... oh, OK, yes, thank you.' Stella lifted a doughnut with the tips of her fingers. A martyr to manners – she didn't have a sweet tooth – eating it would be torture.

Jack loved doughnuts, he tucked in.

He'd seen photographs of Cassie Baker's mother in Mercer's file. One taken five years after Cassie had 'left home', taken at Karen Baker's wedding in which Trudy, in cerise with cascading curls, upstaged the bride, pale and unremarkable in a meringue dress that gobbled her up. The second photo accompanied an interview Trudy had given to the *Daily Express* after the discovery of Cassie's body in 1999 and finding that she'd been dead twenty-two years. Grim-faced and staring off as if into a better happier time, it was in the image genre of mothers of murdered children. Riven with pain – her daughter discovered at Belas Knap days earlier – Trudy was a ghastly travesty of her present-day self. 'Time stopped when Detective Chief Inspector Mercer said my baby girl wasn't in London, married with kids, but dumped like rubbish in some old grave. I pray the police find the other poor girl so Bryony's mum won't go through what I'm feeling right now.' No one had told Trudy – or she had not retained – that Bryony Motson's mother had died three years before.

'Would you tell us about Cassie?' Reaching for another doughnut, Jack tore himself away from a diamond engagement ring on the screen. They'd agreed he would lead.

Trudy Baker was plank-thin, parchment skin stretched over cheekbones. She had eschewed the jam doughnuts, saying she was weight-watching. Jack supposed she got a vicarious pleasure from plying guests with forbidden fruits.

'She knew her own mind, bless her.' Trudy sighed. 'She ran off when she was ten. The police found her in Gloucester Cathedral trying to cadge a fag. She shoplifted – just lipstick and sweets – and at fifteen she went to Bristol. No, I tell a lie, that was sixteen, when her dad got her home. The other time, she came back, skint, tail between her legs.' She leaned forward and adjusted the doughnut plate. 'Her and that Spicer girl, what a pair.' She gave a sigh of undisguised pride. 'My Cass wasn't a stick-in-the-mud, she shook us all up. One in a million.'

Jack bit into his doughnut. Jam squirted onto his trousers, just missing the pink fabric of the armchair.

'I'll get you a cloth.' Trudy Baker eased off the sofa and left the room.

Stella wrapped her doughnut in tissue and secreted it in her rucksack. Jack made a mental note to ask her later if he might have it.

Trudy returned with a damp J-cloth and before Jack could take it off her began dabbing at his trousers. 'Lucky they're black, lovey, still you'd better bung them in the machine tonight to stop them staining.' Finishing, she chased up flecks of castor sugar on the table.

'You were saying about Lauren Spicer,' Stella prompted.

'Lauren is a stuck-up madam. Not a patch on Cass. She needed Cass to breathe life into her. I was married with a baby at their age. Karen's nicely settled with grandchildren. Cassie could have had that.' For a moment Trudy Baker's face was clearly a mask that expressed a more palatable emotion than never-ending grief. Then the impression was gone and her smile appeared genuine.

'Do you still see Lauren Spicer?' Stella was writing in her Filofax.

'Every week. She does my nails and monthly hydrotone facials.' Trudy rose, and swiped up a packet of Silk Cut and a Bic lighter from a shelf scattered with pink and blue shells and sea urchins like those in the print on the wall. Lighting a cigarette, she slid open a glass door and went out onto the patio.

Stella joined her. 'Paul Mercer has died.'

'Was it his heart?' Trudy dragon-puffed smoke from her nostrils.

'I expect so.' Stella hated cigarette smoke, but nothing betrayed this.

'A release. It was terrible seeing him like that.' She drew on the cigarette. 'I warned him, keep on with this business and it'll kill you!' Clasping an elbow, cigarette held aloft, Trudy wandered among large tubs of hydrangeas.

Trudy Baker didn't seem upset by the news of Mercer. Jack hooked loose a lump of dough from the roof of his mouth with a finger and went out to the garden.

The cigarette bobbed on Trudy's lower lip. 'You'll be baling out of this investigation too. Don't blame you.'

'We'll do our best to find your daughter's killer, Mrs Baker.' Like her dad, Stella knew better than to make rash promises.

'I told Paul, unless you bring Cassie back to life, finding who killed her is no odds to me. She's dead. That's all that matters. Craven's doing time, leave it.' She contemplated her cigarette fitted between two fingers.

'Paul Mercer didn't believe Matthew Craven was guilty,' Stella said.

'He was guilty of sniffing around Lauren. He was guilty of hiding my Cassie in that horrible Belas Knap place.'

'Didn't Craven leave Cassie?' Jack asked.

'He said so. Cassie wasn't around to argue, was she. Take it from me, she ended it. Lauren was always snapping up her leftovers. Craven wouldn't have liked being jilted.'

'Did you know Matthew Craven well?' Stella looked up from her notes.

'Know him? Chance would have been a fine thing. He was too lazy to come in and wait for Cassie when they was going out. He'd skulk out there on the lane.' Trudy Baker ground out her cigarette in a pot of mint. Jack noticed it was dotted with other butts. He edged closer and nipped out a stub when she was busy lighting another one. He secreted it in a poo-bag to examine later. Was it conceivable the Watcher was Trudy Baker?

'What about this heart-throb Karen told the police about?' If Stella had seen him, she gave no sign.

'Cass probably made him up.' Trudy Baker blew out a cloud of smoke.

'She made him up?' Stella echoed. 'Did you tell Paul Mercer that?'

'I'm only guessing, she liked to wind up her sister.'

'Mercer believed "Heart-throb" was Brice. Did you?' Jack followed up.

'Charlie had a girl already, I never saw him with Cassie.' Trudy Baker ripped a leaf off the mint and sniffed it. 'One thing about Cassie, she never two-timed. Her men were beefcakes, the rugby player sort like Craven. Not that he is now. Looks like a lamppost. Charlie's a bantamweight. Know what I think? This Heart-throb fellow was that prince who'll whip you up and carry you off to where the streets are paved with gold. Not some local lad like Matty Craven. She met her heart-throb, rode to London and lived happily ever after.' Crushing her cigarette underfoot, Trudy Baker went inside and returned to her sofa.

Jack and Stella looked at each other. His own thought was reflected in Stella's expression. Trudy needed to imagine her daughter living it up in London with a prince charming. Not dead and buried in Belas Knap.

He was startled by a cry, strangled and piteous. It came from a plastic monitor on the table. Stanley chorused in time to the cries, his howl almost human.

'Ignore!' Trudy Baker commanded. Stanley was quiet. 'Liam's woken from his nap too early. He'll go off.' As if Liam was a heating system.

'Did Cassie have enemies?' Stella said.

The possibility of anyone hating his twins enough to kill them scared Jack witless.

'Whoever killed Cassie was her enemy. Other than him, everyone loved her. God knows, she could drive you mad. What she put us through running off, cheeking teachers, but still she was pure diamond.' A shadow deepened her smoker's lines. 'Our Karen's another kettle of fish. Not a peep out of her all these years.' Jack thought grimly that Trudy hadn't had a peep out of Cassie either.

The crying escalated to a scream.

'Is he OK?' Stella nodded at the monitor.

'Give in and one day he'll have his wife at his beck and call. Got kids?' Trudy Baker raised her eyebrows at Stella and Jack as if they were a couple.

'Um, actually…' Jack saw it would be easier to tell Stella about the twins with someone else there.

'No.' Stella would find the clamour grating. Jack wasn't confident Bella would tolerate their children crying. She needed peace to draw. How would she work with children there needing attention? He'd comfort them if it meant spending his life chasing after them. He'd care for their every need.

'Mercer never mentioned that Brice had a girlfriend.' Stella wasn't deflected. 'I read that Brice had been staying at his aunt's house in Winchcombe in 1977. Was the girlfriend there too?'

'She wouldn't let them stay with her, right old bat, that Phyllis Brice, ruled with a rod. Talk about having enemies! His girl was one of a gang, up at Belas Knap. I saw them when I was walking the dog.'

'A gang of who?' Jack raised his voice above the monitor.

'Campers. Kids.'

'Did you tell Mercer about the campers?' There had been nothing in the case files about anyone camping at Belas Knap.

'Nothing to tell. They'd gone before Cassie went.' She eyed the monitor as if it was recalcitrant.

'Why did you think Brice had a girlfriend?' Stella wasn't letting it go.

'Honey was Cassie's lab, not that Cass fed her, took her to the vet's or walks. I was up on Belas Knap and Honey goes nosing off round the hill. I went after her and found two tents. Beer cans, vodka bottles, they'd had a fire and no doubt treated the place like a toilet. Honey went into one of the tents. Charlie was there with some girl. *Starkers.*'

The screeching from the monitor reminded Jack of Lucie's budgerigar.

'The little blighter's not leaving off. I'll have to settle him.'

Jack told himself he'd love his children more than himself. Were they to die, his life would be over.

'… Jack?' Stella had been speaking.

'Sorry?'

'Did you read anything about the campers at Belas Knap?'

'No, but Trudy said she never told Mercer. She said they'd left Winchcombe by the time Cassie Baker vanished. They weren't potential witnesses.'

'These were Brice's friends. His girlfriend could have been a character witness. It's odd she's never come forward to be eliminated as a suspect.' Stella ran a hand through her hair, making it stick up. Jack imagined stroking her black locks, twirling them in his fingers. He snatched up the last doughnut.

'Unless she did it.' He licked sugar off his fingers.

A shadow from the garden fell across the carpet. They both jumped. A woman stood in the doorway. She wore a denim shirt and her hair was tied back from her face, which wore a confused expression.

'Where's my mother? Who are you?' There was nothing confused in her tone.

In his mind Jack recited,

I am the family face;
Flesh perishes, I live on,
Projecting trait and trace
Through time to times anon,
And leaping from place to place
Over oblivion.

He said, 'I can see that you and Cassie are sisters.' In the shape of the woman's nose and the succession of expressions passing over her face – annoyance, anger then faint pleasure – Cassie Baker lived on in her sister.

Karen Baker slid shut the patio door. 'Cassie was better-looking.'

'We're private detectives, hired by Paul Mercer to find out who killed your sister.' If a compliment was fished for, Stella missed the hook. She got up to greet Karen.

'We know who killed her.' Karen Baker stalked across the room and began piling the crockery onto the tray. She paused at the empty doughnut plate with a chilly look.

'We did hope to talk to you.' Stella remained standing. 'Cassie talked to you about meeting a man she called her "heart-throb". Can you remember anything more about what she told you?'

'It was forty years ago. No, I can't. It was just Cassie's way. No one gives you a car and a house.'

'Is that what the mystery heart-throb promised?'

'He said, "I'll only ever love you."' Karen examined her nails, polished in sparkly blue. Had she too been to Lauren Spicer's beauty salon? Jack wondered. Possibly, because Karen said, 'Lauren's who to ask. They were thick as thieves. Cassie told her everything. No one danced with me at that disco because I broke my arm playing hockey against Bishops Cleeve,' she added with fleeting rancour. She looked around as if she'd lost something. 'Is my mum having to deal with the baby?' Her recriminatory tone suggested that Jack and Stella should be dealing with Liam. Jack felt amorphous guilt, as if along with his unborn children, he was responsible for the crying baby.

'You didn't ask the identity of the heart-throb?' Taller than Karen Baker, Stella drew herself up to her full height.

'No. Do we have to dredge this up? Cassie thought she was better than me. Well, she wasn't.' Karen hugged herself and scowled.

The sitting-room door banged open and, with the urgency of a police raid, Trudy Baker burst in. She carried a bundle swaddled in a blue cellular blanket, a large white teddy bear wedged under an arm. She sat down on the sofa and unwrapped the blanket, revealing a baby.

Stanley stared at the creature, dressed in a blue onesie with pink mice ears, his tear-stained face twisted in misery as he continued to bawl.

'He's teething.' Trudy Baker bounced the baby up and down which, Jack saw, only increased his wretchedness. 'Karen was the same, so was Rich, this boy's dad. They'd scream at the drop of a hat.'

'Not like that, I didn't.' Karen made no attempt to relieve her mother of the boy who must be her grandson.

Jack stretched out his arms. 'Let me try.'

Trudy Baker thrust the baby at him. Tentatively cradling him, Jack cooed, 'Hel-lo Leee-am!'

Liam went quiet. Jack felt profound happiness as the little boy gazed wonderingly at him.

'He likes you.' Trudy had seemingly lost interest. A great-grandmother was maybe a generational step too far. Karen Baker dabbed a finger in the sugar on the doughnut plate and licked it.

'It's like when someone tries to get the cap off a bottle, they pass it on and someone else does it easily.' He affected modesty.

The boy's body went rigid. He emitted a yell so loud that Jack's eardrums popped. The thing in his arms was a screaming mass.

Two hands relieved him of the writhing bundle.

Silence.

A queen on the stripy sofa, Trudy Baker nursed her coffee mug. Karen Baker sat hunched beside her. Stanley lay sprawled on the carpet at Jack's feet. The baby was propped in the crook of Stella's arm. He gripped her forefinger in his tiny fist and beamed at her with what could only be described as adoration.

If Jack hadn't known he was in love with Stella Darnell before, he knew it now.

'This young woman you saw in the tent with Brice, why didn't you tell Mercer about her?' Stella waggled her finger up and down, lifting the boy's arm as he held on. He giggled delightedly.

'The girl was embarrassed. I couldn't put her through more shame. I told you, didn't I, Karen?'

Karen nodded. 'She should have been embarrassed. Belas Knap isn't the place for that sort of thing. I'd have had words with Richard if he'd done that with Janice.'

'You have to remember, Stella. The police found our Cassie in 1999. By then that girl would be a grown woman, married with kids. Paul and his team would have bugged her with questions. She wouldn't need her husband hearing she went with a murderer on Belas Knap! Your dad would have lost it.' Trudy nudged Karen who nodded again. Jack had the sense that they often sat together on the sofa in what looked like quiet companionship.

'When Cassie ran off to London, Dad went ape. Got drunk, ran his lorry off the road in Gretton and smashed his leg. He couldn't climb ladders after that. Cassie wasn't even in London.' Karen finished as if Ralph Baker's accident was an overreaction.

'I told Paul, in 1977 I lost a daughter and gained a teenaged son. Ralph was a useless husband and father.' Trudy looked at Stella. 'Little mite's taken to you. Never seen him that good with his mum, but Janice should never have had kids, should she, Kaz!'

'Richard changes him, does all the night feeding. She's always down Beauty Heaven dolling herself up.' Despite her comment, Karen's tone was of indulgent equanimity.

'How did you know the campers had gone by the time Cassie vanished?' Stella was pulling faces at the baby. Yet again Jack had imagined he'd got the measure of Stella, but she wrong-footed him. Now she was Madonna and Child. Would Bella surprise him and be the perfect mother?

'I went up there with Honey and they'd cleared off. Apart from the burnt grass from the fire, no mess, nothing. That would have been the girl clearing up.'

'Can you describe her?' Jack wanted another go with the baby, but Liam looked content in Stella's arms.

'She was stark naked!' Trudy said again. 'So was Charlie! Long hair. Not dark. She had the grace to put on a T-shirt, I remember it was the Rolling Stones, with those horrible lips. Our Cassie was a Quo fan. Me too. After she went, I got her Rick Parfitt's autograph at a concert. Ended up giving it to you, didn't I, Kaz. When the Quo went on Live Aid I expected Cassie to ring and sing down the phone that she was rocking all over the world! She was a laugh.' Trudy Baker's voice caught. She put a hand to her mouth.

Silence. Everyone contemplated the empty doughnut plate.

'How did you know the man was Charles Brice?' Stella spoke first. She was letting Liam play with her watch. Large-faced with a silver strap, it had belonged to her dad. Jack was worried the baby would break it.

'I didn't know it was him until Phyllis introduced him to me in the grocer's. He had a cheeky grin on him!' She smiled at the memory. 'Reminded me of Ralph at that age.'

'Do you think we could speak to your husband?' Stella asked.

'He's in Five Trees Nursing Home. Can't hold a spoon. Or won't. If he's not there, he'll be in the Corner Cupboard. He can hold a pint. I doubt he'll tell you anything. He can't recall how to tie his shoelaces, can he, Kaz!'

'He's all right, Mum,' Karen mumbled irritably.

'That's the care home owned by Lisa Mercer!' Jack said.

'Yes, poor thing has to put up with him when her own father wouldn't go near the place.' Trudy bit the inside of her cheek then stopped as if conscious of creating facial lines. She snapped to attention. 'That girl in the tent. She'd only gone and had "CB" tattooed on her arm. No man's worth that. Wherever she is now, even if she's got it taken off, she'll have a scar.'

'Tattoos are stupid,' Karen announced.

Jack guessed that, aside from the terrible loss, it would be hard having a sister who was murdered. Cassie might be dead, but she'd always dominate the family.

'Paul was a good man. If not for him, Cassie wouldn't have had a decent burial. He called Charlie evil. But sorry, there's no way you can tell me the bloke who made those shelves is evil.' Trudy Baker pointed at a cabinet with the hi-fi, from which emanated Perry Como's 'Moon River'. 'Beautifully made, not like Ralph's DIY dog's dinner!'

'Charles Brice made those?' Used to entering a variety of homes, Stella remained neutral about taste and the degree of tidiness. Jack recalled Beverly's phrase *Think cleaning, not compliments*.

'The problem is?' Trudy Baker fixed on Stella, eyes as dark as marble.

'I didn't realize you knew him.' Stella, who had faced down bullies at school and charmed unpleasant clients, was unfazed by the basilisk glare.

'He's my handyman. I said to Paul, Charlie couldn't hurt Cassie. It was Ralph's fault.'

'What was?' Stella stroked a lick of hair off the baby's forehead. The gentle gesture belied her absolute attention to Trudy's every word.

'Ralph drove Cassie away, saying she needed a proper job and going on about her wearing make-up. Once she was big enough to argue, she was off. They'd had a steaming row that day. If you ask me, you should leave Charlie alone and have a proper look at my ex.'

Perhaps reminded of her connection to the baby, Karen Baker got up and, sweeping around the table, took him from Stella. As if a switch had been thrown Liam gave a furious shriek. Stanley woke up and barked. Jigging her grandson, Karen went out into the garden.

Jack caught Trudy's murmur, 'Charlie's got a feel for wood.'

Perry Como sang how it was impossible to stop a baby crying and in that moment Jack felt that the little boy's sobbing expressed all the pain Jack had ever felt.

Chapter Twenty-Four

Jackie's car triggered security lamps and Barry's drive lit up a white BMW coupé parked beside the black Shogun. Every window blazed with light. Barry's flamboyance found expression in a hacienda-style villa (dubbed by Graham 'the House of a Thousand Lights') off the A406 in Ealing.

Jackie had told Graham she had to go over details of premises Barry had found for Clean Slate. True, but Graham wasn't fooled, she could have talked to Barry from the office. As she ascended shallow semi-circular steps framed by ornate columns, Jackie wished Graham had challenged her; a pithy remark about his brother would have been better than stolid silence.

She pressed the bell. Big Ben chimes clanged inside. Barry's wife Yvonne answered the door. When Barry suggested coming to the house, Jackie had assumed Yvonne was out.

'Jax! He didn't say you were coming. Nothing new there!' She air-kissed Jackie.

'I did tell you, darlin'.' Barry Makepeace was running down a beige-carpeted staircase that extended from the centre of a gallery above. All he needed was walk-on music.

Ceiling spots illuminated walls on which hung gilt-framed mirrors that multiplied the effect. Strangely, given what a romantic he professed to be, Barry disliked mood lighting.

'Come to my snug.' Barry opened a door off the hall.

'I've got a ladies' meeting at the golf club. Jax, another time, yeh?' A black crocodile handbag on her shoulder, her spray-tan orange in the bright light, Yvonne blew Jackie a kiss and tossed it towards her with a cupped palm. She shut the door behind her with a crash.

Jackie was fairly certain Barry's flirtations were just that, yet she felt for Yvonne Makepeace. She was the recipient of exorbitant presents, cruises to Australia, safaris in South Africa, a new car every year and limitless credit on an array of plastic, yet whenever Jackie saw Yvonne with Barry she sensed she'd interrupted a quarrel. Generally, Jackie felt relief that she and Graham led such a harmonious life. Or had.

Barry and Yvonne had three children and four grandchildren. There was always some party being thrown to celebrate someone's birthday. Graham said Barry's personality was off-the-peg, with nothing original or unique about him – Jackie felt that was harsh. Barry was a warm kind man. Accepting the ice-cold drink he poured her from his lavish bar, she settled onto a leather chesterfield. The last time she'd been in Barry's snug was three years ago to sign probate papers. Frank Makepeace had hoped appointing her as his executor would encourage a rapprochement between his sons. It had grieved both parents that Graham disliked his brother. It wasn't natural, Frank said. Jackie hadn't cited Cain and Abel, Will and Ed Grundy in *The Archers* or her twin cousins who'd hated each other since birth. Loyal to Graham, she'd resisted agreeing when Frank said how Barry wanted Graham to like him. Barry needed to be liked. He was indiscriminate about who did the liking. Sipping her vodka and lime, Jackie considered that the sibling problem was the least of it.

'I'd have brought the office stuff in tomorrow.' Barry tweaked his grey cotton trousers (nothing off-the-peg about his clothes) and joined her at the other end of the chesterfield, legs stretched towards an enormous mahogany desk on which was an enormous computer. Jackie had known why, after Stella cleaned his house, she'd been reluctant to hand over the job. Apart from the dust-proof vitrine of Barry's golfing trophies to the right of the chesterfield, every room was clutter-free.

Jackie's voice was muffled by leather and thick carpeting. 'We must go to the police.'

Barry leaned across to her and, smiling, brushed her wrist with the side of his thumb. 'That's a bad idea.'

Chapter Twenty-Five

'I don't see why you'd get a man who might have murdered your daughter to put up shelves.' Her face bathed in rays from the setting sun, Stella sat back in her chair, legs outstretched, sipping her second glass of Merlot.

'Trudy might have forgiven Brice. People do.' Jack tried to concentrate. He was struck again by Stella's looks. Not the pre-Raphaelite splendour of Bella Markham that, dare he admit, had palled. Stella's beauty was all of her. Her Roman (and hyper-sensitive) nose, tousled black hair sleek as a cat's and a steady gaze that could see into his soul. This last bit was likely nonsense. Jack topped up their glasses. Stella's perception was less hit than miss and she didn't hold with the existence of a soul.

After cold chicken and salad around a rusting old table on flagstones stained by moss, Jack washed up the supper things in water heated in a saucepan on the calor stove. Tomorrow they'd have to find somewhere else to stay in Winchcombe.

Contemplating his wine, a rich red in the evening sunlight, Jack knew he'd do without his beloved District line and the River Thames if he could live with Stella in the country. He breathed in the scent of apple blossom drifting across the patio from the orchard. From one of the trees, a blackbird warbled a cheerful song.

'Trudy Baker supported Mercer when he was accused of gross misconduct, but all the while she thought Brice innocent. That's inconsistent.' Drinking her wine, Stella seemed less concerned tonight to keep a clear head. She had picked a bouquet of rosemary and lavender from wooded bushes growing by the wall of the house next to where she'd parked the van. Every now and then she stuck her nose into the rough and ready posy and inhaled deeply. Fancy Stella noticing plants, Jack thought.

'Trudy never actually said Brice was innocent,' Jack reminded her. 'I think it's healthy she's not ravaged by revenge. Some people are eaten up by hatred for their loved one's killer.' He wondered if he was one of those.

'She seemed to accept Matthew Craven killed Cassie,' Stella said. 'She wasn't nice about him.'

'When something as cataclysmic as murder happens, relatives must have to find faith in verdicts. They have to trust the legal system got the right person. Murder is a senseless yet complex act, those left behind need a simple solution. Words like "guilt" and "evil" sew it up nicely.'

'I don't think Trudy had time for Mercer beyond being so grateful he found Cassie.' Stella bent and stroked Stanley who lay at her feet.

'It must be hard to let go of the hope your daughter is alive and take on that not only is she dead but she was murdered.' Faced with bitter reality, Jack chose fiction every time.

'It must be hard for Karen, the daughter who never ran away. She was obedient and caused no trouble. Even though she's alive and Cassie's dead, she could always have been envious of the attention Cassie got. And still gets – after all, we were there today about Cassie, not Karen.' Stella sipped her wine. 'There were no pictures of Cassie in Trudy's living room.'

Diverted by the doughnuts, Jack hadn't spotted that. 'Maybe Trudy can't bear to be reminded of what happened to Cassie. I did notice she didn't portray Cassie as perfect.' He'd never heard Stella explore what it was like to be another person; at the time she hadn't seemed aware of Karen Baker. It could be the wine or the approaching twilight. Or had clean air, hills and fields released a new Country Stella? 'Trudy made Cassie real to me. I wish I could have met her.'

'What if Trudy argued with Cassie and hit her? Photos on the wall would be a daily reminder. She could have pointed up Cassie's faults to justify killing her.'

'How would Trudy have got Cassie's body up to Belas Knap?' Jack got Stella's thinking. It wouldn't pay to make an enemy of Trudy Baker. Behind the cheery décor and smooth sounds of Perry Como was a tough woman who nursed a bitter wound. He observed, 'She let the baby cry.'

Stella swilled her wine around in the glass. 'Trudy went up to Belas Knap with the dog. Easy to suggest Cassie come with her and kill her there. Maybe it was an accident, a quarrel that got out of hand.'

'She couldn't have moved that blocking stone in the chamber by herself.'

'It could be why she likes Charles Brice. Maybe he helped her. Or more likely Matthew Craven and it's why she's particularly nasty about him. If Trudy murdered Cassie, no wonder she's happy to pin the guilt on Craven and keep the case closed.'

Jack felt a thrill; Stella was exploring psychological consequences. He suggested, 'If Craven had admitted guilt he might have got parole sooner. It could mean he's innocent.'

'Craven was eighteen when Cassie died. Even if he didn't kill her, he put that stone by her body. He knew what happened to her all that time. That's as good as murder.' Tipping her chair dangerously, her voice ethereal in the dwindling light, Stella reached down and grasped a stalk of cow parsley from between the flagstones. Never off the cleaning clock, she shook the roots free of soil and hurled it towards the orchard.

She was thinking aloud. 'Trudy Baker said Ralph wasn't a good dad. Less than ten per cent of femicides are at the hands of strangers. Did he return from Bristol that night after all?'

Femicide. Stella – who never read anything except cleaning catalogues and articles on cleaning – was spouting facts on homicide. He *loved* her!

Jack checked himself, the wine was making him soppy. Stella hated men to be in love with her, he'd seen others make that mistake.

Stella shifted her chair into a last scrap of sunlight closer to the house. 'Ralph Baker may have started drinking because his daughter was murdered. Or because he murdered her.'

'He wouldn't be the first father to murder his child,' Jack agreed. 'Brian Motson could have murdered his daughter too, twenty years after Cassie was killed by hers. Small towns and villages must seethe with unexpressed emotion. Mercer has a daughter, maybe he couldn't contemplate a father doing that to his child.' Nor could he, Jack thought with a shudder.

'Let's take stock.' Stella got up and, picking up the empty wine bottle, went inside.

Jack caught a whiff of Stella's perfume as she passed and breathed it in.

Stella sat at the long oak table. She'd lit four of the candles they'd bought after visiting Trudy Baker, from a hardware shop on the high street that sold all anyone could need, from light bulbs – Jack wished they needed them – to mothballs and garlic crushers. They'd stocked up on other sources of light and heat, candles, boxes of matches, firelighters and bundles of kindling. They'd forgotten to buy torches.

Jack nestled into his chair at the other end, they were a team.

'Where's Mercer's notebook?' Stella asked.

Jack fumbled amongst the papers at his end of the table. He found it and, getting up, came and gave it to Stella.

'By rights we should have left this for Lisa Mercer.' Frowning, Stella leafed through the notebook. 'Mostly Mercer's jotted down facts. I do that when I'm trying to work out a problem. It clears the mind. He's put the dates when Cassie and Bryony were last seen. Cassie went missing in the summer, Bryony in the winter, so no connection there.'

Looking over Stella's shoulder, Jack's eye was drawn to 'Terry's Girl' written beside Clean Slate's Shepherd's Bush address. He'd missed that when he'd flipped through it at the detective's cottage. Stella was looking at the collection of symbols on the inside cover.

$$\text{\sout{L=MC ??}} \ SBHH = L/GS? \ TC \checkmark$$

'Isn't "MC" a maths formula?' he wondered.

'You're thinking of Einstein's theory of relativity, that's $E=MC^2$. Matthew Craven's initials are MC, yet what would he mean by L=MC with two question marks?'

'Two suggests an expression of more than doubt. I put two question marks when I can't believe something can be true,' Jack said.

'He's crossed it out. Twice. So perhaps he decided it *wasn't* true. In Roman numerals, L is fifty and MC is one thousand, one hundred. If it's an equation, it doesn't make sense.'

Who knew Stella was hot on maths? The Spreadsheet Queen, of course she was numerate. 'He could have crossed it out then added the question marks. L wasn't equal to MC then it was equal and Mercer found that extraordinary,' Jack pondered.

'The crossing out includes the question marks. He posed the question to himself and then decided it wasn't true. Perhaps the "SBHH = L/GS?" with a slash is a correction of the first section of the formula. In Microsoft Excel a slash is a mathematical operator, denoting divide. He's still put a question mark.'

'Meaning he decided the first formula was wrong and it *might* be the second.' Head spinning, Jack leant on the corner of the table.

Stella flipped back through the notebook. 'I reckon he wrote it recently, just before he died. The handwriting is weak, the pen's hardly touched the paper compared with these earlier pages where it's firmer. There is the possibility this may have nothing to with the case. Maybe Mercer did puzzles in his spare time. My mum does.'

'Lisa said her father was obsessed with the case.'

Stella returned to Mercer's last entry. 'I'm over-thinking. These are initials. "MC" is Craven and "L" must stand for Lauren.'

'Or Lisa. How would Lauren equal Matthew Craven?' Jack pulled a face. 'One person can't equal another.'

'People are equal to each other. Or they should be.' Stella was copying out the formula onto a page of flip-chart paper. 'It could mean that they were together and then not. Which is true. Lauren Spicer withdrew her alibi for Craven when she heard he'd put the stone next to Cassie's body.'

'Stella, you're onto something!' Jack squeezed Stella's shoulder without meaning to. He let his hand linger. *One two three…* Then retreated to his end of the table.

'Let's sleep on it.' Stella turned to her Filofax. 'So, taking stock, in June 1977 Cassie Baker left the Jubilee disco early. We know she went to the disco, out of about a hundred people, loads of them saw her dancing with Lauren. No one saw her leave. Lauren Spicer went off with Matthew Craven at the end of the evening. But three people saw him leave earlier. He was alone. He told Lauren he was going "to find Cassie". Later he denied saying this, he'd wanted air. When Lauren retracted her alibi she told police he'd said it.' Stella was speaking without looking at the papers piled between them. 'Cassie was seen on the bridge on Vineyard Street. Possibly going home or was she waiting for Heart-throb Guy? What we know is she met her killer and was buried at Belas Knap. The interval from the moment she was sighted on the bridge to when she was found could have been hours, even weeks. Did she walk to the long barrow alive or was she carried there dead?'

'Trudy Baker called Brice a "bantamweight", he couldn't have lugged her body there alone. Craven was a beefcake.'

'Being a bantam doesn't preclude strength. Even if she knew her killer, would she have agreed to accompany him to a remote burial site? According to the files, it's a steep path through woods. Let's go there after we've seen Ralph Baker tomorrow.'

'Good idea.' Jack wanted to go to Belas Knap regardless of it being the crime scene. It had been a place of ceremonies celebrating life as well as death. It would be special to go with Stella.

'If Craven planned to murder Cassie it was odd to advertise that he was leaving by telling Lauren. Why not just slip out?' Jack said.

'Craven's barrister made that point in court. He suggested it was a sign of innocence, not guilt. Cassie's skull was smashed in.' Stella looked suddenly stricken, although the night before she'd examined copies of X-rays of the injury without apparent emotion. 'Mercer said the murder was premeditated. It has to be said that impulse killers tend to leave clues. Nothing has been found at Belas Knap.' She put down her marker. 'It would be good to meet Charles Brice. Get a sense of him.'

'If we approach Charles Brice, he'll know we're investigating him and if he's guilty he won't help us. Right now we have anonymity on our side.' Jack thought of the dead crow, the drone at the ruined house, the cigarette butts and the mystery photograph of Stella. And the scarecrow. Did they have anonymity on their side?

'Brice might be willing if he thinks we'll clear his name. If he's behind all the things that have happened he's onto us already. We mustn't be tempted to *not* think him guilty because we're keeping an open mind. Mercer could be right and Brice is a murderer. If we could be a fly on a wall in Charlie Brice's house,' Stella sighed, 'we'd know if he was a murderer. Two flies.'

Was someone a fly on their wall? He'd been slow. The picture of Stella was meant as a threat. Someone knew that Stella was important to him. Nothing in Stella's response suggested she'd realized this. But Stella wore very little on her sleeve.

A ghastly mewling echoed through the house. For an absurd second Jack pictured Liam, a horror-film baby lurking in one of the empty rooms. 'What was that?' His shout blew out one of the candles.

Neither of them moved.

'It was Stanley,' Stella said eventually.

The dog stood in front of the unlit grate, his eyes black. As they watched, he opened his mouth and made the dreadful cry again. It was like he'd been possessed.

Stella got up. She was opening the door to the hall before Jack could stop her.

'Stella, no!' Jumping up, Jack knocked over his other candle. He slapped at the flame as it licked the edge of a photograph of Bryony Motson. The ten-year-old, in a festive cracker hat, knelt by a Christmas tree. He ignored splashes of wax scalding his skin.

The sitting-room windows rattled as if something had been thrown against the glass. Dimly aware that all the candles had blown out, Jack headed after Stella.

A clattering. He was hit in the face by something sharp, yet soft. He ducked.

'A bird has got trapped.' Stella was cool as a cucumber.

Flailing, Jack swept his hand up and down the wall for the light switch before remembering there wasn't one.

'It's panicking. Could you bring me a candle?'

Jack felt his way back into the sitting room and immediately jarred his thigh on the corner of the table. As he grew used to the gloom he saw it wasn't pitch black outside. Lozenge-shaped panes suspended in the darkness were mauve. Something passed the nearest window. Jack shrank back. It was a branch and it was metres from the house. His sense of perspective was shot. Pulling himself together, Jack travelled his hand over the table until he found a candle. He fumbled to light it. The flame flared. He put it to the wick. When it caught, Jack, trembling, made for the hall. The movement put out the candle. He went back to the table and, sweat pricking his brow, began the arduous process again. This time cupping the frail flame, he set off as if in an egg and spoon race, one step, pause, another step, pause. The room seemed to go on for ever. At last Jack raised the candle and pulled open the thick oak door. Only then did he realize he could hear nothing beyond.

'Stella?' The glare of the flame accentuated darkness outside the sphere of light.

He was in time to see Stella walk out of the front door, her arms in front of her like a sleepwalker, hands clasped. She could be in an arcane ceremony. She dissolved into the darkness.

The candle went out as he went to go after her.

Moonlight cast a sallow gleam over the drive. Stella opened her hands. Jack saw a giant bird; black against the sky, it soared towards the new moon.

'Another crow. Maybe there's an actual nest,' Stella said. 'At least this one lived. I don't understand how it got in. All the windows were shut. It must have been while we were outside.'

'A crow is a symbol of luck. They look out for predators.' *And intruders.* The bird had chosen Stella, she would be safe. Jack clawed his hair back off his forehead. The night was muggy and even in a thin cotton shirt, he was hot. 'Crows are messengers. They urge you to develop the gift of second sight.'

'First sight would be enough,' Stella said. 'Let's go to bed. I'm dead on my feet.'

Don't say that! Jack stifled the words.

The kitchen door had been shut while they were eating.

Across the fields came a strange call. Short on bird knowledge, Jack's nocturnal ornithology was limited to owls. And crows. The sweeping of a breeze through the woods made his skin crawl. So much for countryside quiet, there was less noise on a London street.

Stella and Jack went around the house checking locks. He bolted the kitchen door and slotted the iron bar across the front door. They carried their candles up the stairs.

On the landing outside their bedrooms, holding the light up – her profile, giant size, projected onto the wall – Stella asked, 'Will you be OK?'

'Oh yes! Will you?' The photograph of Stella in the kitchen flashed up. He blinked.

'Yes, but you don't like birds in confined spaces.'

She'd remembered him telling her that scared him. He tried to sound casual. 'I've got over that.'

'Good. That's good.' Stella continued lighting his face with her candle.

The next thing happened so fast that later Jack wasn't sure it *had* happened. Stella darted forward and kissed him. Before he knew it she'd gone into her bedroom and he was alone on the landing. His lips tingled where her lips had brushed them, light as a moth.

Stella's door was ajar. An invitation? Jack reached to the handle then let his hand drop. It would be for Stanley to go in and out. Not for him.

Jack lit his way into his own room and placed the candle holder beside the bed. Some people made the mistake of assuming the intensity of passion they felt for another could not be experienced without reciprocation. Stella was a no-nonsense woman, she didn't do hints and hesitations. If she wanted him he'd be in no doubt of it. The look in her eyes did make him doubt. Love skewed reality, it made fiction out of fact.

Jack dragged his shirt over his head, folded it and laid it on the chest of drawers. No one loved him. Not like that. If Bella had felt anything like love for him, she didn't now. The love between children and parents could be the strongest bond. His children would never know him to love him.

The woman who had loved him was long dead. Jack's memory of his mother was as flimsy as gossamer, her ghostly presence less and less a comfort.

Jack was certain he would lie awake all night, but the second his head hit the pillow he fell fast asleep.

Chapter Twenty-Six

Stella watched helplessly from the shore as Stanley chased along the bank of Chiswick Eyot. Water rippled over the causeway until it was submerged. The air reeked of river mud. A crow perched on a post and screeched.

A messenger of death.

Stanley barked, the strident *rrouooff* meant danger.

'*Fuck* off!' The cyclist's shout was amplified in the suffocating quiet.

If Stella called Stanley, he would attempt to swim across the widening strip of water. The currents were deadly and he'd be swept away. Freezing water lapped around her ankles. Stella slipped on giant cobbles. And woke up.

The barking was real. She flung out of bed and smacked into a wall. Her shoulder smarted with pain. Her palms traced cold plaster. A picture hung in front of her. Trees, silver in the moonlight. Not a picture, she was looking out of a window. Stella remembered where she was.

Stanley's barks were the same as in the dream. Danger! Stella shuffled into her trainers and, laces loose, felt her way to the door and down the stairs. The house had a held quality as if waiting for something. Stella put an ear to the living-room door. She heard the clock ticking. There was no clock.

'Don't move!' the voice whispered.

'Jack?' Stella grabbed Jack's arm. His skin felt warm. 'What's happening?'

'I came to see why Stanley's barking.' Jack covered her hand with his and gripped it.

'Where is he?' Stella moved away and peered out through one of the side lights in the hall.

Jack began pulling up the bar on the door.

'Don't! Stanley'll run out!' she warned.

'He must already be outside.'

'How did he get out?' Stella was sure they shut all the doors and windows when they went to bed. 'Did you let him out?'

'Of course not.'

'I'll get the torch from the van.'

Stella had indeed understood the message implicit in the picture sent to Jack's phone. Unwilling to trouble Jack with her thoughts, she'd deduced that someone out there had her in their sights. As she crept past the living-room windows she was mindful with every step that at any moment she could be attacked. Had she and Jack played right into their enemy's hands?

The van appeared luminous in the half light. Stella unlocked the passenger's door and rummaged in the glove box, yielding the Maglite she kept there. She reassured herself it would double as a cosh. *A blunt instrument.* Not that it would need to, she insisted inwardly. Stanley barked at spiders and dogs on the telly. Still Stella couldn't shake off her dream of Stanley trapped on Chiswick Eyot by the rising river. His bark had not been about a spider.

She shone the torch along the drive. It was empty. She should have asked Jack to wait for her. Stella whispered fiercely, 'Jack?'

Stanley began barking in earnest. Whoever was out there would see her torch. This was the countryside, dwellings were few and far between, nothing but fields and woods and ditches. There was no one for miles.

Stella tripped on her trailing shoelace and pitched forward. Saving herself from falling, momentum propelled her along the path. At last her legs gave way and she crumpled to her knees. The torch rolled into the undergrowth, lighting a patch of nettles. Someone stood over her. They'd been there all along. Stella scrambled up. 'Who are you?'

She found the torch and aimed it wildly at their face. There was no face.

Jack raced towards the barking. Moonlight washed everything grey like a photographic negative. The night breeze was cool against his skin. He should have waited for Stella. But he'd been useless with the crow in the hall, he had to save her now.

Jack's fantasy of princely bravery fought with cold fear. With each step, his being urged him to turn tail. His head was filled with the buzzing of the drone, all around him were phantom lights of cigarettes. He blinked them away. He knew he was rushing into a trap, but he kept on.

Something brushed his ankle. Stanley! Jack grabbed at him, but Stanley streaked away into the darkness. The little dog wasn't running away. He was leading Jack to the source of the trouble. Jack blundered after him.

'Don't move!'

Jack forced himself to stop and work out where the voice was coming from. He'd lost his sense of direction.

'Keep still or you'll make things worse for yourself.' It was Stella.

Her voice came from the direction of the lane. Jack plunged through the wood. He tripped on tree roots and brambles scratched his skin, his hands pushing against the air urging him on. He saw a light ahead.

Jack had always believed Stella's lack of fear would land her in trouble. A stickler for the law, she tackled a trespasser, a litter-bug or someone parked in a disabled space. Deep cleaning had made her fit, she was tall and strong and capable. Keen to avoid the fact of mortality, Stella behaved as if she was immortal. No matter how fast Jack ran, the light got no nearer.

'Stay where you are.' Whoever it was wasn't staying where they were. Jack's heart beat so hard it felt it would give out. *Why wasn't Stanley barking?*

Two figures were struggling by the barbed-wire fence. He stopped and, scrabbling on the ground, found a thick branch. With crazed strength, he broke it in two. He had only surprise on his side. Raising the stick he yelled, 'She said, *don't move!*'

Distantly Jack registered a sting as barbed wire strafed his bare arm.

'Way to *go*, Tarzan!'

It couldn't be.

'Lucie, please hold my torch.' Even in extremis, Stella was polite. She was crouched by the fence. '*Please* keep still.'

Jack was dazzled by light.

'Jacko! What a sight for sore eyes.' Lucie May was caught in the wire. A rucksack on her back, she resembled a giant snail.

'Lucie, what are you doing here?' Jack panted.

'I'm your em*bedded* reporter,' Lucie cried.

'Entangled, more like.' Stella was snipping at Lucie's nylons with the scissors on her Swedish penknife.

'Hah-de-hah, Miss Marple,' Lucie wheezed. 'Ouch, *careful*! I paid a friggin' fortune for these tights.'

'It's your tights or you stay on this fence. Now, Lucie, please bend down as far as you can go and slip the strap of your rucksack off. I'm holding up the wire. You'll be safe.'

'Jack's naked chest's gone to your head. Or to somewhere else!' Lucie May jerked an arm. The rucksack fell onto the ground, narrowly missing Stanley.

'Where's Endora?' Lucie was suddenly serious.

'What's Endora?' Stella asked.

'Not what, who. My venerable bird!'

'Your bird?'

'Lucie means her budgerigar.' Jack remembered the yellow bird perched in the Murder Room.

'You've brought a budgie with you?' Stella asked without a trace of incredulity.

'Here's looking at you, kid.'

Jack felt feathers brush his head and then a sharp dig on his cheek.

'The crow is back!' he yelled.

Lucie moved the beam of light off his torso to his face. 'She likes you!'

Twisting his head, Jack saw the 'crow' peering at him, plumage bright yellow in the Maglite's glare. He wanted to dash the thing off his shoulder, the scratching claws set his teeth on edge. Instead he managed to say, 'Hello, Endora.'

'She escaped! *Naughty* girl! Stanley could have eaten her.' Few were more adroit than Lucie at creating a crisis and blaming others for the consequences.

'Come this way please,' Stella called. Endora launched off Jack's shoulder and with a whooshing flew towards the cage Stella was holding up and in through the open door.

'She never comes when I tell her to.' Lucie was munching on a carrot.

'Let's get inside the house.' Stella fastened the cage door.

In single file they trudged up the drive. Jack lugged Lucie's extremely heavy rucksack, Stella held the cage, Stanley trotting beside her. Lucie, waving the torch at the darkness ahead, appeared to swim along in front. She stopped.

'Who's that?' She grabbed Jack's bare arm, her nails sharp as Endora's claws.

'It's a scarecrow,' Stella said.

'It's moved.' Jack was filled with fury. Someone was playing games with them.

In the torchlight the scarecrow seemed to be walking towards them down the drive.

'Great! We've got bloody Worzel Gummidge!' Lucie twirled

around the straw effigy, as if she could work her charm upon it. Jack felt momentarily better; extraordinary though it was, for once Lucie's gung-ho attitude was a relief.

Finally ensconced on the sofa, Lucie busied herself concocting a nippet from ingredients in her rucksack. Endora perched on Jack's shoulder as he hefted Lucie's bag upstairs. He stood for a moment in the candlelit passage, grateful that Stella was putting Lucie at the other end of the house. The bird made chuckling sounds in his ear. He turned to her and before he'd considered the words, he confided to her, 'I'm going to be a father.'

Endora gave no sign she'd heard and with a flap, she swooped back down the stairs.

Jack put a shirt on and did another sweep of the house to make sure the windows and doors were locked.

'You've got dressed, shame!' Lucie said when he returned. She clacked her teeth and took a slug of gin. 'I do hope you two aren't paying for this dump!'

'Lisa Mercer arranged it. It's free. Paul Mercer has died so we'll have to move.' Jack encouraged the embers in the fireplace to flames and heaped on more logs. He sat down in an armchair. Stanley leapt onto him. Seeing them as through the window, he imagined himself and Lucie in a David Hockney painting, two dulled figures and a dog. He spotted advantage; Lucie liked her creature comforts: 'There's no electricity, no lights, no hot water and we found a dead crow. It's terribly basic.'

'Like my house,' Lucie said obliquely.

He should have guessed that Lucie could rough it. She'd be in her element.

'Stella, there you are, we were starting to pine, weren't we, Jackabub!'

'Your bed's ready when you want it.' Stella sank into the other armchair and to Jack's astonishment she accepted the gin and tonic Lucie held out for her.

'I hope nobody died in it.'

'I expect someone has died in it.' Stella took a gulp of her drink. 'People die everywhere.'

Jack rubbed his face. The artist who captured this tableau should be a surrealist.

'Speaking of corpses, you two look dug up.' Lucie appeared concerned.

She wasn't wrong. Dark circles raccooned Stella's eyes, one cheek was streaked with earth and her hair stuck out in clumps. She looked like Jack felt. They'd barely slept in the last twenty-four hours, someone was watching them and now they'd had a scare. Still, Jack thought, even dishevelled, Stella could cut it.

'What did Matthew Craven tell you?' Stella was blunt.

'That was a secret.' Lucie looked thunderous.

Jack hugged a cushion. His hatred of confrontation had infuriated Bella. Stella and Lucie under one roof would be tricky.

'What did he tell you?' Stella said.

'He gave me the slip.' Lucie swished ice in her glass with her devil-headed swizzle stick. 'He left the day before. He's in the wind.'

'So why are you here?' From anyone but Stella the question would have been antagonistic. She was merely curious.

'Don't get your knick-knacks twisted, me and Endora will be silent mice in the corner. I've got my book to write – *Closing the Coffin Lid, Fifty Years of Murders Unsolved.*' Lucie blew kisses at the bird who was pecking at the mantelpiece. Stanley had gone to sleep. The non-human creatures, at least, were accommodating each other.

'Unless I'm needed.' She slid a coy glance at Jack. He felt a pang. Lucie was always 'doing' a book that never got done.

'Maybe, if you didn't mind, you'd go to the library in Cheltenham on Monday,' Stella asked her. 'There's a ruined house across the fields that we found. It's close to where Cassie Baker was last seen. Perhaps you'd check out who lived there. They are potential witnesses to her murder.' She sucked on an ice cube. 'We need to trawl local newspapers for what else was happening around here in the summer of 1977 when Cassie disappeared with the mystery heart-throb, and in December 1999 when Bryony failed to catch her bus. Fetes, bazaars, fairs, shows, country stuff. Who would have been in Winchcombe? Pull out maps, photographs, we've got the bones of the story, but no background. Jack and I will handle interviews. We can put everything together tomorrow night.'

Lucie tapped the gin end of her swizzle stick against her front teeth. 'Yes, all right.' Jack would have supposed that if anything could make Lucie leave, it would be having to answer to someone else, but Lucie agreed without protest. 'On one condition.' But not without strings attached. 'Whoever finds him, Matthew Craven is mine.'

'No conditions. You're either on the team or you're on the M40 back to Hammersmith.' Stella finished her drink. 'I'm off to bed.' Stanley leapt off Jack's lap and went with her.

'Me too.' Jack couldn't muster Stella's stern tone.

'Have fun, darlings,' Lucie told them.

As he closed the door, Jack saw another tableau. The sofa, crimson curtains open to the night. The dark green walls absorbed the light of the solitary candle. His eye was drawn to the yellow plumage of the budgie dozing on Lucie's forearm and a pinprick of light glancing off her nippet glass.

Unobserved, Lucie's features had slackened, gaining her years. Her eyes betrayed sadness. Lucie had come to stay, he thought, not to take over the case, but because she was lonely.

Still Jack wondered, hovering outside Stella's bedroom, what might have happened between himself and Stella if they were alone.

Chapter Twenty-Seven

'Café, Wi-Fi, air-con. Twenty-four-seven security for when you girls work late. Take the fifteen thousand square metres and sublet. Kick 'em out when Clean Slate expands. The flat frontage, high ceilings and cool windows offer the genuine warehouse vibe. Little bro can drop you at Turnham Green, Jax. What's not to like!' Barry, swish in a blue silk suit and fresh as a daisy on this Monday morning, rocked on his heels as he regarded Beverly assiduously writing in a notebook decorated with pink hearts.

Jackie, dwelling on her talk with Barry on Saturday – he'd been intractable – the rift with Graham and that Stella and Jack were still in Winchcombe, couldn't envisage Clean Slate benefiting from any vibe. Only the round-the-clock security would impress Stella.

'And the price?' Beverly enquired.

'I'll sort that.' Barry fiddled with a lock of his hair. A childish trait that saved him from being a creep.

'What does "sort" mean?'

'Just that, Bev. I'll get you a sensible figure.'

'Yeah, but what's a sensible figure?'

Jackie felt pride. Bev wasn't awed by incontinent charm or good looks (at sixty-three, Barry was old enough to be Beverly's grandfather). Beverly needed no protection from Barry Makepeace.

'The list price is five k, but I'll ensure you guys get more bang for your buck!' Barry flashed perfect teeth at Beverly.

They were in a bright airy kitchen area with sink, cupboards and cavities for a fridge and microwave. On the ground floor were showers and a bike room. No one at Clean Slate rode a bicycle, but the proposed office move was for new staff. *New staff.* Jackie felt a welling up of dread. She'd encouraged Stella to get new premises, but this yawning space – 'full of natural light' – was too much for a Monday.

'There's no such thing as a free lunch.' Fresh from her 'Inhabit your Authority' course, Beverly wore a terrible frown.

'The landlord owes me. Don't you worry your pretty…' Jackie was relieved, for his own sake, that Barry was sufficiently a new man to leave the sentence there.

'You're saying five k per calendar month.' Beverly was writing. 'There's cash-flow to consider. Even thriving companies go down due to late payment.'

'Clean Slate will sublet to me.' Barry was prompt. Jackie doubted Bev's tenacious questioning had bounced him into it. This was his plan. What was he up to?

'It's still a risk,' Beverly said.

'Clean Slate is *fam*-ly. I'll handle the risk.' Barry did an *EastEnders* accent.

Beverly wrote, 'Subletting possible. Risk.'

'I wonder if we shouldn't opt for the six hundred square metres upstairs. It's ample for three years until, as you said, there's a break clause.' Jackie saw a chance to get Barry alone. 'Let's see it. Bev, be a love, scoot down and feed the meter.'

Beverly's footsteps on the metal staircase merged with a police siren reverberating against the 'cool' windows. Barry's phone beeped.

'Got to take this.' He strode out after Beverly. 'Grant! Didn't I say never…'

Alone, Jackie began to feel the white brickwork had a prison vibe. The air-conditioning was making her sinuses ache.

'I've put on an hour.' Beverly was back. 'Where's his Barry-ness?'

'He took a call.' It irked Graham that Barry took phone conversations without leaving the room, his booming voice meaning that they had to be quiet while he was talking. Graham said he was showing off. Barry had gone outside this time. What was special about Grant? 'We must go. We'll discuss the move when I'm back. I'll drop you at the office.'

'I've just… OK.' Heaving aside the concertina gate into the lift, Beverly asked, 'Where are you going?'

'Winchcombe.'

Chapter Twenty-Eight

Lisa Mercer supposed they were coming to return the Crow's Nest key. Stella wasn't happy with what had amounted to deception, although they would be truthful when they got there. She agreed they 'come to my office at nine thirty a.m. sharp'.

Five Trees Nursing Home was three 1940s mock-Tudor houses knocked together on a leafy lane behind Winchcombe library. Stella and Jack had left the van at Crow's Nest and walked into town, because of Jack's thing about learning the terrain and Stella hoped Stanley – she wouldn't leave him with the budgerigar – would be less inquisitive if he was tired.

They'd watched Lucie May drive off to Cheltenham library, her twenty-year-old Volkswagen Beetle's exhaust belching fumes and emitting bangs. Stella was surprised when Lucie had acquiesced to her task list. Relieved, too, because when they interviewed Cassie Baker's father, three would be a crowd.

Lisa Mercer sat at a pine veneered desk smelling of Pledge Wood 5 in 1. From the carpet emanated the scent of shampoo (Rug Doctor).

On the wall behind Lisa was a nursing hygiene calendar of a barge on a river. A gloomy old man in a cardigan looked out from an Age Concern poster which said, 'No one should have no one.' Stella battled briefly with the double negative, gave up and resorted to the list of 'Care Home Hygiene Dos and Don'ts' stuck on the back of the door. One 'don't' was stinting on the quality of cleaning materials. Stella agreed. She applauded the top 'Do'. *It takes ten seconds for patients and loved ones and inspectors to decide about your establishment. We are influenced by what we see, hear and smell. You want that first impression to be positive.* It had taken Stella five seconds to decide Lisa Mercer's care home was at least clean.

'... naturally I'll pay expenses and cover anything you've spent while here.'

'There's no need—' Stella began.

'There's every need. You were brought on a wild goose chase. The least we – *I* – can do is ensure you're not out of pocket. Have you brought the key?'

'We'd like to continue with the case,' Jack said.

Lisa Mercer stared at Jack. Stella saw he wasn't a reassuring sight. Pale, his hair mussed, he'd not shaved because Lucie had broken his razor. His shirt was creased, but that was normal. His shoes were dirty, which was not.

'I told you. My father's obsession died with him. I'm sorry you wasted your time, and that you found him like that yesterday. He died sooner than I expected. You owe him and, certainly me, nothing.'

Jack beamed. 'We don't expect a fee. We owe it to Cassie Baker and Bryony Motson's families to find out the truth. We met Trudy Baker.'

Too late, Stella saw he'd said the wrong thing.

'Trudy Baker!' Lisa Mercer straightened things on her desk: a stapler, a hole punch, a box of tissues. 'Matthew Craven's done time for Cassie's murder. Trudy got a grave for Cassie. That's enough for her. Don't start on about getting her justice, she's after nothing but a quiet life. If you want to help her you'll leave Winchcombe now.' She flicked through a block of sticky notes branded with the same disinfectant Stella's company used at the hospice.

'It was Trudy who suggested we talk to Ralph Baker.' Still

smiling, Jack might as well abandon being the 'good guy', Lisa Mercer wasn't impressed.

'You're wasting your time. Trudy's washed her hands of Ralph. Karen Baker hardly ever comes. I don't blame them. He goes on about Cassie being his angel when Karen does come. I'm an only child, but it doesn't need imagination to work out that your dad going on about your sister would annoy you.' Lisa snatched up the hole punch and brought it down on the desk like a gavel. Stella had said something similar, Jack thought.

'Ralph Baker might remember something,' Stella said.

'He doesn't know what he had for supper last night. I don't want him upset, it's more work for my staff. If you bring up my father, believe me you'll upset Ralph. Being a bad apple, he hates do-gooders.'

'Does Mr Baker get other visitors?' Jack enquired chirpily.

'None at all.' Lisa Mercer said it as if it was a personal achievement.

'No one should have no one,' Stella said accidentally.

'Perhaps it would be stimulating for him to meet us,' Jack agreed.

'I'm sure it will be. And seeing as Trudy suggested it,' Lisa said tonelessly.

'As you know, my father helped your father with the case.' Stella went in at another angle. 'He was going to tell me who my dad suspected killed Cassie and Bryony when we came back the next day, but unfortunately—'

'He went and died,' Lisa snapped wryly. 'I wasn't privy to his work. I can't help you. I do know they fell out and Terry Darnell stopped coming to Winchcombe.'

'Your dad didn't tell us that.' Stella sat forward.

'If he'd told you your dad wouldn't help, you'd have refused,' Lisa said. 'Maybe he was going to come clean when you saw him the next morning. Although I doubt it.'

'Maybe.' Stella found her heart was pumping against her chest. Why had Terry stopped helping Paul Mercer?

'We'd love to keep renting Crow's Nest. Who should we contact?' Jack stepped in.

Nowhere in Winchcombe would accommodate three people, a dog and a budgie. They'd agreed it was easier to stay put.

'Henry's family have had it for generations. We had enough trouble keeping that Spicer woman away.'

'Lauren Spicer?' Stella shouldn't be surprised. Winchcombe was a small world.

'Interfering biddy.'

'You mean she wanted to rent it?' Still winded by the news about Terry, Stella vaguely thought renting the ramshackle house didn't fit with her profile of the beauty salon owner.

Lisa Mercer's frostiness softened at the idea. 'Fleece him, more like. She's been after knocking down Crow's Nest. She preys on lonely old people, Dad, her old teacher; that old lady who pulled her up by her bootstraps, I tell Henry, "At your age don't do anything you don't want to." Luckily I have power of attorney.' She made this sound like a happy accident.

Stella noticed Lisa Mercer was referring to her father as 'Dad' and not 'Mercer'. Had Mercer's death made her feel less angry with him? Stella could understand that. Since Terry's death she felt she knew him better.

'Crow's Nest pays for Henry to live here.' Lisa tweaked the sleeves of her red 'flight-attendant' jacket.

'Surely the nursing home costs more than rent for Crow's Nest?' Jack asked what Stella was thinking. Five Trees must be about five thousand a month. Mercer cannot have paid much for them to stay.

Lisa Mercer stood up. 'Henry can't live in that old house on his own. He likes it here. You can stay for a hundred per week – that will cover Henry's trips out.'

Jack protested. 'That's daylight—'

'Here's enough for two weeks.' Stella laid most of the notes from the bundle Paul Mercer had given her beside the hole punch.

They followed Lisa Mercer up twisting stairs and along a corridor with a patterned carpet also fragrant with Rug Doctor. Easy Hygeine's Power Blast spray, scented with Floral Breeze, had recently been fired into the atmosphere. Stella was back in the world of smells that she knew.

She glanced into the first room. An old man lay in a cot bed, mouth open and eyes staring unseeing at the ceiling. A television blared. In another room a tense woman of about Stella's age sat opposite a white-haired woman in an armchair who was asleep. Perfectly still, the younger woman balanced a cup and saucer on her lap. They passed a lounge, people of various ages sat in a circle of armchairs, clutching slices of sponge cake. Stella heard hoots of laughter. A regal woman in a pastel blue jacket and skirt was ripping gold paper off a present with the urgency of pass the parcel. Stella's mother often said she'd kill herself before she went into a home, implying Stella planned to put her in one some day. Stella had no such plan.

'Jean's ninety-two today. She's one of my favourites,' Lisa Mercer remarked over her shoulder. Stella, who discouraged her staff to have favourites, hoped none of the other residents were listening or were too deaf to hear.

'Here we are.' Lisa tapped on an open door and strode in, slamming shut a door to a toilet as she passed.

A man was propped against cushions in a Parker Knoll chair. A gold watch on his wrist, in a baggy grey tracksuit, he was toothless, his jutting chin nearly touching his nose. Unlike Jack, he'd shaved, or had been shaved. Ebullient jet-black hair (that recalled Grecian 2000) was combed and oiled in a strict side parting. Hazel eyes – sharp and intense – flicked over Stella. The same eyes as the photographs of Cassie Baker.

'Who've you brought me?' Baker's tongue lizarded over cracked lips.

'Stella and Jack. They're visiting Winchcombe and wanted to meet you.'

This was true, but it made them sound like tourists taking in Ralph Baker along with Belas Knap and the Winchcombe Folk and Police Museum.

'You have fifteen minutes.' Lisa Mercer left the room.

'Sit!' Baker looked pleased to see them. Stella disliked the duplicity involved with being a detective. Feeling fraudulent, she dragged over a chair to face him. She suggested Jack have it, but Baker wheezed, 'I decide who sits, lass.'

'We've been asked to look into your daughter Cassie's death, Mr Baker.' Spotting a hearing aid on the window sill, Stella raised her voice.

'Who asked you to?' Baker asked, munching his lip.

'We decided ourselves.' They couldn't mention Paul Mercer. More lies.

'What an angel, they broke the mould after her.' Grimacing, Ralph Baker tilted a pearly framed photo on the sill towards them. Stella was familiar with the image: Cassie Baker, the year she died. The picture was cut from a newspaper. Didn't Baker have an original?

'When did you last see Cassie?' she asked.

'Last night.' Baker drank from a plastic beaker with a non-spill lid.

'I'm sorry?'

'Never tell a fella you're sorry.' Ralph Baker patted Stella's knee with callused fingers.

'You saw her last night?' Stella kept her tone level.

'In my dreams, darling. She's with me all the time, her dirty laugh! My little girl.' His eyes were red and rheumy.

'Apart from in your... when did you see Cassie in real life... when you were awake?' Stella gave a rictus smile. This was going badly. Jack was as still as a post. They'd agreed she'd lead and he was sticking to it.

Thankfully, Ralph Baker carried on blithely, 'I had a job down Bristol way. Clifton. Or I'd have got my hands on him before he hurt her.'

'What were you doing in Bristol?' Stella knew why, but wanted to hear Baker's version.

'Just said, lass, I had a job. Plastering ceilings. Those high ones are a killer. You ever plastered a ceiling, mate?' Baker's expression suggested that Jack would be hard-pressed to recognize a ceiling.

'No.' Jack's tone implied he'd like to try.

'Does your neck in.' Baker took another sip of water.

'You said he hurt her. Who do you mean?' Stella asked.

'Heart-throb, Karen said she called him. Truth be told, there wasn't no one good enough for Cassandra. Trudy blames me,' he bleated at the photograph.

'Was the heart-throb Matthew Craven?' Stella noticed the knuckles of Ralph Baker's hands were tattooed with 'Love' and 'Hate'.

'Lauren reckoned not.' He ran a finger along his top gum. For a moment Stella recalled Liam, Ralph's great-grandson.

'When did Lauren say that? Did she know who the heart-throb was?' Stella asked.

'She said it wasn't Craven, Cassandra had got rid of him. Lauren was always picking up my girl's leavings. They all sniffed after Cassandra, those lads.' He looked at Jack.

Seeing a clock by his bed, Stella noted they had ten minutes left; so far the interview had netted nothing.

'Did you get on with Cassie?' She turned back to him.

'She was Daddy's girl.' He rubbed at his nose with a palm.

'What time did you finish plastering the ceiling in Bristol, Mr Baker?' Stella returned to her initial question.

'Six, maybe. I went for a drink.' No mention of the 'mistress'. Either Ralph Baker was sidestepping the truth or he'd forgotten.

In the garden below, an elderly woman in a white cotton jacket and colourful skirt was reading a newspaper on a bench. She held her straw hat on with the flat of a hand although the branches of trees and bushes were still.

'What time did you get back to Winchcombe?' Stella tried another approach.

'After midnight. Everyone was in bed.' He ran both his hands through his hair as if getting ready for a night out. 'I was seeing someone, OK? Me and Trudy, we were having our difficulties.'

'Who was that?' Four minutes to go.

'Marilyn, like the actress. "Diamonds are a girl's best friend!"' Jigging his hands, he crooned to Cassie's photo.

'Would Marilyn vouch for you?'

'She would, except she passed years ago, cancer or the like. One minute here, the next gone.'

'Paul Mercer has died,' Jack told him.

'He's one to talk. Should have been hung.' Baker interleaved his fingers and flexed them. Hate was uppermost. 'Bloody coppers!'

'Do you think Charles Brice killed Cassandra?' Stella remembered Bryony Motson's father's complaint to the Police Complaints Authority that Mercer's conduct had allowed Bryony's killer to escape trial. Why hadn't Baker complained?

'Someone killed her. He's out there breathing air while she's mouldering in the ground. Mercer wanted me for it.' Ralph Baker scratched his chin as if this baffled him, but Stella caught a glint of pride in his eyes.

'Time's up!' Lisa Mercer was in the doorway. Stella had the fleeting impression she'd been there a while. She was a minute early.

'We've all made mistakes.' Baker put on a smile. 'Lise! Sorry to hear about your dad.'

'Thank you, Ralph. Please leave Mr Baker in peace,' Lisa Mercer told them.

As Stella got up, Ralph Baker snatched hold of her wrist. His grip was surprisingly strong. 'This isn't for the likes of you.'

'What do you mean?' Stella couldn't move.

'Let sleeping dogs lie.' Ralph Baker let go of her. His gaze rested on the photograph of his long-dead daughter. Stella felt worried by something, but couldn't think what it was.

'I'd say Ralph rivals Brice as prime suspect,' Jack said when they were walking along the high street. He lingered as Stanley lifted his leg against a lamp-post by a hairdresser's called Head Room. 'I wouldn't have liked to get on the wrong side of Baker when he had his teeth in.'

'Being a suspect would get him attention.' Stella was thinking of Baker's look of pride. 'He's the only one of the family who's given interviews in the last ten years. If he killed Cassie I think he'd have given himself away. He strikes me as someone who makes mistakes.'

'His memory isn't that bad. He recalled Marilyn well enough.'

'It's the short-term memory that goes as you age.'

'He gave off a violent aura. No wonder he and Cassie argued. He must have driven her mad.' Jack spoke as if he knew Cassie.

'My dad would have given off a violent aura if I'd been murdered.'

'Don't say that!' Jack looked winded.

Stella got what was worrying at her. 'Lisa said my dad fell out with Paul Mercer. Apart from with Mum he never argued. Maybe Dad suspected someone else. Mercer didn't like his version of events and refused to see him. I think Mercer would have objected if we'd not followed his instructions.'

'Lucie might know.' Jack gave Stanley a liver treat for no good reason.

'I'm sure she'd have said,' Stella said. 'Lucie likes to talk about Terry.'

'Ralph Baker thought you were a sight for sore eyes!' Jack laughed.

'That's nonsense.'

'You never notice when people like you,' Jack said.

Stella could still feel Baker's vice-like grip on her arm. 'He didn't want me on the case. I didn't like his comment about Cassie's dirty laugh. Cassie might have run away because he abused her.'

'I can see that,' Jack said. 'Maybe he abused Bryony too. Men like that don't stop at one.'

Jack and Stella wended their way along the Old Brockhampton Road in silence. Only when they were in the kitchen drinking tea (the more tasty for the water taking so long to boil) did Stella muse, 'Baker said "He's one to talk." He implied Mercer had done something wrong.'

'We know he did something wrong, he was kicked out of the police.'

'It sounded personal.' She drank her tea. 'Probably nothing.'

'In films, when detectives say something is nothing, it's usually something. He could have been jealous, Trudy was full of how Mercer had found Cassie and "brought her home". She had no time for Baker.'

'You always say people are jealous. It can't be the reason for everything.'

'I think it can,' Jack said sagely.

'Terry's rule was everyone's guilty until proved innocent. Convenient that Marilyn was his alibi and has died.' No death was convenient, Stella reminded herself. Except murder.

'He called her Daddy's girl. That's always creepy. Or maybe Cassie discovered his affair with Marilyn and threatened to tell Trudy.'

'Baker had means, he had a van and he's still strong.' Stella rubbed her wrist. 'He could have carried her up the slope to Belas Knap. He was local. He'd have known about Belas Knap.'

'I don't see him as a budding archaeologist,' Jack said.

'He didn't have to be. Craven could have helped him move the stone. He might even have suggested the chamber.' Stella cut some bread off the loaf they'd bought at the baker when they got the candles. She buttered them both a slice. 'We need a ruse to see Charles Brice. He's the Great Unknown.' She didn't know where the name had come from, it made Brice sound like a music hall act.

'He's a carpenter, let's call him out to give an estimate for shelves or a new door. There's enough to do here!' Jack was excited.

'More than enough.' Stella looked askance at the warped cupboards, peeling wallpaper and broken wainscot. 'The place is falling down, it needs more than a bit of carpentry and he'll see that straight away.'

'A scenario rings true if the players pull it off,' Jack counselled.

'Better to be honest and say we're detectives. Brice might know already. He could be moving the scarecrow, watching the house, flying the drone. Even the crow.'

'He'd be too smart to drop cigarette butts. If Paul Mercer was right, Brice has got away with two murders in the last forty years. Why show his hand now? Ooh, that reminds me…'

Jack went into the living room and came back with the evidence bags of butts.

'No such thing as a coincidence!' Flourishing the bag with the three stubs he'd found by the gate, he laid it on the table. 'These are Chesterfield. The brand Trudy Baker smokes.'

'Lots of people smoke Chesterfield.' Stella was impressed he'd noticed. She'd been avoiding secondary smoking when she was with Trudy.

'Aha! But how many wear red lipstick?'

'There isn't any lipstick on those butts.' Stella didn't want to spoil Jack's argument.

'What's this?' As if it was evidence that could be contaminated, Jack manipulated one of the stubs through the bag. On the filter was a faint stain of pink.

'OK. But do you really think Trudy Baker spied on us? She's in her seventies, it's hard enough for younger people to stand about in the open for the time it takes to smoke…' Stella dotted her finger over the bag, 'three cigarettes. For the average smoker that's over an hour's worth.'

'For a chain smoker, it's ten minutes max.'

'Trudy Baker only smoked two in the hour we were there.' Stella had noticed that.

'She lit one from the other then the baby cried.' He tapped the bag.

'Why would she watch us?'

'She could have been with Charles Brice. He built her shelves and the way she talked, he could do no wrong,' Jack said. 'It strengthens the idea that she killed Cassie and he helped dispose of the body.'

'We absolutely need to see Brice.' Stella got up from the table and put their empty mugs on the draining board. It was half a lifetime to boil a kettle for two bits of crockery. 'Lucie could help.'

'How?' Jack had wandered to the door.

'She's always saying my dad rated her ability to get people on her side. She could lure Brice into conversation. She got close to Terry, he wasn't close to many people. If Brice knows about us, he might not realize Lucie is with us.'

'Lucie's not taking over our case,' Jack snapped. 'If Brice likes young women – Bryony was young enough to be his daughter – however much Lucie lures him, Brice won't take the bait. She could be his mother.'

'No she couldn't and anyway so what if she's older!' She was older than Jack, Stella thought to herself. She snapped back at him, 'I didn't mean like that! I'll do it. I'll track Brice and study his movements.' She saw her chance to prove to Jack, to Terry, to herself, that she took detection as seriously as cleaning. 'I'll strike up a conversation as if I'd just happened to be there. It's the next best thing to being a fly on the wall.'

Chapter Twenty-Nine

'If we could be a fly on a wall in Charlie Brice's house we'd know if he was a murderer.'

Jack repeated Stella's remark to himself as he tramped along the lane into Winchcombe. It justified his decision.

Lisa Mercer predicted the case would kill her father as it had killed his marriage and his relationship with his daughter. It mustn't 'kill' Stella. Pacing the house last night, hearing Lucie May's snores – she claimed she was an insomniac – he'd agonized. When Stella said she would find a way to meet Brice she'd frightened him. Passing Sudeley Castle's gatehouse, Jack rebuked himself. He'd told Stella to take detection seriously. Now she was taking it too seriously and planned to walk into the arms of a man who, if crossed, could be dangerous. Stella had little experience of tracking a criminal. Brice was clever and ruthless. Despite living under a cloud of suspicion, he'd stayed in Winchcombe. He dared his enemies to confront him. Stella wanted to be a fly on his wall. *No way.* Jack would be the fly. Lucie May's unexpected arrival did at least mean Stella wouldn't be alone in the house.

Jack had sworn to himself that he'd never lie to Stella. But this was a special case. He'd told her he had to do a driving shift on the London Underground. He'd be back tomorrow.

'Never kid a kidder!' Lucie had once told him. A company girl, Stella hadn't questioned his stepping up when his work called. Passing the bus stop for the 606 to Cheltenham, Jack told himself he was a total shit.

Winchcombe library's car park gave a view of Brice's cottage on the corner of an adjacent lane. Jack took up position by a sign listing parking charges, as if he might be consulting it. Moments later he was rewarded: Brice came out and strolled along as if taking the air. He'd left his van – a white Peugeot Partner identical to Stella's – outside his house. This suggested he wouldn't be gone long. As a guest of a True Host, Jack didn't need long.

Jack had known of a plumber who neglected his home for his work, and hoped here for rotted wood with dried putty falling away. He was disappointed, Brice had restored and painted the sashes. The windows held fast. No weeds grew between block paving. An ornamental bench in a corner of Brice's front garden looked handmade. Jack had said to Stella, if Brice murdered Cassie Baker and Bryony Motson, he'd not got away with it for nearly forty years with carelessness. He guessed that, with a pall of suspicion hanging over him, Brice got little work, he'd have time on his hands.

Perfection was accentuated by a tiny flaw. Jack circled Brice's cottage twice before he found it. Ivy spreading over the ground at the back of the house gave when he trod on it. Not the softness of leaves, but a springiness that was yet firm. He teased away a fretwork of stems and found a trapdoor. The ivy was filthy with dust and cobwebs. It was a long time since Brice had lifted the hatch. In the notes Jack had read that Paul Mercer's interest in Brice led to vandals spraying 'Murder House' on his fence some years ago. Yet he hadn't sealed all means of entry.

With the penknife Stella bought him for his birthday (it matched hers), he cut foliage around the trapdoor, careful to keep it in place. To a casual glance it would appear undisturbed. Although, if Brice were a True Host it would be the first thing he'd check. Jack was working in the dark, Brice was an unknown.

A True Host is a psychopath who enjoys the journeying to a murder as much as the act itself. If Brice was a True Host he would look for the slightest change in his environment. In a game of hide and seek, Jack knew, the seeker and the person hiding are in mutual contention. The trapdoor could be a trap.

'If we could be a fly on a wall in Charlie Brice's house we'd know if he was a murderer.'

Jack had lived as a 'guest' in the homes of True Hosts. The odds of solving this cold case – ice cold – were slim, they needed to dig deep.

He worked fast. If Brice had gone shopping, he might be back soon. Stella had chaffed with impatience while locals and tourists chatted at counters in the greengrocer, mulled with the butcher over cuts of meat and caught up on the news. Brice, guilty or not, would avoid idle conversation – that gave Jack fifteen minutes max.

Gingerly, he snaked head first into the gap. If Brice kept a slathering hound in his cellar, he was literally entering the jaws of death. A grimy ladder. He clasped a rung and performing an acrobatic movement got his feet on the ground. The hatch closed, plunging him into darkness. Jack had only ten per cent battery on his phone, but he had no choice but to use it.

The cellar stretched the length of the cottage. Jack tripped and looked down, seeing a collection of implements – a scythe, a wooden-framed sieve, trowels, a small fork without a handle – scattered on a flooring of pallets. He took another step and something rushed past, screeching. *A rat.* It was all Jack could do not to join in. He stifled a sneeze.

He shone the torch ahead of him. Something tall was covered by a tarpaulin. *The scarecrow.* Jack forced himself to breathe evenly. He whipped off the canvas and revealed a pile of wooden crates. The top one was crammed with more tools, rusting and broken. Behind this was a door. Jack eased behind the crates and pushed on the door. It juddered aside. Stone steps, the treads worn. He ran swiftly up.

Light leaked through a grille above a door at the top of the stairs. Attached to the wall was a fuse box. A gap at the bottom of the door would allow room for a rat. He switched off the phone-torch, and running his hand down the wood found a keyhole. He couldn't see through. The key must be inserted. Jack had lock picks, but had left them in London. Blessing Stella for her inspired present, he isolated the smallest blade on his army knife and slotted the tip into the keyhole. If the key was turned slightly in the lock he could do nothing.

He pushed the key, it shifted. He eased it again. He heard clinking. Brice was back! It wasn't Brice. The key had dropped out of the lock onto the kitchen floor. He crept down a couple of steps and crouched at eye-level with the top step. He peered through the gap beneath the door. The key lay by a chair leg a metre away. It was out of reach. He needed something to retrieve it. A coat hanger might do, but obviously he didn't have one.

A draught whooshed under the door. Dust flew into his eye, he blinked it away. Footsteps. Someone in boots stomped into his view. This time it was Brice. A tap ran, a match was struck. The flare of a gas ring. The boots approached the door. *Close*, Jack could see the scuff marks on the toe.

True Hosts could detect another presence. Jack tried to blank his mind to make himself non-existent. His heart pounded so loud Brice must hear. A second later there was no chance he'd hear it. The theme for *Mission Impossible* filled the kitchen.

'Hello?' Brice's ringtone. Jack forced himself to ignore the key, his own awareness of it could draw it to Brice's attention.

'From Yellow Pages, that's a first!' Brice had the smooth dark chocolate voice of an actor. From gaps in the conversation, Jack guessed he was writing down what the caller was saying.

'... I know the road. I've never seen inside... Now? As it goes, you're lucky, I can... See you in ten.' From 'off-stage' Brice swiped keys from a table. The boots, a lace trailing, were back. To Jack, his ear literally to the ground, Brice's steps were as loud as gunfire.

Two hands, clean and elegant, tied a knot in one of the boots. Jack heard the man's breathing. Only a flimsy door separated them. *Brice's boot was next to the key.*

A person checking a room for an intruder instinctively looked at head level. When Brice saw the key and opened the door Jack would have seconds. He'd never make it to the cellar, never mind the garden. Brice would be there before... Eyes screwed shut, Jack came close to praying.

Jack stifled a shout when Brice kicked the key. It shot across the floor right up to the crack in the door. As he waited for Brice to pick up the key, Jack forced himself not to move although he wanted to run back down to the cellar. Silence was his only hope.

The boots left his sightline. The key was still there. Brice couldn't have noticed it. Moments later Jack felt the draught again. A diesel engine revved. Brice had gone to see the caller. Prompt service, although Jack considered again that Brice wouldn't be inundated with jobs. After Jack's mother was murdered, he knew his dad's engineering contracts dried up.

He whispered through the keyhole, '*Coming, ready or not.*'

Chapter Thirty

Contrary to Jack's belief, Stella wasn't such a 'company girl'. She was irritated that he'd accepted the shift on the Underground. He had every right, it was she who'd decided to take the case for no fee. Still, they were a team. Jack had been angry with her for focusing on cleaning instead of crime. Now she was being a detective, he'd gone to London to be a train driver.

Watching a fly crawl up the jamb of the front door, Stella was reminded of her comment about being a fly on Charles Brice's wall. Lucie was in Cheltenham and Jack had gone to London. It was up to her to come up with a way of staging an encounter.

She'd watched Jack walk off down the drive until he vanished amongst tall oaks in the wood. He'd explained he was only leaving because Lucie was there. He'd asked if she minded. She said she didn't. Now, surrounded by nature, Stella realized she did mind. Since when was Lucie May company?

'*Here's looking at you kid!*' the budgie screeched. Her cage hung from a beam in the living room. There was Endora and Stanley. Quite a crowd really.

She glanced up at the chimneys. The stacks were topped off with chicken wire, the sides green with thick ivy. A protection from crows.

She caught a snatch of the Old Brockhampton Road two

hundred metres away. The spot from which someone – surely not Trudy Baker – had staked them out. The scarecrow was at the top of the drive. It hadn't moved since last night. Somehow that was more sinister.

The fly buzzed past her. The countryside was full of insects and birds. This thought reminded Stella of the dead crow in Jack's bedroom and the live one in the hall. The birds could not have come down the chimney. How had Stanley got out in the night? She felt a frisson of fear. Although Lucie was out, Stella felt grateful after all that she was here. She remembered Terry's saying, *There's more than one possible explanation for anything. But in the end there is only the one reason.*

'*I'm going to be a father!*'

Stanley, basking in the sun on the drive, opened an eye and shut it again. Stella hadn't known a budgie could have such a loud voice or, for that matter, talk at all.

She went inside the house as an idea formed. She'd dismissed Jack's suggestion about getting Brice to estimate a job as far-fetched. Jack said a scenario was as plausible as you made it. Stella dealt with enough implausible clients demanding crazy cleaning tasks. She could make the implausible plausible.

Stella wasn't an actor, but until her dad died, she hadn't been a detective. She used the last of the battery juice on her phone and Googled the number. She felt guilt at going behind Jack's back. She mitigated this with the thought – brief and treacherous – that Jack had lied to her, he wasn't at work, Stella knew he'd gone to see Bella. Some team.

'*I'm going to be a father.*' Endora clung to the bars of her cage. There were droppings on the plaid rug and along the mantelpiece.

'Please be quiet.'

'*Please be quiet!*' The voice might be a recording of Stella, so precise was the imitation.

With 25 per cent battery left, Stella punched in the number.

'Hi. I'm Stella, please could you come and do an estimate?'

'*Hi. I'm Stella, please could you come and do an estimate?*'

Chapter Thirty-One

The first thing was to 'secure a point of egress'. Jack had half an hour. Brice had told his caller that he'd be there in 'ten'. Twenty minutes' return travelling time. Twenty to do the estimate. Forty minutes. Jack shaved off ten to be on the safe side. Enough time to get his bearings and find a 'guest-space'.

One thing he'd learnt from Stella was to be methodical. Stella tackled murder cases according to the lore of her cleaning manual, 'stain by stain'. Jack's 'stains' were, Establish Egress, Scope Premises, Hunt for Clues, Establish Guest Space. Stella liked acronyms. ESHE, not that Stella could know. She'd never countenance him being a fly on Brice's wall. In this way Jack entered a property without bothering the host.

He started in a brick lean-to off the kitchen. Washing machine, drier, a rack held upturned wellington boots, rubber waders, above hung high-vis waterproofs. The vandals hadn't caused Brice to hide the window key. It lay on a shelf beside a bottle of turps. Jack unlocked the casement, tried it and shut it without locking it. Egress Established.

He started the Scope of Premises from the top floor to ensure where the occupants were or that he was alone. True Hosts generally lived by themselves. They couldn't make relationships.

Soundlessly, in his rubber-soled brogues, Jack tested the staircase for creaks.

The bathroom suite was brown, a legacy of the seventies. Two bedrooms. Brice used the larger one at the front for carpentry. There was a lathe on a bench. Peg-boarded walls were hung with saws, a wrench, hammers and other fearsome instruments that Jack didn't recognize. A gleaming petrol-powered chainsaw was propped against a wall. Brice took care of his tools.

The claw hammer looked new. If Brice had killed Cassie Baker, he wouldn't have kept the hammer he'd used to smash in her head. The room smelled of sawdust and glue, a pleasant smell. Was it the smell of a murderer's lair?

In the bedroom next to a single bed, a chair served as a bedside table, carrying a radio, a new retro Bakelite alarm, and a cassette of dental floss. No cigarettes. If Brice was their stalking smoker, he didn't smoke in bed. Nor did he read. The room lacked anything personal, there were no photos of family or Brice himself. The stark décor wasn't the minimalism Stella favoured, it felt temporary. Brice had lived there for thirty years, but his bedroom looked no more than a billet.

Jack returned to Brice's lair, certain this was where he'd find a clue. He opened plastic drawers in a cabinet labelled with fixings of Brice's trade: 'screws', 'nuts', 'rawl plugs'. The contents matched each legend. Fifteen minutes. No time for a meticulous search, he'd look if Brice went out for longer.

Jack couldn't resist the tin of loose-leaved Earl Grey from Betty's Tea Rooms in Harrogate that was on top of the cabinet. He kept a biscuit tin in his house for his treasures. Were these Brice's treasures? So far the house was a disappointment. Jack felt illogical annoyance, as if the taxi-driver-turned-joiner had let him down.

He prised off the lid, finding that there was an inner lid to keep the leaves fresh. The objects were random and motley, not like trophies of a crime, a glue stick, a pot of Vaseline, a cloth for cleaning glasses from Specsavers, a rounded stone with a hole in it, a plastic clothes peg and a lock of hair pinned to a card framed with hearts. The miscellany from a tidying spree. Not the spoils of a murder.

Amongst a tangle of paper clips, a British Leyland key fob and beige Post Office elastic bands, was a small teddy bear. It was brown with a white bib and paw pads. Jack put it to his nose and gave a long sniff. This was Stella's job, with her superhuman sense of smell. He only caught a stuffy odour and maybe the faintest hint of perfume. He wished Stella was there. As he looked at the bear, Jack felt tingling. *A sign.*

By dawn on their first morning, when the candles had died and streaks of sunrise cut across the sky, he'd been dropping with tiredness from reading all night. Unlike Stella he never made notes. He had a photographic memory. Not only did Jack recall salient facts and snippets of apparent irrelevancy, he retained the rest. At the time he'd felt the poignancy of Bryony's bear an emblem of innocence.

Jack didn't believe in coincidences. There was only one explanation that the bear in the tin fitted the description of the bear that Bryony's father had won at the Mop Fair, which it seemed she'd kept into the cusp of adulthood. It was the same bear.

Mercer's team had searched Brice's house. No DNA or hard evidence was found to link Brice to either young woman.

Until now. Jack couldn't show the bear to Stella without revealing how he'd come by it. Like everything Brice had said to Mercer before his arrest, the bear was inadmissible. Jack shouldn't be in Brice's house. He shouldn't know about the bear. The last time he'd got information in a way Stella would call illegal (because it was), Jack resolved he'd never do it again. He closed the tin and laid it on the cabinet.

He tucked the bear into his trouser pocket.

There was no roof space and no attic, the wardrobe was small. Jack crept back down the stairs to look for his 'guest-space'.

A shadow darkened the frosted glass in the back door. Jack cursed himself. Time had passed. He'd been distracted by the teddy bear. Stella was never distracted from her method. Stain by stain.

The figure cupped hands either side of their face, trying to see inside.

'Charlie. You there?'

Jackie?! Jack felt his limbs turn to water.

Jackie rattled the door handle. Soaked in a flop sweat, Jack backed against the fridge. In normal circumstances he'd have been overjoyed to see Jackie. Even now, he wanted to fly out and fall into her arms. But circumstances were not normal. He couldn't explain why he was in Charles Brice's house. Worse, he wouldn't have to, Jackie would know. She'd be disappointed he was getting up to his old tricks.

She did know. She'd seen Stella and between them they'd worked it out. They knew him. Miserable, Jack sank to the floor by the fridge.

Jackie would see the trapdoor. Jack crawled across the kitchen to the cellar door, thinking to lock it and cut off the entrance.

'Charlie, please let me in.' Jackie thumped on the kitchen window. Pleading. He'd never heard Jackie make a plea for anything.

Jack's phone buzzed. Jackie. He felt actual terror. His thumb hovered over 'call reject'. *She knew he was there.* Never would he reject Jackie's call.

'Hey, Jackie!' A toad's croak.

'Where are you, lovey?' Jackie's voice was louder through the window than the receiver.

'Didn't Stella text?' So cheery he sounded nuts.

'Stella's not picking up. Where are you?'

'London.' Jack had the sensation of the floor tilting.

'Why? What're you doing there?' Had Jackie noticed she'd said 'there' and not 'here'? She'd have no intention to lie.

'I told Stella I was in London. Actually, I'm not...' Anguished, Jack pressed a fist into his forehead until it hurt.

Silence.

'Jackie, I'm sorry. It was stupid, I'm in Brice's house. I can see you. Listen, the thing is I've found…'

Dead air.

The phone battery had gone. Jack heard music. Elton John's 'Tiny Dancer'. It was Jackie's ringtone for Graham. His throat constricted, with Stella and Stanley, Jackie and Graham were his family, the song was synonymous with them. The music was still playing. Jackie hadn't answered. He peeped around the fridge. Jackie was looking at her phone as if it were a grenade about to explode.

She chucked the phone into her handbag and went around to the front of the cottage. Jack got to the living-room window in time to see Jackie latching the gate. She appeared to be looking at him. He shut his eyes. When he looked again, she wasn't there. Jack had been so bound up with his own guilt at being in the house, it only occurred to him now to wonder why she had come to see Brice. *Charlie*. Jackie knew Brice. How could that be?

Jackie belonged in a life of bright loving warmth. Sunlight flooded into Brice's cottage, but Jack dwelt, like Orpheus, in the nether world of death and duplicity. He did not want Jackie down there with him.

Jack was startled by the landline telephone ringing. Automatically, he went to answer. When he stayed with True Hosts, he had to resist entering their lives. The answering service clicked on.

A rushing noise. Jack made out wailing, distant and amorphous. A 'pocket' call. The message ended. Someone had realized their phone had accidentally connected. Then the phone rang again. The wailing was more distinct, like angels singing. There was the rushing. *It was breathing*. The phone wasn't in a pocket, someone was holding it to their mouth. Jack strained to hear.

Then, loud and clear, 'It's me. I heard about Chief Inspector Mercer. Please could you call?'

Click. The message ended.

Jack's neck tingled as if with electricity. A sign of pure gold. Although the caller was curt, a woman he was sure, the tone was diffident. The woman knew Mercer had died. She'd referred to him by his title which suggested she'd known of him as an officer. Mercer's death had prompted her to ring. Jack sensed she was seldom in touch with Brice, although he had no reason to think this. If the woman was the person who'd helped Brice get Cassie to Belas Knap and to kidnap Bryony Motson, they probably had an agreement not to contact each other. Jack was more than aware that women were not angelic Madonnas (except for his mother), but that a woman could kill another woman disturbed him. Brady and Hindley, Fred and Rosemary West. A woman as part of a supposedly kindly couple had more than once lured victims to their deaths.

Who was Brice's mystery woman? He could find out. Jack dialled 1471 and wrote the number on the inside of his wrist. It was a mobile phone number.

Jack could have kicked himself. If Brice did redial – a True Host would – he'd guess someone had used his phone. Brice was likely to hear the woman's message and call her. That would erase last number redial. Likely, but Jack never banked on the likely.

Jack could call the woman, but that would show his hand. His best hope lay in identifying the background sounds. He tried to replay the singing in his head, if it even was singing, but only heard 'Tiny Dancer'. He needed to hear the message again.

About to press play, Jack stopped himself. He was getting reckless. Since meeting Stella he'd curbed his visits with True Hosts, and now he was out of practice. If he played the message, the '1' on the machine would become '0'. Brice wouldn't see he had a message. The woman would call again and say she'd left a message. Brice would remember the cellar key lying on the lino. He would know he'd had an intruder.

The answer was so simple Jack nearly congratulated himself out loud. He opened the cellar door, letting light flood the top of the staircase. He flicked down all the switches in the fuse box. The answer machine beeped and clicked as the power went down. Jack flipped the switches up. More beeps and clicks.

Brice must return any minute. Jack replayed the message. He made no more sense of strange, ghostly singing beyond the oblique familiarity of a dream. His eye fell on a wire beside the telephone. A phone charger. This time he couldn't stop himself. 'Yesss!' The charger was Samsung, like his own. Jack plugged in his phone. The wait until the lightning bolt on the battery icon changed from 0% to 1% was agonizing. Finally, he could open his audio app. He recorded the message. He unplugged his phone and flicked down the switches on the fuse box. This time he left them. Brice would assume something had tripped them.

Time to go.

A scrap of paper lay beside the phone. Jack recalled Brice's saying, 'I know the place!' He'd got the impression Brice was writing down what the caller was saying. He picked up the note.

'Crow's Nest – shelves.'

While he was being a fly in Brice's house, Stella had gone with his bonkers idea and got Brice in to do an estimate. Jack smarted, his plan had depended on him being there. He was adept at subterfuge; honest as the day, Stella was not. He spun about the room. He'd left Stella alone. *Not alone, Stella was with a murderer.*

Jack's point of egress was the front door.

Chapter Thirty-Two

'Are you sure? Shelves would pretty much be holding these walls up. Or else they'd bring them down!' Charles Brice sucked on his teeth as he scrutinized the corner in the living room where Stella had said she wanted him to erect shelves.

She had raised the same objection when Jack had suggested the idea.

Brice still looked like Malcolm McDowell. Was he Bryony's 'film star'? His eyes were so bright it was as if they had a light shining behind them. He had fine features and would indeed look good in a film. Stella was groping for a response, when Brice said, 'Sorry, but I don't want you wasting your money.'

'Where would you suggest they go?' Stella wished Jack was here, he'd go into superfluous detail and sound plausible.

'What are they for?'

'Books.' Jack would have arrived at Paddington and be on his way to Earl's Court to pick up his train. No, he was going to Kew to see Bella.

'What sort of books?'

Stella had expected Brice to measure up, and give a ballpark sum while she surreptitiously logged gestures, tics and scars, his smell and everything he said in her Filofax. Mentally, she'd noted the brushed cotton shirt, ironed jeans, polished CAT boots and clean nails. She planned to drop in questions when Brice was off his guard. Now he was asking her about books. The only one she'd read – skim-read – was *Wuthering Heights*. And volume one of The Forsyte Saga. What sort were they? She hazarded, 'Old ones.'

'Old ones. You're thinking hardbacks?' His eyes seemed to burn into her. 'Large or small?'

'Does it matter?' She was wasting his time. She'd have to give him the job.

'Made-to-measure avoids gaps between the books and the shelves and looks neater. Importantly, it cuts down on dust.'

His eyes never leaving her face, Brice waited for her answer.

'No gaps please,' Stella said.

'*I'm going to be a father.*' Endora was jumping up and down along the bar in her cage, making it swing wildly.

'Christ, that scared me!' Brice turned around. He didn't look scared. 'What's your bird's name?'

'Endora. She talks nonsense.' Vaguely thinking it was what you did with birds, Stella cast about for a cloth to toss over the cage and silence her, but she'd used the only one to cover the case files on the table.

Brice was looking through the bars at Endora. 'It's a shame she has to be in a cage, but with a dog...'

'She belongs to a friend. She'll let her out when she gets back. Stanley's not interested.' Stella had told Brice she lived alone. Brice was being more chatty than she'd expected. Nothing in his manner suggested he knew her real motive for asking him to come. This should have made her relax, instead the ice only seemed to get thinner.

'Do you want them free-standing?'

'Who?'

'The shelves. So that should you move, you can take them.' Impassive, he cast about the room, chill with damp and rot. Crow's Nest was virtually uninhabitable. Following his gaze, Stella saw the pages of flip-chart paper stuck to the bare stone wall. She'd covered the case papers but forgotten the timeline and the list of suspects. Her skull tightened as if her brain would burst.

'Yes. No. I might sell.' Stella looked to Stanley for help. But – a sign he sensed no danger – Stanley was asleep on the settee. She moved so that she was facing the wall.

'Isn't this place owned by some chap in that old folks' home in Winchcombe?' Brice's eyes were back on her. His voice a low rumble, 'I guess he died.'

'I meant renting.' Stella looked away first. So far he was asking all the questions.

'*I'm renting!*' Endora pecked at the bars.

'I'll let her out.' Stella had a vision of Endora disappearing over the fields until she was a speck in the sky. She flung wide the cage door. Endora soared over their heads and alighted on the door lintel.

'She'll appreciate a wall behind her, birds like to feel secure.' Brice wrote something in his estimates book. Nothing suggested he'd seen the timeline.

'Don't we all!' Stella said, although until this moment she'd not thought about feeling secure. She had made one basic, but very stupid, mistake.

'Her cage is Victorian. You might advise your friend that while it's ornately beautiful, Endora could get her head stuck in the bars, and that's an exposed nailhead. At least your friend lets her out. Birds in cages can have temper tantrums and get moody because they're unhappy.'

'You are informed.' Stella agreed about cages, but was inclined to protect Lucie May from criticism. The fancy cage implied that Lucie cared very much about her new pet.

'My aunty kept a budgerigar. Despite her wittering on at it, it never said a word. This one's intelligent.' He reached up and nudged Endora's puffed-out chest with the back of his forefinger. Endora swooped down onto his shoulder.

'She talks all the time.' Stella heard herself exaggerate.

'They repeat what their owner teaches them. Is your friend about to be a father?'

'She's a woman,' Stella told him.

'Endora will have picked up some random remark. When I was a teenager in London I came down here to feed my aunt's bird. I left the window open and it escaped.'

Extraordinarily, Endora had led them to the subject Stella was wondering how to broach. 'Did your aunt live in Winchcombe?'

'You don't know about me?' He blew kisses at Endora.

'No.' Jack said the trick was to believe your lie. She wasn't close to believing hers.

'Some call me the most hated man in Winchcombe, you've done well to miss the gossip. I assumed it was why you'd called me.' He pronounced 'assumed' with a 'sh' like Terry had.

'No! I saw your ad in the Yellow Pages.' The timeline seemed to glow on the wall behind him.

'*I saw your ad in the Yellow Pages*,' Endora crowed.

Stanley came and sat at Stella's feet.

'She's a tape recorder! You'd better not have any secrets.' Brice grinned. 'Don't tell me you haven't heard of Cassie Baker?'

'The name rings a bell.' Jack said keep the lie to a minimum. Not that it mattered now.

'She was murdered in Winchcombe in the seventies. I took police to her body, it was up at Belas Knap, not far from here. New Year's Eve 1999. Paul Mercer, the detective, got it into his head I murdered her because this other girl had just gone missing and I knew her. All I did was repeat what a passenger told me.' If Mercer had seen the timeline he was a consummate actor. Either way, he appeared relaxed about telling her people thought him a murderer.

'I suppose people confess all sorts in the back seat of a taxi.' Stella tried being chatty too. Her throat was tight, her voice felt strained. Jack was miles away. Lucie was only in Cheltenham, but had said she'd be out all day. At the time Stella had been grateful, now she longed for her to walk in.

'You knew I was a taxi driver then,' he said.

'You said so.' *He had not said so.*

'You made the leap. Smart.' He looked genuinely impressed.

'Then what happened?' Stella asked brightly.

'My passenger was an estate agent called Matthew Craven. He'd been the dead girl's boyfriend. He told people they'd split up. The case was a no-brainer, he went down for it. Actually, I heard Craven just got out.' Brice was challenging her to claim ignorance.

Endora flew over to the window and pecked at the glass. Tap. Tap. Tap.

'Paul Mercer has died.' Stella made an offering to appease a God. She shouldn't know that. Her plan had unravelled, she was tangled in a horror of her own making.

'I know.' Brice snapped open a measuring spool. He thrust the aluminium tape against the wall up to the ceiling. Retracting it, he jotted in his estimates book. 'I presumed that galvanized you into ringing.'

'Why would that be the reason?' A genuine question.

'People want to tell their mates a murderer made their shelves. That he drank out of their mugs and shook their hand. One lady showed me a pencil box she'd bought from the arts and crafts shop at Broadmoor. She'd convinced herself it was made by the Yorkshire Ripper. Is this what you're looking for?'

'No, I—' Stella didn't want anything made by a killer. Her mum, a walking dramatist, talked about being scared stiff. But being scared didn't make you stiff, it turned your insides to liquid and extinguished your senses. It was like no pain Stella could imagine. Losing her balance, she took hold of the mantelpiece.

Brice appeared oblivious. He handed her his estimates book. He'd drawn a shelf unit with a cupboard at the bottom as she'd stipulated she wanted when he arrived. His sketch was so life-like it could be in an art gallery. Her speech rubbery, she felt his ice-blue gaze. 'That's good. I mean, it's what I'd want. What I *do* want.'

'What kind of wood?' Moving closer to her. She smelled him. Warm skin cleansed with Moulton Brown's Black Pepper. No aftershave.

Brice ran his hand up the wall by the fireplace. 'This is oak panelling. It limits choice – for example, pine would clash. If you're watching costs, I can supply a perfectly acceptable oak veneer.'

'Oak veneer please.' Jack would hate veneer. He liked things – and people – to be real. 'Did you kill Cassie Baker?' The country silence pressed in on the empty house. Outside, the trees were still. Through the window, the scarecrow faced out towards the fields.

'You're the first to come out with that. Most clients go on about Belas Knap being historical and avoid what they're *dying* to ask.'

'I've never been to Belas Knap.' She and Jack had planned to go that afternoon. Before he left her and went to London.

'Great views. I love it up there. That used to wind up Mercer. He was my shadow until he couldn't walk. It's a climb, it damn near killed the poor sod!' He got out his phone. 'Give us your email, I'll send you a price. What's your full name, Stella?'

If Stella told him her name and address, he'd Google her and a short breadcrumb trail would take him to articles about the cold cases she'd solved. If he'd seen the timeline he'd do that anyway. This was why Jack kept incognito, although he was recorded forever on the internet as the boy whose mother was murdered. 'Stella Makepeace.'

Brice frowned. 'How are you spelling Makepeace?'

Stella faltered through each letter.

'"A" before "e". Unusual.'

How often did she write Jackie's surname? Stella echoed Jackie, 'Peace like *War and Peace*.'

'There's an *old* book! And email?'

'We don't have Wi-Fi. No electricity.' No one to call for help.

'Can't you get emails on your phone?' he asked pleasantly.

'No! Yes. The battery is nearly dead.' Stella was seeing stars dancing in her eyes and felt faint.

'Not a problem. I'll pop it in your letter box on the lane. I can't get up to the house, it's like Fort Knox!' He grinned again.

'I'll show you out.' Stella flung wide the door to shield the timeline.

When Brice had gone, Stella flew back into the living room. She ripped the flip-chart pages off the wall. Some detective. Rule one, do not invite the suspect into the Major Incident Room. The wall where she'd said she wanted shelving was stained with black splodges of damp. Brice had acted as if she'd been evasive about her email address because he'd told her he was a murder suspect. If so, he'd believed she knew nothing. He hadn't seen the timeline. After all, she'd been plausible.

Endora was in her cage, so much for wanting freedom. Stella's phone battery was down to 5 per cent. She put it in save mode. That gained her another two hours.

She'd learnt nothing concrete from Brice's visit. Jack and Jackie didn't think her great on nuance, she missed the meaning behind tiny actions and expressions. Still, she'd read Brice to a T. He was clever, perceptive and confident. Bundling up the paper, Stella drifted to the table. The qualities that Paul Mercer had ascribed to Brice. The profile of a man who'd committed the perfect murder, twice.

The estimates book lay beside the covered mound of papers. Brice had forgotten it! Stella opened her phone, he couldn't have got far. She stopped. As a cleaner she'd never dream of snooping in a private notebook. As a detective... Terry's words whispered in the quiet,

'*On a house search, open address books, daily diaries, read shopping list pads. Start at the back, that's where we hide the interesting stuff.*'

Sitting at the table, Stella opened the estimates book with the care of a safe-cracker. The pencilled sketch reminded her of Bella Markham's botanical illustrations. Instead of a flower – each part separate for the botanist to examine – Brice had drawn from life. A church surrounded by graves, headstones jutted out from long grass. Willow fronds hung around the edges of the book, as if Brice had drawn from beneath the tree unseen. In the next sketch his ears of corn (or whatever) in a field were better than Bella's. Beyond the field, a drystone wall, broken by a stile, led to a long low mound. At the front of the drawing was a sweet chestnut, Stella recognized the long glossy leaves with pinking-sheared edges from her childhood tree-book. She carried the notebook to the window and tipped the page to the light. Under the tree was a figure in trousers and fleece. Brice had drawn a scarecrow. Not *a* scarecrow, he'd drawn the scarecrow standing outside the window grinning back at her.

Stella photographed the sketches with her phone. Focusing on the last one, again she pondered: scarecrows were meant to scare birds off crops. Why put one on grass under a tree?

She flipped through the book. Three-quarters full. Brice did have plenty of clients. He'd built shelves, cupboards, even staircases, every job illustrated in painstaking pencil.

While she waited for Brice to answer the phone, Stella recalled he'd said she was the first client to ask if he killed Cassie Baker. Brice hadn't answered the question.

Chapter Thirty-Three

Jackie wandered along the high street in a time warp. The stone-built shops, some half-timbered, striped awnings and wrought-iron signs were still there. A woman browsed in the window of a florist, two men stood by the war memorial, one, his hands on hips, listening unhurriedly to the other man talking. The butcher was still on the high street. So was the pub where they'd all gone one night. A red bus signed to Cheltenham trundled down the street. There were more cars, but nothing on the scale of Chiswick High Road. Winchcombe was timeless.

Many times, in a recurring nightmare, Jackie had walked through Winchcombe. She would wake sweating and angry but, feeling Graham beside her in the bed, sink back in relief. This time she was already wide awake.

Jackie stopped outside Beauty Heaven. Irritated by the name, she dwelt on adverts with smiling women, no lines, perfect teeth and glossy hair, propped amidst Guinot and Clarins anti-ageing creams. Jackie saw her beautician niece, Hannah, once a fortnight to keep her own nails manicured and tinted a pale pink. She caught her reflection in the glass, no amount of creams would wipe away the lines of nearly sixty years.

The salon door opened and a man in a shabby Barbour came

down the steps and, turning, gave someone behind him a kiss. A woman appeared, her complexion as flawless as the adverts. Bright red lips, blue nail vanish. She said, 'Fabby job, thanks. Catch you laters, Charlie!'

Charlie.

Wide mouth, full lips on the edge of a grin. She wouldn't have had to hear his name to recognize those eyes. Age hadn't raddled him nor altered that easy stride. She was about to go after him when the woman spoke to her, 'Coming in, dear? We've got a fifty per cent offer on pedicures. Today only.'

'You're all right, thanks.' Jackie moved along the street and then stopped dead outside a shop selling paintings of horses. Oh. My. God. Swishy silks and a styled blonde bob had replaced the skinhead look of two-toned skirts and tasselled loafers, but voices change little with age. The woman on the steps was Lauren Spicer. The anger of her nightmares coiled like fire. Wrestling with the ghost of an emotion, Jackie passed under the town clock and entered North Street in time to see Charlie Brice going into a coffee shop.

She waited a short interval and then followed him inside. She ordered an iced coffee.

'Is anyone sitting here?'

Alone at a table, Charlie Brice was breaking up the heart shape in the whipped milk of his cappuccino. He didn't look up. 'Good to see you, Jacqueline. Got you a coffee.'

'You saw me!' He'd always called her by her full name – he pronounced it Jack-*leen*. Charlie had to be different. Jackie sat down opposite him, her back to the café.

'You don't need a session at Beauty Heaven!' Malcolm McDowell eyes drinking her in.

'Why didn't you say something?'

'Lauren may seem like a kitten…' He spooned froth into his mouth and dabbed moistened lips with a serviette.

'You're still with Lauren Spicer.' She imagined dashing the cappuccino off the table and all over the floor.

'I've done her a nice set of shelves.' Brice rested the bowl of the spoon on his lower lip. 'Does Graham know you're here?'

'No.' She saw her mistake and compounded it. 'I'm about to call him.'

'Don't let me stop you.' His eyes glittered.

'Usual sandwich for you, Charlie?' The warm demeanour of the man in trimmed black beard and glasses didn't mitigate Jackie's nightmare.

'Marky Mark!' Brice crowed. 'You know what, I'll have your pastrami special. It's a special day!'

'Good for you.' If the man knew about Brice's past, he didn't show it. 'Take away?'

'I'll eat in. Jacqueline, I'll treat you. Mark's sandwiches are sensational!'

'No thanks.' Jackie waited until Mark was out of earshot. 'Charlie, you must go to the police.'

'Why would I do that?' Brice asked pleasantly.

'You know why.'

'Listen, hun, Mercer's dead, he died yesterday. Craven's out on licence. It's over.'

'They're still looking.' Lifting her coffee cup, Jackie was annoyed to see her hand shake. Anger, not nerves. It drew Brice's attention. He reached out and stilled it.

'It left a scar then.' He brushed her wrist with a finger. 'Graham not approve of tattoos?'

'It's not obvious.' But it was. With a tan, faint marks in the shape of a shamrock showed white against her skin, the initials showed when she was cold. She snatched her hand away. Jackie considered that the self that had got her skin tattooed was long a stranger; if she had ever known her.

'Some scars never heal.' He looked briefly solemn. 'Listen, Jacqueline. Mercer's gone. His carers found him dead. The police know Craven's their man. It really is over.' Brice chinked his cup against hers. 'Finito!'

'Who told you all this?'

'Winchcombe's brimming with secrets and lies. Lauren told me he'd died. In that salon she soaks up all the goss.'

'News does travel fast. Anyway, they weren't carers. Mercer hired detectives. It was them who found him.'

'Detectives?' For the first time Brice showed concern.

'Yes.' Jackie felt queasy. She put down her cup.

'Jacqueline, dead men don't pay, these detectives will have packed up and gone to the pub.'

'Stella's doing it for her father, Terry Darnell, the cop who helped Mercer.' Jackie saw she'd got to Brice. His eyes were steely.

'Stella, you say? Who's the other one?'

'I may be wrong.' Jackie back-pedalled. Brice's mobile rang.

'Hey!' The jaunty tone wasn't reflected in his impassive features. The effect was chilling.

'I left it there? What an idiot! I'll come and get it now.' Brice waved at the counter. 'Marky, give my sandwich to this good woman. I'll take four fruit tarts.' He gathered up his keys and opened his wallet, withdrawing a twenty-pound note. 'Catch you later, Jacqueline! I take it you'll be around for a bit.' He took a box from Mark the deli owner, paid and left.

Jackie watched Brice negotiate buggies and shopping trolleys out of the deli onto the street. Too dazed to see the pastrami sandwich placed before her, Jackie saw only that coming to Winchcombe was a profound mistake.

Chapter Thirty-Four

'This is it.' Brice lifted up a panel in the stile and beckoned Stanley. He let it drop like a guillotine a second after the little dog jumped through. Refusing Brice's help, Stella climbed up onto the stile. Feeling for the lower step, she still ended up facing the way she'd come. Brice had made it look easy. She turned in time to see Stanley chasing to the top of a mound.

When Charlie Brice returned to collect his estimates book he'd suggested he showed her Belas Knap. 'If you trust being with a murderer!'

She didn't trust him, but she didn't want him to know so had no choice but to agree. After a long climb through woods that echoed with birdsong, then a twenty-minute walk across a field full of sheep and a footpath through more woods, they arrived.

A notice by the stile described Belas Knap as a particularly fine example of an Early Neolithic long barrow. Thirty-one bodies were found buried in the four chambers by archaeologists excavating in the Victorian times. Stella had pictured a tourist attraction complete with car park, ticket kiosk, ice-cream van and a teashop in which to shelter from the sun. The sun had gone in and Belas Knap turned out to be a boring old hill.

No tourists. They were alone. Terror returned, creeping through her like flames taking hold. If she were to escape him, she'd have to be clever. Too late. The time for cleverness had been when Brice invited her to Belas Knap. A remote hill with only sheep to hear her shouts.

She'd left a note saying where she was going and who with. She caught Terry's voice, *'When alone with a suspect avoid antagonizing them.'*

Jack said you got away with a murder by being careful not to make a mistake. It had been no mistake that Brice had forgotten his estimates book. After all, he'd seen the timeline and he'd laid a trap. Too confident, she'd walked into it.

Had Cassie and Bryony been as confident? No pushover, it wouldn't have been easy to pull the wool over Cassie's eyes. Yet someone had done more than that. Was that someone Charles Brice? Stella's calves began to tremble, her body was a mass of spasm. She wrapped her fingers around her Swiss Army knife and told herself that if he attacked her, she was prepared.

In the distance, hills blurred into clouds. The sound of sheep cropping grass in a field on the other side of the drystone wall was too loud.

'This was the forecourt.' Brice pointed back down the steps.

Out of the shade of the woods, the sun beat down. Stella's head thumped. Her hands were clammy. She wiped her forehead with her sleeve and feigned interest. 'People must have lived in this area for thousands of years.'

'Exactly! This long barrow dates from about 3000 BC. The Victorians removed the bodies. It's wrong to disturb a grave.' He pointed to a hole in the side of the mound. 'Over there is where Cassie was buried.'

Even from two metres away, Stella could smell the musty air inside the chamber. Her thoughts raced. He knew the area much better than she did. If she ran, she'd have to carry Stanley or he'd nip at her ankles thinking it a form of play and slow her down. No matter what she did, Brice would catch up with her.

'We'll picnic there.' Charlie Brice ran back down the mound and stopped at the stile. He tapped it as if testing its strength then climbed over into the field beyond. He flapped open a rug onto a cluster of speedwell and daisies in the shade of a tree. Stella noticed he tapped the trunk before leaning back on it. Three times. The odd gestures, as if he was superstitious, chilled her to the bone with fear. With or without Stanley, she couldn't have run anywhere, her legs wouldn't carry her.

'Picnic?' Stella couldn't make sense of the word.

'Tea, and I got fruit tarts from the deli.' He grinned up at her. If she ran, she'd have a head start. She could pretend she needed the loo. Absurdly, Stella was horrified at the idea of going in a bush, not that she'd actually pee. But the nimble way Brice had leapt over the stiles told her he'd quickly gain on her.

She clambered clumsily over the stile, fear had made her no more dexterous. As she turned around, the sun came out.

Brice sat in dappled shade, his back against the tree trunk. He poured tea from a flask into a travelling mug and smiled. He had laid strawberry tarts, richly coloured syrup glistening in the sunlight, on a doily on the rug. The tea was how she liked it, milky, not too hot.

Before she could stop him, Stanley snuffled over and snapped up the nearest tart. He scampered over to the nettle bed out of reach.

'Oh ! He never does that!' Although true it sounded false. Dangerous. Brice would perceive a trashing of his hospitality.

'*Only antagonize or humiliate a suspect in pursuit of a likely outcome.*'

'He's a dog, it's what they do. I shouldn't have put them under his nose.' A breeze lifted Brice's fringe. His eyes were as blue as the sky. 'Like a film star,' Bryony had told her flatmate, Jenni. Had Mercer let himself confuse the nasty roles the young McDowell had played with the character of the man he failed to arrest? So far he'd been nothing but charming. Terry had also urged her to trust a hunch.

'*Start from the heart and back your theory with corroborated evidence.*'

Eating a strawberry tart and drinking the best tea she'd had for ages, Stella's hunch was that Charles Brice had murdered no one. But was that because, like Paul Mercer, she couldn't bear to be wrong?

Sated and unrepentant, Stanley came back, settled on her and set about washing his toes.

'Mercer would be stuck behind there for hours while I snoozed or read the paper.' Brice nodded at a hedge of blackthorn bordering the field. He fixed piercing eyes on Stella. 'You ever been stalked?'

'I don't know.' Jack said to assume someone was following you. An ex-boyfriend had kept tabs on her for a while, but she wasn't going to tell Brice that.

'A good stalker then!' Brice cleaned his hands with a wet wipe and offered her the packet.

Suddenly, Stanley catapulted off her and bolted across the field. Stella shielded her eyes to see what had got his attention. There were sheep in the next field, but with the hedge she'd thought it was OK to let him off his lead. Her senses dulled by fear and heat, she was slow to see the tractor that had come into the bottom of the field five hundred metres away. Stanley was a scrap of apricot, but for his plumed tail, barely discernible in the brown grass.

'Stan-ley!' Her shout was swallowed up in the hot heavy air. A huge cylindrical shape appeared on a trailer behind the tractor. It rolled along the flat bed and dropped onto the ground. It was making bales. If one of those things landed on Stanley he would die.

As if in slow motion, she made out the little dog running towards the tractor. He was dwarfed by the gigantic tyres. Yaps of outrage carried across the field. The man in the cab hadn't seen him. The tractor trundled on. Stanley was going to run in front of it.

Stella gave her whistle a shrill blast. Kirsty, Stanley's trainer, had said, *'Once the red mist comes down, your dog will be deaf to instruction.'* Stanley had fixed on his quarry. He was galloping to certain death and Stella, blundering over the grass as if through water, knew she couldn't save him.

Brice passed her with loping steps. Shirt billowing, he belonged in *Chariots of Fire*.

Stanley was leaping and cavorting around the machine. A bale narrowly missed him and, distracted, he barked furiously at it. The tractor moved inexorably on. Stella pushed beyond her limit, muscles on fire, all the while feeling she was slowing down.

When he got no response from the bale, Stanley resumed his chase of the tractor. He darted at the gap between the wheels. Stella screamed, expressing all the grief and pain and desperation in her heart. The scream sliced through the lazy sounds of summer.

The tractor stopped.

Charles Brice was bellowing at the driver, a man with grizzled grey hair, his eyes sunk in a puffy red face. 'Didn't you hear us shouting?'

'Heard her, proper banshee, your girl!' Languidly the driver pulled his headphones down to his neck.

'You were going to crush her dog. She bloody well let you know.' Brice's eyes were flaming. His hands were balled into fists.

Shattered by adrenalin coursing through her, Stella could hardly lift Stanley. She gathered him to her and pressed her face into his fur, breathing in the unfamiliar scents of nature. He twisted around and slathered her with an avid tongue.

'Ask me, they should both be on a lead, Charlie-boy.'

Brice flapped a hand at the man and stomped away across the field.

'Thanks for stopping,' Stella told the driver, but his headphones were back on and the cab door was shut. She clipped on Stanley's lead and set off after Brice. She saw the abandoned picnic rug, Belas Knap rising behind the drystone wall. She gave an icy shiver.

Brice had halted. Stella met his searing gaze. Framed by the tree – a sweet chestnut – and the stile, it was the sketch in the estimates book. Charles Brice had drawn Cassie Baker's grave.

Chapter Thirty-Five

Sun shining on the gold signage lent Beauty Heaven the desired celestial appearance. There was a saying, 'Smile and you feel like smiling.' A beauty therapist, Lauren Spicer liked to paint a smile on her customers and improve their well-being.

Winchcombe did the rest. The town had begun the inevitable rise in desirability as the well-to-do of London and the south-east, unable to afford the Slaughters, the Rissingtons or the Barringtons, widened their net. In addition to the influx of week-enders, Lauren benefited from holidaymakers keen to build a pamper into their Cotswold experience. Her business was thriving. She was thriving.

Lauren eased a towel off a rack, flapped it open and refolded it. She lifted the soft fabric to her nose. The scent of lavender mingled with cotton pleased her. She laid the towel back. Three Jessica gels were out of number order, she swapped them back. The new junior, in a permanent sulk because she fancied herself too posh for tidying or laundry, would have to go.

Upstairs the doorbell tinkled. There were no appointments booked, it must be a 'walk in'. Lauren heard Rosie, her receptionist, greet the customer and offer them a cup of the lemon-infused water. Lauren straightened the chairs each side of the nail bar – one of a warren of treatment rooms in the salon's basement.

Lauren flicked a speck of dust off the client chair. She loved this bit when she welcomed her clients into her special space, the clean white walls lined with bottles of varnish and treatments for every nail condition and oozing with the sounds of South American pipe music. Smoothing down her Beauty Heaven tunic, she stationed herself at the foot of the stairs to greet the woman as she came down. Her own smile ready.

'I'm Lauren. Here to care for you. Sit down for me.' Her tone was lilting, caressing even.

'Pleased to meet you.' Her client clacked her teeth as if snapping an insect. 'I am Endora. I told your girl I want a manicure. But tell me about your facelifts, for a friend, you understand.'

Lauren spoke confidentially. 'Tell your friend that we offer a non-surgical facelift. Any wrinkles are smoothed and drooping muscles tightened. We re-educate the jowl upwards to an original position. We can achieve much in one session, but for dramatic results I'd recommend a course of ten.'

'Sounds just what she needs.'

'Just a manicure or would you like your gels refreshed?' Lauren asked sweetly.

'Yes I want a new colour.' Her customer scowled at an advert for Clarins face cream and criss-crossing wrinkles around her mouth deepened.

Lauren fanned out a swatch of gel colours painted onto finger-like spokes over the counter. 'You choose your shade, Endora. I'll be back.'

When Lauren returned with a bowl of warm soapy water and a pile of folded flannels, Endora had isolated a spoke. Pop Princess, a vivid pink that when in the right mood, Lauren herself favoured.

'You have beautiful skin.' Lauren turned over Endora's right hand as if to read her palm.

'Do I?' The inflection betrayed that she knew this perfectly well.

Lauren Spicer swathed each of Endora's fingers in cotton wool soaked in alcohol to remove the gel and secured them with caps of tinfoil. She placed new editions of *Elle* and *Country Life* in front of Endora. 'Have a flick through while they cook.' She went upstairs.

In reception, Rosie was stacking a holder with newly printed loyalty cards. No such thing as loyalty, Lauren frequently observed to herself. Now she asked, 'Any messages?'

'Mr Birch the solicitor rang. He said he supposed you knew Paul Mercer's died.' Rosie's sing-song delivery went well with tootling pipe music.

'Why should I care?' The question was more to herself. Why did she?

Gazing out between the Clarins adverts to the street, Lauren recalled the lady nosing outside the shop at lunchtime. Charlie had known her, she was sure. She returned downstairs and sitting back on her stool enquired conversationally, 'What brings you here?'

'My ancestors lived in Winchcombe. I've come to find them.' Endora waggled silvered claws.

'Where did they live?' As she removed the foils, Lauren was careful not to pry. It was a safe question, an ancestor was sufficiently remote to be acceptable.

'In some place called Belas Knap. Have you heard of it?' Endora said airily as she cocked her head with apparent fascination as Lauren scraped off the old crimson gel from her nails.

'Belas Knap is an ancient monument.' Finger by finger Lauren clipped dead skin from around each nail then began massaging Endora's cuticles with an electric implement that sounded not dissimilar to a dentist's drill.

'They're ancient ancestors.' Endora made a flitting motion as if already the subject was exhausted. She fixed Lauren with a gimlet eye. 'Have you and your husband got a break coming up?'

'I'm single.' Lauren gave an on-off smile as she picked up an emery board and swished it over each nail.

'Truth be told, I'm getting over a death.' The corners of Endora's mouth drooped.

'I'm sorry.' Lauren was sorry. With renewed intent she whipped a file over the top of Endora's nails. 'Life's a business.'

'I heard someone died at Belas Knap many moons ago.' Endora yawned.

'Death is everywhere.' Lauren proffered one of her neutral phrases. Thirty years of women keen to off-load problems as she massaged their faces, covered them in mud and steamed them to a turn, had enabled Lauren to pick a path across the treacherous marsh of gossip and slander.

'It was thirty years ago this week since my best friend died. We were in the sixth form. The pain is fresh as a daisy. I've come to Winchcombe to reach back into the past. Meditate on the meaning of life. Treat myself. Think of her,' Endora said bravely.

If Lauren suspected Endora's facial lines put school nearer fifty years than thirty, she betrayed nothing. Lauren liked to give her clients a little of herself. 'My friend died when we were sixteen. You never forget, do you?'

'Certainly not. My friend was mugged, she died from horrible injuries.' Endora was fervent.

'Bless you! That's horrible. I hear you, Endora. It's no secret in this small town, but my friend was Cassandra Baker. Cass was the girl they found up at Belas Knap. When it's sudden like that and violent too, you can't get your head around it. Cass was my bezzie mate. Trauma leaves its mark.' Lauren was as soothing as a dove as with practised speed she set about applying pink coats of Pop Princess.

'It put me off getting close to anyone. When someone leaves you like that. You learn not to trust,' Endora cooed. 'I was to blame. If I'd been with her…'

'Not your fault. There was me cross because Cass had gone to London without me and she nicked my make-up. Every cloud… You and me, Endora, we've learnt to put things in perspective.' Lauren clicked on the ultra-violet drier and guided Endora's hand under the heat – she would never dream of saying that mention of her long-lost friend had whipped up pain barely dormant. Lauren's clients did not pay good money to hear about her feelings.

'I was cross with my friend for dying!' Endora eyed the beautician beadily.

'That's part of grieving,' Lauren reassured.

'I heard that the man who murdered your bezzie mate is out free as a bird.'

'If he showed up here, I wouldn't trust myself.' Lauren fed Endora's hand into the heater.

'He hasn't then?' Endora wheedled.

At that moment a curtain at the back of the room flapped aside. A man with a buzz-cut, in a shirt and sagging jeans, his pallor a grey that no amount of Clarins could rectify said, 'Thought you'd done.'

'Stay in the back.' Lauren was momentarily flustered.

The man vanished behind the curtain. Somewhere, a door shut. Lauren continued the treatment in silence, grateful that Endora was suddenly absorbed in an article about a dog show at Sudeley Castle.

Lauren removed Endora's hand from the drier. 'Would you like almond oil?'

'Mmm, please.' Endora bobbed appreciatively. Dotting each nail, now a vibrant pink, with oil, Lauren sought to raise the client's 'exit mood'. She enquired brightly, 'What's your line of work, Endora?'

'I breed budgerigars.' Lauren's customer gave a corncrake cackle.

Lauren flicked the sign to 'Closed'. She shot the bolts top and bottom and pausing by the door, looked out at the street. The pub opposite was filling up, smokers milled on the pavement. Next door, Phil in the hardware shop was trundling in his racks of gardening gloves and walking socks. Watching him clasping a pile of doormats, it came to her. The woman in the street was Jackie Redmond. Jackie *effing* Redmond.

Charlie Brice had seen her. Lauren Spicer shuddered as a cold trickle of perspiration ran down her back.

Chapter Thirty-Six

A lark twittered in the sky. A breeze rustled trees in the woods and the scarecrow's scarf.

Jack had the impression of returning to Crow's Nest after years – as to the ruins of Mandalay or Thornfield Hall. He'd been away three hours. Stella's van wasn't outside. The front door was open.

'Stella!' He raced up the stairs. Her bed was made, her pyjamas (Stella wore pyjamas) were folded on the bed. A well-thumbed textbook on the bedside table. 'Murder Investigation Manual'. The pages were stuffed with sticky notes, he read 'Preserve Scene'. Stella hadn't needed his urging to be a detective, she'd been one all along.

Jack ran next door to his room. He took in his hastily made bed, the bag in the corner. Yesterday's shirt was folded on the window sill. His cursory attempt at tidying was nothing to Stella's army drill order. He'd seen it as tempting fate to make himself at home.

Lucie May's bedroom might have been subjected to a police search. Tights dangled over open drawers. Clothes were strewn over a warped clothes horse and over the top of the door. Her bed looked like she'd slept restlessly, sheets twisted, a blanket on the floor.

'Stella!' Hurtling down the back stairs, Jack fought tears of frustration. This was his fault.

No one in the sitting room. In the kitchen he heard a low whine. The drone! He flung himself out to the patio. 'I know you're there. You arsehole! Don't you touch her!'

'Ooh, I say, Jacko, you'll frighten Endora!' The whine had stopped.

'*You arsehole!*' Endora's cage hung from a branch of a stunted apple tree.

Lucie wore a sleeveless safari jacket – the numerous pockets bulging – and a wide-brimmed hat. She appeared to be hoeing grass in the orchard. The hoe wasn't a hoe.

'What is that?' Jack panted.

'My Treasure Hunter!' Lucie said. 'My sister bought me a metal detector for my birthday. First time she's given me something I want. Usually it's thermal underwear and pot plants. See what I've found!' She motioned at a heap of bottle tops and a drinks can on the table where he and Stella had eaten supper last night. *In another time.*

'Where's Stella?' Jack whirled full circle. 'She had Charlie Brice here.'

'I got a free magnifying glass and special gloves for handling treasure! Practice makes perfect. If Bryony's buried around here, I've got the perfect tool with which to find her!'

'Lucie. Where. Is. Stella?' Jack enunciated as if to someone with little English.

A shadow fell across the flagstones. There she was. 'I should never have left you—'

Jackie stood at the edge of the orchard.

'Mary Poppins!' Lucie clutched her detector under her arm like a machine gun. 'Why are you here?'

'I could ask you that,' Jackie replied.

'I live here.' Lucie beamed.

Jack wanted to ask Jackie too, and why she'd been to see Brice. But it was impossible to ask without giving himself away.

'Where's Stella?' Jackie asked Jack.

'I don't know! She called Charles Brice.' He shouldn't know that.

'How come?' Jackie demanded.

'She got him to do an estimate for shelves,' Jack mumbled.

'Isn't that priceless! Ask a handyman to put up shelves in a house that's falling down! Fantastic, that girl's got front!' Lucie crowed.

'So why isn't Stella here?' Jackie was too calm. Jack wanted someone to get the urgency. Stella was in danger!

'She's on a date with Mr Murderer!' Lucie pulled a ball of paper out of one of her pockets and thrust it at Jackie.

'"Gone to Belas Knap with Charles Brice. Won't be long,"' Jackie read out. 'Charlie is *not* a murderer,' she told Lucie. Jack noticed she didn't look convinced.

'Hello! "Charlie", is it?' Lucie hugged her metal detector. '*Charlie* has taken her to that Neanderthal grave.'

'*I'm going to be a father!*' Endora chanted from the tree. Jack willed her to be quiet.

Everyone looked up. Apparently minding her own business, the budgerigar was dancing along her swing.

'Take that budgerigar indoors,' Jackie commanded. 'It's too hot out here.'

Jack unhooked the cage from the branch. Endora flew up to the bars and squawked, '*I'm going to be a father.*'

'She keeps saying that. Garry must have been talking crap at her. My nephew with kids? Call social services!' Lucie was rifling through her 'treasure'.

Jack took Endora into the sitting room and attached her cage to a hook in the beam. He was loath to utter a word in front of her.

'Why isn't she back by now? We need to get to Belas Knap! Stella's in trouble. Lucie, you should have called me!' Forgetting his worry about Endora, Jack yelled.

'I did. You chose not to answer. Anyway Panic-Pants, it's time

222

you understood Stella's got grit. No one builds a cleaning empire by being a fainting filly. Chill, poppet!'

Jack dialled Stella's number.

'I tried her before I rang you,' Jackie said.

'This is Stella Darnell. I'm sorry I—' Jack nearly flung the phone at an apple tree.

'Let's see where she is.' Lucie's phone was in a silver case that looked bulletproof.

'How can you know?' Jackie went over to Lucie.

'My app gives me her precise location.'

'You're tracking Stella! Does she know?' Jackie was no longer calm.

'No point telling someone you're tailing them! How dumb is that? Here we are...' Lucie moved into the shade to get sunlight off the screen. '*Whoa*, Stella's left Belas Knap, she's on the move!'

'We need to go,' Jack heard himself shout.

'Why are you tracking Stella?' Jackie was indignant.

'I'm a journo, we follow the story. Stella's is honey to a bee. OK... she's on a lane. Slowing down. Turning right. No left. Everything around here's the same. Hedges, cow pats, barns, deer.' Lucie squinted at her phone.

'Are you tracking me too?' Jack asked.

'Of course, poppet.' As if Jack would hate to be left out.

'That's not right,' Jackie said.

'Horn in your reins, Brown Owl. Us chickens turn a blind eye when Jack o'Lantern's flirty-girty with the law. Were I not trailing Stella we wouldn't know where she was.' She looked at Jack. 'Or would we? Jackaranda, when you arrived, you didn't know Stella had left a billet-doux, yet you knew who she was with. Forgive me, but last thing I knew you'd gone to London to see the Queen.'

'We must go!' Jack pictured the teddy bear trophy. 'Brice killed Bryony Motson and he'll kill...' Jack couldn't finish the sentence.

Chapter Thirty-Seven

'Go right!' Lucie yelled. 'Hot damn! You missed it.'

'You need to give me notice, I've got a queue of cars behind me.' Jackie was patient.

'Notice? I don't know where Stella's going!' Lucie protested.

'I thought the point was you know exactly where Stella is at all times.' Jackie backed into a field. Her Nissan Juke easily accommodated them all, including, at Lucie's insistence, Endora in her cage and the metal detector.

'I can see where Stella is *geographically*, weirdly I just can't read her mind. That's more Jackaroo's thing. Shitty *shit*!'

'What?' Jack leaned forward between the seats.

'The blue dot's gone.'

'It can't have!' Jack banged the armrest.

'Keep your wig on. Where are we?' Lucie squinted out at a hawthorn hedge so close to the window, it blotted out the view.

'Isn't there a street sign?' Jackie made sarcasm the new polite.

Jack minded less that Lucie had tracked him and Stella, he minded very much she'd lost her.

'Found her. She's by a railway line, what's she doing? Hurry, Jackie. Put your foot down!'

Jack stopped himself telling Jackie the same thing.

'*Here's looking at you, kid!*' Endora's shriek ripped through the car's interior.

'Where *is* she going?' Jack's phone was dead. What if Stella was trying to call him? She wouldn't call, she supposed he was in London.

'Faster!' Lucie jigged on her seat.

'Brice won't hurt Stella,' Jackie said. She glanced at Jack in the rear mirror. *She was frightened too.*

'Bryony Motson was never found...' His voice cracked. 'He took her teddy—'

'*Left!*'

Jackie had taken the car onto another lane before they all realized the instruction came from the budgerigar.

A tractor roared around the bend. Jackie slammed on the brakes. Jack grabbed the cage as she thrust the gearstick into reverse. Turning in her seat, Jackie clasped the back of Lucie's headrest and with her advanced driver's skill, steered backwards, avoiding ditches. She pulled off the road by the entrance to a wood.

'Hell's bells,' Lucie grumbled.

'What?' Jack was a frayed rag.

'The dot's here. But Stella isn't.' Lucie peered out through the windscreen.

Jack released the belt and jumped out of the car. He ducked under an arch of willow fronds.

The little church was surrounded by headstones, green and barnacled with lichen. Insects buzzed, from a distant field came the persistent call of a sheep. A gate stood open. Jack slipped through. He crept up to the porch.

Inside the church, the air was chill. In daylight trickling in from stained-glass windows Jack made out the ghostly images of saints and a greyhound giving chase to a fox painted on the stone walls. Next to the pulpit was a donation box. A blackboard was chalked with an invitation to leave messages for loved ones. Someone had written, 'Maria found peace at last', 'Sleep with the

Angels our dear Diana'. Jack found 'I'm coming, Tabitha Twitchet' faintly sinister.

He grabbed the chalk, thinking to scrawl 'Stella, I'm sorry.' *Words.* Bowing his head in a semblance of prayer he ran down the aisle and into the porch. Something dragged at his leg, making him yelp. Stanley!

Stella was kneeling beside a mausoleum set within railings rusted brown. She was reading an inscription engraved in gold lettering on the granite.

CASSANDRA BAKER 1959–1977
SPECIAL DAUGHTER AND SISTER
DORMIAT IN PACE (1999)

'You answer your phone? Where's Brice? How come you saw him without me?' Jack bombarded Stella with questions.

'What's Dormiat mean?'

'What? Oh, sleep. Brice, where is he?'

'Sleep in peace. I wonder what Karen thinks of this huge tomb. Maybe there's room for them all.' Stella got up. 'Charlie? I asked him to drop me here. I wanted to see where Cassie is buried.'

'We tracked you.' Jack drew breath. 'Lucie's got a tracker!'

Stella looked out across fields to where a tractor was moving slowly up and down. She remarked, 'She's been tracking us for months.'

Chapter Thirty-Eight

'How come you knew about the church?' Jack asked Stella. 'It's not in the files.'

They were all in the Winchcombe deli, huddled at a corner table, out of earshot of other customers. They'd got permission from Mark the owner to charge their phones in sockets under the table.

'It was in one of Brice's sketches.' Stella told them about the drawings in Brice's notebook. 'I realized he'd drawn Belas Knap when—' She couldn't bring herself to tell them about Stanley and the tractor, it was her fault for letting him off the lead in the countryside.

'That one of the sketches is the deposition scene points to guilty,' Jack said.

'Surely that Charlie has pictures in a book his customers are likely to see proves he isn't,' Jackie said.

'I wasn't meant to see it.'

'Yet you did.'

'OK, enough of this rooting for "Charlie". There's something you're not telling us, Jackie Makepeace!' Lucie knocked back her second espresso. 'Fess up.'

'*Fess up. Fess up,*' Endora squawked from her cage on the table, causing a conversational lull in the café.

'I went out with Charlie in my last year of school when he lived in Hammersmith.' Jackie jolted as if hit by a charge of electricity. She looked at Stella and Jack. 'Only for a few weeks. Actually, he was good at art then. Good at most things.'

'Go, girl!' Lucie hooted.

'He came top in history. Charlie could have gone to Oxford to study Classics, he passed the entrance exam, but instead he left school and got a job at a petrol station. Then he went travelling in a van.'

'That's why he knew all about Belas Knap,' Stella said. 'He knew the names of things and what they were used for. They didn't bury their dead in one place, they put different bits in different places and then dug them up.' She sipped tea as she recalled Brice striding about the mound describing Early Neolithic ceremonies held in the forecourt. It was after the tractor incident. For a reason she couldn't explain she had become convinced Brice was innocent. Her fear of him had gone.

'I'd hate to come across bits of my father dotted about. Dead means dead in my book.' Lucie poked a stick of carrot into the cage. The budgerigar, examining herself in a mirror fixed to her perch, ignored it.

'I was going out with Charlie before Cassie Baker was killed.' Jackie clutched Jack's arm. 'I was going to tell you both. We camped in Winchcombe in 1977. Charlie had an aunt who lived here.' She pulled a wallet of photographs developed in Boots from her bag. 'These are of our holiday. The photo-booth strip of me and Charlie was taken when we first started going out.'

'You've shagged a murderer.' Lucie pulled the wallet over to her and began flipping through the pictures. 'How cool is that!'

'*You've shagged a murderer.*' The silence in the café was absolute.

Jackie pulled a face. 'Don't say that! I don't think he's a killer.'

'You don't sound certain.' Jack spread his paper serviette over the top of the cage.

'The Charlie I knew in 1977 didn't act like a murderer.' Jackie shook her head.

'If murderers acted like murderers, they'd be caught before they murdered.' For once Lucie said what Stella was thinking.

'I know that!' Jackie flared.

'How did you meet this bloke who killed two innocent eighteen-year-old girls on their way home from a night out?' Lucie was ready with her reporter's notebook.

Why hadn't Jackie told them about Brice? Stella didn't talk about her exes, but if one was a murder suspect she would have told Jackie. She tried to marshal her thoughts, but they were a jumble. All she saw was Charlie Brice's eyes flashing at her and his grin. He said he had liked winding Paul Mercer up, had he played her too?

'Graham and I were childhood sweethearts. Charlie was his brother's best friend. Barry and Charlie are three years than older us. Not that Barry admits he's over sixty.' Jackie's hands were clamped under her armpits as if she was freezing. She was watching Lucie's busy shorthand.

'Charlie pretty much lived at the Makepeaces' from when he was fourteen; Graham's parents treated him like a son. Charlie's dad drank, his mother left when he was five. He never saw her again. He slept in Barry's bedroom and was more like a brother to him than Graham. Charlie said the family saved him from going into care.'

'Your own family's like that.' Lucie was filling page after page with frantic hieroglyphics. She waved her pen at Jack and Stella. 'You've got these two under your wing.' Like a blue moon, Lucie's compliments were rare.

'One day after maths, Barry told me Charlie fancied me. I already liked him, he was a laugh and there was something daring and dangerous about him. He'd been a skinhead, Doc Martens, Crombie coat with silk hanky, the lot. He went around with the tough crowd, but he also hung out with me and Graham's friends, hippies in Biba and Laura Ashley and urine-soaked afghan coats.'

'How did that happen?' Stella was horrified.

'How did I get together with Charlie?' Jackie's eyes had

darkened as if she'd gone back to that time. She looked at Stella as if she was a stranger.

'She means the pissy coat.' Lucie flipped over a page. 'Stell, baby, you were too young for loons and T. Rex.'

'At some lower-sixth disco I watched Charlie dancing to Stevie Wonder. It was "Boogie on Reggae Woman".' Jackie lifted her cup to her lips, then without drinking went on, 'By then he was into electric-blue suede brothel-creepers and Levi drainpipes. He'd let his hair grow a bit. He was bopping to the beat, miming the words, eyes shut. Then he was dancing towards me, he never took his eyes off me. Up close, I smelled his ginseng cologne…' Involuntarily, Jackie pinched her nostrils.

'The Root of All Evil.' Lucie lifted Endora's serviette. 'The strapline for the advert. Just saying.'

Jackie didn't appear to have heard. 'Charlie whispered that line in the song about wanting to do it until you holla for more. I got goose-bumps. No boys in our year danced like that, not even Graham. I was stupid. *Stupid.*' Jackie snatched the serviette from Endora's cage and began tearing it into strips. 'He can't be a killer.'

'Fancy Pants could boogie, so couldn't have whacked anyone over the head?' Lucie crunched on a crudité. 'Myra Hindley may have knocked 'em dead in Gorton's British Railway Club, it didn't make her a saint!'

'He drew Belas Knap where Cassie was buried?' Jack looked cross. 'He took Stella there.'

'He didn't "take" me. I went on my own accord,' Stella protested. No she hadn't. Had she been stupid too? She was struck with a thought: 'You're the girl Trudy Baker – Cassie Baker's mother – saw in the tent with Brice!'

'A woman came in the tent after their dog. We'd got used to being alone up there. I had nothing on, it was awful, embarrassing, although she was OK about it. So that was Cassie Baker's mother.' Jackie repositioned the salt and pepper pots.

'There's nothing in the files about you being in Winchcombe. Mercer believed Charlie was here, but had no proof.'

'I should have told you, Stell.' Jackie laid a hand on Stella's. Without quite meaning to, Stella removed her hand.

'Never mind these two, how come you didn't tell the local constabulary?' Lucie waggled a carrot.

'Cassie Baker's body was found twenty-two years after she was murdered. There was nothing significant about my stay in Winchcombe beyond that I broke up with Charlie.' Jackie bridled. 'At the time I was upset, but by 1999 it was trivial to me, I loved Graham. Except it wasn't trivial to Graham.' Jackie lined up a sprig of lavender in a glass phial with the salt and pepper. 'I've told him a million times: I was young, it meant nothing. When they found Cassie Baker, it raked it all up. How if Charlie hadn't two-timed me, I wouldn't have gone with Graham. It wasn't true, but in 1999, the millennium, when people were reviewing the last century and wondering what the future had in store...' Tailing off, Jackie bit her lower lip. A bead of blood appeared.

'So, that a girl's body was found inches from where you and Charlie were dirty dancing rather took a back seat.' Lucie put down her notebook.

Jackie stormed at her. 'Shut up, Lucie! Of course not. Graham isn't that cold-hearted.' She took a breath. 'Far from it.'

'You were teenagers, why did – does – it matter to Graham?' Stella had always supposed Graham was the love of Jackie's life. If anything had, the assumption gave her security.

'The agonies of betrayal and jealousy burn deep,' Lucie intoned. 'Your Graham would have suffered in the next-door tent.'

'When Charlie led Paul Mercer to Cassie Baker's body, why didn't you go to the police? Even if it upset Graham.' Stella felt another kind of fear coil within her. After this case, her life would never be the same.

'By the time I heard they'd found Cassie Baker's body, Matthew Craven had admitted he knew she was buried there. They'd solved the case. Why tell the police I'd been in Winchcombe two weeks earlier? It was the holiday season, the place was teeming with tourists. They didn't need us adding to their work.'

'Good of you.' In one snap Lucie devoured her carrot.

'How come you were camping?' Stella asked for the sake of asking as she pondered on agonies burning deep.

'We'd left school. It was meant to be Charlie and me going off by ourselves, but the next thing I knew, Barry and Graham were coming. Barry and Charlie were inseparable so that was no surprise. Graham had just passed his driving test and bought an ex-TV licence detector van. The boys used him shamelessly as a gofer. He's never forgotten. I was glad he was there, I already liked him. Still,' she admitted, 'I'd wanted Charlie to myself.'

'Three dishy hunks. Lucky you!' Lucie produced a pistol-shaped lighter from her bag, spinning it on her forefinger.

Stella turned to Jack. 'How come you're here? Don't you have a driving shift?' *Why didn't you tell me you're seeing Bella Markham again?* Betrayal? She unplugged her phone and set Jack's on to charge. *Jealousy?*

'I didn't go.' Jack had ordered a cheese sandwich, but not touched it.

'Why not?' Everything was upside down. Jackie and Graham were a byword in happiness on which she depended. Jack was being odd. Stella gripped the edge of the table.

'Shame you gave the carpenter his book back.' Lucie took a bite of Jack's sandwich. 'We could've had a squiz at his etchings.'

'You can.' Stella passed her phone to Lucie. 'I photographed them.'

'That's our scarecrow!' Jack was looking over Lucie's shoulder.

'Scarecrows all look the same.' Lucie tweaked the image larger.

'Actually they don't. The humanoid ones tend to be—' Jack began.

'It's got the same hat.' Stella hadn't seen the detail in the actual drawing. 'Whoever moved it couldn't have got it to Belas Knap by car, you can't drive there. It must have been Charlie after all.' She felt disappointment. So much for an open mind.

'Don't forget Matthew Craven's out of prison,' Lucie said.

'He's not allowed to come anywhere near Winchcombe,' Stella said.

'You're not meant to murder people either, maybe that didn't stop him.' Lucie wriggled in her seat as if she knew something. Stella was about to ask her when Jack's phone buzzed.

The vibration sent the handset travelling about the table. They watched as if, like a spinning knife, where it came to rest would seal someone's fate. Jack stared too. Stella caught the name on the screen. *Bella*.

'Money on Madam Scalpel wants you back!' Lucie finished Jack's sandwich and pushed the plate away. Despite her pithy remark, she was looking at Jack with concern.

Jack pulled the cable from the phone and practically ran from the café. Stella caught him say, 'Bella, I'm so glad you...' before he reached the street. He *was* back with Bella. Stella felt uncomfortable. Jackie hadn't told her about Brice and Jack hadn't told her about Bella? She tried to tell herself she didn't mind. It didn't work. She did mind.

Jackie put up her hands. 'Stella, I'm so sorry I didn't tell you and Jack about all this straight away. Charlie couldn't have hurt Cassie Baker.' She paused. 'I'm certain.'

'You can't be certain,' Stella heard herself say. Only hours ago she too had reached that conclusion. Now she was certain of nothing. Except that Jack was back with Bella.

'... when Lisa Mercer walked into Clean Slate, I even toyed with turning down the case. But I've been nagging you to build up the detective agency, so I couldn't do that.'

'I was on Craven's case before you guys.' Lucie rested the butt of her pistol on her lip. Stella was sure Lucie was hiding something. She reminded herself never to forget that for Lucie the story came first.

Stella too had exes she'd rather forget, but until now had supposed Jackie had always been with Graham. That she'd gone out with Charlie Brice, the man with glittering blue eyes who could run like the wind, put Jackie in a new light.

Jackie continued, 'Charlie told me he had an aunty near Winch-combe. He'd always given out he was an orphan, I was curious to meet her.'

'Charlie's Aunt.' Lucie examined the barrel of her gun. 'So he lied to you.'

'Not a lie exactly. I guess he didn't feel connected to his aunt,' Jackie said. 'The plan was to camp in her garden, but when we got to Winchcombe, it turned out Charlie had never told her we were coming. She made it clear what she thought of girls who went away with boys. We drove around looking for somewhere to pitch the tents and found Belas Knap.'

'You camped in a death chamber!' Lucie sounded impressed. 'Spook-ee!'

'We didn't see it as spooky. I thought it was romantic, like Stonehenge.' Jackie stopped.

'What?' Lucie demanded.

'I'd forgotten. Charlie gave me a pebble with a hole in it. I threaded a thong through it and wore it round my neck.' Jackie tucked a strand of hair behind her ear.

'That's what Matthew Craven left next to the body!' Stella exclaimed. 'You're saying Charlie knew about stones being lucky?'

'Charlie read up on ancient rites and rituals. He was already superstitious, never used an umbrella, avoided cracks in pave-ments, touched ten things when he came in a room, bit like Jack.'

'He was tapping wood on our picnic!' Stella remembered Brice touching the stile and the tree trunk. 'It was creepy.'

'He must have got wet a lot.' Lucie was writing again.

'That means he too understood the significance of putting the stone in the hole in with Cassie Baker's body. Maybe Mercer was right and Brice did frame Craven?'

'After I caught him with that girl, I said he could keep his luck.' Jackie gave a tight smile. She looked about to cry. Stella had never seen her cry.

She asked, 'So how come you split up? Don't answer if you'd rather not. Did he tell you?'

'Do answer,' Lucie urged.

'One night we were in a pub in Winchcombe, the Sun Inn on the main street. Graham and I left early, neither of us were drinkers. The boys came back late. After that they often went there. Graham once said he reckoned Barry had met a girl. But Barry was engaged to Yvonne, he wouldn't have been unfaithful.'

'Are we talking about Baz Makepeace?' Lucie rolled her eyes.

'Go on.' Stella was inclined to agree with Jackie, she liked Barry.

'I loved hanging out at Belas Knap. It had a special atmosphere. Charlie and Barry would go off in Graham's van and stagger back, stinking of booze, tripping over guy ropes. They dented Graham's van. He was pretty cross. The holiday was something of a disaster.'

'Sounds like all my holidays,' Lucie confided to Endora who was dozing on her perch.

'One evening Graham and I decided to walk into Winchcombe. Charlie and Barry had taken the van. It was the actual night of the Queen's Jubilee. Not the date of the disco when Cassie disappeared.'

'Aha! So you're not that convinced Brice is innocent,' Lucie said.

'How can I be?' Jackie banged the pepper pot on the table, waking Endora and Stanley. 'I went out with him for a few weeks and until today I hadn't seen him since. I just don't see it, that's all.' Jackie was shaking.

'Go on.' Stella touched Jackie's hand.

Jackie gave her a tiny smile. 'As Stella knows, the route from Belas Knap is through woods. It was June, like now. Idyllic, bird-song, the scent of flowers…'

Picturing Stanley and the tractor, Stella wouldn't have said 'idyllic'.

'Graham and me, we never ran out of things to say. Charlie didn't talk much, only to explain stuff. That time with Graham outside the tents was the start of everything.'

Lucie had no truck with feelings, she glanced at her watch. A Fitbit. Stella imagined Lucie more concerned with counting nippets drunk than paces walked.

'We heard noises. Grunting and shuffling. An animal, I thought. Graham tried to hurry me on. I had to look. In a clearing I saw Charlie, his pants down, doing it with a girl we'd met in the pub on the first night.' Jackie repositioned the salt and pepper pots. 'I now know her name was Lauren Spicer. She was stunning. I was no match for her.'

'The delightful dame in the beauty parlour!' Lucie exclaimed. 'Cassie Baker's best friend. I think you could give her a run for her money, sweetheart!'

'How do you know she's delightful?' Stella noted Lucie's second compliment to Jackie.

'She did my nails this morning.' Lucie spread her pink manicured hands down on the table.

'When were you going to tell us?' Jackie was getting her own back.

'I just did. She's still upset about the girl's death.'

'What did you find out?' Stella wasn't angry that instead of researching information in Cheltenham library, Lucie had gone to the beauty parlour and interviewed a suspect.

'Nothing, except Ms Spicer's good at her trade.' Lucie curled her nails like a cat about to pounce on a bird. 'She gained nothing by Cassie's murder and lost a friend. Cross her off your list.'

'I think it's too soon to eliminate suspects. But thanks for that, Lucie,' Stella said. Whatever Lucie was hiding, it had to do with her visit that morning.

'What happened after you caught Charlie-boy with his pants down?' Lucie said.

'I ran. I didn't stop until I reached Winchcombe. Graham chased after me. He was so kind. There was no sign of Charlie. I wanted to go home. Graham said he'd drive me that night. We tried all the pubs looking for Barry to get the van, but couldn't find him. Eventually, on the way back to Belas Knap, we came across the van on a verge near where you're staying. No sign of Barry. Graham had a spare key. We returned to Belas Knap, packed up and left.'

'You left Barry and Charlie stranded?' Stella couldn't imagine Jackie doing that to anyone.

'Barry couldn't say anything, he didn't want Yvonne to know he'd gone off.' Jackie was talking like a robot. 'Charlie came to London and pleaded with me to make up. He cried, sent me flowers and letters.'

'He was pissed off he'd been caught. My hubby was the same. Weasels. Bet you stuck to your guns!' Lucie fired a flame from her gun-lighter at the ceiling.

'I returned his letters unopened and threw away the flowers. In the end, Charlie bought Graham's van and went off. I never saw him again. Not until today outside Lauren Spicer's salon.'

Lucie clapped her hands. 'He's still with her! *Shit-bird*. Yet you don't think he's the killer!'

'For one reason,' Jackie said. 'Charlie wasn't in Winchcombe when Cassie Baker went missing.'

'How do you know when she died?' Lucie asked.

'Police think Cassie went to Belas Knap on the evening of the disco. That was the Saturday after the Queen's Jubilee. I remember it because that was when Charlie stood outside my house until dawn. My dad told him to go.'

'So why didn't he tell Mercer? It would have ruled him out. Your father and you could have alibied him.'

'No one knew he needed an alibi. Craven was charged, not Brice.'

'Brice knew he needed one. Why didn't he ask you?' Lucie said.

'I don't know.' Jackie rubbed at her face. 'I don't have a clue.'

'Maybe because he knew you couldn't alibi him for the actual time he killed Cassie. Maybe you got that date wrong.' Lucie began on another carrot.

'Who was the girl Barry may have cheated with?' Stella asked.

Before Jackie could answer, Lucie exclaimed, 'Lordy, did some-one *die*?'

Jack, arms folded, his face chalk-white, was standing by the table.

Stella was on her feet and beside him without realizing she'd moved. 'Sit here.'

'No one died.' Jack sat down heavily and, with the urgency of an allocated task, began rolling the salt cellar between his palms.

'Have a nippet.' Lucie whipped a silver hip-flask from her bag and sloshed gin into Jack's empty water glass.

He shook his head, while mechanically he raised the glass and drank the gin. The two dots of pink pricked his cheeks. He picked up the salt container again.

'Are you OK?' Dizzy with a feeling she couldn't name, Stella put her hand on Jack's arm. She felt toned muscle through the fabric. In a sleeveless jumper, wire-framed reading glasses tucked into the front of his crumpled shirt, Jack looked like a distraught professor.

Jackie leaned across the table and stroked back Jack's fringe. 'What's happened, love?'

'It's hot.' Jack didn't protest when Lucie emptied her flask into his glass.

'Was that Bella Donna?' Lucie chirped.

'No.'

Although she'd seen Bella's name on his phone, Stella believed him.

A police car sped down North Street, siren blaring. Only Stella heard Jack say to her, 'There's stuff I need to tell you.'

Chapter Thirty-Nine

'Wait for me!' Lucie was penned into the kissing gate.

'Take off your rucksack,' Jack called.

Lucie, wrestling with the gate, didn't hear. Jackie went back for her. She craned over the railing and eased the straps off Lucie's shoulders. This wasn't easy as Lucie refused to keep still. At last Jackie heaved the rucksack over the gate. 'Blimey, Lucie, this weighs a ton. We're not going on a hike!'

Lucie reclaimed the rucksack and, crippled by her new walking boots, limped up the footpath after the others.

There had been no opportunity for Jack to talk to Stella after the café because Lucie had jumped into her van before he could. This was both a relief and a stress. He'd travelled back in Jackie's car. She'd asked if he was OK without referring to the phone call. He'd lied again. He said he was fine. Jackie hadn't believed him, but said nothing.

He'd thought – as Lucie had – the call was from Bella. Her name was on the screen. It was from Emily, her best friend.

'Bella's had the twins, Jack. A boy and a girl as expected.'

'Oh! Are they...'

'Everyone's fine, Jack.'

'Thank Bella for getting you to ring me.' He cleared his throat.

'Actually, Jack, look, I'm so sorry. Bella doesn't know I've phoned. She'd be furious if she did.'

'Delete my number from the "outgoing calls" or she'll find out.' Jack went into techie mode as he explained to Emily how to do this. Bella hated deception, even for good reasons. She wouldn't think that Emily telling Jack was a good reason.

On the way back into the café the impact of Emily's news had hit him. He had children. A boy and a girl. He had children...

'Who put that there?' Lucie's raucous tones carried across the field. She skidded her boots along the grass as if skiing.

'Put what where?' Jackie asked her.

'Sheep shit! This is a footpath, for crying out loud. There's muck everywhere.'

'Sheep can't read,' Jack said.

'Ha-de-*hah*! Farmers can. It's all over my boots. How far have we got to go? I'm wondering why we're walking to see a ruined cottage when we live in one?'

Stella was by a stile in the third field. Draped over her shoulder, Stanley eyed the straggling group with baleful button eyes.

'Bally hoo! We're staggering about in a bog to give this doggie a trot out and you're lugging him along like a handbag pug!' Leaning over the stile to get her breath, Lucie glowered at the patchwork of fields as if surveying a battle scene.

'The crop is attracting bees,' Stella replied. 'He was snapping at them. He could be stung.'

The humming was insidious and pervading. Jack looked properly. Stretching away amidst pale yellow flowers, petals twitched as hundreds of bees alighted on them.

'Bees are pollinators for clover,' Jackie said. 'Clover's a cover crop, it regenerates soil with nitrogen.'

'Someone listens to *The Archers*!' Lucie sounded impressed. Since the café Jack noticed Lucie appeared to view Jackie in a new light.

'*Farming Today*,' Jackie said.

They left the field of bees and after another stile came across a signpost, 'Belas Knap, 2 miles'. Across the field was the old house.

'I've been here!' Jackie stopped.

'Me too,' Stella said. 'We came the day we arrived.' It was the first time she'd responded directly to something Jackie had said since Jackie told them about her relationship with Brice.

'This is where Charlie's aunty lived. He planned for us to camp here. As I said, the aunt would have none of it. A shame, I remember rather liking the look of her. She was feisty and fierce.' Jackie smiled at the memory.

'Are you sure this was the place?' Stella put Stanley down and let him off his lead. He shook himself and, nosing after a scent, scampered towards the house.

'Absolutely.' Jackie was striding over to the railings around the house. 'The window on the right was the living room.'

'Do you know what happened to the aunt?' Jack said.

'I should imagine she's dead. She was late fifties then, although to us kids that was old. She'd be nearly a hundred. I wonder who owns it now. I shouldn't imagine she left it to Charlie. There was little love lost from her side, at least.'

'You were going to find out at the library?' Stella turned to Lucie. 'Did you actually go there?'

'One step at a time.' Lucie flashed her pink nails at Stella. 'I did find out that the old house is owned by SBH Holdings Ltd.'

'I remember the garden was gorgeous,' Jackie said. 'Coming from London, I'd never seen a proper country garden except in a Ladybird book. Flowers, sweet peas on sticks, one section was veg and salad, with a perfect lawn. A quintessential country cottage. Such a shame it's fallen into disrepair.'

They were startled by a stuttering like a lawn mower.

'Someone's there.' Stella gripped the railings.

'Where's Lucie?' Jack said.

Through a 'window' in the wall, Lucie May drifted. She moved rhythmically as if doing a dance. Into the frame and out.

'That's why her bag weighed a ton. She brought that metal detector!' Jackie burst out laughing.

'She shouldn't be in there and not with a metal detector,' Stella groaned. 'I'll tell her to stop.'

'Good luck with that.' Jackie was still laughing.

Stella climbed the fence and jogged across the rubble. At the corner of a free-standing wall she halted abruptly. The metal detector buzzed on. Stella was waving at them.

'Come on!' Jackie was already over the railings.

'Look at this,' Stella said when they reached her. She held out her phone.

'It's one of Brice's sketches,' Jack said.

'Look there.' Stella pointed to where Lucie was sweeping the detector to and fro. In khaki jerkin and combat pants, she might be mine-sweeping a devastated land.

'Now look.' Stella held up the phone.

'Brice sketched *that* field!' Jack got it.

'Why? The other drawings were related to Cassie Baker. There was the church where she's buried now and Belas Knap where she was found,' Stella said.

'Is it where Bryony is buried?' Jackie suggested quietly.

'Look!' Jack whispered. Knee-deep in nettles, arms out-stretched, was a scarecrow. *The* scarecrow.

'Someone playing a joke,' Jackie reassured him.

'It's not a joke.' Stella told her about the drone, the scarecrow and the cigarette ends.

'That's not all.' Jack swiped to the photo of Stella on his phone.

'Someone came up to the kitchen door while I was making breakfast,' Stella told Jackie. She sounded upset. Not good. As Lucie had said, little rattled Stella. 'Jack thinks it's Charlie.'

Jack hadn't said that, yet Stella was more right than she could know. Brice must know they were here to trap him. He was playing tricks on them. Jackie had no idea what a lucky escape she had had all those years ago. Although, he had kept the stone with a hole that he'd given her in the trophy box in his workroom so he still cared about her. Jack felt a chill as if a cloud had gone over the sun. The sky was clear. Jackie must keep away from Charlie Brice. Stella too.

'When I saw Charlie, I told him Mercer had asked you to look into the case. He seemed genuinely surprised.'

'You told him?' Stella stared at her.

'I'm sorry. But in all honesty, I don't think Charlie did anything. He has no cause to scare you. Lisa Mercer was sure her dad was wrong. I do agree someone is out to make you leave. That photo of you is no joke. I think you should book into one of the pubs in town.'

'Bryony Motson.' Stella hadn't been listening. 'I've been assuming the sketches are related to Cassie, but there are tall nettles.'

'And knapweed,' Jack offered. He was trying to 'learn nature'.

'Nettles grow higher where there's a body. Bryony Motson could be buried there.'

The detector switched to a higher pitch, a solid distinctive whine.

'Treasure!' Lucie stabbed the hardened ground with her trowel, tossing soil aside. Stanley joined in. Practised at digging, he was more effective than Lucie.

'Lucie, we shouldn't be here.' Stella's tone was resigned, Jack thought. Lucie had the bit between her teeth.

'Here we are!' Lucie handed Stella a bottle top.

'Watney's Pale Ale.' Stella read the cap.

'You come at treasure from different angles. The sound defines the object.' Lucie went back to scooping from the hole. 'An uninterrupted signal is a circular disc of metal. It should have been a coin, not a beer bottle top.' She sounded cheated.

Stella said, 'Watney's doesn't exist now. It was a London brewery, did they distribute down here?'

'They might have,' Jack said. 'Whatever date Watney's ceased being sold in off-licences gives the latest date it could have been dropped.'

'Charlie drank Watney's Pale Ale,' Jackie murmured.

'This was his aunt's house, he stayed here. It's not extraordinary you've found something loosely linked to him,' Stella said.

'You said Phyllis Brice wouldn't let you stay.' Lucie switched on her detector and hovered it indiscriminately in a metre radius.

'Charlie Brice told me he stayed here while his aunt was away and fed her budgie,' Stella said.

Jackie shouted over the din, 'Barry told Graham they both stayed here after we left.' She shrugged. 'Probably with Lauren Spicer.'

The detector's whine rose. Lucie switched it off and this time let Stanley do the spadework.

Stanley grubbed up his find and clenching it in his jaws, clambered out. As Lucie made to grab his muzzle, the dog gave a blood-curdling snarl, eyes black as marble, whites showing.

'He's possessed it.' Stella came forward.

'Possessed, you mean! Tell him it's mine,' Lucie protested. 'Finders keepers.'

'Actually, you must give ten per cent of the value of any treasure you find—' Jack began.

'Listen up, Legal Larry.' Lucie cracked apart her metal detector as a sniper might dismantle a rifle after a clean shot. 'He's stolen my treasure!'

'We have to convince him we don't care.' Scattering liver treats in her wake, Stella walked across the rubble. Everyone trooped behind her.

In minutes Stanley had abandoned his find and was eating his way back along the trail of treats.

Lucie moved faster than Jack thought her capable. 'It's a key!'

'It might have been to the door, but since there isn't one, we'll never know.' Disconsolate, Lucie gazed into Stanley's hole.

Stella took the key. 'It has a code. We might be able to trace the cutter.'

'That will help how?' Lucie said. 'What has this key to do with the murders? Cassie was found at Belas Knap and we don't know this is where Bryony's buried…'

'We don't not know,' Jack said. 'Brice could have gardened for his aunt. Easy to dig a hole and return at night with Bryony's body. If his aunt had seen him, Brice was clever, he'd have had an explanation ready.'

'Or Craven,' Stella objected. 'He was an estate agent. He could have managed the sale of this place. Or Ralph Baker, he lived up the lane.' She paused. 'The key was dangling from Stanley's mouth. How was that possible?'

'Because your dog is a magpie,' Lucie snorted.

'It should have been between his teeth.' Stella began scanning the ground. 'There must have been a fob.'

'Brilliant!' Jack loved Stella's brain.

In the early-evening light, the four of them conducted a finger-tip search along the cracked concrete.

'Found it!' Stella teased aside blades of grass.

'Looks like a pet tag.' Jackie was beside her.

'It's too heavy.' Stella rubbed a metal disc on the knee of her jeans. 'I think it's a coin.'

'I said so!' Lucie exclaimed. 'The detector's never wrong. We're in business!'

Jackie said, 'You said it was dangling from Stanley's mouth; he couldn't hold a coin and the key.'

Stella pulled a tissue from her pocket and rubbed at the coin. 'It's an old penny.'

'What year?' Lucie was no doubt dreaming of an *Antiques Roadshow* jackpot.

'Nineteen fifty-five.' Stella held up the coin. 'Two years after Queen Elizabeth came to the throne. This is her first image. There's been six on currency during her reign.' She resumed cleaning. 'The copper's oxidized, it must have lain here a while. Strange, it's not worn, it can't have been in circulation.'

'Who knew you were a royalist!' Lucie said.

Jack said, 'It can't be related to Cassie's murder – when she died, there was decimalization. Maybe someone dropped it soon after it was minted.'

'There's a hole. And here's what it was attached to!' Stella picked up a rusted ring by her boot.

'It must be significant.' Stella scraped at the penny with a blade from her penknife.

'Maybe it was the year Brice's aunt was born?' Jack suggested.

'She was about fifty in the seventies,' Jackie said.

More than ever, Jack wanted to be alone with Stella. This was what they did well, late nights sipping hot drinks, chewing over evidence. He asked Jackie, 'Did she have children?'

'Charlie called her the Maiden Aunt so she can't have been married. There was no mention of children.'

'If it was given to someone to commemorate their birth year they'd be sixty-two. How old's Brice?' Jack asked.

'Same as me and Graham, fifty-eight. We were born in fifty-eight. I never saw Charlie with a key. He didn't count his father's flat as home. No idea if the Makepeaces gave him a door key. I guess I could ask Graham.'

Jackie wouldn't want to ask Graham. Jack was sorry. He'd wanted their marriage to be perfect. A happy story like those his mother used to tell him.

'Where's Lucie?' Stella groaned.

They found Lucie at the back of the house struggling for balance on a heap of rubbish set long ago for a bonfire. She was pulling frantically at a branch. Jack was reminded of a member of a search and rescue team at an earthquake site.

'I've found the front door!'

Jack scrambled up to her. 'Are you sure?'

'I'm not sure. You'll learn that detection is about conjecture as much as nibbling at hard science. But who paints internal doors black?' Lucie glanced at Jack. 'Don't answer that. Grab this side. One two *three*!'

'Careful!' If Lucie let go of the door she would tumble backwards. It was held by tangles of ivy and brambles.

'One, two, *three*!' Lucie said again.

Jack winced as the slab of wood thrust into his chest. Stella was beside him. She grabbed hold and together they manoeuvred the door off the heap onto the grass. Smacking her hands free of grime, Stella tried the key.

'It doesn't fit.'

'That's a sign,' Jack said.

Lucie said, 'Aunty Phyllis had the lock changed. Portentous!'

'It slims down possibilities.' Stella was unperturbed. 'The key could have been lost here any time over the last sixty-odd years. The condition of the coin suggests at least ten. When I was six I buried some newly minted coins in the garden for spacemen to find. I dug them up four years later when I'd run out of pocket money. The coins hadn't deteriorated as much as this penny.'

Jack felt touched that the little Stella had left money for spacemen. He'd once buried a piece of lucky green glass but that was about hoping the glass would bring his mother back.

'We might get close to establishing when this was dropped.' Stella trudged back to the house. 'When was the renovation work begun? I don't suppose you found that out in the library, Lucie?'

Lucie was wandering about the remains of the rooms, singing to herself. 'They don't keep records of building work. For planning permission, I need to get on to the council.'

'The key was under this broken concrete, which suggests it was there when work began. The lock on this door is old and, despite what you said, Lucie, I'm betting Phyllis Brice never changed it. Winchcombe isn't a hot crime spot. I don't think this key ever fitted a door in this house. I reckon it belonged to someone visiting or trespassing… like us. Or—'

'Or to Cassie Baker's murderer.' Jack completed Stella's sentence.

'A giant leap.' Lucie tucked her detector into her rucksack.

'It is,' Stella agreed. 'Nothing links this house to Cassie Baker or Bryony Motson and if it did, we'd never trace all the visitors Charles Brice's aunt had from 1974 to when she left twenty years ago. Let's stick to facts and keep our parameters tight.'

'It's the only lead we've got, don't knock it,' Lucie said. 'This

Aunty Brice was a recluse, it should be a doddle to find her friends.'

'Who said she was a recluse?' Jack asked.

'She'd have had to be scintillating company for me to traipse all the way out here for a cuppa.'

Stella said, 'Thanks to Lucie, we know when Phyllis Brice sold up. Her house is on the way to Belas Knap. She was on holiday when Cassie Baker was murdered. Jackie thinks Brice stayed here with Lauren Spicer. It could be where Cassie was killed. Her home is over that hill.' Stella pointed towards the Old Brockhampton Road. 'This puts the time the key was dropped no later than 1999.'

Heaving up her rucksack, Lucie asked, 'Are you playing tricks on us, Stella Darnell?'

'Not intentionally. Why?'

'Where's that bloody scarecrow?' Lucie sounded nervous.

Evening sunlight washed over the tall nettles. There was no scarecrow.

Chapter Forty

'I don't need to ask where you've been.' Still in his work trousers and shirt, tie loosened, Graham leaned against the sink. It was exactly midnight.

'Winchcombe,' Jackie said anyway.

'Did you see him?' Graham clasped the back of his head as if the question was jerked out of him.

'Yes.' Wearily, Jackie got up, tested the kettle for water and flicked it on.

'Are you still in…' Graham unhooked her 'Best Mum' mug off the mug tree.

'Do I *really* have to answer that?' Eyeing her husband, his face contorted with misery, Jackie saw she did. 'I'm not still in love with Charlie. I never was. Gray, we were kids. Any feeling I had for him went that day we saw him with Lauren Spicer in the woods. I had no right to mind, let's face it, you and I were getting together anyway.'

'Why did you go to Winchcombe then?'

'I had to tell Stella and Jack. And yes, to see Charlie, not because I'm in love with him, but because I wanted to find out the truth. Did he kill those women?'

'And?'

'He's hiding something.' Jackie looked in the fridge. She felt empty, she'd eaten nothing since leaving Winchcombe, yet she wasn't hungry. She shut the fridge door.

'He's guilty.' Graham gave her a mug of tea. 'Why do you think Charlie knows something?'

'I'm probably being silly.' Sitting at the table, Jackie warmed her face in the steam from the mug.

'I doubt it.'

'It's the way he was. So calm, cocky even. If a detective hounded me for years, I'd be a wreck.'

'He was always cocky. Kids at school were scared of him. I was.' Graham sat opposite Jackie.

'You were scared of Charlie?' Jackie had never known Graham scared of anyone or anything.

'I was in Barry's room once, looking for a record he'd borrowed. Charlie came in. He was angry. Not normal angry, quiet, seething. I was terrified.'

'You never told me.'

'It was hardly a chat-up line saying your ex scared me! You know what he was like. Doesn't say much. Keeps it all inside. Then suddenly charming. Mum loved him. I know you think I'm jealous, but I can see him killing a girl if she didn't do what he wanted. Was it worth going back to Winchcombe?'

'I think so. I went for a walk with everyone before getting in the car. We found that house where his aunt lived. Remember? She shooed us off. I felt sorry for Charlie, my aunties and uncles were always so welcoming.'

'I don't blame her. Would we want a bunch of teenagers taking over our house?'

'We've had teenagers taking over this place many times.' Jackie raised her eyebrows. 'It could be where one or both of the girls were killed.'

'Does Stella think it was Charlie?' Graham set a lot of store in Stella's opinions.

'She's keeping an open mind. I think Jack does. Actually, never mind Charlie, Jack's definitely holding something back.'

'Jack's always got a secret! If Charlie did kill that poor girl the only way he got her up to Belas Knap was in my van.' Graham had unclipped his watch and was trailing the bracelet over the backs of his fingers. A sign that he was upset.

'Cassie Baker could have been killed in that cottage. Bryony Motson too. It's isolated and the nearest house is where the Bakers lived. The mother's still there. That reminds me, Lucie found a key attached to an old penny in the grounds. I said I'd ask: did Charlie have a key to your house? A long shot, but it might be a clue.'

Graham snapped on his watch. 'What date was the penny?'

'Nineteen fifty-five. We wondered if that's when the owner married or had a baby. Or was their own birth year.'

'Jax, there's something I haven't—'

The phone rang. Jackie and Graham jumped. A call after midnight was bad news.

'Hello?' Jackie put a finger to her other ear although Graham was silent. 'Yvonne?' Out of barely intelligible speech punctuated by sobs, Jackie got the gist. 'We're on our way. We're coming!'

'What's happened?'

'Barry collapsed. He's in hospital.' Jackie took his hand. 'Graham, he's unconscious.'

Chapter Forty-One

'We should add Barry.' Stella laid the suspect list on the table between them.

They were in the sitting room. Lucie May and Endora had gone up for an early night. Stanley was snoozing in front of the fire. It might have been a scene of domestic harmony, but for the fact that Jack and Stella were discussing murder.

'Jackie said Barry Makepeace was in London. And Brice,' Jack said.

'At the end of the day, Jackie can't be objective. Barry's family. Actually, I don't think she's sure about where either of them were. All those nights they went into Winchcombe and she stayed with Graham. Although I can't see him as a killer.' Stella added Barry's name. She didn't fancy interviewing him.

'Let's take Trudy and Karen off,' Jack said after they'd stared at the list for a minute. 'How have they benefited by her death?'

'What about the lack of pictures of Cassie?' Stella said.

'There could have been a shrine to Cassie upstairs. Like we said, they were real about her. She brought life to the family,' Jack said.

'No motive.' Stella drew a line through the two names. 'Speaking of fathers, let's see if Brian Motson can conjure up Bryony for us like Trudy and Karen did around Cassie. Like them, he's still in Bryony's childhood home. A place called Broadway. That sounds nice and busy. Let's go in the morning.'

Missing London, Stella would be hoping to find a resemblance to Hammersmith Broadway. Jack suspected she'd be disappointed.

He read from Mercer's notes. '"Brian Motson, single parent. Aged sixty-two. Brought up only child after wife died when Bryony was ten. Bank manager at the Lloyds Bank in Winchcombe."' Jack was an only child, brought up – if that was the word for being sent to boarding school – by his widowed father.

'Sixty-one.' Stella tapped the list. 'Brian Motson was born in 1955.'

They looked at each other.

'The age of the penny,' Jack said at last. 'What would his motive be?'

'Bryony found out her dad killed Cassie and was going to report him so he killed her?'

'But why kill Cassie?'

'Was he Heart-throb? In 1977 Motson was twenty-five. We found the penny at Aunt Phyllis's ruined cottage. Motson was a local bank manager, he may have gone to discuss giving her a home improvement loan. Bank managers have to be meticulous. Like murderers, they can't afford to make mistakes.' Stella batted a hand. 'It's crazy to conjecture this penny key-ring is related to either murder. We don't know if Cassie Baker went to Phyllis Brice's house. The only people we know did are Brice, the Makepeace brothers and Jackie.' She clicked her pen on and off.

'Motson has an alibi for when his daughter vanished. He was at a conference in Harrogate and was seen at breakfast in the hotel the next morning.'

'Nowhere have I read that Motson had an alibi for when Cassie Baker went missing,' Stella said, as if this had just struck her.

'Mercer said he might not see us,' Jack said. 'Motson got Mercer sacked.'

'If you were Motson, what would make you agree to see us?' Stella asked Jack his sort of question.

'If I thought we'd find my daughter's body…' He shuddered at the words.

'He'll want closure,' Stella said. 'Mercer prevented him getting it. Closure is what we can offer.' She paused. 'If Motson killed Bryony, he won't need closure. His response to our request to see him might be a clue to his guilt or innocence.' She began writing. 'I have to add Jackie, Graham and Barry Makepeace.'

'You're kidding!'

'If we didn't know them, they'd be prime suspects. We were suspicious of the mystery campers not telling the police they'd been there. Now we know who they are, we should still be suspicious. Jackie could have told us sooner. She could have gone to the police, why didn't she?'

'She told us why.' Jack hadn't thought he could feel more bereft.

'Did that satisfy you?' Stella looked at him over the candles.

'OK, put them on.'

'Even with losing two, we still have six suspects,' Stella said. 'Jenni Wiles didn't have an alibi. She had no motive either. Since she's now died, we can't rule her out or rule her in.'

'If we found Bryony Motson's body, it would bring the investigation to life.' Jack was thinking of the field by Phyllis Brice's old cottage.

'It's like looking for a needle in a haystack.' Stella picked up the candle holder. 'My brain is tired. I'm going to bed. Night.' She glided into the darkness of the hall. Jack watched the door shut and heard her footsteps on the old wooden stairs.

Shortly after, Jack heard murmuring above. Stella was on the phone. He didn't like not knowing who she was talking to. Stupid to mind.

Since suspecting they were being watched, they'd drawn the curtains. Jack pulled one back. Fiddling with the catch – rusted, it wouldn't stop an intruder – he pushed wide the casement.

The moon sent bluish light across the woods. As he watched, a fork of lightning zig-zagged across the horizon. *One hundred, two hundred, three hundred*, Jack reached six hundred before he heard a rumble of thunder.

The air was laden with the scent of wheat. Breathing in a lungful, he smelled the approaching rain. He caught something else. *Cigarette smoke*. He plunged over the sill and jumped down onto the drive. The crunch of gravel was like a smattering of gun pellets. He'd advertised his presence. He stopped and listened.

From the hills came a piercing cry. Jack had learnt it was a vixen mating. He sniffed. Stella would identify the brand of cigarette. He looked back at her window. It was shut. There was no light.

'Stella left you on your lonesome, Jack?'

Jack stifled a fox shriek. Where the scarecrow should have been hovered an apparition, the firefly glow of a cigarette bobbed inches from his nose. Lucie.

'You're smoking!' Jack hissed, mindful of Stella sleeping metres above them.

'We each have our little secrets, Pusskin!' The corncrake cackle. 'You know mine. Now you're going to tell me yours.'

Stella wasn't asleep. After talking to Vicky, she was lying dressed on her bed brooding at moonlit diamond shapes projected through the leaded window. Vicky had told her that Patty Hogan was unconscious, the end was approaching. 'Her heart packed up. At least she's out of pain. She's going to a better place now.'

'You think?' Stella had been fascinated that a nurse, who dealt in medical facts, believed in an afterlife. Stella tended towards the idea that once you were dead, you were dead, although she couldn't shake off the sensation that sometimes Terry was watching her. He wasn't there tonight. She felt alone.

Vicky had said, 'The good go to Heaven. If there's justice, sinners will be consumed by fire.'

'Patty wasn't all that nice to her family,' Stella had said. Mindful of the danger of naked flames since being in Winchcombe, she didn't want anyone to be consumed by fire.

'Patty will persuade St Peter to open the pearly gates, she has the gift of the gab. Believe me, compared to some parents we see in here, Patty's a saint! We have one woman, effing and blinding at her son. Calling him a wastrel and saying she ruined his life. She'd tried to have him put in care when he was a teenager.' Vicky had gone quiet. Stella guessed she'd breached confidentiality rules. Then Vicky had asked, 'How's it going down there with the detective work?' She hated talk of murder, but she'd pretended interest.

Stella had given her an outline of progress, or lack of it. 'We might have found where Bryony Motson is buried. Trouble is, we can't go digging in fields ourselves, we might destroy evidence. At some stage we'll have to hand what we find to the police. But we need solid proof to get them interested. It's a bit chicken and egg.'

She thought of Patty Hogan, unconscious in the hospice. Apart from being a detective and a cleaner, Stella had become a befriender. She'd let Patty down. If she'd been reading her The Forsyte Saga, Patty might not have died.

She got off the bed and, undoing her shirt, peered into the dark outside. There was a lamp-post on the pavement opposite her bedroom at home, Stella wasn't used to the impenetrable black of the countryside. Not black. As she stared, it resolved into contours and defined forms. There was someone there.

A dot of orange light. The smoker was back! She crept closer to the glass. There were two people huddled together, they were talking. Standing in a splash of light, they hadn't bothered to hide. One person turned. Stella was unsure which she minded most. That Jack was talking privately with Lucie May.

Ridiculous to mind that.

Or that Lucie had started smoking again.

Chapter Forty-Two

'Here you are.' Jackie handed Graham a coffee from the machine. He took it and, head down, elbows on knees, held it as if that was his job.

On the drive along Uxbridge Road to Ealing Hospital and for the two hours they'd been waiting on moulded bucket chairs in A&E, Graham had spoken once to say, 'He might die.'

Jackie hadn't been able to refute this. The doctor had called it 'an angina attack' and they were doing tests. She didn't know if Barry might die.

Two people were allowed by his bed in intensive care at one time. This was Yvonne, his wife, and Maxine, the eldest of their three children. One daughter lived in Australia and was trying to get a flight out of Perth, their son Joe was on his way. Graham and she could only wait.

Jackie wasn't surprised by Graham's catatonic reaction. He'd spent most of his life dissing his older brother, but when push came to shove, siblings stuck together. She'd always feared that if Barry died first, Graham would take it hard. She didn't like being right. She sipped her own coffee. On television, characters were rude about drinks from vending machines, but this coffee – if she didn't think of it as coffee – was welcome.

'Dad wants a cup of tea!' Clutching a pair of high heels as if she was trying them on in a shoe shop, Maxine sat next to them and burst into tears. Through her sobs she told Graham, 'Mum says you can go in. She's gone to the loo. Both of you.'

Maxine might be in her thirties, but she looked as she had at the age of three, small with big eyes. As she had then, Jackie got Maxine a hot chocolate then she and Graham followed a yellow line on the floor to intensive care.

Barry looked thinner. His features were lean and contoured, a throwback to his teens. Locks of blonded hair fanned around his head on the pillow. Hushed voices, monitors beeped, a screen showed various green waving lines.

Calm until this moment, Graham clutched Barry's hand, as if Barry or he would slip to the floor if he let go.

'Jax! You're out late!' Barry enunciated with care like an old man.

'It's always you that keeps me up, Baz!' She gave a tight smile. 'You gave us a scare.'

'I'm tougher than old boots, me!' He shut his eyes, a faint smile playing on his lips.

'You OK?' Graham asked. 'Listen, I wanted to ask, when you were in—'

'Calm, little bro, you're not inheriting yet!' Barry winked and squeezed his hand.

'We'll let you rest.' Jackie touched Graham's shoulder. Staring at Barry, Graham didn't move. 'Gray, come on!'

'Get him out of here. He's annoying the hell out of me.' Barry gave his brother's hand a pat.

Maxine was asleep across three chairs when they returned, her head on her mother's lap.

'He's got to take it easy. He works too hard.' Yvonne was tight-lipped. 'He doesn't listen to me.'

Jackie sloughed off suspicion that 'too hard' was the work Barry did for Clean Slate. Yvonne was one of those people whose silences made you paranoid. Avoiding saying that she couldn't see Barry easing up, Jackie told her, 'He'll listen now, Von.'

The next minute mother and daughter were crying on Jackie's shoulders. They held her so tight, Jackie could have relaxed her legs and stayed upright. Kleenexes doled out, she sent them back to Barry.

In the car park, Graham leaned on the roof of the car. 'Barry had one.'

'Had what?' Graham was in shock. She too was shattered by the adrenalin rush and although no one had voiced it, Barry wasn't out of the woods yet.

'A penny.'

'Darling, I've lost you. What are you saying?' Jackie couldn't reach Graham over the top of the car.

'When we were born Mum and Dad gave us pennies as key-rings. They were minted the year we were born. Mine was 1958.'

'I've never seen it.' The bonnet was still warm from the drive to the hospital.

'As a boy I thought it was naff!' Graham gave a bitter laugh. 'I've got it somewhere.' He ran his finger around a bird-shit stain on the roof. 'Barry used his all the time. Then one day he said he left his key in the front door and it was stolen. Dad had to get the lock changed. Charlie said it was his fault, he always stuck up for Barry, but Dad made Barry pay.'

'What are you saying, Graham?' Jackie's stomach curdled.

'Barry was born in July 1955.'

'So what? Since his key was stolen from your house it means it's not the penny Lucie found this afternoon.'

'Barry could have lied to my parents.' Graham rubbed at the bird-stain with a tissue.

'Is that likely?' Jackie unlocked the car. 'Barry wasn't in Winchcombe when Cassie Baker disappeared. Nor was Charlie. Or I don't think he was.' Jackie remembered Lucie casting doubt on her memory. If asked in a court of law, could she swear she knew it was that Saturday Charlie was outside her house? She opened the car door. 'Graham, get in. Leave this now. Not with Barry so—'

'What if Barry met Cassie Baker? We have to tell Stella and Jack.' Graham gave the cleaned roof a slap with the flat of his hand. In the bleak orange lamplight, Jackie could see the stain had corroded the paintwork.

'It's just speculation.'

'I've wondered since they found the body in the tomb. He was definitely unfaithful to Yvonne. And now this penny?' He rested his forehead on his fist. 'My brother's a murder suspect. God, I'm glad Mum isn't alive to see this!'

'You never told me you suspected Barry was with Cassie Baker.' All those years she'd thought Graham possessive. A quality not evident in any other part of his life.

When they were in the car Graham said, 'You know of course that Jack and Stella will already have us as suspects. We should have told Mercer years ago about camping in Winchcombe.'

'Barry said not to bother. We'd create work for the police. He said it again the other evening when I saw him.' She saw Graham register that she'd spoken to Barry.

'He would, wouldn't he!' Graham was cold-faced. 'There's one way to sort this once and for all.'

'Not now, Barry's too ill!'

'When's a better time to ask? After he's died?' Graham spat out.

'Don't *say* that!' Jackie waited until Graham clipped on his belt, then before he could change his mind about tackling Barry, reversed out of the bay. 'I'll ring Stella tomorrow and tell her about the penny.'

'It's tomorrow now.' Ever the back-seat driver, Graham was watching the wing mirror, brake foot tapping. 'He's *my* brother, I'll call Stella.'

Chapter Forty-Three

'I haven't changed a thing.' Brian Motson considered his daughter's bedroom with what Jack thought unalloyed pride. Jack wondered if one day he might show off his own daughter's bedroom to visitors. His daughter wouldn't know him, so no, he would not.

Motson still lived in the house off a side street in Broadway, which he'd shared with his daughter until Bryony moved into a flat share weeks before she disappeared on the way to her bus stop in 1999. Jack had supposed that Stella, hoping for a conurbation, might have been disappointed by the picturesque village ranged along a broad street (hence the name, he guessed) of teashops, gift shops and the sort of plush hotels that had stags' heads on wood-panelled walls.

It was Tuesday morning, fifteen minutes early for their eleven o'clock meeting with Brian Motson, Jack and Stella had stopped at a bookshop on the main street and bought an ordnance survey map of the Winchcombe area.

Jack and Stella had wanted to examine Bryony's bedroom without Motson there. But after a tour of his house (including greenhouse and shed), he'd presented the room, like a National Trust guide revealing the best bit.

Far from refusing to see them, Brian Motson had welcomed

them and over the last half-hour hadn't stopped speaking, as if the chance to talk about Bryony was rare.

'I made her leave home. "Strike out on your own," I said. She was a daddy's girl. Would have been even if Mum hadn't passed. You've got to be cruel to be kind. Everything's as she left it so that when she visited, she didn't feel forgotten. With her gone, why change it?'

Motson was short and slight, a once-white cotton jacket, cuffs fraying, sagged on his sloping shoulders. Cream-coloured trousers (now matching the jacket) with light coffee-coloured shirt buttoned to the neck and home-dyed blonde hair, had Jack not known Motson was a retired bank manager he'd have guessed out-of-work actor. A grey brush moustache betrayed a stricter air. Motson was sixty-one, but had the stoop and gait of an older man.

'I'm not sorry Mercer's dead.' He'd said this several times. 'When my little girl went, he was in here, pulling out drawers, opening cupboards, prying into her things as if she was the criminal. The man was a fool and he did for my Bryony.'

'Did you let him visit after he left the police?' Stella turned from the window where she'd been watching Japanese tourists decamp from their coach in the car park opposite.

'I did not. He asked. I reported him. He got a warning. Spilt milk can't be poured back in the bottle. I suppose you want to look too.' Before Stella could answer – the cleaner in her didn't look at people's things – Motson flung wide the wardrobe.

'I got her clothes back from that flat she took on. The police fiddled with them, fingering everything. I had them cleaned and hung back the way we had it.' He stroked his moustache with the side of a forefinger.

'What do you think happened to Bry— to your daughter?' Stella avoided using a victim's first name to a relative. It implied a relationship she hadn't had. Jack believed that referring to the victim by name kept them real for loved ones. Stella was leading on this interview.

'She's dead.' He was pulling open drawers. 'And her killer's a free man.'

'You didn't think she'd run away?' In their meeting, Mercer had talked of Bryony's kidnap.

That morning, Lucie still in bed and Endora out of earshot in her cage in the sitting room, Jack battled with how to tell Stella he knew Bryony was dead and it was Brice who had killed her. He'd said nothing. He and Stella were prised further apart by a secret of his own making. A secret that had gained leaden weight when he shared it with Lucie.

The night before, Lucie had challenged him.

'So, turtle dove, my tracker put you in the middle of Winchcombe when you should have been in London. Coincidentally, the blue dot stopped in the street where Charles Brice lives. We don't believe in coincidences, do we?'

He'd confessed – it felt like a confession – breaking into Brice's house and finding Bryony's bear. He'd omitted the answerphone message left by the woman who didn't give her name. Now, in Bryony Motson's bedroom, Jack pondered again on the woman's identity.

'... Mercer knew Brice had my little girl. He sacrificed her for a dead girl. He sought fame and fortune. His greed killed her.'

'How was that?' Stella asked.

'He tipped off the press that he'd found his man. He should have arrested Brice as soon as he suspected him and given him a grilling at the station. He broke every rule in the book. Bryony could be mouldering in a drainage hole to this day. Brice has only to sit tight. Without evidence he's got nothing to fear. I saw that daughter of Mercer's in the Co-op this morning. She had no time for Mercer. She was a lovely little girl. He didn't deserve her.' Motson spoke in a clipped monotone, his accent suggesting New Zealand or South Africa, although Jack knew he'd grown up in Cheltenham. Jack wouldn't have liked to have had Motson refuse him a bank loan. Bad news was made worse by the manner in which it was delivered.

'Have you met Charles Brice?' Stella said.

'I keep a wide berth. We have police to uphold our laws. If you pin this on Brice, I won't stand in your way. He took Bryony in his cab, opened her legs, fucked her and hid her, planning more fun later. It's too late to prove it. Mercer saw to that.' Motson stroked his moustache.

'You think it was Brice?' Stella was looking at the bed. The *Ghostbusters* duvet and heap of cuddly toys evoked a long-lost childhood.

'He had something to do with it. Sickening to think of someone else's hands all over her. Have you got children?'

He was looking at Stella. Jack stared at his shoes.

'No, we haven't.' Stella rarely answered for them both. She nodded at the toys on the pillow. 'Isn't that the teddy bear you told the police was missing?'

Jack stared at where Stella was pointing. For the craziest moment he imagined the bear had got by itself from Brice's workroom to Bryony's old bedroom. It lay in the centre of the pillow, button eyes looking at the ceiling.

'No, naturally it isn't. I bought her another one.' Motson took hold of the bear. 'I found the exact one. The internet is marvellous. Bryony took it everywhere. That bastard has got it. They like keepsakes, these people. I won it for her at a fair. I was her hero.' He sat on a chair by the bed. 'I read to her. Every night. All of Enid Blyton, *Black Beauty*. Girls' stories. These days girls are told to be ashamed of being girls. My Bryony was proud to dress like a queen. She should never have grown up or she'd still be here.' He squeezed the bear, manipulating its legs and arms and twisting the head around. If the bear could feel, Jack imagined it in pain. He quelled the urge to rescue it. Motson was closer to the truth than he could know.

'Your wife died when Bryony was twelve.' Stella stated a fact and waited.

'We managed the loss. Bryony was going to be a bank manager. I said, nursing's too good for you. The Abbey National snapped her up.' But for a twitch of his moustache Motson's features were stony. 'Have we finished here?' He put the bear back on the pillow. Face down.

'Why have you kept Bryony's bedroom intact?' Stella asked.

Jack was impressed. Stella dared to go where he dared not.

Beads of perspiration blossomed on Motson's forehead. Could be nerves, but just as likely it was heat: the window was shut and sun streamed in.

'It's all I have.' Motson tapped his front teeth as if the action was a code. 'It's not one of those ghastly shrines. I have no other use for the room. It's Bryony's and that's that.'

'Do you believe Bryony might come back?' Stella's expression gave nothing away.

'She might as well be dead.' He walked out.

With the speed of a gunslinger, Stella whipped out her phone. She took shots of the room. She dropped the phone into her bag and left.

Jack turned the bear over. It regarded Jack. It seemed to say, 'We know we are imposters.'

'That was more like a little girl's bedroom than an eighteen-year-old's.' Stella nestled into her seat. 'Bryony only left there months before she vanished, she was grown up.'

Jack and Stella were back at the corner table in the Winchcombe deli, charging their phones and sipping drinks. They sat side by side, backs to the wall.

'Going by the file photos, the room in Bryony's flat was adult,' Jack observed. 'I suspect that even before she went, Motson kept her a little girl. Some people can't bear to see their children grow up, he said as much. Others want them adult from day one without the fuss of nappies and nursery school and baby babble.'

'Mum got cross with Dad for getting me babyish stuff, dolls, etc. while I was still young.' Stella was mildly surprised by Jack's view on babies. Jackie had once said he'd frozen emotionally at the age he was when his mother died. That made him about three.

Fanned out on the table was a selection of black-and-white photographs. Stella pulled one across. 'Bryony's room in her flat was less tidy than her childhood bedroom.'

'Motson probably tidies it.'

'He probably painted it too, the decoration looked fresh,' Stella said.

'Whatever Motson said, that bedroom looked like a shrine. Look how he replaced her bear.'

'He described her body being trapped in a drain.' Stella picked up another photograph of the flat bedroom. A small room, the single bed, wardrobe, a slim bookcase and dressing table with a chair slung with clothes made it look crowded. 'I'd have expected Motson would be unable to voice what might have happened to her.'

'He struck me as uncompromising. I'd guess over the years he's imagined many appalling scenarios. My hunch is that the bedroom was less a shrine than a fantasy. When Bryony moved out she was going to nightclubs and we know she met at least one man in a pub. Maybe she left to escape his fairy hopes for her.'

'Working in a bank is hardly a "fairy hope",' Stella retorted.

'Buying another bear isn't facing reality,' Jack said.

'We've got no motive for Motson. Nothing justifies him as a suspect, but something about him didn't add up.' Stella was puzzled by something, but couldn't put her finger on it. She continued looking at the photos, stopping to swipe through the ones she'd taken on her phone.

'Motson was one of those parents who express grief with action, a vacuum that has to be filled. He waged war on Mercer and got him sacked. It would haunt me if my daughter disappeared, I can't imagine functioning, and if not for having another child I'd want to die.'

'He doesn't have another child.' Stella glanced at Jack. Perhaps he was confused with Cassie Baker's parents who still had Karen.

'No, I meant...' Jack broke off.

Stella saw what was puzzling her. She lined up the pictures of Bryony's bedrooms, in her Winchcombe flat and her childhood room in Broadway, and placed her phone displaying the bookshelf by the window at one end. She tapped the CID's picture of Bryony's bedroom in her flat. 'Look at that bookshelf.'

'I saw those children's books in her Broadway bedroom,' Jack said eventually.

'Yes.' Stella slid forward her phone and enlarged her shot of the bookshelf. 'Except where is *The Hobbit*, and those Narnia ones? She's acquired *The Silence of the Lambs*, *Captain Corelli's Mandolin* and Bridget Jones since she moved to Winchcombe. And Delia Smith. Mum made me buy that for Dad one Christmas, she said he couldn't boil an egg. None of those children's books which are visible in my shots of her bedroom are in her Winchcombe flat.'

'Motson could have given them away?' Jack suggested.

'Why do that while taking care to keep the room intact? Besides it's the other way around. He has them.'

'He prefers to remember Bryony as a little girl. Too young to go clubbing or read gory thrillers. Now he's free to portray her how he likes. So no books with sex or violence? Out goes *Silence of the Lambs*.'

'There's no sex in *The Lion, the Witch and the Wardrobe* and *Worzel Gummidge*. They're missing. Motson told us the bear was missing. He didn't mention her books.'

'Probably forgot. She could have dumped them when she moved. It's not like she'd have been kidnapped with them.'

'Look at this one.' Stella dabbed at a faded photostat copy of Bryony sitting cross-legged in a fleece and tracky bottoms on the bed in her Winchcombe flat, her back against the wall, smiling at the camera. 'Those bookshelves to Bryony's right must have come from her bedroom in Broadway, which we'll call

"Motson's Shrine". The shelves are in all the shots of the two rooms.' Stella grabbed her Filofax from her rucksack. 'So there's the bedroom in Bryony's Winchcombe flat, that's her "Adult Bedroom". And her bedroom when she was little and living in her father's Broadway house, her "Child Bedroom".' Stella wrote down each legend and added 'to' and 'from' years beneath. 'Where's that picture of Bryony as a young girl that Motson gave to the media?'

Jack pulled it out from under the others. 'I didn't get why he did that, she's about nine here, miles younger than she was when she went missing. And she has long dark hair. In the picture Jenni the flatmate gave the media she'd had it cut short and spikey.'

'Maybe her dad liked her having it long and when she left home she could do what she liked.' Stella was silent as she digested the stark fact that Bryony's freedom had literally been short-lived.

'That fits in with the "keeping her young" thing.' He sounded tired. Stella was surprised, Jack usually loved hunting through clues.

'See those gaps on the shelves in her adult bedroom? There are a couple on the top and on the shelf below.'

'I have gaps in my bookshelves.'

'Yours are at ends of shelves, these are random as if books were taken out. Question is, who took them and where are they?'

'There's nothing in the file about missing books.' Jack would have a photographic recall of Bryony Motson's papers.

'I doubt anyone noticed. Jenni Wiles might have taken them, but surely unlikely. They'd only known each other since Bryony answered the ad for the room. I am surprised Motson didn't notice them missing.'

'Many fathers wouldn't know what their kids were reading.'

'He said he read to Bryony every night when she was little. He's painstakingly reconstructed her bedroom, even replaced the teddy bear. He was a bank manager, I'd expect him to notice gaps.' Stella was tired too. She tried to grasp an already vanishing half-formed theory.

'It's those!' Jack tapped the photo of Bryony at nine. 'That Worzel Gummidge paperback in this picture of her child's bedroom isn't in the police shot of her Winchcombe adult's bedroom.'

'It *is* in my picture of Motson's Shrine.' Stella tweaked her phone screen. In the pixelated image they made out words on the narrow spine of one of the books: '*Worzel Gummidge* by Barbara Euphan Todd.'

She felt a plunge of disappointment. Her hunch had hit a dead end.

'I had that book…' Jack was saying. 'Actually no, not that edition, I had… Oh!'

'What?' Stella clutched at the spark.

'*Worzel Gummidge* is different! This copy in Motson's Shrine is newer than the book in the picture of Bryony as a girl. The book to the right of her head in Child Bedroom is the same edition as mine, published after it was on television. The spine's torn, looks like she gave it some welly. Maybe she lost it and replaced it?'

'Except it's not in her Winchcombe flat. Nor is that one, *The Box of…*' Stella enlarged the picture on her phone.

'*Delights*!' Jack exclaimed. 'I wanted to be Abner Brown, he's the baddie!'

'It's a different edition to the one in Child Bedroom and it's not in Adult Bedroom either.' Stella articulated her fast-reviving hunch. 'This explains the gaps on the bookshelves in the CID picture of Adult Bedroom. After Motson got back his daughter's stuff, he ditched her grown-up novels and replaced these kids' books. He knows full well that they're missing!'

She scribbled on her Filofax and, finishing, slid the result across to Jack.

Books	Child's Bedroom (Broadway)	Adult's Bedroom (Winchcombe)	Motson's Shrine (Broadway)
	1981–1999	1999–1999	2016
Worzel Gummidge	TV Edition	Missing	Later edition
The Box of Delights	✓	Missing	Later edition
The Lion, Witch and Wardrobe	✓	Missing	Later edition
Adult novels, Bridget Jones, etc.	✗	Present	Missing
Teddy Bear	✓	Missing	Motson Replaced

'Charles Brice must have gone to Bryony's flat and taken her books along with her and her bear?'

'When Bryony's bag was found, there were no books. If it was Brice. My money's on Brian Motson. He couldn't bear for her to grow up. He sees her coming out of the nightclub and picks her up from the bus stop. Gets out of the car, they row. He dumps the bag to make it look like kidnap and hides her body.'

'She would have trusted Brice too. And what about the bear?' Jack pointed out.

'We've only his word for it that the bear in her room isn't her bear. He wouldn't co-operate with Mercer. I think we should tell the police.'

'He co-operated with us. He could have hidden the bear.' Jack slid the Filofax back to her. 'Stella, I've something to te—'

'Broccoli and goats' cheese quiche and cheese roll!' A woman in a yellow 'Winchcombe Deli' apron was holding two plates.

Jack and Stella had forgotten they'd ordered food. As Stella hastily gathered up the photos her phone rang.

'Hi Graham.' Five minutes later, the call over, Stella leaned across to Jack, 'Barry's in intensive care. He could die.'

'That's awful.' Jack dabbed up crumbs of pastry from his plate. 'Why was Graham calling? I'd have expected Jackie to ring.'

'He wasn't calling because Barry's in hospital. Or not just that. He said when they were young Barry had a penny key-ring for the year he was born. 1955. Graham told Jackie that when he came back from Winchcombe after the camping, Barry was on the doorstep. He'd packed his key and couldn't be bothered to go through his bag...' Stella tailed off.

'What are you saying?' Jack had finished his quiche.

Stella put down her cheese roll. 'Graham's thinks Barry met a girl when they were in Winchcombe. Graham didn't want to know because Barry was engaged to Yvonne. He said if it was Cassie and she was pushing Barry to dump Yvonne, he doesn't know what Barry would have done.'

'People commit murder if the spot they're in is tight enough.'

'I remember Jackie saying Barry worked for his father-in-law's insurance brokerage after school. If his boss had found out Barry had cheated on his daughter he wouldn't have been able to take over the business and become a millionaire.' Stella sighed, 'Mercer was fixed on Brice like it was personal. We've only been working this case a few days and already we've got a football team of suspects. It strikes me the only person who didn't murder Cassie Baker is Charles Brice.' She shook her head. 'I can't see Barry as a murderer. He's nice.'

'Nice people kill.' Jack nodded at the cheese roll. 'Are you going to eat that?'

Chapter Forty-Four

'Barry is not a murderer!' Jackie assured Graham.

'Come on, Jackie, you don't know that.'

It was nine o'clock in the morning. Jackie and Graham were back in the hospital car park. Graham was dressed casually in leather Adidas trainers and a pink cotton shirt worn outside his boot-cut jeans.

'I've known him practically all my life and you've known him all yours. We'd know,' Jackie insisted. Perhaps they did. *Perhaps they always had.*

'The Yorkshire Ripper's sisters didn't know he was the Yorkshire Ripper. People don't know what their family gets up to. We've no idea what our sons are doing at this moment.'

'Nick will be asleep still and Mark will be in the office,' Jackie said.

'Did we have any idea Emma would leave Nick? Yeah, OK, you did, but you get what I mean.' Graham reached into the car and placed the parking ticket on the dashboard.

'There's probably a simple explanation for the penny. When he's better Barry will give it to us,' Jackie said.

'Simple, yes. Barry had a fling with Cassie Baker when we were in Winchcombe. He went to that house, the penny proves it.'

'You're running ahead, the penny doesn't prove Barry knew Cassie Baker.'

'Charlie knew Cassie Baker's best friend Lauren Spicer. We both know that. Odds are my brother was shagging her! Why didn't he go to the police?'

'Why didn't we tell the police we were there?' Jackie said.

'Because we weren't there. But actually, yes, when they found Cassie Baker's body we should have gone to the police. That night he was round at ours, Barry didn't want you to tell Stella that Mercer's daughter came to the office.'

'Nor did you.' Jackie reminded him.

'I'm no better than my brother. I suspected he was up to something and I never looked closer. I told myself I didn't want to think about that time when I had to watch you and Charlie all over each other. All the time, Barry was getting to me. The only reason he'd have stayed out all those nights was because of a girl.'

'Stop it, Gray!' Jackie told him. 'That key-ring might not belong to Barry.'

'It's his key.' Graham narrowed his eyes and looked across to the hospital building.

'And as I've said, so what if it is? We all went to the aunt's house. She let us use her loo. Barry could have dropped it then.'

'Why say he left it in our front door? A lie that got him into trouble.' Graham waved thanks to a car that paused to let them over the zebra crossing outside the hospital.

'I won't believe he's a murderer.' Jackie shouldered through swing doors into the ward. 'When he's better, we will get the truth.'

'Why wait until he's better?' Graham spoke between gritted teeth.

'Graham! He's far from strong enough.' Jackie pumped a bottle of alcohol cleanser on the wall and massaged it into her hands.

'Exactly! Catch him off guard.' Graham went to the nurses' station. 'We've come to see Barry Makepeace.'

The nurse, a young woman with an earnest face and heavy

black glasses, consulted a whiteboard behind her. 'Barry Make—He's gone.'

'Gone?' Jackie slipped an arm around her husband's waist. Throughout their conversation, neither of them had considered the possibility that Barry might have died.

'Self-discharged. He said he was better, why block a bed. Thoughtful, but he had a CT scan booked and he was far from well.' The woman snatched off her glasses.

'Couldn't you stop him?' Graham demanded.

'Don't.' Jackie squeezed Graham's arm.

'He had the capacity to decide for himself. He said he'd get tests done privately.'

Graham and Jackie had to stop themselves running from the ward. In the foyer they met Yvonne with a man that for a crazy second Jackie thought was Barry from twenty years ago. It was Joe, his son and business partner. In an expensive blue suit with fine chalk stripes, holding an attaché case, he might have come to get his father to sign an updated life insurance policy. Or a will.

'He's gone!' Graham shouted. 'Where is he?'

'What?' Joe went ashen.

'Gray, for goodness' sake! He's fine, love. Barry has discharged himself,' Jackie reassured her nephew. Yvonne said nothing.

'He'll be at home.' Suddenly Jackie was sure that the house of a thousand lights was the last place Barry would be.

'We've come from there.' Yvonne thrilled with tension. 'I know exactly where he is.'

Her son was on his phone: 'Marcia. Joe. My mother is with me. I'm checking on Dad, is he there... has he rung?... Best you say, yeh?... OK. Email me his diary, he'll have gone to a meeting.'

Jackie had the fleeting conviction that she wouldn't want to work for Joe Makepeace. Like his father, Joe disliked events slipping from his grasp, but unlike Barry he didn't employ tact or charm in the clear-up.

'He never listens to me.' Yvonne was struggling not to cry. The effort gave her a wild staring expression.

'Yvonne, where would Barry be most likely to go?' Jackie asked her softly.

No one spoke as they digested the question. Joe tapped a pointy shoe.

'He's with *her*.' Yvonne sprang to life.

'Mum, really, truly, there is no *her*.' Joe's tone expressed extraordinary kindness for a man who squashed spiders as soon as look at them.

'I suggest going home and waiting for him,' Jackie said. 'We'll go to ours in case he comes there.'

In the car Jackie had a flash recall of Barry taking a phone call the last time she'd seen him. She asked Graham, 'Does the name Grant mean anything to you?'

Chapter Forty-Five

After leaving the Winchcombe deli, Jack had announced he was going to Crow's Nest to check on Lucie. Stella was irritated that Lucie had to be checked on. This was their case. Stella knew full well that Lucie's objective wasn't to solve the case, but to find Matthew Craven and get a scoop. In the process she wouldn't hesitate to stomp over any sensitive situations. In that sense maybe Jack was right to go and check on her.

Outside the Winchcombe Folk and Police Museum (what on earth was that?), at the junction with North Street and the main road, Stella had to step clear of a silver Jeep Defender that, without braking on the corner, mounted the kerb. A policeman's daughter, Stella turned to catch the number. 'G4 SPIC3'. Jack would like it for his list. Gas-pic? She continued along the high street. G for something. Spice maybe. Easy to remember, silly if you were going to drive badly.

Stella rang Beverly. She asked her to find out who Phyllis Brice had sold her house to in 2000 and, if the elderly woman was still alive, where she was now. Stella read Beverly the 'equation' at the back of Mercer's police notebook. ~~L=MC ??~~ SBHH = L/GS TC ✓. Bev liked puzzles. Stella updated her on the case.

'... I'll call you later, Bev.'

'Totally on it!'

Beverly's gung-ho spirit could make Stella fretful, it spoke of deleted files and wiped hard drives. However, standing in the lunchtime sunshine, she was sorry to say goodbye to Beverly. Jack had introduced Stella to the concept of home, but only since being in the country – with no internet and a murderer nearby – did Stella appreciate it. Home included Clean Slate's office with Beverly at her desk.

While talking to Beverly, Stella had taken hazy notice of Beauty Heaven on the other side of the road. Now it struck her, Lucie wasn't the only one who could go undercover. Stella caught a gap in the traffic and, muttering 'Heel' to Stanley, she crossed over. As she led him into the salon she was greeted by a familiar voice.

'Look who it is!' Charlie Brice lounged beside a life-size cut-out of a woman with a gleaming complexion. Ankle propped on a knee, he was grinning. 'Ready to put up your shelves whenever!'

'What can I do for you?' A woman behind the counter, her complexion identical to the cut-out, smiled. A smile largely to do with accentuated eye-liner. Stella knew from the file photos this was Lauren Spicer.

'You've come for a pamper!' Charlie Brice said.

'Ye-es.' Stella felt herself teetering on a high wire with no safety net. She had a haphazard grasp of nuance, yet she got the impression Brice had fed her a prompt. She caught the words 'dry and flaking nails' on a poster behind Lauren Spicer. 'My nails need doing.'

'What were you wanting, darling? Manicure, pedicure, geleration, file and polish, paraffin wax?' Lauren uttered the list in a melodic tone as if calling an infant class register.

'Geleration.' Stella didn't fancy anything involving combustible fuel.

'With or without manicure?'

'With. Without.'

Although he hadn't moved, Stella sensed Brice tense. Why should he care?

'Let me know when you want those shelves,' he murmured.

'You haven't sent me an estimate.'

'Not sent an estimate? You're losing your grip, Chas,' Lauren Spicer said.

'I'd better crack on with it.' He scratched Stanley under the chin.

Lauren Spicer asked for Stella's name. Just in time she remembered Brice thought she was Stella Makepeace. He tipped a hand and left the salon.

'Would you like a glass of water, Stella?' Lauren asked.

'Thank you.'

Lauren Spicer held open a door behind the cut-out woman. Stella envisioned walking inside and never being seen again. Stanley nosed through. Stella followed. The door shut with a hiss. At the bottom of some stairs, the walls were lined with pictures of more brightly smiling women. Others showed hands and feet with nails decorated in vivid colours. Strange fluty warbles came from all around her. The air smelled of a cleaning product Stella hadn't encountered. More than the woozy music and the glacial smiles, this disturbed her. Unused to perfumed oils and unctions, Stella was never going to identify the wafts of geranium oil.

'Sit here for me.' Spicer pulled out a stool by a counter covered in a white cloth on which were bowls, bottles, tubs of cream and a heap of flannels. She gave Stella a beaker of water.

Opposite a chrome rack packed with white towels were two white leather armchairs with footrests. The leather reminded Stella of the house in Bollo Lane where they'd first met Lisa Mercer. It was less than a week ago, but felt like a lifetime.

'We don't allow dogs, but as you know Charlie...' Lauren's tone was lilting.

'I can come back.' Stella had made a spur-of-the-moment decision and, as with such decisions, it was a mistake.

'Don't worry. Your gorgeous little doggy has a lovely soft wool coat – who knitted you, darling? – he won't affect our allergic clients. Besides, you're the last one.' She began filling bowls and arranging metal contraptions. 'I wanted to buy Crow's Nest. The old man wouldn't sell.' She spoke as if it was of no consequence.

'It needs a lot of work,' Stella said by way of consolation. She didn't say that Lisa Mercer had already told her. She felt hopeful: minutes in and Spicer had brought up personal stuff. Sitting in the clinically sealed atmosphere of Beauty Heaven, Stella doubted that Spicer would actually have wanted the ramshackle draughty house that smelled of damp and dead creatures. She'd have wanted the land. She saw Lauren, like Stella herself, happier with a new-build.

'Are you buying it?' Mercer began working Stella's cuticles with a short sharp instrument.

'No. Renting.' Her story must tally with what she'd told Brice.

'There are nicer places to rent in Winchcombe.' She smiled sweetly.

'We wanted to be in the countryside.' Stella said the first thing that came into her head and the last thing she'd ever wanted.

'Creepy, I call it! Where are you from then?' Lauren was tweaking snippets of skin from around Stella's nails. Unsettling though it was, Stella had to look.

'London.' Stella had gone undercover without a persona.

'I hate London, dirty and too many people.' Lauren trimmed each of Stella's nails. She flannelled her fingers then dipped them into the sudsy water. 'You've got lovely hands. Soft skin and nicely shaped fingers. What treatments do you use?'

'Water.' Stella had a feeling this was the wrong answer. 'And soap. I wear gloves to clean.'

'Get a cleaner, that's my motto! No creams.' It was unclear whether last was a question or a statement. Lauren Spicer towelled Stella's hands dry then began working a pink cream that smelled of rose into her fingers, tugging on each one as if testing it was fixed on properly. Cream must be OK.

'Yes. Cream.' Stella guessed you didn't turn up at a beauty salon and admit you never used moisturizer. Terry, or more likely Jack had said, *When undercover, find a point of commonality.*

Stella agreed about the cleaning motto. 'Have you always lived in Winchcombe?'

'Born and bred.' Lauren began filing Stella's nails. Swish swish.

'I suppose you have lots of old friends if you've been here all your life.'

'People have moved away or died.' Not an answer. Swish.

'Died?' Stella feigned what she hoped was a mix of sorrow and surprise.

'My best friend was eighteen when she passed. Bless her.'

'That's young, cancer, I suppose.' It didn't sit well with Stella to probe. She guessed that on her undercover mission to the salon Lucie May had done a better job.

'Murder.' Swish swish.

'Goodness. Don't say more if you'd rather not.'

'It was a… little while ago.' Lauren had seen she'd be revealing her age. Presumably that, as the proprietor of a beauty parlour, she must imply she had the gift of eternal youth. 'It was a big story. You're too young.' Lauren treated Stella to a special smile. 'In 1999 Cassandra Baker was found buried in some ancient monument up the road from here. We last saw her in 1977, it was a shock to discover she'd been there dead for twenty years. Funny that Charlie didn't tell you. It's his claim to fame.'

'He came to do an estimate.' If Spicer compared notes with Charles Brice, she'd realize Stella was pretending ignorance. 'He did mention it.'

'The man who killed her is just out of prison. Everyone deserves a second chance, don't you think?'

'If he was guilty. Charlie did say Mercer thought it was him.' Lauren Spicer knew Craven had been released. So much for Lucie's scoop.

'Matthew Craven *was* guilty.' Spicer increased the speed of her filing, whizzing the emery board over each of Stella's nails.

'Did you know him?' Stella tried a wide-eyed expression. She was leaning towards the view that Craven had killed Cassie

Baker after all. And that Brian Motson had murdered his own daughter.

'He was my boyfriend. Small town, choice is limited.' Lauren flapped at a cloud of nail dust. 'When they'd found her, Craven asked me to tell the police a little fib about where he was the night they think she was killed.' She tapped at the file as if adjusting mercury on a thermometer. 'See, I never thought it was really him. I'm telling you because you'll hear gossip, better you hear it from me.'

'We trust our friends,' Stella opined.

'More fool me. What colour are you going for, Stella?'

'Colour?'

'On your nails, what shade gel?' Lauren fanned out a swatch of tints painted on plastic in front of Stella.

Geleration. 'Perhaps I'll keep them bare, empty...' Stella pricked with heat. Beautifying came with a whole new vocabulary. She should have mugged up.

'As you like. Me and Cassie were going to run a salon in Cheltenham. She said London, I said Cheltenham, start there, build outwards. I thought she'd gone without me. I often think of how Cassie would love this place.' She did a Clarins smile and deftly dotted each of Stella's nails with drops of almond oil.

A voice spoke from the shadows. 'I'm off now.'

Taken by surprise, Stella jerked her hand away from Spicer.

'You scared her!' Spicer gave a throaty laugh. Her eyes remained impassive.

'Sorry, babes.' A man, with 'Beauty Heaven' on a T-shirt outlining a six-pack chest, was crushing an empty Evian bottle between his palms.

'You didn't scare me.' Blond locks. Deep tan. Stella was looking at a young George Michael. She hadn't heard him approach. The geleration colour swatch became multiple fingers pointing at her. Stella was in a foreign land.

'That stuff in the back needs sorting.' The man tossed the crushed plastic into a chrome swing bin by the nail counter.

'I said, I'll deal with it. I'll be all right. *Go.*' Lauren massaged Stella's hands, working the ligaments a little hard, Stella thought.

Balancing on his haunches, the man grabbed Stanley's head and scrubbed it heartily. 'Who's this cute chap?'

Stanley's moustache twitched, his lip curled. Stella glimpsed teeth. Stanley's tolerance for petting was limited. 'Actually, he can bite, best not to—'

'He won't hurt me.' The man went on ruffling Stanley's head.

Beneath the fluty music Stella heard a growl. With her left hand clasped in Lauren's she was powerless when Stanley snapped at the man's finger.

'*Ouch.*' Nursing his hand, the man leapt up.

'She told you not to touch!'

'My fault.' The man didn't achieve sincere.

'I'm so sorry!' Stella managed. The calming music tootled on, the white walls, the women with glacial smiles became oppressive. Stella felt far from calm.

'Don't apologize, Stella. The dog was protecting you. Please excuse me.' Lauren ushered George Michael up the stairs.

Stella caught the hiss of the outer door. Silence. She knew that when a dog does something wrong the owner should ignore it. Telling Stanley off would be to give him attention. She counted to ten and was about to look at him when her phone rang.

Beverly. She didn't want to talk to her in the salon, but it was rare to have both a strong phone signal and battery. She couldn't afford to wait. An eye on the staircase, Stella took the risk.

'I checked that house!' Beverly was speaking so close to the microphone Stella had the sensation of breath on her ear. Nervous that in the deathly quiet Beverly's voice would carry, Stella cupped her hand over the earpiece. 'Guess what, Charles Brice's aunty isn't dead. She's massively old, older than my nan was. But she's alive.' There was silence, during which Stella guessed Beverly was digesting the fact that a person could be younger than another person but die first. Something Stella herself could find hard to grasp. '… She's ninety-one and in an old people's home in Winchcombe. I've got the details, wait a sec…'

'Five Trees,' Stella whispered.

'You know!' Beverly was disappointed.

'Just a guess.' Stella strained to listen for Lauren Spicer's return.

'She's called Phyllis Brice – as you know too – and she sold the house to SBH Holdings. Are you in a library? Is that why you're whispering?'

'No, in a beauty parlour,' she hissed.

'Oh! That's nice.' Beverly would be recalibrating her view of Stella.

'Anything else?' Stella heard a sound. So slight, she could have missed it. Stanley. She looked behind the white leather recliner where he'd scampered after biting George Michael. *He wasn't there.*

'So, SBH Holdings is owned by Lauren Spicer. I guess you know that too.' Beverly sounded downcast. 'So that thing you told me – 'SBHH' – is Spicer Beauty Heaven Holdings.'

'Brilliant work, Bev.' Stella nearly forgot to be quiet. Beverly, unlike Lucie, didn't balk at doing plodding research.

'There's more, Matthew Craven and Lauren Spicer were business partners.'

'How do you know?' Stella was scouring the nail bar. Where was Stanley?

'I looked on the dark web.' Beverly was casual.

'What?' Was that even legal?

'Joke! I checked with Companies House. Craven stopped being a director when he went inside so she's taken on another one. He's called Grant Smith. He's quite young.'

George Michael.

'You are a Wonderhorse!' Stella used Jack's name for her. She looked behind the rack of folded towels, hoping to see a remorseful poodle. Nothing. She noticed a white curtain along the end wall. She pulled it aside.

'Stella, that's not all. A thought, since we're keeping open minds...'

'Go on.' Stella was beginning to think having an open mind was overrated. Was it easier to follow Mercer, fix on an idea and test every fact against it?

'What if Bryony isn't dead?' Stella listened to Beverly and then closed the line.

Beyond the curtain was a passage. At the far end a dimmed ceiling spot spilled faint light onto Stanley snuffling along the bottom of a door.

Stella crept along the passage and grabbed Stanley's trailing lead. Her fringe dropped forward into one eye, making it smart. She shoved it back and smelled the almond oil that Lauren had rubbed into her nails.

Stanley grasped his end of the lead between his teeth and embarked on a tug of war. Stella gave in and moved towards the closed door. Stanley was her excuse to check out the salon. Terry, and the murder manual, said that talking wasn't enough. *To build a profile, check out where the target lives, where they work, learn what they do and how they do it.*

Any moment now, Lauren would come downstairs. Stella opened the door.

The body lay face up on a white sheeted table, hands by the sides, stark features outlined in the soft lighting. A man with short hair, in jeans and a Beauty Heaven T-shirt.

Stella became aware of the music swelling as, keeping Stanley on a short leash, she stepped over to the bed. She placed a manicured finger on the man's neck. Prepared for stiffened cold skin – this wasn't her first corpse – Stella was shocked to feel a pulse.

The man rose up. Stanley barked.

'I thought you were dead.' Stella stifled a bark of her own as the man swung bare feet over the side of the bed and stood up.

She didn't need an introduction. The last picture she had seen was taken seventeen years ago, but the thin foxy features, lank hair and unshaven chin were little changed. The man now standing by the door, cutting off her exit, was Matthew Craven. The boastful estate agent imprisoned for Cassie Baker's murder.

Craven was shorter than Stella. She'd rather expected a murderer (or suspected murderer) to be tall. His thick arms were dark with tattoos. A tabloid identikit of a killer. Stella resisted putting a hand to her nose as a rank odour of stale sweat hit her. She caught a tiny click as Craven swung shut the door.

'My dog bites.' Her throat was paralysed, she was paralysed.

'Sure he does.' Craven grabbed Stanley's head and shook it. 'A proper little Rottweiler, aren't you, boy!' He lifted Stanley up. He spoke with a nasal twang that Stella rather expected of a murderer.

She watched, hawk-eyed and breath held, for the tell-tale warning signs of anger. Her heart plummeted when, instead of sinking his teeth into Craven's neck as she found herself willing him to do, Stanley started washing Craven's face. Stella heard the rasp of his tongue as he slathered across Craven's stubble. Her disgust was eclipsed by the implacable realization that she was trapped with a murderer. She dare not try to escape and call Lauren because while Craven was enduring Stanley's attentions, she knew he wouldn't hesitate to break her dog's neck. As she was thinking this, the door burst open, just missing Craven.

Lauren Spicer was in the doorway. 'You've seen him! Now leave and go and write up your filth!'

Stella gaped. Lauren wasn't shouting at Craven. She was looking at Stella.

'Filth?' Relief and panic coursed through her simultaneously, tottering against the treatment bed, Stella vaguely thought of cleaning.

'Who rents a tumbledown wreck? You must think me an idiot! You fooled Charlie, but not me. You didn't come for a pamper, *Lucille bloody May*!'

'I'm not Lu...' Even as they felt about to give way beneath her, Stella thought on her feet. Keeping Stanley in the corner of her eye she braced her shoulders. 'You an idiot, *babes*? No way! But who knew Craven was snoozing in your boudoir?' She blew a puff of imaginary smoke at the ceiling. 'What if the cops found out he's breaking the terms of his release?'

'What if they did?' Craven rubbed his face against Stanley's fur. Stella had to stop herself flying at him. If she showed Stanley she was scared he would attack Craven. Glancing at Lauren, Stella was astonished to see, from her expression, that the beautician was thinking the same thing.

That stuff in the back needs dealing with.

George Michael-Grant had meant Matthew Craven. Lauren had reassured him she'd be 'all right'. She was like Stella, she thought she could handle anything. And, like Stella, Lauren was out of her depth. Stella was their only hope.

'Face it, love, we're going to press on with this anyway. "No Comment" is boring, readers make up the rest and the rest is *way* worse than the truth. Why don't you give me your side of the story?' She smiled at Craven. She had to make him think she put Lauren in his camp; if he sensed she was helping her, he'd trap them both.

'Get out,' Lauren Spicer whispered at her from behind Craven. Her eyes were pleading. Stella couldn't leave without Stanley. Lucie the Reporter wouldn't leave without a juicy quote.

'First question. Why is Matthew Craven, the man who killed your best mate, in your massage room? Second, what's your relationship with Charlie Brice and with Paul Mercer?' Stella saw Stanley tense. He didn't recognize her. She didn't recognize herself. Fear barely kept at bay, Stella felt herself getting into Lucie's stride. 'Third, why would you do Mercer's shopping?'

'Say nothing, Laurie, it's none of her business,' Craven snarled.

'Don't call me "Laurie",' Lauren told him.

'Let's look at that vanishing alibi.' Stella-Lucie steamed on. 'Now you see it, now you don't. You said you were shagging this gorgeous fella. Then you find out Craven's slipped a good-luck charm next to his ex's body and bish-bash-bosh goes your alibi and lover-boy's on remand. Then he has a chatette with another con through a sewer pipe between cells and, Bob's your uncle, down he goes for fifteen years. Now he's here napping in your parlour. What happened inside, Matty? D'you get religion? She dobs you in and you're all palsy-walsy, how does that work?'

'Leave now!' Lauren Spicer retreated down the passage.

'Paul Mercer was your only friend, Matt. He said you were innocent as a baby. Now he's dead. Was he right or was he wrong?' Stella-Lucie sang the last words to the tune of the Clash's 'Should I Stay or Should I Go'.

'I said go,' Lauren shouted.

'I should do as she asks.' Matthew Craven opened his arms wide as if about to be frisked and Stanley fell to the floor.

He landed badly, paws splaying. Squealing with pain and gazing sorrowfully at Stella, he held up a front paw. She snatched him up and strode into the passage. Her back tingled with the certainty that Craven would stick a knife into her. *One, two, three.* Halfway along the passage she allowed herself a glance behind her. Craven lay on the bed, hands behind his head, staring at the ceiling. Stella had an image of him in his prison cell, waiting out the years.

Lauren Spicer drummed the banister rail as she waited at the bottom of the staircase. 'We've had years of you lot camping out in Winchcombe, filling up the parking bays, staking out the pubs, making our lives a misery. We're a tight community, real people with lives. You wheedle your way in and then print lies, twisting the truth into trash. Leave us alone!' As she frogmarched Stella upstairs, Lauren raised her voice as if she needed Craven to hear her. By withdrawing her alibi, Spicer had consigned Matthew Craven to a life sentence. That would make anyone, guilty or innocent, scary. Lauren was in danger. Grant Smith had known that too.

'Lauren, come with me now, I can't leave you there. With him.' Stepping onto the pavement, Stella forgot to be Lucie. She turned around in time to see a hand flip the sign to 'Closed'.

Stella pushed on the salon door. Lauren had locked it. Stepping back to the kerb she rang the number on the signage above the window.

'No one at Beauty Heaven can attend to you right now...'

It was early-closing day. Awnings had been retracted, the pavement had emptied. Stella wandered along in an agony of indecision. Should she call the police?

She stopped outside the butcher's window. Instead of cuts of meat, an array of model farm animals, pigs, sheep, cows and a chicken larger than the rest were displayed. Dimly Stella thought how country people weren't squeamish about associating a lamb chop with a lamb.

By the time the police arrived, Craven would be gone and Lauren – and Grant – would deny he'd been there. Stella had lied about her identity. Lauren had status in this 'tight community'. It would be Stella's word against theirs.

G4 SPIC3

Grant for Spicer. Grant Smith, the man who had taken Craven's place as a director of Lauren's company. Had he taken Craven's place in more ways than one? Was that what Spicer was scared that she would tell him?

Stella called Jack.

'Lucie! What have you done— Stella, hey!'

'*I'm going to be a father*,' Endora yelled in the background.

She fought disappointment; Lucie was there. 'Could you meet me at Five Trees?'

'Copy that. On my way.' For some reason, Jack put on an American accent.

Stella was outside the nursing home when her phone rang. It was Lisa Mercer.

'The detective got the last laugh!' Her voice grated down the receiver.

'What detective?' Stella considered her manicured nails.

'My excuse for a father. He's only gone and left everything to that Spicer bitch. Just for shopping at the Co-op!'

Chapter Forty-Six

After Jack left Stella, he drove back to Crow's Nest. He should have stayed with Stella, they were meant to be a team, but he'd made a mess of that and now must find Lucie May and try to save things. 'Lucie!' He jumped out of the van and sprinted around the house to the back.

He expected to see Lucie in the orchard with her metal detector, but the trees were silent and empty. At his feet, a bee buzzed in the petals of an evening primrose, the sound amplified in the hot, heavy air.

The kitchen door was locked. Through the window, Jack could see Endora in her cage on the table. He caught himself about to ask the budgie to open the door.

'Lucie! We need to talk!' He banged on the door. Giving up, he raced back to the drive. The front door was open.

'Lucie?' She hadn't said she was going out. Lucie knew they had a stalker, yet she'd left Endora on her own with the door unlocked. Jack rushed along the hall to the kitchen.

'*Where's Lucie!*' the bird shrieked at him.

'You and me both.' Jack unhooked the cage and carried it into the sitting room. The papers on the table were in the same neat piles as when he and Stella had left after breakfast. Lucie was adept at covering her tracks. Around him the silence swelled.

He let Endora out of her cage. She fluttered onto his shoulder and, as he climbed the stairs, began studiously nibbling at his ear.

'Lucie!' Even in the day, little light reached the corridor. The smell of dead crow still lingered.

Jack hadn't been able to tell Stella why he needed to 'check on', as he'd put it, Lucie. After his and Lucie's chat in the garden last night, he'd been feeling as bad as if he himself was a murderer. The enormity of his betrayal to Stella burnt as if his skin was flayed. He would show Stella the teddy bear. She'd understand why he believed Charles Brice was the killer. She'd realize it wasn't Brian Motson. If it meant she never wanted to see Jack again – it would mean that – at least Stella would have all the facts. Knowledge was power and he'd given power to Lucie at Stella's expense.

With foreboding, Jack went into Stella's room. No Lucie. Despite the closed windows, the air smelled fresh, of Stella's perfume and furniture polish. A fly buzzed lazily around the ceiling. Another lay dead on the window sill beside a candle holder, the wax burnt to a stub. Jack opened the casement and, pinching up the dead fly, tossed it out. He waved and flapped at the live fly until it flew out through the aperture.

He scanned the room. He was sure that, taking care not to disturb a single object, Lucie had taken advantage of Stella's absence to go through her personal things. He felt angry, but he was no better. Stella's murder manual was by the bed; she'd read more since he last looked.

Lucie wouldn't have stopped at Stella.

Jack raced along the passage to his own bedroom, Endora soaring above him. Jack ripped open his bag. With Endora watching attentively from his bedhead, he unzipped his washbag. Razor, toothpaste and brush, deodorant, dental floss. He plunged his hand into every pocket. He turned the canvas grip upside down and shook out the contents. Underwear, books, the washbag. Although Lisa had told Stella and him they could stay, Jack hadn't unpacked. Hanging his clothes in a wardrobe was akin to sending him to boarding school. Frantically, he ran a hand around the grip's lining. Someone had taken Bryony Motson's teddy bear from his bag. He knew exactly who that someone was.

His phone rang.

'Lucie! What have you done— Stella, hey!' He dashed perspiration from his forehead.

'*I'm going to be a father,*' Endora yelled.

Jack mouthed 'Shut up!' at Endora.

'Could you meet me at Five Trees?'

'Copy that. On my way.' In a fluster he did a Philip Marlowe voice.

He tried to call Lucie. The answering voice invited him to leave a message.

'Ring when you get this. We need to talk. *Now!*'

He clambered into the van. Taking a bend on the Old Brockhampton Road, Jack was startled by Humphrey Bogart.

'*Here's looking at you, kid.*'

He'd forgotten to put Endora back in her cage.

Chapter Forty-Seven

'You're a Wonderhorse!'

Yesss! Beverly was ecstatic. Stella had never called her that before. Alone in the office, she permitted herself two spins of her chair.

Someone was watching through the glass in the door.

That insurance company upstairs had left the latch up again. Beverly knew that if anyone was in Clean Slate by themselves, they must not let a casual stranger into the office.

'Can I help... Oh hi!' Beverly opened the door.

'What are you up to this morning, Bev?'

Smiling warmly, Barry Makepeace wandered over to Beverly's monitor and looked at the screen. In grainy black and white, Cassie Baker's face smiled back.

'I'm doing research for Stella?' In 'Wonderhorse' mode, Beverly's upward inflection at the end of sentences, trained out of her by Jackie, was back with a vengeance.

'What sort of research does a cleaning company do?' Barry was pleasant. He dabbed at sweat on his face with a silk hanky although the room wasn't yet warm.

'It's for this case Stella and Jack are working on?'

'How's that going?' Barry wheeled Jackie's chair around the desks and sat down next to Beverly.

'I've tracked down some vital information.' Beverly hovered behind her chair. 'Jackie's not in this morning. She left a message, she didn't say why.'

'No worries. You're handling the office search, aren't you?' He sat back in his chair as if he was out of breath from running.

'Well...' Puffed up though Beverly was by Stella's praise, 'handling' overstated her role. With Jackie not being there, she could handle it now. 'How can I help?'

'I've found another couple of places. One's in Ealing. The other's in Olympia. Worth a look.' Regarding Cassie Baker's long-ago smile, Barry gave a yawn. 'What did you find out for Stella?'

Beverly was clear the case was confidential, but Barry was part of Jackie's family. It would be OK to tell him. Plus he was in Winchcombe with Jackie and Graham when they were kids. That made him a witness. Beverly might elicit something from him that would make her even more of a Wonderhorse. Sitting down, she decided to tell Barry her theory.

'I'm thinking the key to this is the "heart-throb". Karen Baker, Cassie's younger sister, told the police Cassie said she'd met a bloke she called a heart-throb. So who was this bloke? Paul Mercer thought it was Charlie Brice. He had a thing going with this girl Lauren Spicer so Stella doesn't think it's him.' She rubbed her chin ruminatively. 'I'm not so sure.'

'Karen could have made it up. She was just a kid.' Barry was still looking at the fuzzy image of the dead girl. He drew a breath as if winded. 'Maybe Karen got it wrong and Cass said she wanted to *meet* a heart-throb.'

'Karen's had years to admit she made a mistake and never has.' Beverly thought that Barry shouldn't call Cassie 'Cass'. On the anniversary of when Madeleine McCann went missing, Stella had complained the papers called the little girl 'Maddie' like they knew her. Thinking again that, since Barry was a witness, she shouldn't waste an opportunity, Beverly asked, 'You guys were camping at that time. Did you meet Cassie?'

'Stella asked me that.'

'And you said?'

'You're good, Bev! I said we were staying outside Winchcombe. It was some weeks before.'

'You did go into Winchcombe, didn't you?'

'For sure. We did a bit of food shopping, the pub, got fish and chips, we didn't mix much.'

'You went to the pub. What about then?' Beverly considered that she should make Barry a hot drink, he looked like he'd run a marathon, but you could ruin everything by interrupting an interrogation.

'There were girls. But the thing is, Bev...' he swivelled so that his knees bumped against Beverly's chair, 'I was engaged to Yvonne. I was spoken for, as we used to say. Charlie Brice was more of a one for the girls. He was with our Jackie and getting off with Lauren Spicer at the same time! Jackie dumped him. Gotta say he deserved it. Our Graham didn't waste his time, drove her home and married her!'

'Do you think Brice is the killer?' Beverly fired a direct question.

'I have no idea, Bev.' Barry tweaked the collar of his shirt at the back, wincing as if in pain.

'I've got a hunch.' Beverly went to the whiteboard, wiped clean since the case meeting. 'I'm thinking that the heart-throb and the killer are not the same person.' She wrote 'Killer' and 'Heart-throb' on the board. 'I think *he*,' she drew a heart around 'Heart-throb', 'is innocent. He didn't kill anyone, but is too scared to come forward in case he's jailed for what *he* did.' She boxed in 'Killer' with a rectangle.

'Got me there, Bev!' Barry raked a hand through his mane of hair. Beverly noticed he wore a plastic bracelet like the one her nana had on in hospital. After she died, Beverly kept the bracelet. Her mum had called her morbid.

Beverly got up and flicked on the kettle. 'I'm thinking Heart-throb isn't from Winchcombe or someone would know him. Being summer, and the Queen's Silver Jubilee, there were tourists. Mr Mercer's team interviewed loads and crossed them off. Jackie said the police didn't know you guys were there. Obviously Mr Heart-throb wasn't Jackie and no way was it Graham cos he loved Jackie. That leaves Brice. But...' Beverly was pleased, she'd got several pieces of the jigsaw for Stella and Jack.

'What about me? I was there too, don't forget.' Barry raised one eyebrow. He got up and joined Beverly by the kettle.

Outside, a bus stopped. Several passengers looked into the window of an office above a mini-mart and idly noticed two people silhouetted through the glass. The bus continued its stop-start journey along Shepherd's Bush Green to the Holland Park interchange.

'No way was it you, Mr Makepeace.' Beverly drew herself up. She suspected Barry Makepeace wasn't taking her seriously. 'Tell you what, I'd really like to meet this Brice, I'm sure I'd know if he's a killer.'

'I bet you would. Why don't you?' Barry leaned against the filing cabinet.

'I can't go to Winchcombe without permission.' Beverly was firm.

'I'll take you. That counts as permission.'

'That's kind, but Brice knows you. He'd guess I had an ulterior motive.' Beverly didn't want to tell Barry that his permission didn't count. He liked being one of the Clean Slate team.

'I bet you could come up with something, you're good at that. Offer him cleaning, ask for directions. You'll be great. Think how pleased Stella will be.'

Watching a number 295 bus pull out into the middle lane on the green, Beverly buzzed through pros and cons. No cons. The biggest pro was, if she identified Heart-throb, Stella would make her a permanent Wonderhorse. 'Let's do it.'

Beverly wrote a note to Jackie. Downstairs, she locked shut the street door after her. Some might call this shutting the stable door after the horse – Wonder or otherwise – had bolted. Beverly, sinking into the comfy upholstery of Barry's Shogun, fixed on nailing Charles Brice and Mystery Heart-throb, wasn't one of them.

Chapter Forty-Eight

'I'll sue her for every penny!' The words fizzed between Lisa Mercer's clenched teeth.

'It does seem odd.' Stella risked a response. When Stanley was like this it was best to say nothing or he got worse.

'You say she did his shopping,' Jack asked. 'Was that all she did for your father?'

'What are you implying?'

'Did she help out around the house?' Endora sat on Jack's shoulder. Stella had been about to ask why he'd brought her when Lisa Mercer beckoned them into her office. So far, Lisa hadn't appeared to have seen the budgie.

Outside, a woman was loading a holdall into a Ford Fiesta with 'Hair Today' stencilled on the side. Stella observed it was an unwise name for a hairdresser, especially if you had clients in a nursing home. She tuned back to Lisa Mercer.

'That bitch was there every day cooking crap for him, washing his soiled pants. She'll have rooted in his stuff and got his will. Even as a kid Lauren got men round her little finger. Flashing her nails, simpering, they wet themselves. She *groomed* him!' Lisa stormed.

Stella couldn't picture Paul Mercer – however unwell – at the beck and call of anyone, even Lauren Spicer who she knew was no pushover. If Terry had been housebound and someone helped him, Stella supposed she'd have been grateful. She remembered she'd left Lauren alone in the salon with Matthew Craven. She should go back. Coming back to Winchcombe, Craven was breaking the terms of his bail.

'I know what she'd say. I neglected my poor infirm father for old people who pay hard cash. You don't know the half!'

'It's easier to look after other people's relatives,' Jack said. 'Speaking of which, we understand you have Charles Brice's aunt residing here?'

Residing? Stella looked at Jack. He was paler than pale. In the deli yesterday, Jack had said he wanted to talk to her. It must be about getting back with Bella. She wasn't sure she wanted to know. He hadn't mentioned it at breakfast.

'Try having a copper for a father.' Lisa flung a glance at Stella, perhaps recalling that, as Terry Darnell's daughter, Stella had tried having one.

'My dad...' She had a succession of childhood memories of times with her dad, climbing over park gates at night and collecting conkers. When her wellington boot stuck in river mud he'd saved her from sinking for ever. Terry had taught her to ride a bike. He took her to see the horses at Hammersmith police station.

'There's me, a whisker from having to turf out my old people.' A shadow passed across Lisa Mercer's face. She patted her hair, styled not, Stella guessed, by Hair Today.

'You knew Lauren Spicer when she was a little girl?' Stella picked up on Mercer's earlier remark.

'I did not *know* her! I was a baby when she was little,' Lisa snorted. 'Her mother was a single parent, never saw her with a man. She'd leave that girl alone at night and go cleaning. Mercer and his mates were too soft to charge her mother with neglect. He even babysat her in the station on Gretton Road. Social services should have waded in and removed Lauren. As it was, she saw more of Dad than me. Now look what's happened!'

'That must be rotten for you.' Jack wouldn't point out that far from abandoning her baby at home, Lauren's mother had left her with the police. If he could babysit his twins, he'd never leave their nursery. If only... he pulled himself up: 'If we could just get a family perspective on Charlie Brice... And talk to his aunt.'

'Phyllis will put you straight on Lauren Spicer. The trouble she had with her! No one visits Phyllis except that Charlie. He'll be after whatever she's got left.' Perhaps because Lisa had seen benefit in them getting Phyllis Brice's low opinion of her new enemy, she relented. Getting up and smoothing her skirt she said, 'This way.'

They passed down the carpeted corridors, left and right, up some stairs and down others. Endora rode on Jack's shoulder, swaying with his steps with the skill of a motorbike pillion passenger. Glancing into the rooms, Stella saw the man in the cot was lying in the same position as on their visit to Ralph Baker the day before. She hoped, if the home closed, he wouldn't be dumped just anywhere.

Phyllis Brice sat by herself in the lounge where they'd met Ralph Baker. A smell of lavender wafted in through doors onto a garden. This time the lounge was scented with Jangro Luxury Wax Furniture Polish; Stella was distantly gratified that Lisa didn't stint on cleaning materials.

A group of elderly people – Stella recognized Ralph Baker among them – sat around a table under a tree singing to Dusty Springfield's 'You Don't Have to Say You Love Me'.

'These two people are friends of your nephew, Phyll. You can tell them to go away,' Lisa Mercer informed her before going away herself.

Phyllis Brice was peering through a magnifying glass at a complex line drawing of a flower. On the table beside her was a box of coloured pencils.

'Any friends of that rapscallion can stay.' Phyllis Brice began shading in the line drawing. Stella was impressed by her steady hand.

'We're not friends,' Stella said before Jack came up with some story involving words like 'residing'. 'We're Stella and Jack and we're investigating the disappearance of Bryony Motson and the murder of Cassie Baker. We understand you knew her, Miss, er Ms Brice.' Stella was surprised to see the woman wore lace-ups, as if about to go out. She'd imagined the ninety-something incarcerated at Five Trees.

'I hope you're not here to try to implicate Charles in murder. He's had enough bother in his life.' She looked sternly at Jack as if he specifically would implicate her nephew.

'We're keeping an open mind. But it's looking increasingly unlikely that Charles was involved.' Stella hoped she was speaking the truth. Glancing at Jack, she expected him to agree. He said nothing. 'I understood that you knew Cassie?' Old people forgot things.

'I coached her in maths, that's not knowing her. Stella is a lovely name. You look like you're a bright star.' Phyllis Brice sharpened a light blue pencil. Wood shavings fluttered to the floor to join others there.

'Thank you.' Terry had once called her his 'little star'. Stella was momentarily thrown off course. 'Did Lauren come to your house or did you go to hers?'

'They all came to me: Cassandra, Lauren and Michael, Matthew, Karen. Most of their homes were ill-suited to study.'

In their deliberations, Phyllis Brice had figured only as the aunt of a suspect and the owner of the ruined house. Not in her own right with a life and a career. Stella asked, 'What was your job?'

'I taught mathematics at Cheltenham Ladies' and gave private lessons to local children at the Winchcombe Abbey Primary. Gratis, you understand. This is a tight community.' Phyllis Brice had used the same phrase as Lauren, Stella noticed as she watched Phyllis colouring in a petal. 'It was a tragedy about Cassandra. Terrible. That girl was a proper trencher girl, she should have had such a life. Never got two plus two to make four, although sharp as a pin in all other respects. No one deserved that. Girls like her write their own bad endings.'

'Do you think your nephew had anything to do with her murder?' Jack asked.

'Is that a double factor spangle?' Phyllis Brice eyed Endora through her magnifying glass.

'I, er… I wasn't great at maths so…' Jack rolled his eyes. 'Long division was a mouse's tail to me.'

Stella intervened. 'So, you knew Lauren Spicer too?'

'Breed. Looks like a spangle.' Phyllis Brice was peremptory.

'I don't know.' Jack twisted his head to squint at Endora as if he expected her to answer. Which she might, Stella thought.

'There's a cat here. An efficient mouser. She'd think nothing of swallowing your bird.'

'She stays on my shoulder,' Jack reassured her.

Stella flung him a look. *Since when?* 'Lauren Spicer—'

'She was as bad as Cassandra, they were thick as thieves. The answer was to keep them apart. I told them, "You're here to learn or you can leave." Cassandra did leave. Lauren stayed. That girl was smart. Smarter than my pupils at Cheltenham. She's done well with that fusspot place. She is a madam, though – fancy claiming to educate your jowls!' She scrutinized her flower. 'Lauren could have been Stephen Hawking. The feeling she had for numbers took my breath away.' She began shading in another petal in red. 'I forgive people most things, but I can't forgive Lauren for smashing up my home.'

'How did she do that?' Stella was still contemplating the idea of Lauren Spicer as a brilliant mathematician.

'She badgered me to sell to it her. I couldn't manage that garden. Know when you're spent, my mother always said. I had no choice but to plant myself here. Pass the burnt umber, please, dear,' she asked Stella.

'She smashed it up!' Stella hovered over the case of pencils in search of something singed. Jack picked out a browny-orange pencil.

'She had to be top dog. I'd see it with the ones from unfortunate homes. Especially single-parent families with no firm father figure to hand.' She tested the point of her burnt umber pencil. 'Lauren wanted to make my house into a palace. She failed to see that it already was.'

'SBH Holdings.' Stella was briefed by Beverly.

'Spicer Beauty Heaven. Imagination isn't Lauren's strong point. She's a businesswoman, but hubris has always been her foe. She paid an architect to design a hideous monstrosity. An absurd cocktail of Cotswold chic and a motorway service station. She mortgaged her salon, it bled her dry. The place is a ruin.'

'Have you been there?' Stella thought of the mudded ruts surrounding the cottage.

'I use surveillance. Marvellous thing. I thought drones were for bombing innocent countries, but for a reasonable sum one can have a quadcopter. Mine buzzes about giving one terrific views of the landscape. My cottage looks like someone else's drone dropped a bomb on it.'

'*I'm going to be a father,*' Endora shrilled.

'Who taught you that, birdie?' Phyllis Brice turned to Jack. 'Are you going to have a child?'

'She belongs to a friend,' Stella explained. 'She picks up nonsense.'

'Be jolly careful what you say in front of her. Budgerigars – the ones that talk – are terrific mimics. You have your own surveillance there!'

'Did your nephew Charles often stay with you?' Jack was steering the subject back. They were a team.

'He appeared one day in 1977 with a hoard of friends, expecting to stay. One lives on one's own for a reason. Why do they think when one's old and never played bingo in one's life, one wants to spend afternoons shouting "Full house" and singing Beatles songs? I crave peace and solitude. At least one can retire to one's bolthole and Lisa runs a marvellous ship, she keeps away halfwits and treats me like a person. I suppose she told you that idiot of a policeman cut her from his will. How dare he put Lauren first? I'll say this, despite his mother, Charles made his own way. Never asked for a penny.'

'He never stayed with you?' Jack prompted.

'I recall the question, Mr Man! That summer, Charles wasn't interested in knowing his venerable aunt. I shooed him and his gang away. But neighbours told me he was in my cottage while I was on my annual holiday. My lupins were trampled.' She filled in the flower's centre which Stella knew, from her murder case in Kew Gardens, was the stigma. 'No lupins there now.'

'Can you remember his friends' names?' Stella wondered for a mad second if, capable of flying a drone, Phyllis Brice had the strength to move a scarecrow.

'Lauren was one "friend", the silly beezum buzzed about Charles, the boy from the big smoke. He had this old van the BBC had used to nose into homes to see if we had a TV licence. Drones are the thing, you can go up to windows and around corners. Charles went abroad in that van. I didn't see him for years. Pass me the black, please,' she asked Jack.

'You said earlier that girls like Cassie Baker script their unhappy endings. Would you say more?' Jack asked one of his elucidation questions. Stella struggled to avoid questions that invited yes or no.

'I understand your insinuation, man. Wrong! I do not mean that Cassandra was "asking for it". She was an adventurous creature, she wanted more than these lovely streets of Winchcombe could give her. Cassandra and Lauren saw those London boys as a meal ticket to the gold pavements of the capital. Cassandra Baker wasn't clever like Lauren. She led Lauren into trouble. Slacking school, running off, drugs and drink, no doubt. Cassandra traded on her looks. You use what you've got. But if you do, chances are that you'll come a cropper, as, with those looks you know, Stella.'

'I'm not—'

'False modesty is tedious, dear. Aquamarine for the outer

petals, don't you think?' She held up the colouring book. 'You're both presuming that I've gone gaga. Doing this helps hand and mind co-ordination and it keeps me sane.'

Stella had actually been thinking she'd like a go. 'Was Cassie – Cassandra – with a boy from London?'

'Years later, Lauren let slip she'd been at my cottage with Cassie and a couple of lads. She meant Charlie, of course. She apologized! Lauren eating humble whatsits is like spotting a white squirrel.'

'Was the other one called Barry?' Jack asked.

Stella had put off this question. For Jackie and Graham's sake – even her own – Barry couldn't be a killer.

'Smarmy young buck, the sort who has the world scoffing out of his hands. Prince Charming. Good at maths though.'

'How did you know?' Jack asked.

'He was in charge of their money. When they landed here, I let them go to the lavvy and have tea. I heard him telling the others what they owed to the halfpence. He was too well behaved for Lauren. I can see Cassandra hooking him. Like her dad – that Rrr-afe thinks he's God's gift.' She rolled the 'r' on Rafe as she directed her aquamarine pencil at the garden where Ralph Baker was singing along to Perry Como. Stella remembered Como playing at Trudy Baker's. Apart from having children together, it seemed the couple shared a taste in music.

'Did you tell the police?' Stella guessed not or it would have been in Mercer's file and he would have put Barry (Prince Charming was a good name for him) in the frame. Or would he? More and more she was suspecting that Mercer had it in for Brice and that cogent evidence had little to do with his being Mercer's prime suspect.

'None of what my students said to me was Paul Mercer's business, especially after he was drummed out of the police. I found out recently that Lauren stayed there too while I was on holiday. Tssk! I will tell you that she also admitted that Cassandra was also at my cottage with Goldilocks the Bursar. Naughty lot.'

Phyllis Brice blew shavings off the blade of her pencil sharpener with a surprisingly violent puff.

'Lauren said Cassie stayed in your cottage?' Stella accidentally gave Stanley's lead a tug. He shot up and growled. She hushed him.

'Well, it wasn't Lauren who trampled my lupins, she had green fingers. Please go now, it's time for my zizz.'

'One last thing, if you don't mind, Miss Brice. Does the name Grant mean anything to you?' Stella got up. This woke Endora, sleeping in the crook of his neck, her head under a wing.

'Lauren's latest. He's a masseur at her parlour. The women flock there, including that lot out there.'

'Does this Grant smoke?' Jack asked.

'I doubt it. I gather he's one of those "my body is a temple" types. Whenever I'm in there he's sipping some hideous green liquid from a pint glass.'

'You go to Beauty Heaven?' Stella exclaimed.

'My mother said keep your hands and hair in order and the rest will follow. That's all she kept in order, but good advice nevertheless. Lauren gives me a discount.' For a second the severity in her features softened.

'Have you seen Matthew Craven since he was released from prison?' Stella asked. Had Lauren confided in Phyllis Brice?

'There's a boy who did his best. Isn't that right, birdie?' Phyllis Brice pointed her pencil at Endora.

'Craven was imprisoned for murder,' Stella said. The old woman had known Matthew Craven as a boy, perhaps she couldn't accept that he'd grown up to be a killer.

'Ah, but is he a killer?' Phillis Brice spoke as if she'd read Stella's mind. With that, she laid down her pencil and closed her eyes.

Chapter Forty-Nine

'My brother can't be a murderer,' Graham said as Jackie pushed on the street door to Clean Slate's office. Between intervals of brooding silence, as if trying to convince himself, Graham had repeated this as Jackie drove them across Hammersmith from Charing Cross Hospital.

For once the door was locked. Jackie was surprised. Beverly had texted first thing to say she was in the office, but usually staff from the upstairs company arrived later and left it unlatched. 'Barry will explain why he discharged himself.' Each time she said this, Jackie was less confident that when they heard Barry's explanation, they'd feel better.

The Clean Slate office door was also locked.

'Whatever he is—'

'Bev must be in Stella's office.' Peering around the Clean Slate sign, Jackie rapped on the glass. 'She'll have popped to the mini-mart.' She let them in.

'She's left you a note.' Graham took a torn sheet off Beverly's keyboard. He handed it to Jackie and stood reading it over her shoulder.

The words swam before Jackie's eyes.

Gone undercover with Mr Makepeace. Phone on divert.
Love and kisses Bev ☺) xxx

She became aware of Graham shouting, 'He's kidnapped Beverly!'

Dimly, Jackie took in Graham's leap from apparent certainty that Barry wasn't a murderer to conviction he was a kidnapper. She pointed to the emoticon. 'Bev always puts in a smiley face. She wouldn't have done that under duress.'

'He's lured her. She's just his type!' Graham was puce.

'What do you mean "his type"?' Jackie rounded on him.

'He likes blonde women.' Graham sat down heavily on Jackie's chair. 'He's having an affair with Marcia, his PA.'

'Joe told Yvonne there wasn't anyone else!' Even as she protested, Jackie felt enormous disappointment. She'd been blinkered. No one was that much of a flirt without at some stage acting on it.

'Joe was protecting his mum. Except that Yvonne knows.'

'How long have you known, Gray?' Jackie didn't expect Graham to tell her everything, no one could live like that, you'd never get any living done. However, she'd taken it as read they shared major stuff. In the last twenty-four hours she'd discovered that this wasn't true. Barry having an affair with his PA was major.

'Since this morning.'

'Has Barry been in touch with you?' Her mind was in a whirl.

'No. But it was the way Yvonne was so sure, and the way Joe emphatically put her right. You heard him telling Marcia to say it would be best she said if Barry was in the office. That was code for "Don't be loyal, if he's with you, fess up!"'

Jackie clutched at the slenderest of straws. 'If Barry's having an affair with Marcia, he won't be after Beverly.' She leaned around Graham, picked up the receiver and rang Beverly's mobile. She willed her to answer.

'Hey! This is Bev, tell me what's going on with you and I'll be right back.'

'Bev, when you get this call, ring. There's a love.' She kept her tone modulated. It wouldn't help to panic Beverly. She stuffed the note in her jacket pocket and gathered up her bag. 'We must go to Winchcombe.' Jackie hustled Graham out and set the alarm. 'God, I hope we're not too late.'

'This is my fault. I suspected Barry—'

'You are not your brother's keeper!' Jackie shouted as they took the stairs to the street. 'I'm just as much to blame. All that matters right now is that we find Beverly!'

Chapter Fifty

'It's moved!' Stella rounded the bend in the drive and stopped by the scarecrow.

'Brice.' Jack stared out of the windscreen, the glass was spotted with dust. In the few days they'd been in the country, Stella's pristine van had got spattered with mud and dotted with seeds.

'I think it's Craven. We haven't found anything that points the finger at Charlie. The opposite. Phyllis Brice thinks he had nothing to do with it.' Stella scooped up Endora and, cupping the bird in her palms, elbowed open the van door.

'We could hide the scarecrow.' Jack wanted to burn it.

'There's no point. Whoever is out there will find some other way to get to us. We need to get to them first,' Stella replied stoutly. He could tell she was as uneasy as he was.

When Stella had told him about her visit to Lauren, Jack was shocked. Twice since they'd come to Winchcombe, Stella had put herself in jeopardy. It was little consolation that Jack knew Matthew Craven wasn't a murderer, although he sounded a nasty piece of work. Both times, Jack had been to blame. If he hadn't gone to find Lucie in Crow's Nest he'd have been there. Jack unclipped Stanley from the jump seat. 'Stella, there's something I haven't told you.'

'Brice said Lauren Spicer's clever. This killer is clever; Brian

Motson is hiding something. He's number one for his daughter's murder.' They walked around the side of the house. The sun beat down on the weed-strewn gravel. Flooded with light, the house might be a luxury mansion. Thinking of the dim rooms, the twisting passage and the staircase in a cupboard, Jack knew it was anything but luxurious.

Stella waited while he fiddled with the key and pushed opened the front door. She followed him into the kitchen. Given she'd been trapped in a beauty parlour a couple of hours earlier, she was remarkably calm. 'Lisa Mercer sounded fit to kill Lauren Spicer, but Lisa was a baby in 1977 so she isn't a suspect. I'll take Jackie and Graham off our list. Since they told us about Barry Makepeace—'

'Stella!'

Stella flinched. Not that calm. He felt dreadful for frightening her.

'Sorry. Listen, I've got to tell you.' Jack had the sensation of sliding towards the edge of a cliff. 'I went to Brice's house.'

'Was he there?'

'No, you don't understand.' Jack was cold and sweating at the same time. He clasped his hands to stop them shaking. 'I got in through the cellar when Brice was with you.' Barely pausing for breath, Jack told Stella step by step (stain by stain) how he'd got into the cottage. How he'd managed to unlock the cellar door and get into the kitchen. How he'd found the teddy bear. How he was sure it belonged to Bryony Motson. He told her that in a tin of trophies he'd seen the stone with the hole in it that Jackie had given back to Brice when she chucked him. He told her about the answer machine message. 'I know it was wrong. All of it was wrong.'

'Have you got it?'

'What?' His tongue felt as if it had swelled up to fill his mouth.

'The recording of the message. Is it on your phone?' Stella was looking at him. Jack thought he knew her, but her expression was unreadable.

'Oh! Yes, here.' He pulled his phone out of his trouser pocket. 'We played it a few times, but...' Jack heard his mistake.

'"We"?' Stella echoed.

'Lucie. She listened to it.'

'You told Lucie?' Stella's tone was neutral.

'Not told, as such.' Pusillanimous. He'd been delighted by the word when he came across it as a boy at school, and relished reasons to use it. Here was one. He was pusillanimous. An abject coward. 'Lucie tracks us so she knew I hadn't gone to London, she got it out of me.' Jack bit back tears. To cry would be to sink to the lowest low. There were no excuses.

'Please play me the recording.'

'Right. OK.' Jack's fingers trembled as he swiped to the audio file. It lasted ten seconds.

First the ghostly music, then the voice, fading in and out. 'It's... I heard... Chief... Mercer. Please call...'

'She's heard about Mercer and wants Brice to call.' Jack remembered the live message. 'Does the background noise give a clue?'

'Sounds like the theme for *Star Trek*.'

'I thought that!' Jack agreed. Although he hadn't thought it. 'What about the woman? Is it Lauren Spicer or Lisa Mercer, anyone you recognize?'

'I couldn't hear. Hang on.' Stella took his phone and left the room.

Jack found Stella in the van. She'd attached his phone to a cable plugged into the dashboard and turned on the ignition.

The ethereal sounds drifting out of every speaker did resemble *Star Trek*. Jack judged the woman's voice fractionally clearer. He was as tense as a wire, much rode on the recording helping the case, or his transgression was unjustified. Stella didn't condone breaking into Brice's house, stealing a teddy bear and eavesdropping on a private phone call. She was giving him rope.

The recording finished.

'Lauren Spicer's accent is from round here,' Stella said

eventually. 'Lisa Mercer's less so. It could be her. She has referred to her father by his name. Although never by his old rank. The quality's bad, but I'm pretty sure it's not Lisa or Spicer. It does sound slightly familiar.'

'I'd say her accent was muted, neither posh nor regional. I think it was genuine, not like she knew she was overheard.' Horrified by his mention of overhearing, Jack added, 'If Bev is right, she could be Bryony Motson.'

'True. How would she know Mercer was dead? You were there only two days ago. He died four days ago. It wasn't made public until yesterday.'

'This is a small town, Brice knew about the death when you went to Belas Knap with him.' His continued resentment that Stella had gone to the long barrow without him was far from fair.

'She obviously knows Brice, but her message implies he wasn't the one who told her about Mercer. It's like she's telling him. Why does Mercer's death mean they have to talk?' Stella gave him back his phone and got out of the van to return to the house.

'She could be his accomplice.'

'When I met Charlie, I couldn't imagine him killing Cassie. Sounds stupid, but it's a hunch and sometimes you have to go with a hunch. I think I was right.'

'It doesn't sound stupid,' Jack said. He wanted to say that nothing about Stella was stupid.

'Whoever it was didn't know you were listening, yet she was careful to keep it short and not give her name.'

'She knew Brice, she didn't have to say her name.' Jack was loath to argue.

'Even when you phone a person you know, you say who you are.' Sitting at the dining table, she looked at him over the case papers. 'Let's see the bear.'

Jack passed her the photo he'd taken of the bear in Brice's bedroom. If only he could turn time back to the first night when they had truly been a team. But even then he'd had a secret. He couldn't think how to tell her about the twins. His twins.

'It does look like that teddy Brian Motson showed us.' Stella tweaked the picture bigger.

'It's too much of a coincidence.'

'You don't believe in coincidences.'

'That's why I believe Brice killed Bryony. Her father said she took it everywhere. It wasn't in her handbag. Like we said, no mugger would leave fifty quid in a purse and steal a stuffed toy. The person who took it had to be her killer.'

'Maybe Bryony didn't take it everywhere with her. Brian Motson could be lying.' Stella drew a ring around the name Brian Motson in her Filofax. 'His grief could be a sham. Or regret for killing his own daughter. Did you find the missing books: *Worzel Gummidge* and the Narnia stories?'

'No, but killers only need one totemic object. He kept the bear.' Jack hated bringing Stella back to the cold fact that he'd been in Brice's house.

'Why did you take the bear?'

'I was stupid, Stella. When I found it, I knew he must be the killer. I had to think of a way to incriminate him.'

'I see.' Stella squared off a pile of witness statements. 'It already incriminated him by being in his box of trophies.'

'If he'd got wind of our suspicions he'd have removed it. Jackie had told him we were here. It was a matter of time.'

'Mercer's been here all along suspecting him. I doubt he was worried about us coming to Winchcombe. You found it easily. If Mercer had convinced the police to search his house they'd have found it too. It doesn't add up.'

'It was idiotic of me.' Jack was suffused with shame.

'It has complicated things,' Stella admitted. 'Okay, so where is this bear? Or did you mean it was a photo?'

'That's the thing.' Jack gripped his chair as if it were about to eject him. Stella wore an expectant expression, devoid of judgement. 'It's gone.'

'Gone? Where?'

'It was in my bag and... now it's not.'

'Someone's stolen it.' Stella was businesslike. 'It's time for the police. Someone left us a dead crow, keeps moving the scarecrow, watched the house. The drone might have been Phyllis Brice but she didn't take that picture of me. Now they've stolen Bryony's teddy. Only Brice could know you took—' Stella stopped. 'You told Lucie!'

Jack wiped a hand down his face. 'I came back to tell her we must return the bear. She's vanished. Don't tell the police, Stella, not until we've found Lucie.' He had no right to ask Stella for anything. 'I don't know where she's gone.'

'I do.' Stella was already out of the door.

Chapter Fifty-One

'The police said Cassie was killed by someone she knew. She wasn't easily fooled, Stella says. That limits the people who could have murdered her. Cassie Baker was cool for a girl from the countryside, she kept running away. I'd never dare.' Beverly pushed hair from her face as a breeze whipped through the open car window. They were driving along a country lane. There were no other cars although ten minutes ago Barry had nearly knocked a horse over. Hedges on either side were so high that Beverly couldn't see where they were. She preferred the seaside.

'It's not the only way to be cool.' Barry stopped to let someone pull onto the road. At last they arrived at a town called Burford.

'I'm never fooled,' Beverly said, and then wondered if she'd know when she was.

She had stopped looking at the speedo. Barry Makepeace – 'Barry please, Bev' – had done eighty miles an hour on the M40. If she went that fast in her car, a fifteen-year-old Fiat Panda, it would fall to bits. Not that she did speed, a car was a lethal weapon, Jackie said.

'I was thinking I could pretend to do a survey. Maybe on having limited Wi-Fi connection. Jackie says it's a rural problem. It'll give a reason for asking Charles Brice lots of questions.

'I'd start with simple ones about how often he emails and how long it takes to send a file and then one about Cassie Baker.'

'If things get nasty, shout and I'll save you.'

'I won't need saving,' Beverly replied stoutly. 'If it comes up I shall say I think he's innocent. Jackie does. I reckon Brice has a good idea who the killer is.'

'Why would he protect someone and take the flak?' Barry rested his head on his palm, his elbow on the window sill. Beverly was talking through the case to get her theory clear and to keep him awake.

'He would if he's being blackmailed. Or maybe he's protecting a relative, like a brother or a son. I'd die for my little brother.' Beverly hadn't considered this until now.

'Charlie doesn't have a brother or a son.' Barry drained the Starbucks coffee they'd got in the service station. His name, in black felt pen, was scribbled on the cup.

Beverly had finished her cappuccino. The barista had spelt her name wrong, although she'd said it was Beverly with two 'e's. 'Maybe he can take the flak. Stella said he gets more work because people think he's a murderer.'

They passed a sign that said Winchcombe was in two miles. They passed a house, the first for ages. Someone had put out a stall displaying boxes of cherries for sale. Beverly supposed it was like leaving a sofa on the pavement in London, hoping someone would walk off with it. Surely most people would take the cherries without paying. She was startled by Barry.

'Put the window up, Bev, we'll use the air-con.'

Ten minutes later, the Shogun passed along the main street in Winchcombe.

Had Beverly glanced to her left as they passed the Five Trees nursing home, she might have seen a man and a woman walking a small apricot poodle, deep in conversation. The sun would have been in her eyes, she may not immediately have recognized the couple. But, a dog lover, she would have known Stanley's sprightly gait. The man's hands were cupped, as if he held something precious in them. The man glanced at the sleek black car with privacy windows that hid the occupants, one of many four-by-fours he'd seen in Winchcombe. Later, when it no longer mattered, his photographic memory would recall the car and precise time he'd seen it.

At the end of the town, Barry swung the Shogun onto a winding country lane. The sun had gone in. Grey clouds and a canopy of branches brought on a premature dark.

'We've gone through Winchcombe.' Beverly didn't like to be rude, but it needed saying. She didn't think Barry was his usual self.

Barry said, 'I'm going to show you something.'

All the way from London, something had scratched at the back of her mind. Now it came to the front. Barry had called Cassie Baker's sister 'Karen'. How did he know her name? Maybe he'd read it at the time Cassie Baker's body was found. He'd known Brice at school, he'd have been interested. But it wasn't like Karen Baker was a suspect so how come he'd remembered her? And he'd called Cassie 'Cass'. You only did that to a name if you knew a person.

Doubts buzzed about Beverly like hornets. Stella hadn't given her permission to interview a suspect. Jackie had said Barry Makepeace was against Stella taking the case, why was he putting himself out? *Cass*.

The hornets became a swarm. Beverly blurted, 'Oh. My. God. You killed Cassie Baker!'

Chapter Fifty-Two

Half past five in the afternoon, clouds had extinguished the sun, dissolving Winchcombe to a dream and capping the hills. In the meadows and at the fringes of fields, mauve scabious, purple thistles and the yellows of hop-trefoil and silverweed were bleached to pastel shades. If not for the balmy temperature, it could be autumn.

Stella parked in a lay-by on the edge of Humblebee Woods. 'This way.' She climbed the stile and, threading Stanley's lead through a gap, clambered down the other side facing backwards. Jack hopped over as if he crossed stiles all the time.

They trudged in silence up the path wending between oak and chestnut trees. Last night's storm had turned the ground to mud. Stella wore her steel-capped 'cleaning' boots, but Jack had on his smart lace-ups.

'Be careful,' she warned.

Before he could reply, he skidded. Stella caught him before he went down.

'Thanks.'

She was minded to hold onto Jack's arm, but suddenly he whizzed on up the track, clearing tree roots, skirting puddles, so it was all she could do to keep up. He must be cross he'd told her about the bear and she'd spoiled his plan. She should mind that he had broken the law. As she followed Jack in the failing light, an incident from her childhood presented itself. At primary school she'd informed a teacher two boys were 'trespassing' – a word learnt from her dad – in the girls' toilet. The teacher told the boys off and said Stella was 'absolutely right' to let her know. Stella had been right, but it hadn't made her happy. The boys and several girls were cross at her. Stella knew when she and Jack found the teddy bear she would feel no better. She tried not to think what Terry would say. She imagined herself telling him that Jack had given them a break in the case, they needed it.

They followed a footpath called the Cotswold Way around a field and over another stile, which again Stella climbed back to front.

'Brice is strong now, then he was only twenty and had all night.' Stella pictured Charlie Brice racing towards the tractor. Did running demand strength or stamina? She didn't remember the route from coming here with Brice. She'd followed him blindly. She'd have expected to be there by now, had she led them the wrong way?

There was the beep of a text. Stella fished in her Barbour pocket. 'Patty Hogan's died.'

'Who?'

'The woman I visit in the hospice.' After Vicky's call the night before she should have expected the news.

'The one who asked you to read John Galsworthy to her?'

'Yes.' Stella felt suddenly weary. 'I told the hospice I was going away. This means we won't reach the end of the saga, Patty won't know what happens.'

'That's what I'd mind about dying, not knowing what happens next,' Jack said. 'Didn't your friend Vicky say Patty Hogan knew the novel, she wanted the familiar in her last days?'

'When I said I was going to Winchcombe, Vicky acted like she disapproved. She doesn't like talking about murder.' Vicky must think her a bad befriender for leaving Patty. She must speak to her.

'Funny to mind talking about murder when you nurse the dying,' Jack commented.

'Most people don't like talking murder.'

At length they came to the sign, 'Belas Knap Long Barrow'. Moments later there was the stile Brice had offered to help her over, as if at her age she needed assistance.

Jack sprang over it. 'Take my hand.'

'Thanks.' She took his hand. Before she knew it she was on the other side facing out. Stella doubted that, without Jack, she could do it again.

Jack and Stella made their way up the steps of the mound. Stanley nosed at mushrooms growing on the top.

Low clouds threatened rain from the west. Stella looked beyond the ash tree to the field where Stanley had chased the tractor. Cylindrical-shaped bales were dotted at what looked like random intervals. She pictured Stanley barking at the machine as bale after bale rolled off the trailer, and held tight to his lead.

In the grey light the mound had a menacing aspect. Tapering at one end, it was like a crouching monster imprisoned within a low drystone wall. The area that Brice had called the forecourt was in shadow. Stella tried to imagine an Early Neolithic ceremony there, but beyond furs and cudgels (which might be Stone Age) she could not.

Lucie May wasn't there. They were alone on Belas Knap. In front of them the fields stretched away to meet the sky with not a building in sight.

'Lucie!' Jack slithered down the slope. Stanley tried to follow and was jerked back on his tight lead.

Sticking out of the mound directly below them was a pair of legs clad in thick black tights, ending in plush Tatra walking boots.

Lucie lay on her stomach, half in half out of the chamber where Brice said they'd found Cassie Baker's body.

'Lucie, are you OK?' For the second time that day Stella felt a prone body for a pulse.

'She's dead,' Jack wailed.

Behind them, Stanley, getting over what had amounted to whiplash, was coughing.

'Ssssh!'

'I didn't say anything.' Stella couldn't feel signs of life.

'*Ssssh.*'

'Lucie!' Stella and Jack shouted.

'What are you doing there?' Stella asked.

'Listening,' Lucie's voice boomed from within the chamber.

'Where is the teddy bear?' Stella asked.

'Listening to what?' Jack craned towards the opening.

Lucie scrabbled out backwards. Jack and Stella helped her to her feet.

'To the atmosphere. A murder story's as much about the place where the murder happened as the characters.' She brushed herself down. 'Belas Knap has strong vibes. Death is not far away.'

'It's not a story. It's about real people.' Stella thought of Lauren Spicer's words to her earlier in the salon. Jack had stopped her calling the police. If Lucie was OK they needed to discuss Lauren. 'Please tell us what you have done with the bear?'

'I've planted it!' Lucie headed off around the mound.

Stella called after her. 'What do you mean "planted"?'

'Oh my days, for brainboxes you two can be slow! Where Stella told us they found the body.'

'You can't frame Brice. He's innocent.' Stella wouldn't go to those lengths for a result.

'No he's not!' Jack shouted.

Stella got on her hands and knees and crawled into the burial chamber. She negotiated what Brice had called the 'blocking stone'. The boulder cut out most of the light. Less than two metres from Jack and Lucie she felt deep underground. The air was stale and smelled of rotting earth. She shuffled forward. Something moved. She froze. Stanley. She was still clutching his lead. She relaxed, grateful for his woolly warmth. She encountered cold roughness, it was the back wall of the chamber.

'Where did you plant the bear?' Her shout was swallowed in

the chamber. She wriggled around, mindful of squashing Stanley, until she was sitting against the rear wall. Groping for her phone she found the torch app. Reading the case notes, she'd imagined roughly hewn stone and mud. But the walls were of lengths of stone packed together.

She heard scraping. Thin light seeping around the stone vanished. Her torch app dazzled Jack when he came around the boulder.

'Lucie says it's behind one of these stones.' He sounded disembodied and far away. He crawled into the cramped cavity beside her. He trained the beam around the chamber. 'This is a giant jigsaw! I'll get Lucie.'

'We'll find it.' Stella didn't want Lucie joining them. 'Lucie's left-handed, isn't she?'

'Ye-es. Ah!' Jack got it. 'She'll have hidden it on the left.'

'She must have found a loose stone, she'd never have got one out otherwise. Let's assume she started on the left. I'll hold the phone, you do the testing.' Stella was keen to test each stone herself, but was keener still to get back to normal with Jack. Giving him the best job was a start.

The task was laborious.

'Got it!' Jack said after what seemed to Stella like ages.

She heard the grating of stone on stone and shone the wavering light downwards.

'Here you are.' Jack passed her the soft toy.

Stella held the teddy bear centimetres from her nose. Too close and she'd smell the fibres and not what clung to them. She gave several short sniffs. 'Lavender.'

'There was a bag of lavender in Brice's box of trophies,' Jack said.

'There's another scent. Perfume. It's faint and mixed with earth, which will be from here. I know it though. My friend Liz wore the same one at school. Revlon something. Wait, oh!' She paused. 'It was called Charlie.'

'That's a sign,' Jack breathed.

For once, Stella was tempted to agree.

She pocketed the bear. She thought of the two boys given detention for going into the girls' toilet. It wasn't about being right. 'Let's ring that number.'

'What number?'

'The woman who called Brice when you were there.'

'It will give us away. Stella, we don't have to. I shouldn't have overheard—'

'We'll pretend it's a wrong number when she answers, I get them all the time. It's a solid lead, we can't waste it.' Surprisingly, despite being huddled in a hole, her phone signal was strong. Lucie would say it was the vibes.

Jack read out the telephone number.

Stella and Jack scuffled closer to each other in the burial chamber and listened to the ringing. A bright electronic voice greeted them, 'I'm not here at the moment...'

Stella cut the line. 'Let's see if anyone calls back.'

Lucie was perched on the drystone wall. A fine rain had begun to fall, her squashy rain hat gave her the look of a ghost of a bygone country woman. Stella ran a hand down her face, she was thinking like Jack.

Her phone rang. It was Vicky again.

'Hi, Stell, you called me.'

'I shouldn't have come here. I shouldn't have left Patty.' Stella scrubbed at her hair.

'If I lived like that I'd never leave the hospice. You have your own life, Stella,' Vicky reassured her. 'How's it going there?'

'We're close to getting it, I think.' *Were they?*

At the stile she stopped. Jack said the Early Neolithics used bones of the dead in their ceremonies. They took the dead with them into life. Patty Hogan wanted to be cremated. *'I don't want the kids lamenting over my grave.'* Like Terry, Patty would cease to exist.

Jack and Lucie had gone on ahead. Stella climbed the stile perfectly even without Jack. She glanced at her phone. It was too soon to expect the mystery woman to call back. She might not call. Stella paused on the path and swiped through her call history, tempted for a moment to ring the woman again. Incoming and outgoing calls swam before her eyes, they made no sense. As she stared at them, a hunch began to form in her mind.

Wind moaning through trees on the footpath evoked the *Star Trek* theme.

The background sound on the voicemail from Brice's mystery woman wasn't *Star Trek*. Her hunch taking shape, Stella knew exactly what it was.

Chapter Fifty-Three

'Where are we going, Jackie?' Unknowing, Graham echoed Beverly's question to Barry an hour earlier. 'Didn't you say Charlie lives in the town?'

'That's not where they've gone.' They had left Winchcombe and joined the Old Brockhampton Road, passing the entrance to Sudeley Castle. Jackie was grim-faced. 'Let's be honest, Gray, neither of us knows what your brother is capable of.'

'Jesus, there's no way...' Leaning forward in his seat as if it would help get them there faster, Graham groaned, 'If he's hurt her, I'll kill him with my bare hands.'

'Join the queue.' Jackie was grave. 'Barry knew Cassie Baker. He was away all those evenings. You didn't care because it gave you time alone with me. And I was too bothered by what Charlie was up to. Charlie was definitely hiding something when I talked to him in the deli. If he didn't kill Cassie Baker, he's protecting the person who did. When we were kids, who did Charlie get in trouble for? Who was like a brother to him? Beverly has found something out and whatever it is, Barry doesn't want her telling us. He has to silence her.' Jackie swerved close to a ditch as a tractor roared by.

'He's my brother.' Graham was stating a fact, not making an argument.

Jackie honked the horn at a blind corner. Ahead, one wheel in a ditch, the bonnet buried in the hedge, was Barry's Shogun. Jackie drew up behind it. 'I think Barry's taken Beverly where he took Cassie Baker. To Aunt Phyllis's house. Come on!'

Graham and Jackie struggled across a field ploughed the year before and left fallow. They teetered and tripped on clods of earth dried hard by the summer sun. No sun now. On the horizon, storm clouds hung over the woods beyond Belas Knap.

The flat light had levelled shadows and detail. The free-standing walls appeared as a stone henge. At the top of the track, they broke into a run.

'Beverly!' Jackie's voice hung in the still air.

Graham vaulted the railings surrounding the ruined house. She was clumsy, sweat-slicked hands slipping on the metal.

Graham was bending over someone amongst the rubble. Jackie saw Beverly's blonde hair.

For the first time in her life Jackie Makepeace screamed. A stillness pushed the insides of her skull. She made her way over the rubble of Cotswold Stone and through what had been the front door into Phyllis Brice's cottage.

'... I went to that house where Jack and Stella are staying. There's no one there and there's no phone. Mine has no signal.' Beverly stood, hands on hips, frowning down at Graham and Barry.

Jackie whirled around. 'I thought he'd killed—'

'I got him breathing. His heart stopped when he got here.'

Jackie looked to where Beverly was pointing. The blond hair was Barry's. Graham was cradling his older brother in his arms.

'He's already had one heart attack,' Jackie said. Under her breath she added, 'I think this second one just saved your life, Bev.'

Chapter Fifty-Four

'If you want to crack a case, you got to play dirty. Rules get in the way.' Lucie hung Endora's cage from the sitting-room beam and flung herself in her armchair by the fireplace.

Rays of sunlight slanted through the diamond-shaped panes, turning the brass surround in the grate to gold. The reek of damp was offset by stale woodsmoke from last night's fire. Stella rather liked it.

'Lucie, I won't frame Brice. The bear could be a coincidence.'

'Jack doesn't believe in coincidence. Nor did Terry.' Lucie sulked from her corner.

'Well, I do. Coincidence is in the eye of the beholder. Thousands of people must own that make of bear and they didn't murder Bryony Motson. I can't shake the image of Charlie Brice racing across the field after Stanley.'

'So you decide a man isn't a murderer because he'd rescued your dog?' Lucie said.

'I know it sounds mad. But something doesn't add up. Sorry, I know you guys meant well.' Stella let Endora out of her cage. The bird flew out and, with a soaring fly-past, took up her perch on the mantelpiece.

'Stella, you've *nothing* to be sorry for!' Jack couldn't bear

Stella to apologize. She was his beacon, his gold standard. If she capitulated to his ways they were lost.

'We need watertight evidence it was Charlie. We have as much evidence that Cassie Baker was murdered by Barry. He lied about losing the penny key-ring and Graham said Charlie supported his lie. Where was he on those evenings when he and Charlie went into Winchcombe and left Graham and Jackie at Belas Knap? Where was he when they found Graham's van on the Old Brockhampton Lane?' Stella was looking at her phone. 'Paul Mercer never followed up other leads for Bryony. When the case was re-examined, any leads had gone cold. You didn't find Bryony's children's books at Brice's house, yet they're missing. Who took them? Then there's Matthew Craven. Lauren looked frightened.'

'Don't sweat it, Stell. Nothing scares that lady, she's made of flint.' Lucie held her nails up to the dying light. 'Damn fine beautician.'

Jack wandered over and glanced over Stella's shoulder. She was checking train times from Cheltenham. *She was going to leave. She was planning to interview Barry without him.* He'd blown it. He would tell her everything. He'd be totally honest. But not now, not with Lucie (or Endora) listening.

He shut the curtains and piled logs in the grate for a fire. If he made Crow's Nest homely perhaps it would persuade Stella to stay. He berated himself, he and Lucie had, like Mercer, jeopardized the case. He put a match to the kindling and closed off the fireplace with a sheet of newspaper to encourage the flames. He hadn't considered the aftermath of stealing the bear. He hadn't dwelt on what would happen next.

Seated at the table, Stella was scrutinizing the police notebook they'd taken from Mercer's house on the day he died. He felt the ghost of relief. She wasn't going anywhere tonight. He joined her at the table.

'SBHH is Spicer Beauty Heaven Holdings.' Stella pointed at the formula Mercer had written in the hours before he died.

'L means Lauren and MC is Matthew Craven!' Jack wanted to get Lucie out of the room, but she was nestled in her chair, warming her stockinged toes in front of the fire.

'It's Mercer's version of shorthand. He was too ill to manage more,' Stella said.

'Or he didn't want his killer to read it,' Jack said. 'Not much of a code. It simply depends on possessing knowledge which the killer probably had.'

'We know Craven is in Winchcombe from when I had my nails done.'

'You said she seemed scared of him.' Dimly Jack noted he'd never have imagined he'd hear Stella say, 'when I had my nails done'. The sun had set. The room darkened. He got up and lit the candles.

'She was scared of something.' Stella studied Mercer's cryptic phrasing. 'Mercer could be considering that Craven and Lauren Spicer were an item again. The double question marks mean what you said before, that the idea is unbelievable, which it is. Why go back to a woman who withdrew your alibi and put you in prison?'

'Maybe he has a hold on Spicer,' Jack said.

'Bev said that, until he went to jail, Craven used to be a director of Beauty Heaven. He might have cash tied up in the business.'

'Lady Lauren has Craven by the short and curlies. She's flourished in the sixteen years without him, now he's holed up in her dungeon.' Lucie rummaged under her outsized jumper and produced her notebook. 'She expected he'd be in prison until he popped his whatsits and she'd keep his stake. Most people think life means life. Not to mention Craven will hear that Mercer left her all his dosh and be demanding a slice.'

'SBHH = L/GS,' Stella read out. 'Beverly told me the present director is a Grant Smith. I met him in the salon. He's about your age, Jack, late thirties. Phyllis Brice said Lauren employs a masseur who treats his body as a temple. He looked like George Michael. I saw his car, the number plate's $G4\ SP1C3$.'

'Grant was the name on the coffee cup in Paul Mercer's recycling bin.' Jack got the tingling at the back of his neck. Stella had been spotting number plates. He was warmer and it was nothing to do with the fire.

'Grant and Lauren did the Mercer murder.' Animated, Lucie was writing in shorthand of her own in her reporter's pad. 'Motive and means. Bonnie and Clyde are good for the other murders too.'

'Grant is too young to have murdered Cassie.'

'What does "TC" with a tick mean?' Stella was puzzling over the notebook. 'My dad's initials were—'

There was a banging on the front door. Snatching up the poker, Jack went to the hall. Stella got there before him.

A crowd. In the dark, steeped in Thomas Hardy and stuck in the countryside, Jack saw a troupe of mummers. His spirits lightened at the prospect. The faces came into focus.

Jackie and Graham, supporting a tall man between them, shuffled into the sitting room. Carrying Jackie's voluminous hand-bag as if strolling through the Shepherd's Bush shopping mall, Beverly brought up the rear.

'Oh my days! What happened, Baz? You fall out of someone's bed?' Lucie crowed.

Golden locks, Grecian God features. *'He looked like a heart-throb.'* Jack had no trouble seeing Barry Makepeace as a murderer. Jack and Stanley took up position by the fireplace and eyed Barry. Beverly helped Stella put a pan of water on the stove for hot drinks.

Jackie sat between Graham and Barry. Lucie was slouched in her chair beside the fire, Endora on her shoulder.

When Jack had moved into his house by the River Thames, he'd held a party. Many of those guests were now in the room. Barry Makepeace excepting, they were his favourite people. On that spring evening the atmosphere had been light and full of laughter.

Tonight, the seven who gathered around the fire in Crow's Nest, their faces licked by candlelight, might be strangers waiting for a train. Stella and Beverly plied everyone with hot drinks and sat down on chairs by the door.

'Why are you here?' Stella asked Barry pleasantly. That she liked him sharpened Jack's ire.

'Tell Stella everything,' Graham barked at his brother.

'Good to see you, Stell.' Barry Makepeace flashed Stella an intimate smile. He was clearly Graham's brother. They had the same-shaped nose. But whereas Graham's face was open and easy, Barry's was a mask of pre-planned expressions. The older brother was one of those people who can look ill and gaunt and still cut the mustard. Jack's dislike of him deepened.

'Barry shouldn't be here,' Jackie announced. 'Last night he had a heart attack. This morning, he discharged himself from hospital and brought Bev here. They went to the ruined house where he fainted. Bev brought him round.'

'You tried to kill Bev,' Graham snarled at his brother.

'Barry was sweet. He wouldn't let me drive.' Beverly shook her head.

'Why would I kill Bev?' Barry protested.

'Tell Stella and Jack the truth.' Graham was jiggling as if he needed the loo. Jackie put a staying hand on his knee, but when she removed it the jiggling resumed.

'I killed Cassie Baker.' Barry buried his head in his hands.

It seemed to Jack that the room shifted like taut elastic. A candle sputtered and died.

'This is mint! When did you kill her? What with? Why?' Lucie cried with glee.

'*I'm going to be a father.*' Endora swooped around the room.

'You're lying.' Stella's voice cut through the mayhem.

'I killed her.' Barry spoke through his palms.

'What was buried with Cassie?' Stella asked him.

'What do you mean?' Barry slowly sat back. Jack wasn't fooled by the show of emotion.

'What did you put in the burial chamber with Cassie?'

'Nothing. It wasn't like that.'

'Barry, stop this bollocks!' Graham shouted. 'Tell the truth. Or so help me, I'll make you...'

Jack had never heard Graham lose his temper or swear.

'I didn't bury anything with her!'

'Exactly. You didn't kill Cassie,' Stella said.

'If it wasn't for me she'd be alive.' Barry's face crumpled.

'How is that?' Stella asked him.

'I shouldn't have left her. If I'd taken her to London with me, she'd still be alive!'

'No, you bloody should not have left her. Tell them!' His own emotion only too real, Graham moved to the edge of the sofa, away from his brother. 'Get on with it. Tell them who you are,' he said.

Unable to contain herself, Beverly leapt up and crossed to the fireplace. 'He's Heart-throb! I worked it out. Heart-throb Guy and the murderer are different men.'

'Baz, darling, we know you didn't do it. Murder's too messy for you,' Lucie crooned at Barry.

'He might be acting ignorance.' Jack couldn't stand it. Barry Makepeace was a fake and only he and Graham saw it.

'Barry's a rubbish actor, if he was acting, we'd know.' Lucie was filling pages in her notebook. She could spot a fake too.

'I think this is how it went.' Beverly was being Poirot by the mantelpiece. 'Charlie Brice killed Cassie to protect Barry. You never asked Brice to kill her.' She fixed a stern gaze on Barry, huddled between Graham and Jackie on the sofa. 'But I bet you were relieved Cassie never turned up in London.' Beverly folded her arms. 'I'd follow my heart-throb anywhere.'

'There's a stone with a hole in it in Brice's box of trophies.' Jack was vicariously proud of Bev, she'd trumped them all and cracked the case. He was loath to contradict her theory. 'Maybe it was Brice who left it in the grave at Belas Knap.'

'That will be a different stone, Jack.' Beverly was patient. 'The police kept the stone from the burial chamber. What Brice must have shown you had to be a different stone.'

Jack felt shame; Brice had not shown the stone to him. What would Beverly think of him if she knew he'd broken into Brice's house?

'Charlie showed a stone to Matt Craven when we were all drinking in the Sun Inn.' Barry's voice was so low, they all leaned forward to hear. 'He was with Lauren Spicer. I remember Craven said it was a sweet idea, to help someone into the next life. Lauren took the piss.'

'You met Matthew Craven?' Jackie turned on Barry.

'Lauren was after Charlie, she lured him into bed. Craven wasn't happy. He went off in a snit. It was just me and Cass.'

'No one can be lured into bed,' Jackie scoffed. 'And it wasn't bed, it was in the middle of the woods.'

'And you had no say in the matter? You were lured into bed too, I suppose!' Graham snapped at him. 'And stop calling Cassie Baker "Cass".'

'Cass was the loveliest girl. I always loved her. I first met her that night after you and Jackie went back to the tents. She and that friend of hers were in the pub garden. It was raining, I said, "You'll get wet out there" and they came inside. After that time when Charlie went off with Lauren, me and Cass got talking. One thing led to another. We imagined taking off into the blue. Obviously fantasy. I was engaged and, it turned out, Yvonne was carrying Joe. No way could we live in London like Cass wanted. Yvonne's dad would have killed me. I was trapped. With Cass, I'd have had no money. I stayed with Yvonne and messed up my life.'

'At least you had a life to mess up,' Graham said. 'The nation was looking for "Heart-throb", and all that time you could have told the police. You chose your bank balance over love. Lust, more like.'

'You think I don't know!' Barry yelled at Graham. 'When they found her dead, it was years later. Life was complicated. I'd got the business, the kids in private schools. Yvonne would have been gutted. It wouldn't bring Cass back. They found the killer so why cause unnecessary unhappiness?'

'It wasn't unnecessary. If Mercer was right, it wasn't Craven. You could have saved an innocent man from going to jail!' Graham fired back at his brother.

'*If*. You just heard Bev! Cassie thought Craven was a creep, ten to one he's guilty. I don't recall you rushing to the cops saying we were up there camping? You're not squeaky clean, little bro!'

Jack asked, 'Did you believe Charlie Brice killed her?'

'No! I've said all along, Charlie didn't fancy Cass. He slept with Lauren. He regretted it. He loved you, Jax. Still does. Charlie wanted to tell the police we'd been with two local girls. He's been all for confessing.'

'You stopped him telling the truth?' Jackie exclaimed.

'Charlie was always there for me.' Barry massaged his ankle. 'It's been hell for me. You want to talk about blackmail, Grant got wind from Lauren that I was "Heart-throb". Check out his bank account. The man's a leech.'

'That's the man who rang you when Bev and I visited the warehouse office?' Jackie said.

Barry gave a curt nod. 'He was chasing a late payment.'

'Grant Smith's a masseur at Lauren Spicer's salon. Phyllis Brice told us,' Jack said. 'We think he murdered Paul Mercer.'

'If you didn't know Cassie Baker was dead, why lie about where you lost the penny key-ring?' Graham's voice was hoarse.

'When I realized I didn't have the key, I was shit scared. Like Bev said, Cassie threatened to follow me to, as she said, "the ends of the earth". I knew she'd nicked my key from when we stayed at my aunt's place while she was away. If Cassie came to London, let herself in, she'd wreck everything. I pretended I'd lost the key so Dad would change the locks. Charlie backed me.' Catching a glimpse of himself in the darkened window, Barry began to finger-comb his hair.

'You didn't have the decency to end it?' Penning shorthand,

Lucie's hand careered over the page. 'Instead you turned Cassie Baker into your bunny-boiler!'

'Cassie went on about meeting Mum, she had the family thing mapped out. I didn't want to upset her.'

'Crap you didn't. And all the time Cassie Baker couldn't *turn* your key because someone had stuffed her into a Neanderthal grave!' Lucie hurled her pencil into the fire. A dramatic gesture which left her nothing to write with.

'How was I to know?' Barry dashed away tears. 'I was gutted. If I'm honest, I wanted her to turn up.'

'If you're honest? Steady, Baz!' Lucie snorted. 'Give me your fancy-pants pen.'

Barry took his Montblanc ballpoint from his jacket pocket and passed it to her.

Jack felt a buzz in his pocket. An image text. *Emily.* It downloaded slowly but Jack knew what she'd sent. His heart felt it would give up.

The babies lay under a blanket. Jack recognized Bella's bedspread. It was all he could do not to raise the phone to his lips and cover the screen with kisses. He forced himself to put the phone away and glanced at Stella. Stanley lay curled on the chair where she'd been sitting. Stella wasn't there.

Jack edged across the room and left without anyone noticing. He lifted the latch on the front door and carefully eased it open. He ducked beneath the sitting-room windows and, a terrible idea forming, he ran to the side of the house. The Shogun had been next to Stella's van. The van was gone. *When did she leave?* Jack trawled back through the heated discussion. When had Stella last spoken? His brain was a fuzz.

Someone had left the Shogun's keys in the ignition.

St Peter's church clock chimed eleven as Jack gunned the four-by-four down the wooded drive.

A shape rose up. Jack had no time to swerve. Something hit the bonnet with a dull thump, blocking the windscreen. Jack slammed on the brakes. The mass slid away and fell in front of the fender. In the bright headlights, Jack saw a hat, a fleece and a heap of straw. The scarecrow.

He floored the accelerator again. The Shogun, built to handle rough terrain, barely registered the mess beneath its wheels.

Chapter Fifty-Five

The cottage, etched silver in the moonlight, might have been a lithograph. The black sky was pricked with stars. Every window was in darkness.

Stella slipped through the gate and sprinted over the trim lawn to the back. Out of view of the lane, she risked using her Maglite. Jack had covered the cellar hatch, but eventually she detected a disturbance of ivy and cleared it away before lifting the trapdoor.

Stella was more used to descending ladders than climbing stiles, but entering someone's house without permission wasn't only new, but against the grain. The rungs were rotten. This was worse than a stile. She lowered herself frontways and found herself flailing. She tumbled into the dark.

In the light of her torch were brick walls coated in cobwebs. The foetid air smelt like the chamber at Belas Knap.

Smacking dirt from her trousers, Stella glanced back and saw she'd forgotten to close the hatch. Jack wouldn't have made that mistake. Gingerly placing a foot on the first rung, she pulled on the edge of trapdoor, it thudded down. If Brice was upstairs she'd given herself away. She checked her watch. Five past eleven. If her hunch was right, Brice was in Cheltenham, it was twenty minutes away.

She forced herself to wait a full two minutes. Was Brice waiting too? She pushed behind a tarpaulin draped over a pile of crates and found the door. Holding the torch as if it were a pistol, she went up the stairs.

The key was in the lock. This was the weak point in Stella's plan. She'd supposed Jack adept at picking locks. The idea of him doing this made her shudder, but right now it was a skill she needed. Except he hadn't used a lock pick when he came, he'd said he used the knife she'd given him. When Jack had given her a blow-by-blow account of how he got into Brice's cottage, she'd become impatient, she'd wanted to see the bear. She wished she'd listened properly.

Stella pulled Stanley's plastic feeding mat – decorated with pawprints – from the poaching pocket of her Barbour and slipped it under the gap and out into the room until she could just touch it. The die was cast.

She selected the spring-loaded, locking needle-nose pliers on her knife and manipulated them into the keyhole. It took several goes before the key shot out and landed on Stanley's mat. She'd calculated its trajectory to the centimetre.

She scrabbled under the door. When she'd sent the mat across the floor she had held it between finger and thumb. Now, the mat and floorboard were seamless, there was nothing to grip. She pressed on the mat and tried to drag it towards her. It stuck fast. If Brice came in, he'd see the key on Stanley's mat and guess the rest.

Stella ran back down the staircase and raked the beam around her. Gardening tools, a rake, rusting spades and fork. She'd delivered Clean Slate's 'Get Ready for Spring' package often enough to know what clients kept in their cellars. Stella found what she was looking for behind the ladder. A stack of old paint tins. She prised open the top one – vinyl white – it had dried to nothing. So had the next two tins. She struck lucky with the fourth. Varnish was exactly what she wanted. Stella dipped her finger in and held it over the tin and let the excess drip off. Sitting on the top step, careful not to get varnish on the floorboards, she reached under the door and laid her finger on Stanley's mat. Tacky with varnish the mat stuck. She retrieved it, wiped clean her finger on a tissue and folding it, put it in her pocket. *'Leave no footprints,'* Jack always said.

The scent of Mr Sheen Spring Fresh Multi-surface combined with a coffee aroma greeted Stella in Brice's kitchen. She was gratified Brice had prepared for his guest. *Her hunch was right.* The old telephone was like the one her parents had when she was little. Green plastic with a dial. She heard her dad, *'Riverside 24...'* What would Terry think of what she was doing? Would a man willing to 'nudge the evidence' have failed to solve the big case of his career? No, Lucie was wrong.

Jack had said the workroom was on the right, at the top of the stairs, and that Brice's trophy box was in 'plain sight'. Unable to use the torch for fear of alerting passers-by on the lane, Stella waited to become accustomed to the light. She made a tentative step into the room and caught her calf on something hard. A camp bed – the sort of constructed canvas and rods – was made up next to Brice's work bench. Despite the shooting pain, Stella felt satisfaction. Terry said, *'Trust your hunch,'* and she had.

The luminous hands on her watch read eleven-oh-four. It was more than a hunch. Stella felt guilt. She should have told Jack. Her original argument with herself replayed; she had to do this on her own.

After thirty seconds she realized it would get no lighter. Unlike her house, there was no lamp-post outside, not even London's light pollution. Inside and out, the darkness was thick as cotton wool.

Stella heard a noise. Eleven-oh-seven. Brice shouldn't be here. Tap-tap-tap. Someone was climbing the stairs. She shrank into the shadows as the door swung open. Dark on dark. Stella felt the wall. There was nowhere to go. She breathed in the smell of clean laundered fabric. Shampoo, washing powder – biological – honey soap.

'Jack?'

'Stella!' Euphoric with relief, Jack stepped forward to hug Stella but, misjudging her position, his arms encircled air.

'Where exactly was the box?' Stella spoke as if she'd expected him.

'Here.' Jack retained an image of the room in daylight. He moved around the work bench and, his fingers fluttering over the objects on the shelf, felt the tin. 'Give me the bear.'

'I'd like to see the tin,' Stella said.

'We can't turn on the light. My phone's died.'

'I've got a torch. We'll go into his bedroom, you said it's at the back.' Stella was firm.

Stella had come prepared. 'He could return any minute,' Jack whispered. He had to get Stella away. Brice was dangerous. He had killed at least once as a good turn to a friend. What happened when he wasn't feeling so generous? In his own home, there were plenty of tools for him to be dangerous with.

'We have seven minutes.' Stella switched on her torch.

'What's that smell?' Jack crinkled his nose.

'Quick Shine Hardwood Luster. You can get it at Lakeland.' Stella sniffed the air and said approvingly, 'Charlie's washed the bedding with Persil's Powergems.'

'It seems cleaner than when I was here last,' Jack observed.

Before he could stop her, Stella had emptied the tin out onto the bed.

'These aren't trophies,' she said after some thought. 'We see a lot of this when deep cleaning: locks of pet hair, parents' wedding rings, old coins, people's keepsakes. You must see stuff like this when you clean for us.'

'If police were to find that stone and the bear, it would incriminate Brice.'

'Not if they did forensic tests. I'm betting a DNA test would prove this hair belongs to Brice and Jackie.' Stella shone the torch on a card framed with pink hearts, in the middle was a circle of brown hair. When he'd looked before, Jack hadn't seen the variation in tone. One lock was finer and lighter than the other. 'That's the stone Jackie gave back. These are mementoes from their relationship. Barry said Charlie still loves Jackie. Here's the proof.'

Engrossed, Jack and Stella didn't see the security light outside the cottage come on or hear the click of the gate latch.

They did hear the key in the front door. Jack began throwing everything back into the box. Stella was only here because he'd been stupid. He'd put them both in danger. He hissed, 'Quick, give me the bear!'

'Come with me,' Stella said. 'Bring the tin.'

Jack was momentarily paralysed as, holding the bear as if, like Endora, it were a small live thing, Stella ran down the stairs. Once Brice was in the front room, they should hide in the bedroom and wait until they could creep out of the utility-room window – he'd checked and it was still unlocked. He had no choice but to follow her.

Stella was locking the cellar door. Jack said urgently, 'Let's go out that way. Since we're here, it's quicker than the window.'

'Charlie'll be here in a minute.' Stella might have been reassuring Jack. Vaguely, Jack took in that she had Stanley's feeding mat tucked under her arm.

The light outside gave the living room the quality of a theatre set. Charles Brice's shadow fell across the grass. Any minute he would open the front door. He should have done so by now. Why was he taking so long?

Stella went over and drew the curtains closed. They were plunged into comparative darkness. She had taken the business of being a guest literally. This wasn't how to be in the home of a True Host. She put a finger to her lips – as if he intended to speak!

Light-headed with the imminence of disaster, Jack mouthed at her, 'Stella, we need to go!'

'Come in.' Brice was with someone.

He and Stella could handle Brice: although he was a carpenter and would be strong, they were strong too. Were they a match for two ruthless assailants? Jack's fingers curled around his knife. Stella laid a hand on his arm. She was restraining him.

The room was flooded with light.

A woman in an anorak with the hood up despite it being a dry, warm night came into the room, Charles Brice following her, carrying a small suitcase. Fleetingly, Jack calculated that, with a bag and the woman barring Brice's way, he and Stella could charge them and reach the back door.

'I think this is yours.' Stella was holding out the teddy bear to the woman.

The woman took the bear off Stella. In a tired voice she said, 'I told Charlie you were good.'

Jack knew the voice.

'I'm sorry to ambush you. I couldn't risk you disappearing again. You're good too.' As if this was her cottage and she the host, Stella waved for the woman to sit on Brice's sofa. As she did so, the woman pushed back her hood.

Her hair was no longer blonde or long, nor was it short and spikey. Gone was the face of the careworn teenager in old-fashioned spectacles. This woman with an auburn bob had authority and a warmth lacking in that earlier closed self. Still, Jack saw the ghost in her features, like the 'family face' in Thomas Hardy's poem. Except this wasn't like seeing Cassie Baker's features in her sister's face. It was the ghost of that younger face. Jack didn't need Stella to tell him the woman holding the bear was Bryony Motson.

'I couldn't tell you, Stella. It's not a secret I had the right to ask you to keep.' Bryony Motson held the teddy like a long-lost friend. 'When you told me you were investigating my case I knew this day would come. I knew you'd find me.'

'Why? Paul Mercer spent sixteen years trying to find out what happened to you and failed, why were you so sure we'd work it out?' Stella sat down beside the woman she still thought of as Vicky, her friend who nursed at the hospice.

'When you started volunteering at the hospice, one of the nurses told me you were a detective and you'd solved the Rokesmith case. I remembered reading about you in the papers. I went on the internet and found you'd solved several murders since then. I was scared to meet you in case you'd recognize me.'

'Why would I? I'd never seen you before.'

'When I first ran away, I was frightened of being spotted. I still check I'm not being followed, I have to make myself meet people's eyes. With each year I dare be more confident. But you'd found killers of cases the police had given up on. I imagined you'd be looking for missing persons. I planned to avoid you.'

'From what Stella's told me, far from avoiding her, you hired Clean Slate to clean for your family and hung out in a patient's room with Stella while she was a befriender. You *acted* like a friend,' Jack said angrily. Stella guessed he was cross because she'd not shared her hunch with him. She would explain, she hadn't wanted to ambush Vicky mob-handed. Vicky was her friend. Protective, Stella moved closer to her.

'When I met you in the hospice, I decided I was being silly. You hardly noticed me. When Patty Hogan was admitted, she liked you and me being with her. It would have been selfish to deny her what she enjoyed in her last weeks.' Vicky (she couldn't think of her as Bryony) was turning the head of the bear around, the way her father had, Stella noticed.

'You hired Clean Slate before that.' Jack was persistent.

'We needed a cleaner. Colleagues recommended Stella's company, it cleans the hospice, so it would have looked churlish not to go with it.'

Stella was hoping Jack would get her eye signals to be 'nice guy'.

'You pretended to be Stella's friend.'

Stella got why Jack was cross. He was sticking up for her. 'It's all right.'

'It is not!' Jack rattled Brice's trophies tin. 'Stella, you're too trusting. It's duplicitous to pretend to like a person and it's *criminal* to run away convincing your family and friends that you're dead!'

'I wasn't pretending to be Stella's friend. I had to change my identity. My father put up a reward and the papers added to it. I daren't tell the truth. I can't trust someone not to give me up to the police and claim the money. My children are little, they wouldn't understand. I wanted to trust you, Stella.'

'You could have.' Stella was tracing the pawprints on Stanley's feeding mat. Jack had a point. It was wrong to pretend you were dead.

'No, she could not trust you.' Charlie Brice was still in the doorway, the suitcase at his feet. 'Mercer's dead. You'll get nothing for this job. Bet you're gagging to tell the cops. I saw you both with Brian Motson this morning. When you tell him you've found his little girl you'll be trending on Twitter. You won't just reap the reward, you'll sell the story and toss away your mop!' His eyes flashed at Stella.

Brice had followed them to Broadway. This was the man she'd decided wasn't a murderer. Brice looked angry enough to kill her. She was too trusting. 'We're not interested in a reward. I won't be selling the story.' She looked at Vicky. 'I'm glad you're not dead.' Idiotic, she already knew 'Vicky' was alive.

'You met my father.' Vicky twisted the bear's head as if to pull it off. 'I expect he told you he loves me more than anything. Did he show you my bedroom decorated with girly frippery? Did he say that with me gone, he's waiting out his life?'

'He did say something along those lines,' Stella admitted.

'Why did you run away?' Jack was being a fraction nicer.

'Because this poor grieving father you're so sorry for is a bastard! He's a paedophile!' Charlie Brice squared up to Jack. 'Listen, matey, if you want to be a hero to impress your girlfriend here, walk out of this house with her and keep walking. Here's the deal: forget all this and go home and I'll overlook that you broke into my house to steal my stuff.'

'Why did you leave your handbag and all that cash behind?'

Stella followed her interview plan. 'It's what made Mercer think you were still alive.'

'That was a mistake,' Vicky-Bryony admitted. 'I dumped the handbag to make it look like murder. I meant to take the money, it was mine and I needed it. Charlie had to lend me some. It never occurred to us that Mercer would conclude I'd been kidnapped.'

'I'd have given – not lent – you something anyway, fifty quid wasn't going to get you far.' Brice turned to Stella. 'Time to grab the glory and call the police, Stella Makepeace. Or should I say, *Darnell*?'

Standing up, Stella had centimetres on Brice. 'It won't be us talking to the police. When you do, you can tell them you lied to Barry Makepeace's family about his door key. And moved that scarecrow to frighten us off. While you're at it, you can explain that you spied on us. Show them the sketches of crime scenes in your estimates book. We found your cigarette stubs. Good luck confessing to your aunt that you took a photo of me with her drone.' Stella drew breath. 'You left a dead crow in Jack's bedroom.'

'No! OK, we did have to get to you to go,' Vicky-Bryony said. 'Charlie made the scarecrow and kept changing its position to freak you out. What drawings?' She turned to Brice.

'They're not crime scenes. Or, not intentionally. Belas Knap was where I stayed with Jackie. The happiest time in my life. I sketched the church where Cassie's buried for my Aunty Phyllis, she doesn't believe in God, but loves to go to church. I take her there. The sketch is for a drawing I'm doing for her. And of that field near her house. It's where we buried her dog.' He gave a glittering smile. 'As for leaving my estimates book... No dastardly plan, I forgot it!'

'After the picnic at Belas Knap, Charlie said he'd succeeded in putting you off the scent. That you trusted him. I did worry that he'd underestimated you, Stella.' Bryony beheaded the bear. 'Charlie didn't spy on your house,' she raised her eyebrows at Brice, 'and you don't smoke, do you?'

'Some spy that smokes while they're on the job! I did keep an eye on Stella and Jack about the town.' Brice gave a mirthless laugh. 'And if I found a dead crow, I'd bury it, not leave it in his bedroom.' Charlie Brice sat down next to Vicky. He looked at Jack. 'I didn't take a picture of Stella either. Sounds like someone else wants you both gone.'

Stella had worked that out. She said to Vicky, 'It was Beverly on our team that got me thinking Bryony Motson – you – were alive. When Jack…' She stopped. She wouldn't give away that Jack had broken into Brice's house before.

'I got in here on Monday while you were doing an estimate for Stella's shelves.' Jack turned to Bryony Motson. 'I heard your phone call. There was singing in the background. When I played my recording to Stella, she thought it was familiar.'

'I worked it out when Jack and I went to Belas Knap. I had to see Vicky by myself.'

'Thank you, Stella.' Vicky clutched the bear's head.

'I noticed that your name came up lots of times on my phone.' Stella looked at Vicky. 'You rang last night and told me Patty Hogan was unconscious, later you texted to say she'd died. You called again this evening saying I'd rung you. I'd just replied to your text, I hadn't called you, I presumed it was a slip of the tongue.'

'You didn't leave a message,' Vicky said.

'Jack and I had tried the woman's number he'd got from Charlie's answer machine. I didn't spot that the number was already programmed into my phone and it was you I was calling,' Stella said. 'As I was leaving Belas Knap I remembered where I'd heard the background singing. It wasn't the *Star Trek* theme, it was that choir who sang to Patty in the hospice.'

'I was surprised when you told me you were close to solving the case. You rarely give much away about that side of your life,' Vicky said. 'You trapped me.'

'I hoped telling you we were close to finding Bryony – you – would force you to Winchcombe to see Charlie.'

'That's why you were checking the Cheltenham trains. I thought you were planning to interview Barry without me! What made you so sure Bryony would come?' Jack asked.

'Bryony and Charlie had to stop us going to the police. He couldn't go to London because we'd tail him. On her home turf, Bryony risked being recognized. If it were me, I'd get the last train from Paddington and arrive after dark.' Stella looked at Jack. 'Sorry I didn't tell you.'

Jack made a dismissive motion.

'I vowed I'd only set foot in Winchcombe when my father was dead,' Bryony Motson said. 'He abused me from the time my mother got ill with pancreatic cancer, and after her death. He said if I told the police, they wouldn't believe me. This was before Jimmy Savile. I was the Evil One, selfish and heartless. He made me show I was sorry.' She gave a shudder. 'He was a respectable bank manager, he's still a pillar of the community. He said he'd kill me if I told anyone. I believed him.'

'You were right to,' Brice said.

'He wouldn't let me redecorate my bedroom. He kept it pink. I had to be his little girl. When I moved out, he was livid. I didn't dare go any further than Winchcombe.'

'Can't you go to the police now?' Stella asked. 'You running away is surely proof of what he did. If you don't tell the truth, he'll have got away with it. Winchcombe is your home, you had friends here.'

'Winchcombe isn't my home now. He took it from me. I've got a new life. Rob and two lovely children. New friends.' She tossed the bear's head onto the floor. 'Bryony Motson is *dead*.'

'Vicky has suffered enough. It's not up to her to go over the parapet to put that man away. I've told you, Vic, there are other ways to stop that monster.'

'I've told *you*, only if he goes to prison for what he did. You've done enough for too many people. Charlie has been my decoy.' Vicky gave a sigh.

'Why would you do that?' Jack asked Brice. 'You nearly got arrested for Bryony's murder.'

'When I was a kid, no one looked out for me. Barry and his parents took me in. I want to repay. Vicky deserved her life back.'

'How did you two meet?' Stella remembered that Mercer had said Charlie had inveigled Bryony into his cab, but Mercer was an unreliable source.

'Charlie came in the building society to bank his earnings and one night I hailed his taxi. We got talking. I found myself telling him everything. How I planned to escape when I'd saved enough money. He made me take cash his aunt was giving him as an allowance. He said I could pay him back one day. I have!' She smiled at Charlie. 'It was his idea we met in the pub so someone would see us together. His plan was to put the police off the scent that I'd run away. It nearly went wrong because it seemed that no one had noticed us! After *Crimewatch* was broadcast, that primary school teacher came forward.'

'In 1977 Barry and me made a stupid mistake over Cassie and Lauren. I'd mucked it up for good with Jackie, but I could help Barry. When I took Mercer to Belas Knap twenty-odd years later and Cassie was found, Barry's whole life could have gone down the pan. If Jack had done a proper sweep of the house he'd have found it in the attic!' He winked at Jack.

'Why lead Mercer to Cassie Baker's body?' Jack glared at Brice.

Stella could see Jack was angry. She should have involved him sooner.

'I didn't think I'd led Mercer anywhere but up the proverbial garden path. Craven told me about Cassie's body when I was taking him back to Winchcombe, my last fare of the night. He was pissed as a newt, crying and carrying on.' Brice's eyes gleamed. 'He was always shooting his mouth off in the pub, in my taxi, to anyone who'd listen. How he made his million flogging property, he thought he was "The Man". I was more worried he'd throw up in my cab! Got to say, I never thought Craven had it in him to murder.'

'People go to prison for crimes they didn't do,' Jack said. 'Why risk prison?'

'I hadn't killed Vicky so Mercer couldn't prove I had.'

'If it had got that far, I would have come back.' Vicky touched Brice's hand. 'You were nearly right, Stella, but for one detail. Charlie never murdered anyone. He's the kindest man you could meet.'

Stella would have believed her, had she not met Jack.

Jack cut in, 'I don't understand why Brice has kept the bear. It was a gift from your father, you couldn't have treasured it. And, it seems, you don't.' Jack nodded at Vicky, the bear's head in one hand, its body in the other.

'My father pretends he's the perfect father. Mum gave me this bear.' Vicky seemed unaware she had decapitated the toy. 'It had to be missing to convince the police I'd been kidnapped and likely murdered. Charlie was meant to get rid of it. I didn't realize you kept it. I took some books. I read them to my children. Stella, when you came to estimate the cleaning job, I worried you'd notice them in my bedroom.'

'I did notice them,' Stella said. 'How could I know they were Bryony's books?'

'You did spot that the books were missing in the photographs. That was cool!' Jack reminded her. He asked Charlie, 'Why did you keep the bear?'

'One, Bryony did treasure it. Two, it was effective blackmail. I only had to show it to Brian Motson and he'd have known it was over. I was waiting for the nod!' Brice looked at Vicky. He was still waiting, Stella saw.

'You played a blinder.' Jack rested his hands on the steering wheel. 'Did you mean what you said to Bryony? That you won't tell the police?'

'What's the point? No one gains.'

'The police. They could close her file.'

'You heard Vicky, she's got a new life. Why ruin it? She says she'll tell them when her father dies.'

'She has to live with the secret.' Jack was surprised that Stella was prepared if not to lie, then not to tell the truth. It was more his line.

'She's lived with it for sixteen years. Didn't you say everyone lives with a secret?'

'You don't,' Jack said. Stella was the most transparent person he'd ever met.

'How do you know?'

The church bells chimed half past one. After leaving Charlie Brice's cottage, neither Stella nor Jack felt ready to return to Crow's Nest. They were parked near the war memorial. Metres away on the dark empty street, a solitary light blazed from the Beauty Heaven frontage.

'I hope Vicky trusts me to keep her secret,' Stella said.

'She does.' Jack believed that, after all, Vicky-Bryony was a friend to Stella.

'Charlie Brice didn't murder Bryony Motson,' Stella said. 'I don't believe he had anything to do with Cassie Baker's murder either.'

'Maybe not.' Jack didn't say he'd rather like the police to give Charlie Brice a grilling. No one was that good. 'What about Barry?' Jack felt no warmer towards Graham's brother.

'Looks like Lauren's still in the salon.' Appearing not to have heard, Stella pointed up the street to where light spilled across the pavement. She opened the passenger door and jumped out of the car.

'Where are you going?'

'To pay Beauty Heaven another visit.'

'I'm coming with you!' Jack made to get out of the Shogun.

'It'll be better just me. If I don't return in fifteen minutes, call the police.'

Chapter Fifty-Six

Stella rang Beauty Heaven's doorbell and waited. No one came. She waited some more. A movement.

Lauren Spicer was standing in the shadow behind the reception desk.

'Open the door, Lauren,' Stella whispered. She adopted a Clarins smile.

Slowly Lauren crossed the salon and unlocked the door, blocking the threshold. 'Piss off, Lucie bloody May! I've got nothing to say.'

'I'm giving you the head's up, Lauren. Charlie Brice's going to spill. We've got a meet on Belas Knap. I'm on my way there now. Last chance, soon it won't be me you'll be talking to, it'll be the cops!' Stella heard herself as less Lucie May than *Cagney and Lacey*.

She saw Lauren hesitate. Then she jutted her chin. 'He can say what he likes. It's nothing to do with me.'

'It's quite a lot to do with Matthew Craven though, isn't it!' Stella raised her voice.

Lauren slammed shut the door and melted into the gloom at the back of the salon.

Stella saw a flicker in a room behind the desk. As she'd hoped, Lauren wasn't alone.

Slowly, without looking behind her, Stella meandered down the dark deserted street.

'What happened?' Jack demanded when she slid into the Shogun's capacious passenger seat and strapped on her seat belt.

Stella told Jack what she'd said to Lauren Spicer. 'We're going to meet a murderer.'

'We should tell the police.'

'Tell them what?' Stella asked.

Stella watched the off-side wing mirror as they drove along Winchcombe's high street. It was a week night and cottages were curtained close, the lights off. Those owned by weekenders were dark and empty.

'Someone following us,' Jack breathed.

A car using side lights was fifty metres behind them.

'I should have gone with you to the salon.' Jack accelerated.

'Slow down or they'll know we've seen them!' Stella directed Jack up Corndean Lane. He parked on the edge of the woods below the long barrow.

Through a gap in the hawthorn hedge they saw a faint light tracing the twists and turns of the narrow road.

'We must get there first.'

Despite the darkness, Stella climbed over the stile without Jack's help. She set off up the wooded slope. Jack caught up with her. At last they emerged onto the wide sloping field. Above them, the sky was impenetrable black and dotted with bright stars. It was a clear night. Once they were on the footpath, Jack looked back.

'They're not coming,' he panted.

'They will be.' Stella shone her torch along the path – a holloway with overarching branches worn deep between the trees – to avoid tree roots and jutting stones.

Jack slipped and slithered after her. He fretted. Stella was an expert on health and safety, but her belief in her own capacity to solve problems was itself a danger. He reached the second stile. Her torch had gone out. 'Stella, where are you?'

'Sssh. Up here.' A light flickered over the steps up the side of the long barrow.

'Where's Charlie Brice?' Jack hissed.

'He's not really here. I told Lauren that to make her follow us.'

'You told me too.' Jack felt as if the ground was giving way beneath him. 'Stella, it's time for the police.'

'Mercer wrote "TC" in his notebook followed by a tick. My dad was called Terence Christopher Darnell. His colleagues called him "TC" like "Top Cat". Lisa said our dads fell out. I think Terry told Mercer that he didn't believe the killer was Brice. Nor did he think it was Craven or he'd never have helped Mercer. The tick implies that in the last minutes of his life, Mercer came to agree with Terry. He nearly told me when we visited him. I think Terry had reached a conclusion about the identity of Cassie's murderer that Paul Mercer wouldn't accept. Mercer couldn't tell me because he guessed – probably correctly – that I'd go with Terry's view and refuse the case. Dad was diligent and professional, a good detective. Mercer knew it.'

'Why get you involved if he was worried you'd find out what your dad thought?' Jack asked.

'He was ill and desperate. Maybe he regretted the fall-out with Terry. He did come to Dad's funeral.' Stella turned off the torch. 'After Lisa told us about their quarrel, and reading through the case papers as well as talking to Mercer himself, I got thinking. It wasn't only that Mercer insisted that Brice was the killer, he needed him to be. Why?'

'To divert suspicion from the real killer,' Jack said. 'Stella, do we have to do this up here in the middle of nowhere? Alone?'

Stella continued as if she hadn't heard him. 'Lauren is protecting Craven, or she's scared of him. Or both. I had to lure her up to Belas Knap. People are affected by place.'

'Like Craven lured Cassie Baker,' Jack remarked.

'Listen! Did you hear that?' Stella grabbed his arm.

'Footsteps.' He counted two sets.

Stella switched on her Maglite and trained it on the long barrow's information board. Two figures were by the forecourt of the ancient barrow.

A victim of her own beauty parlour, Lauren Spicer's elaborately applied make-up took years off her. Caught in the powerful beam, Jack could see she wore Dubarry leather riding boots, cords, a brown sleeveless Barbour, her expensively cut hair tied back. She might have emerged from the pages of *Country Life*. Jack was cross with himself for thinking Lauren Spicer stunning. In contrast, Matthew Craven was a sorry creature. No longer a beefcake his jeans hung off him and an oversized army jumper with leather shoulder patches made him look twelve.

'OK, Lucie bloody May, game's over. Where's Charlie?' Lauren's nails flashed red in the beam of Stella's Maglite.

'I'm not Lucie May, my name is Stella Darnell. This is my partner, Jack Harmon.' Stella sounded calm.

'The amateur detectives. Paul told me.' Lauren was sulky. 'Keep your mouth shut, Matt. You've done your time, they can't touch you. Where's Charlie?' She moved out of the light. Stella adjusted the Maglite and captured her again.

'Charlie's told us everything,' Stella said. 'He didn't kill anyone, did he?'

'Leave Craven alone, he's been put through enough. This is harassment.' Lauren looked fit to kill.

Jack saw a True Host. *A person who has killed or will kill.* 'Matthew, what did Lauren promise in return for your silence and the little matter of a fifteen-year prison sentence? Everlasting love? A cut of the ever-fattening cash cow?'

Stella flipped open Paul Mercer's pocketbook and directed her light to it. 'Mercer left us a message before he died. He told us Brice was the killer and had framed Craven, an innocent man—'

'We're out of here.' Lauren turned into the burgeoning shadow.

Stella strode along the burial chamber until she was above the forecourt and flooded Lauren in light. 'That June night, Cassie went with the girl she trusted most, her best friend. She'd been miserable because her heart-throb, Barry Makepeace, the handsome boy from London, had left her. You told Cassie that Barry was coming back for her...'

Jack felt soaring excitement. Stella had solved it. Except here they were stuck on a hill with two killers.

'... he would meet her at Belas Knap that night and take her away. Cassie must have been surprised you were helping because she knew you'd fancied Barry. It wasn't Cassie who took from you was it, Lauren? It was the other way round. Trudy Baker told us you nicked Cassie's clothes. You had to have what she had. Cassie was so happy to be convinced Barry was back she must have forgotten that Barry hadn't liked you. He'd never confide in you. Cassie only cared that her nightmare had become a dream and she was going to live it.'

'This is shit!' Matthew Craven's voice was rich and powerful. He could be an actor, Jack thought.

Lauren Spicer tugged Craven's arm. 'Matt, come on!'

'I'm guessing Lauren hasn't told you what she's been up to while you've been in Long Lartin, Matthew. You've been holed up in Beauty Heaven since you were released, maybe you missed it. As well as being your legatee, Lauren is sole heir to Paul Mercer's estate. What with Phyllis Brice's house and your investment in Beauty Heaven, your girlfriend's worth a few bob! Except she's not your girlfriend. Maybe she forgot to mention Gr— '

'You're talking out of your arse,' Matthew Craven sneered. 'Why would Mercer leave her anything?'

'Why indeed.' Stella wandered down the slope and along to the chamber where Cassie Baker's body was found sixteen years earlier. Jack knew Stella's ruse, it worked with Stanley when he wouldn't let her clip on his lead. Walk away and the dog – or person – follows. Lauren Spicer headed after Stella.

'What did you have over Mercer that caused him to bypass his only daughter for you?' Stella asked Lauren.

'That bitch wasn't his only daughter,' Spicer spat. 'She did nothing for him. I cooked for him, gave him massages, did his shopping. I listened to his nonsense about Charlie Brice. I've got more right to his money than her!'

'Don't let them wind you up, babes.' Matthew Craven had gained in stature. 'Who cares about Lisa Mercer?'

'Paul Mercer was my father. I was born first!' Lauren Spicer stormed. 'He loved Mum more than that Julie Mercer with her airs and graces, and far more than her prissy brat. When he got his heart trouble, Lisa Mercer tried to put him in that home and feed him on slops. Serves her right, she's got nothing! I was his real girl!' Spicer sounded like a little girl. Jack wanted to tell her that the detective hadn't been a father to either of his daughters.

He did see the likeness in Lauren's face to the younger Paul Mercer, before fluid and fat had distorted his stolid police officer good looks. 'That would mean Mercer was in his teens when he had you and—'

'Are you shocked, posh-boy?' Lauren asked. 'They were fifteen when I was born. What do you think the cops would have made of Paul Mercer having underage sex? Thanks to Mum and me they didn't know.'

'You had a hold on Mercer,' Stella said.

'He loved me.' Lauren stepped out of the circle of light.

'You killed Paul Mercer,' Stella said. 'You and your boyfriend were there after us. You gave Mercer his supper. Shepherd's pie – a ready meal, not actually cooking, I should know – what else did you give him? He told you he'd asked his daughter – his *other* daughter – to hire detectives to find who killed your best mate. You had to stop him. You tried to stop us. You and Grant left the dead crow in the house and you let Stanley out one night hoping he'd run off. You had a key from when you tried to buy Crow's Nest.' Stella's voice echoed in the burial chamber.

'You townies scare easily.' Lauren gave a nasty laugh. 'It was a nice little greeting for you. I took a lovely photo of you cooking for your man!'

Stella went on, 'Except you and Grant were careless. You

know Grant Smith, don't you, Matthew? He's a director of your company! Your ex-company since they crossed you off the list.'

'You're not even close!' Lauren thrilled with rage.

'What's she on about, babes?' Craven asked Lauren.

Lauren ignored him. 'Paul had to have Charlie. Ever since he knew I'd been with him he hated him. Charlie knew I was Paul's kid, Paul hated that he knew. Charlie would never have said.'

Charlie Brice had known that Lauren Spicer was Paul Mercer's daughter. Stella had been right: Paul Mercer had needed Brice to be found guilty of murder.

'Paul told me to say I was with Matthew that night. Let Matt off the hook since he hadn't done anything, even though the idiot went and told Charlie where she was buried.'

'He made me tell him Laurie.' Craven was adamant.

'Don't call me that!'

'Your mother told the police – Paul Mercer – you were with her after the Jubilee disco,' Stella said.

'Paul made her lie or he'd have lost his marriage and his precious princess.'

'Why would he have lost Lisa?' Jack asked.

'Mum was with Paul that night. He used to come round for his tea. They all knew down the station. That lot look out for each other.'

'Why did you withdraw your alibi? I don't see you as concerned with honesty,' Jack asked.

'I told you, Paul made me lie and say I was *alone* with Mum. He said Charlie kidnapped that building society girl. No way would Charlie do that. I knew Paul was wrong there too. Your old dad said he was wrong.' Lauren's voice carried over the fields. 'The bastard told Paul it was me and Matt. Paul soon saw him off! He knew I was innocent. Matt got rid of Cassie. This place was your idea, wasn't it, babes. Stick a body in a grave, no one ever looks there!' She gave a nasty laugh.

'Clever Matt, happy to take that credit, are you?' Jack goaded Craven.

'You shut up!' Craven was visibly struggling with comprehension of the exchange. Jack remembered Lucie's comment. She too had been right about Lauren. 'You didn't expect Craven to get out of prison, did you? It scuppered you and your boyfriend's plans.'

'We haven't got plans.' Craven looked at Laura as if this was an issue.

'Jack didn't mean *you*,' Stella said helpfully. 'He meant Grant.'

'Matt, we are *leaving*!' Lauren told him.

'Grant's gay!' Matthew Craven laughed. 'Nice try, lassie.'

'Is that what Lauren told you?' Stella asked. 'There was a coffee cup in Mercer's bin the morning we found him dead.' She aimed her Maglite into the chamber. 'It had Grant's name on it.'

'You and your boyfriend are clowns.' Lauren Spicer was acid. 'A coffee cup!'

'Our job is to ask who knew there are bins behind Mercer's cottage?'

'Anyone would know that!' Craven scoffed.

'Would a passer-by, looking for somewhere to chuck their disposable coffee cup, bother to try a side door and walk around the back of a house looking for a bin? There's one outside the co-op and another in the car park on Bull Lane. Whoever threw it in Paul Mercer's bin had an ulterior reason for being there,' Jack said. 'You both did.'

'Grant's my salon manager. He gave me a lift to Paul's.' Lauren Spicer blazed with fury. She moved to the drystone wall. 'I've had it up to here, we're going.'

'Not yet we're not, Lauren.' Craven leant against the wall. Jack heard creeping threat in his tone. It was no longer 'Laurie'. He wondered if Spicer had heard it too.

Stella twisted the Maglite's beam, making it thin as a laser. It pierced the darkness of the chamber.

Jack saw the blocking stone behind which Cassie's body had lain undiscovered for decades. 'We asked Phyllis Brice if Grant smoked, she said not. We didn't ask if you did. Silly us, eh, Stell!'

'I doubt you smoke between beauty sessions, most customers are revolted by the smell clinging to a smoker after a fag. You wait until the end of the day. The funny thing about some smokers is that while operating military-style tidiness, they can be careless about cigarette butts. You crush yours in a saucer in the yard behind your salon. Round at Mercer's you stick them in a flowerpot by the recycling bins. I noticed it when we visited him the first time. The next morning the flowerpot was empty.' Stella stood aside so that Lauren could see the chamber. Her hair was ruffled by a stirring breeze. Far off came the cry of an animal, strangled and searing.

'He had a heart attack.' Like a moth attracted to the light, Lauren came closer to the lit chamber. 'I went every day, changing shitty sheets, washing and dressing him. I'd get him to the toilet, make his meals. The stink of old people! That evening he told me about hiring you, he was full of it. I lost it: "You stupid old man! I lost my virginity with Charlie when I was sixteen, a year older than you when you spawned me!" He'd have hit me if he could have got out of his chair. Called me a tart. "My own flesh and blood, sleeping with a murderer." Said he was changing his will to his "proper daughter". I told him, "I've never slept with a murderer, Charlie didn't do it."

'"All you do is paint tarts' toenails. You're my worst mistake. Lisa has made something of herself."'

'Your father had vascular dementia, he didn't mean that—' Stella began.

'He meant every word. I told him, "I killed Cassie! Her murderer was under your nose and you couldn't tell. Cassie wasn't a saint, she was a slut!"' Lauren Spicer broke free from the inane salon chat to tell the story she'd bottled up for years. She yelled into the chamber as if Paul Mercer was interred there. 'He fell back. I checked his pulse. There wasn't one.'

From the woods, an owl hooted. And the rustle of animals in bushes beyond the long barrow.

'Why did you kill her?' Stella asked eventually.

'Barry Makepeace couldn't take his eyes off me. Tongue round his ankles then Cassie comes along. Next minute she's planning her bridal gown and going on about a grand London wedding – and I'm left with Charlie. I reminded Barry he was engaged and he dumped Cassie.' Lauren gave a genuine laugh. In other circumstances, Jack thought, it would have been cheering and infectious.

'I put that stuck-up cow right.' Matthew Craven pushed off the wall. 'I told Cassie that Barry would meet her up here. Only for a laugh. He wouldn't come so Cassie would be here all night waiting! Serves her right for putting on fancy airs! I never thought she'd fall for it.'

'Matt had his car so we gave her a lift. When we got up here, Cassie starts on about Barry, how he fancied her more than me.' Lauren might have been recounting a pleasant memory. 'I hit her with a stone.'

'Did you mean to kill her?' Stella asked.

'Duh! Yes. We threw away the stone and hid her in that hole. No one guessed, not until he goes and blabs to Charlie.' Lauren jerked her thumb at Craven and said again, 'She deserved to die!'

'*She deserved to die!*'

An echo resounded across the long barrow. Stella shone the Maglite upwards to the mound. She lit up a figure. Tall, shimmering, robed from head to foot.

'We've got it all, sweetie.' Lucie May whipped a cloth off the figure. Jack felt dizzy. It was the scarecrow come back to life – re-stuffed with a friendly smile – with Endora's cage balanced on its head like fancy headgear. 'You might have got a sentence reduction for no prior intent. But boy, did you have intent! Years for premeditated murder, then add extra for wasting police time and perverting the course of justice. Life will mean life.'

Figures dotted on the long barrow. Jack made out Jackie and Graham, Beverly, and Charlie Brice.

'You can't prove anything.' Lauren backed into the gloom.

'We've each recorded every word.' Jackie held up her phone.

Shouts, lights, footsteps. Endora screeched choice phrases from Lauren Spicer's confession. Chasing through the woods, Jack swore. There were seven of them, yet somehow Spicer and Craven had got clean away.

Chapter Fifty-Seven

Stella took the stile in one go. It was dark. In the confusion she had dropped her torch. Belting along at full pelt, she was aware only of the thud of boots on earth ahead of her. She'd begun by jumping tree roots, but began to realize the ground was flat. She was running beside a field.

Grey streaks appeared in the sky. Dawn was breaking. She'd lost all sense of time. If she raised her wrist to see her watch she would lose momentum. She glanced to her right again. It was the field where Stanley had chased the tractor. The dull sound of footsteps was of her own boots. She had gone the wrong way. *Where was she?*

Stella was about to break step when she heard a voice.

'I'm driving. You and I have got some talking to do.' *Craven.*

Stella increased her pace.

The air was rent by a howl. Stella just managed not to break her step as something light streaked ahead of her on the path. Wildlife, she dimly thought.

She reached another stile and flung herself over. She was caught in a blaze of headlights. They raked over her. Not just over her, and not wildlife. As with a squeal of tyres Lauren's MG turned full circle, Stella saw Stanley streak towards the wheels.

She gave chase. The car careered down the road, Stanley behind it. He could run fast but not fast enough. The MG was drawing away. Stella ran too although she knew it was over. Craven and Spicer had got away.

The track entered thick woodland and Stella was running – plodding, it felt to her – in darkness. She could just make out the pale shape of the small poodle ahead of her. She could feel her muscles, a hot pain that would soon take her over. She knew where she was. She had, after all, come the right way. This was the private road the archaeologists had used in the seventies to excavate Belas Knap. Lauren and Craven were locals, they probably knew all the byways and footpaths around Winchcombe.

The air was split by a roar. Instinctively, Stella ducked. It was one of those aeroplanes they'd heard when they were with Paul Mercer. Except the sound, metallic and like the splitting of wood, didn't sound like a fighter plane. Stella began to run.

She rounded a bend in the track. The air reeked of petrol and burnt rubber. Light spliced through the trees, illuminating the canopy of branches over the track.

Agitated, Stanley ran back and forth at the side of the track, crossing and recrossing spears of shadow.

There had been no plane. The MG had smashed off the track, crashing down a drop of ten metres. The vehicle had hit trees, scarring their trunks, and ploughed a deep gash in the mulch of dead leaves and twigs below. Beneath the soft roof, she made out a hand. A foot. The MG was on fire, its passengers like kindling, beneath it.

Stella could do nothing, she'd break a leg trying to reach the upturned vehicle. She called Stanley. He ran beside as she set off along the track.

There were lights ahead. A car. Two cars.

'Stella!' Jack jumped out of Barry's Shogun. 'We lost them! I've called the police and given them Grant's number plate. They won't get far.'

'They haven't. I know… where they…' Stella bent double as a stitch crippled her. Palms on her knees, she gasped, 'Call… ambulance… fire brigade…'

Chapter Fifty-Eight

'Jack's saying he killed Craven.' Clasping a mug of tea, Jackie sank into one of the patio loungers.

'What? I thought it was the beauty parlour woman,' Graham said.

'He says he should have got to know the area.'

It was late Thursday afternoon. Jackie and Graham were home from Winchcombe. Sun blazed down on the garden. Jackie sat in its glare, seeking temporary respite from her thoughts, Graham was on one of the Jack and Jill seats in the shade of the umbrella. He hadn't moved for the past hour. She had always loved summer afternoons in their garden. Today she felt as if none of it – the roses, the lavender bushes, the smell of newly mown grass – was real.

Too much was real.

'If anything, we're all to blame.' Jackie put a hand to her heart. She'd had palpitations all the way back along the M40. 'It was obvious Spicer would make a dash for it. She died because Craven crashed the car. From what the policewoman told us, he did it deliberately.' Although he never drank before six o'clock, at five fifteen Graham was halfway through his second London Pride. He was drinking from the bottle, one sip after another. She couldn't look.

'Jack said that in London he'd have known every surrounding street and alleyway. Those two are fishes out of water in the country. They'll be glad to get home.' Jackie sipped her tea.

'I wouldn't bet on Stella. This morning as we were leaving, she told me that even after only one week, she liked Winchcombe. Unlike Hammersmith, she can see "the edges", hills in every direction. She said she liked the silence. Who knew Stella would love anywhere that didn't require deep cleaning? Wouldn't surprise me if one day she packed it all in and went to live in some rural retreat.' Graham smiled grimly to himself. 'Her and Jack in a cottage in Winchcombe with roses round the door!'

'Stella saw the car in the woods. She's not used to death, especially so violent an accident.' Jackie wondered if Stella should stay in Winchcombe. Jack had said she and Lisa Mercer had apparently got on well. Jackie blurted out, 'I'm so sorry, Gray.'

'What are you sorry for? Don't tell me you think you killed Spicer too?' Graham put down his bottle.

'I'm sorry for letting this whole business get in the way of *us*.'

'It takes two to not talk. I've never wanted to think back to that time, let alone discuss it. I knew at some level that Barry was involved. I blocked it. Charlie got off with Lauren Spicer, was it likely Barry played gooseberry? Never could resist a girl who fancied him. I just chose not to face it.'

'We both did that. Frankly, Barry's not that hard to read, I should have seen it too. I was bound up with Charlie dumping me. I wiped that summer of 1977 from our history and put out the myth we were each other's first love.'

'You *were* my first love,' Graham remarked without apparent rancour.

'Strictly speaking, you were mine. I liked being seen out with Charlie, he was my John Travolta, so *cool*. I liked other girls being envious. How crap was I! You heard Spicer, she saw that in me. It made her go for Charlie even though she liked Barry better. With you I don't care what the world thinks.'

'I'll try to take that the right way.' Graham drained the bottle.

'You'd better.' Jackie put her face in the sun. 'We'll do this next bit together. Will Barry go to prison?' She knew the answer. Barry had failed to admit he was a material witness in a murder case. A custodial sentence would be mandatory.

'He'll lose the business, his marriage. I doubt the kids will speak to him. For what? A secret affair forty years ago that he dropped not because he loved Yvonne, but for money. There's a moral in there.' Graham got up and stepped onto the lawn, gingerly as if walking into a cold sea.

'He won't lose you,' Jackie said. 'Or me. The kids will come round one day; whatever else, he's their dad.'

'He won't lose me,' Graham agreed. 'Because Mum would never forgive me if I turned my back on him. But my true family is you and the boys.'

'I suppose he *is* going to tell the police?' Jackie was struck with doubt. They'd brought Beverly home. Barry had driven off in his Shogun. They'd decided to trust that he'd go home and tell Yvonne and their children everything. 'You don't think he'd do anything stupid?' Jackie couldn't bring herself to say 'suicide'. Men like Barry held so much store by status and wealth. With all that gone, who was he?

'We've gone over this, he's too practical to do a runner. Where would he run to? He'll take what's coming to him. Personally, I'm worried that he's refused to go back to hospital. There're many ways to be "stupid".' Graham paced the lawn.

'I got the impression that Barry and Cassie being at Phyllis Brice's cottage – defiling it – upset Lauren Spicer more than Cassie being with Barry. Phyllis Brice seems to have been the only person who liked Lauren. She saw her potential.' Jackie sunned herself.

'She didn't appreciate it enough to spot Spicer was a killer.' Graham returned to the seat and sat with his legs outstretched.

'Lucie May will get her scoop.' Jackie struggled out of the lounger and tossed the rest of her tea into a flower bed. Going into the kitchen she noted it was five thirty. The sun was nowhere near the proverbial yardarm, but Graham had it right, it was definitely time for a drink. She got two beers out of the fridge.

'Not if her parrot spills the beans before she's sold the story!' Graham took a bottle of beer from Jackie. 'Mind you, he spouts claptrap. Said he was going to be a father!'

'Endora's a she and she's a budgie.' Letting the sunshine seep into her bones, Jackie held the ice-cold bottle to her cheek. 'Actually, Gray, I've got a theory about that...'

Chapter Fifty-Nine

'Seems I owe you,' Lisa Mercer said. 'Thanks to you I got my inheritance.'

It was Friday morning. Jack and Stella had been in Winchcombe exactly a week and were leaving today. They sat beside each other under a horse-chestnut tree in the garden of Five Trees Nursing Home. Lisa had poured tea and given them each a slice of colourless sponge. There was a water bowl for Stanley.

'You owe us nothing.' Stella didn't care for cake, but it would be impolite to refuse. Her van, packed and refuelled, was out the front of the home. Stella had intended to return the Crow's Nest keys and leave for London. Instead, Lisa Mercer greeted them like old friends and insisted they have tea with her.

'But for you that woman would be alive. Don't expect me to shed crocodile tears. I hope it's hot where she is.'

'When Matthew Craven discovered Spicer planned to go off with Grant, Craven would have killed her at some point.' Stella was firm, Jack had been insisting Spicer's death was his fault, she had to knock that on the head.

'You solved one murder anyway.' Lisa Mercer shot the cuffs of her red blazer. 'Could Spicer have killed Bryony Motson too, I wonder? Brian Motson needs closure, the man keeps her bedroom as if Bryony will walk in one day. He's deluded, poor chap.'

'Maybe she will walk in,' Jack murmured. Stella shot him a look, but Lisa hadn't heard him.

'Lauren Spicer killed my dad when she told him she murdered Cassie Baker. To think all those years he wasted barking up the wrong tree. Your dad had his head screwed on. Shame mine didn't listen to him.'

'It must have been a shock to realize he was wrong.' Stella kept her tone neutral, although she was quietly proud that Terry had realized Lauren was guilty.

'That woman – I shan't say my sister – blackmailed my dad all her life with the fact of her life. He was scared to lose his job. He lost it anyway.' Lisa Mercer examined her newly gelled nails. 'To think of the money I wasted in that parlour.'

'Not a waste, your nails look great,' Jack said. This time Stella caught his eye. He returned to his cake. So far he'd had two slices. 'Your dad couldn't suspect his own daughter. In the end, his children came first. You mattered to him.'

'She wasn't his daughter, her mother and him weren't married.' Lisa snapped her head to one side as if she'd been slapped.

'You don't have to be married to have chil—' Jack began.

'My dad respected Paul Mercer or he wouldn't have helped him. Dad never cut corners or supported anyone who did.' As she spoke, Stella felt this was true, Terry had taught her to work by the book, as he must have done himself.

'Nice of you to stick up for my father, Stella, but Paul Mercer wasn't cut from the same cloth as Terry Darnell. My father lied to guard a secret.' She poured them all more tea. 'Parents are strangers. I know more about Ralph Baker than about my father. Ralph's a reprobate, but he fessed up to Trudy about his mistress and when he did, she kicked him out. My father tried to have his cake and eat it.' She picked up the cake plate. 'Have the last slice, Jack.'

Unable to argue, it was what Mercer had tried to do, Stella bit into her cake and was surprised to find it was delicious.

*

'I forgot to give you this.' Lisa Mercer rushed out of Five Trees as Stella was negotiating the van out of the gates.

Stella looked at the envelope Lisa dropped onto her lap. 'What's that?'

'Your fee. You solved Cassie Baker's murder. It's not fair you don't get paid because Dad's gone.'

'You weren't going to use your own money,' Stella reminded her.

'It's not my own money! It can come out of his legacy. Make sure you bank it. Terry Darnell told my father that his daughter always went the extra mile for no payment. Not this time, girl!' Arms folded, heels kicking out, Lisa ran back into the building.

'That's nice what your dad said about you.' Jack watched Stella stuff the envelope into the glove box and made a mental note to tell Jackie or Stella might not bank it.

'Lisa hardly saw Mercer, she probably got it wrong.' Nevertheless, Jack saw Stella flush with pleasure. She would squirrel the nugget away with the other glimpses of Terry Darnell she'd gathered since his death.

'It would be a detective's worst nightmare finding out that the murderer in a case you're investigating is your own child.' As they drove along the high street, Jack lined up this scenario alongside other horrible parental fates, including not helping your babies grow up. Did that matter if they had happy lives? Would his children have happier lives without him?

They passed the butcher and the florist. A board outside the pub offered an all-day breakfast, another advertised Happy Hour, two Proseccos for the price of one. The newsagent's hoarding read *Jubilee Killer dies*.

'Pull in!' Jack shouted.

Two minutes later they were on the road again. Jack flapped the *Daily Mirror*, *Murder of Jubilee Teen Finally Solved*. 'Lucie May hasn't wasted time.'

'Has she mentioned Vicky?'

He scanned the front page. 'Can't see. I'll read it to you.'

He hoped Lucie had stuck to her word to keep Bryony Motson out of her piece. For Lucie, story came first. Stella had insisted they trust Lucie. Although he often told Stella she was too trusting, Jack loved that she was.

An inset photograph showed Lauren Spicer and Cassie Baker as teenagers, their lavish make-up recalling *The Rocky Horror Show*. Jack hadn't seen it in the file and guessed Lucie had been doorstepping relatives and friends. Another was of the adult Lauren. Her eyes met Jack's. The foxy hollow-eyed look in Craven's arrest mugshot was now as familiar to him as the iconic photograph of Myra Hindley.

'Jack?'

'*Yes*, sorry.' He cleared his throat and began to read.

'"When Lauren Spicer's car smashed into a tree in Gloucestershire woods last night, news spread fast in her home village of Winchcombe. Floral tributes piled up outside her salon, Beauty Heaven. Customers described Spicer as a bubbly lady, who shopped for pensioners. Then it emerged that the 53-year-old had been harbouring a secret which could help crack a murder unsolved for 39 years.

'"On the night of June 5 1977, Cassie Baker left the Queen's Silver Jubilee disco in Winchcombe's Youth Centre. She never went home. A frequent runaway, Cassie's family didn't worry, the pretty vivacious girl had eloped to London with the mystery man she'd told her sister Karen was 'Heart-throb'. It would be the new century before the Bakers learnt the true fate of their daughter.

'"December 18, 1999. Bryony Motson, an 18-year-old Abbey National teller, left Cheltenham's Pandemonium nightclub, bidding friends 'Happy Christmas'. She went to catch the last bus to Winchcombe nine miles away. Bryony hasn't been seen since..."'

Jack skipped the facts of the case. Lucie hadn't embellished and Stella knew them.

'"... Stella Darnell is a cleaner who solves murders. Following the footsteps of her top Met detective dad, Stella's swept many successes into her dustpan. Now she's done it again.

'"The decades-old mystery is solved. Charlie Brice is innocent. Cassie was murdered by her 'Bezzie mate'. Evil Lauren Spicer, jealous of Cassie's new man, killed her. Cowardly Craven helped his depraved lover bury her victim. Struck by a perverse remorse, he returned to the scene of the crime later and laid a good-luck charm, a stone with a hole in it, beside her body. Under her thumb, Craven took the blame for murder.

'"Last night, the pair's sick ambitions ended. With her ace team, Stella Darnell set an ingenious ambush on Belas Knap and tricked the psychopathic manicurist into confessing to murder. Spicer intended to marry Grant Smith, her 'toy boy' masseur. Instead, speeding from the death chamber along a farm track, the ex-con grabbed the wheel of Smith's MG and propelled the demon couple to their deaths.

'"Winchcombe is once more a sleepy idyll in the Cotswolds. Tourists stroll down the street, buy fine local cheeses in the deli, sip pints of Donnington's in the pub or head to Sudeley Castle to see Catherine Parr's tomb. Many climb the hill to Belas Knap. Outside Beauty Heaven, dead bouquets shrivel in the summer sun."

'Lucie did what you asked. She hasn't given Bryony away. Although it means Brice can't be exonerated for Bryony's "murder".' Jacked tweaked his fingers for inverted commas.

'She said he's innocent. Charlie told Vicky he's put up with a cloud hanging over him for sixteen years, he can stick a few more.'

'Vicky's father is sixty-one, he's likely to live another thirty years. I see why Vicky had to disappear, I've done that in the past, but her father could be abusing other girls.'

'Charlie keeps watch on him. Vicky'll come forward in her own time. Lucie's ready for when Vicky gives the word.'

'You're kind about Lucie,' Jack commented.

'Dad loved her.' Stella slowed for a group of cyclists to pass. 'Lucie kept you out of her article too. Are you OK with that?'

'I won't be any use to our team if I lose my anonymity.' Stella would think he meant publicity would stop him sneaking into houses and stealing people's things. Did he mean that?

'I'd like to be anonymous.' Stella shrugged. 'Jackie says publicity's good for Clean Slate.'

'It is.' Jack was rereading the article. 'Lucie's rather overdone the monster thing. Spicer wasn't evil.'

'She wasn't very nice,' Stella said. 'If she hadn't died the judge might have ruled her bad, not mad. Craven was under her thumb.'

'I never trust that phrase. The press reported the Moors killings as if Ian Brady had Myra Hindley under his thumb. From descriptions of Hindley in prison, she was no pushover. The media can't conceive of a woman committing murder. She has to be a monster, in thrall to some man, or mad. Spicer was as sane as me and you. She was resourceful and quite prepared to kill for what she wanted. She had a tough upbringing, but she was no victim. Mercer probably knew Terry was right. Lauren kept Mercer in check.'

'Lauren was a monster. She murdered her best friend,' Stella said firmly.

'Lauren didn't have friends.' Jack smoothed down a crease in Lauren's picture. 'She made alliances to suit her. When Cassie got in the way, she killed her. Lauren was spellbinding to men. It's good she never did go with Barry, he had a lucky escape, such as it was.'

'Did you think she was spellbinding?'

'No!' Not true. Jack pictured the woman by the chamber where she'd buried her victim, and shuddered. As Bella had said of him, Lauren Spicer was 'of the night'.

They lapsed into silence. Stella's expression was inscrutable, Jack had no idea what she was thinking. He was thinking Stella was more spellbinding than Lauren Spicer. He shouldn't say. Stella was funny around compliments. Anyway, could someone be *more* spellbinding?

On the M40 Stella took the slip road to the Beaconsfield

services. While Jack walked Stanley on a patch of grass in the car park, she went to get coffees.

Jack's phone rang. Emily. He felt a sickening lurch.

'Are you still in Whitstable?'

'Winchcombe. We're on our way back. Are the twins OK?' Jack opened his eyes. *Please let them be fine.*

'Yes, they're gorgeous. Thing is, Jack, I've had a chat with Bella. And, well, she says you can see them.'

'See them?' Jack shut his eyes. 'You already sent me a picture.'

'Properly see them. *Meet* them. Bella says you can visit. Is there a chance you could come this afternoon? It's short notice, but with Bella, you know...' Emily meant Bella could change her mind.

'I can! I can!' Jack said goodbye and opened his eyes.

'Can what?' Stella asked.

'London Underground want me to drive tonight.' He couldn't tell Stella about the twins. Not *ever*. It would ruin everything he had with her. However honest he tried to be, like Mercer, like Bryony, and like Barry, he'd always have a secret. The sun shone brightly, but to Jack there might have been an eclipse.

'I took your advice about anonymity.' Stella was holding up two Starbucks cups. One said 'Stanley' the other 'Endora'.

Chapter Sixty

Jack eased around a double buggy parked in Bella's hallway and followed Emily along the passage. His heart smashed in his chest. He was a small boy the last time he'd felt this way, That day, when only the hard plinth of the statue against his back told him he was real, had been an end. Today was a beginning.

'Jack?' Emily paused at the door. Jack had stopped. Emily came back, and tugged on his hand. 'It'll be fine.'

Her tone made Jack think, for the umpteenth time, what a kind little girl Emily must have been. She was still kind. He whispered, 'Thank you, Emily. For... for—'

'This way.' Emily led him into the sitting room. She called merrily, 'Here he is!'

The door shut. Emily had gone. It was all Jack could do not to tear after her.

'Say hello to your kids, Jack.' Bella was on the sofa reading a book. She waved at two Moses baskets on the rug in front of the fireplace.

Jack's legs were as heavy as lead. He shoved his hands in his pockets so Bella wouldn't see they were shaking, then, feeling the pose must appear lackadaisical, took them out again.

The babies lay on their backs. One was asleep, the other was gazing right at him. They were dressed in pale blue onesies. *Boys*.

Why had he thought there was one of each? Jack panicked. Two sons. In the time since their birth, the girl had become real to him. He was nervous of a son, how would he be with a boy? Two boys! He had no trouble imagining himself with a daughter, chatting about this and that. Yet she didn't exist. It was like a death.

'The one on the right's Emily.' Bella was beside him.

'Emily?' Jack peered at the sleeping baby. 'But she's wearing a blue—'

'Don't start with that pink for girls and blue for boys crap!' Bella told him. 'I got a job lot of baby clothes on eBay. I've snipped a corner off Emily's collar so I can tell which is which. See? I can tell anyway. He's always asleep. Sit down, so you can hold Emily. I don't want to wake Justin.'

'Justin? That's my middle name! What a coincidence!' Jack remembered he didn't believe in coincidences. As he sat on the sofa, out of nowhere came the conviction that this was where the twins had been conceived. He banished the vision.

'I know that. You can be a klutz, Jack!' Bella placed Emily in Jack's arms. 'Hold her like this. Man up, she's not made of china. Support her head. Perfect.'

Perfect. 'Is Emily named after Emily?' Jack expected Bella to scoff at the question.

'Of course. Em's their godmother, not that I believe in God, but she does.'

Seemingly having forgotten she wanted him to stay sleeping, Bella picked up the other baby – Justin – and joined Jack on the sofa.

Jack smiled at Emily. 'Wow! She's smiling at me.'

'She's not. Babies don't smile yet,' Bella told him and Jack saw it was true. It was just him smiling and he couldn't stop. '... projecting trait and trace...' He saw his mother's face pass across the girl's peaceful features. '...through time to times anon...' Jack just stopped himself reciting Hardy's poem out loud.

'Emily's got your nose.' Bella broke his reverie.

Jack looked at Bella. She had colour in her cheeks, her curly hair was styled. In a cerise dress set off by a brown bead necklace likely made of dried seeds, it would be easy to suppose motherhood suited her. He guessed what suited her was not carrying twins any more. She'd got her 'self' back. He saw a half-finished botanical illustration on her drawing desk. Surely she wasn't off her maternity leave at Kew Gardens? He took in Bella's words, 'Emily's got *my* nose?'

'She looks like her father. By the way, we're calling her Milly so as not to mix her up with Emily who got here first. Her middle name's Kate like your mother.'

'What about your mother?' Jack could hardly articulate. *She looks like her father.*

'My parents don't feature for the reason they never featured while I was growing up, their names would be a hex. This is Justin Joseph Markham and that's Emily Kate Markham.' Bella was gruff.

'Joseph?' Jack felt a flare of jealousy. Bella had a new man. Some stranger would bring up his children.

'Joseph Hooker. Keep up, Jack!' Bella rolled her eyes.

Jack breathed. Long dead, the nineteenth-century director of Kew's Botanic Gardens was Bella's true love, but was no rival for his children's affections.

'Thank you for letting me be here, Bella.' He watched as Justin opened his eyes.

'Yeah, well, Emily kind of said it wasn't fair to stop you being around. They're your kids too.' Bella bent and kissed Justin on the nose. 'That's all, though, no happy families. I've moved on.'

'"Being around"?'

'We'll make it official. Visitation rights. If you're serious. Being a dad's not for Christmas. Except for my father that's precisely what it was. Until the Christmases ran out. Be like him and you're gone!'

'I won't be like him, Bella. I'll be a real father. I've got a maze in my garden, when they're walking, they might like playing there. I'd have loved my own maze.' Jack pushed back his hair. 'I'll be there for my children.'

My children.

Epilogue

'Sounds riveting!' Vicky whispered from the doorway to the patients' room.

Stella put down the *Daily Mirror*. The article describing which shops in Australia would be shut for the Queen's ninetieth birthday had sent Mrs Stokes to sleep. Stella had read the article to her without taking in a word. She missed reading The Forsyte Saga. Laying the newspaper on her chair, Stella tiptoed from the room.

'All right?' Stella asked when they were in the car park. 'I didn't expect you'd be in for a bit, not after...' She looked beyond the hospice to the Thames, silver-white in the sunshine.

'Nor me you. Didn't you just get back from Winchcombe today? Listen, Stell, I wanted to talk to you. How will you call me Vicky when you know it's not my real name? You hate dishonesty.'

'Easy. You are Vicky to me.' Since their time in Winchcombe, Stella had come to think the business of lies and truth and honesty was complicated. If Jack hadn't found the teddy bear at Brice's cottage, she wouldn't have known the truth about Vicky. If Brice hadn't taken Mercer to Belas Knap, Cassie's body would still be up there. If Lucie wasn't tracking Jack's and her phones they'd never have joined them at Belas Knap.

'I'm glad you know. I can be "me" with you. Still, I'm surprised you came in today. You've only been back from Winchcombe hours ago!'

'The befriending co-ordinator rang asking if I was available. I wondered if, I kind of... hoped I'd see you.' A puffy white aeroplane trail cut across the sky above Mortlake Crematorium on the other side of the river. The plane had gone, already Stella could hear the rumble of another one.

When Stella had dropped Jack at Kew Station at lunchtime – he hadn't wanted a lift to his house – she'd been reluctant to go home. Leaving Stanley with Beverly at the office, instead of catching up on emails, she'd come to the hospice.

'I rang your friend,' Vicky said.

'Jack?'

'Jack's not really just your friend, is he!' Vicky raised her eyebrows. 'No, that reporter, Lucie May.'

Stella was about to say Lucie wasn't a friend when the import of what Vicky had said sank in. 'Are you sure? You were going to wait.'

'It's wrong to wait. Like Jack said, my father should pay for what he did to me. Let Winchcombe and Broadway – everyone – know who he really is. I want Charlie to live his life, he needs to stop looking after others and look after himself.'

'Charlie chose to protect you.'

'His father abused him. He wanted to do something positive. He took me under his wing. But he's paid a price. It's time to stop it. Rob's coming with me to see Lucie May. She'll write the story then I'll go to the police. It gives her a head start. Lucie suggests I contact someone called Martin Cashman based at Richmond police station. She said you know him.'

Martin Cashman had been her dad's best friend. Stella pictured the headline *Grieving Dad is Evil Predator*. 'Lucie tends to go over the top.'

'I saw her article in the *Mirror* this morning. She's welcome to describe my father as a monster. Lucie's arranging a safe house for us. Charlie too. Her story will free us all.'

'Not *all*,' Stella said.

'My father can rot in jail.' Vicky got into her car.

'What did you mean about Jack not being a friend?' Stella asked as Vicky started the engine.

'Anyone can see what he feels for you, Stell.' Vicky leaned out and touched Stella's sleeve. 'I'll never walk out of the room again when you talk about murder! You're a true friend.'

Stella watched Vicky's yellow jeep pass through the hospice gates. *Not just a friend*. Through the open windows behind her came haunting music. The transition choir was singing *Jubilate Deo*.

Jack wandered out of the graveyard and crossed Jackie's street. Squeezing between Graham's Saab and the mud-streaked Shogun he recognized as Barry Makepeace's, he strolled up to her front door. It was on the latch; he was greeted by the aroma of garlic and ginger. From the garden he heard chatter and laughter. He was home.

Wreathed in barbecue smoke, like Lucifer in an apron, Graham was arranging skewered fish and vegetables on the grill at one end of the patio. At the other end, Beverly and Jackie lay in loungers. Stella sat at the table under the umbrella reading a book. Jack put down the bottle of chilled Prosecco he'd brought and flung himself into the seat beside her. The novel was *In Chancery*, the second volume of The Forsyte Saga. Judging from the bookmark, Stella was a third of the way in.

'No Lucie?' He looked around.

'She's coming later. She's got stuff to sort,' Stella said.

'We've found new offices!' Beverly had clearly been bursting to tell him.

'Great!' Jack feigned enthusiasm. He relished change less than

Stella did. He didn't want Clean Slate to be in some glitzy almond-shaped edifice in Docklands.

'It's upstairs from our old office!' Beverly rocketed out of the lounger and, flourishing a tea towel, eased the cork from Jack's Prosecco. 'The insurance brokers are leaving. They got burgled. Yah boo! They left the door open so won't get compo. It's karma, bro!' The cork popped out and flew up into the air. When it landed, Stanley snatched it and cantered off to a private corner of the garden.

'But it must be the same size as Clean Slate's present office?' Jack hated to puncture the mood.

'That's what's brilliant.' Beverly handed Jack a Prosecco and refilled everyone's glasses. 'The space goes across the mini-mart and the dry cleaner's; it's double the size of our place but,' she raised a finger, 'if we keep our office we gain by two thirds. Stella agrees. Downstairs will be our detective agency. Awesome!'

'Awesome indeed!' Jack clinked his glass against Stella's.

'You'll have your own desk,' Stella told him over the rim of her glass.

'I've never had a desk in an office before.' Jack became aware of the warmth of Stella's thigh against his. The effect was electrifying.

'Hold the front page, darlinkas!' Lucie burst onto the patio as if out of a cake. She held a cumbersome square cage in one hand and in the other a magnum of Veuve Clicquot.

'This is new.' Beverly took the cage off Lucie and pulled faces at Endora on her perch.

'Stella got it for me. She said the Victorian one is bad for Endora, sharp corners and what-not.' Lucie flapped a hand. 'Endora loves it.'

'Blimey, Lucie, you've pushed the boat right out! There was no need, we've got a case of booze.' Jackie took the champagne from Lucie and held it up. 'Do I shake the bottle and pour it over you?'

'There's *every* need!' Lucie tipped the rest of Jack's Prosecco into a glass and raised it to the sky. 'It's not every day our Jack's a dad! You kept that quiet, Jackanory!'

'What do you mean?' Stella asked. Jack felt coolness where her leg had been.

'I bumped into the Botanical Wonder pushing a ginormous chariot around the streets.' Lucie whooped. 'Jack has twins!'

'*Jack has twins!*' Endora shrilled.

Jack felt as if he'd been hit on the head, his ears were zinging. Voices were miles away. The seat beside him was empty. Stella had gone. He was dead inside.

A hand rested on his shoulder. Jackie. He turned to tell her. *No really, I'm fine...*

'Congratulations, Jack, you'll be the best dad ever.' Stella kissed Jack on the lips.

Acknowledgements

Many thanks and gratitude to Stephen Cassidy, retired Detective Chief Superintendent with the Metropolitan Police, for sharing some of his considerable professional experience with me and for bringing to life the codes of practice of the Police and Criminal Evidence Act. My thanks also go to retired Detective Inspector Michael Kerslake. Any errors are mine.

I'm so grateful to Andrew Maxted for his engaging 'seminar' on the Early Neolithics as he drove me from Harrogate to Lewes. Andrew's suggested reading of *Britain BC* by Francis Pryor was rich and illuminating. Again, any inaccuracies are down to me.

Big shout-outs to Domenica de Rosa who gave me the title. And to 'The Detective's Parents': Shirley Cassidy, a much-valued reader, and Major Ron Cassidy MBE.

Thanks always go to Frank Pacifico, Test Train Operator for the London Underground for giving Jack a job...

Laura Palmer, my editor at Head of Zeus, is discerning and inspiring. This novel owes much to Laura's considered editing. I'm lucky to work with an ace team at HoZ, including Blake Brooks, Jenni Edgecombe, Daniel Groenewald, Victoria Reed, Chrissy Ryan, Suzanne Sangster, Jon Small and Nikky Ward.

I have fabulous support from my agents, Georgina Capel Associates, specifically I'd like to thank Georgina for her encouragement. Philippa Brewster's wisdom and experience is invaluable, thank you.

Much of *The Death Chamber* was written 'on location' in the special little Cotswold town of Winchcombe. Food Fanatics kept me in lattes and North's Bakery in iced buns and freshly baked bread. I was helped in my research by Marty Kent, Operations Manager at Marchants Coaches which operates the 606 bus route. Marty kindly contacted Rory and Rowena McCubbin of the old Castleways of Winchcombe Bus Company and Vic Robinson, retired bus driver with Castleways, all of whom provided me bus schedules right back to the seventies and specifically for the 606. I found the Folk and Police Museum and Winchcombe's terrific public library a valuable resource.

I get lovely messages from readers, a big thank you to you all. Keith and Gail wrote to tell that me they'd named their poodle Stanley after Stella's dog. A wonderful honour!

My love to Mel, my ever supportive partner and first reader. Oh, and a liver treat of gratitude goes to my walking companion, our dog, Alfred (aka Stanley).

A letter from the publisher

We hope you enjoyed this book. We are an independent publisher dedicated to discovering brilliant books, new authors and great storytelling. If you want to hear more, why not join our community of book-lovers at:

www.headofzeus.com

We'll keep you up-to-date with our latest books, author blogs, tempting offers, chances to win signed editions, events across the UK and much more.

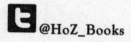 @HoZ_Books

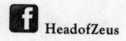 HeadofZeus

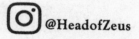 @HeadofZeus